The Second Leonaur Book
of
Great Ghost and Horror Stories

The Second Leonaur Book of Great Ghost and Horror Stories
Twenty-Nine Spine Chilling and Strange Tales

Compiled by Eunice Hetherington

The Second Leonaur Book of Great Ghost and Horror Stories
Twenty-Nine Spine Chilling and Strange Tales
Compiled by Eunice Hetherington

FIRST EDITION

Leonaur is an imprint of Oakpast Ltd

Copyright in this form © 2012 Oakpast Ltd

ISBN: 978-1-78282-048-2 (hardcover)
ISBN: 978-1-78282-049-9 (softcover)

http://www.leonaur.com

Contents

The Listener   7
Algernon Blackwood

The Yellow Cat   31
Wilbur Daniel Steele

Thrawn Janet   49
Robert Louis Stevenson

A Terribly Strange Bed   58
Wilkie Collins

The Man With the Pale Eyes   74
Guy de Maupassant

The Birthmark   79
Nathaniel Hawthorne

The Biter Bit   95
Wilkie Collins

A Witch's Den   123
Mme. Helena Blavatsky

Ligeia   137
Edgar Allan Poe

Chan Tow the Highrob   152
Chester Bailey Fernald

May Day Eve   161
Algernon Blackwood

The Box With the Iron Clamps   181
Florence Marryat

The Clavecin, Bruges   209
George Wharton Edwards

The Diamond Lens   214
Fitz-James O'Brien

The Eyes of the Panther   236
Ambrose Bierce

The Woman's Ghost Story   245
Algernon Blackwood

The Great Valdez Sapphire   254
Anonymous

The Inmost Light   272
Arthur Machen

The Lost Room   298
Fitz-James O'Brien

The Mummy's Foot   314
Théophile Gautier

The Mysterious Card   325
Cleveland Moffett

The Oblong Box   348
Edgar Allan Poe

The Return   359
Algernon Blackwood

The Second Generation   364
Algernon Blackwood

The Secret of Goresthorpe Grange   371
A. Conan Doyle

The Sin-Eater   387
Fiona Macleod

The Sylph and the Father   411
Elsa Barker

The Torture by Hope   415
Villiers de l'Isle Adam

When the World Was Young   420
Jack London

The Listener

By Algernon Blackwood

Sept. 4.—I have hunted all over London for rooms suited to my income—£120 a year—and have at last found them. Two rooms, without modern conveniences, it is true, and in an old, ramshackle building, but within a stone's throw of P— Place and in an eminently respectable street. The rent is only £25 a year. I had begun to despair when at last I found them by chance. The chance was a mere chance, and unworthy of record. I had to sign a lease for a year, and I did so willingly. The furniture from our old place in H—shire, which has been stored so long, will just suit them.

Oct. 1.—Here I am in my two rooms, in the centre of London, and not far from the offices of the periodicals where occasionally I dispose of an article or two. The building is at the end of a *cul-de-sac*. The alley is well paved and clean, and lined chiefly with the backs of sedate and institutional-looking buildings. There is a stable in it. My own house is dignified with the title of "Chambers." I feel as if one day the honour must prove too much for it, and it will swell with pride—and fall asunder. It is very old. The floor of my sitting-room has valleys and low hills on it, and the top of the door slants away from the ceiling with a glorious disregard of what is usual. They must have quarrelled—fifty years ago—and have been going apart ever since.

Oct. 2.—My landlady is old and thin, with a faded, dusty face. She is uncommunicative. The few words she utters seem to cost her pain. Probably her lungs are half choked with dust. She keeps my rooms as free from this commodity as possible, and has the assistance of a strong girl who brings up the breakfast and lights the fire. As I have said already, she is not communicative. In reply to pleasant efforts on my part she informed me briefly that I was the only occupant of the house at present. My rooms had not been occupied for some years. There had been other gentlemen upstairs, but they had left.

She never looks straight at me when she speaks, but fixes her dim eyes on my middle waistcoat button, till I get nervous and begin to think it isn't on straight, or is the wrong sort of button altogether.

Oct. 8.—My week's book is nicely kept, and so far is reasonable. Milk and sugar 7d., bread 6d., butter 8d., marmalade 6d., eggs 1s. 8d., laundress 2s. 9d., oil 6d., attendance 5s.; total 12s. 2d.

The landlady has a son who, she told me, is "somethink on a homnibus." He comes occasionally to see her. I think he drinks, for he talks very loud, regardless of the hour of the day or night, and tumbles about over the furniture downstairs.

All the morning I sit indoors writing—articles; verses for the comic papers; a novel I've been "at" for three years, and concerning which I have dreams; a children's book, in which the imagination has free rein; and another book which is to last as long as myself, since it is an honest record of my soul's advance or retreat in the struggle of life. Besides these, I keep a book of poems which I use as a safety valve, and concerning which I have no dreams whatsoever. Between the lot I am always occupied. In the afternoons I generally try to take a walk for my health's sake, through Regent's Park, into Kensington Gardens, or farther afield to Hampstead Heath.

Oct. 10.—Everything went wrong today. I have two eggs for breakfast. This morning one of them was bad. I rang the bell for Emily. When she came in I was reading the paper, and, without looking up, I said, "Egg's bad."

"Oh, is it, sir?" she said; "I'll get another one," and went out, taking the egg with her. I waited my breakfast for her return, which was in five minutes. She put the new egg on the table and went away. But, when I looked down, I saw that she had taken away the good egg and left the bad one—all green and yellow—in the slop basin. I rang again.

"You've taken the wrong egg," I said.

"Oh!" she exclaimed; "I thought the one I took down didn't smell so *very* bad."

In due time she returned with the good egg, and I resumed my breakfast with two eggs, but less appetite. It was all very trivial, to be sure, but so stupid that I felt annoyed. The character of that egg influenced everything I did. I wrote a bad article, and tore it up. I got a bad headache. I used bad words—to myself. Everything was bad, so I "chucked" work and went for a long walk.

I dined at a cheap chop-house on my way back, and reached home about nine o'clock.

Rain was just beginning to fall as I came in, and the wind was rising. It promised an ugly night. The alley looked dismal and dreary, and the hall of the house, as I passed through it, felt chilly as a tomb. It was the first stormy night I had experienced in my new quarters. The draughts were awful. They came criss-cross, met in the middle of the room, and formed eddies and whirlpools and cold silent currents that almost lifted the hair of my head. I stuffed up the sashes of the windows with neckties and odd socks, and sat over the smoky fire to keep warm. First I tried to write, but found it too cold. My hand turned to ice on the paper.

What tricks the wind did play with the old place! It came rushing up the forsaken alley with a sound like the feet of a hurrying crowd of people who stopped suddenly at the door. I felt as if a lot of curious folk had arranged themselves just outside and were staring up at my windows. Then they took to their heels again and fled whispering and laughing down the lane, only, however, to return with the next gust of wind and repeat their impertinence. On the other side of my room, a single square window opens into a sort of shaft, or well, that measures about six feet across to the back wall of another house. Down this funnel the wind dropped, and puffed and shouted. Such noises I never heard before. Between these two entertainments I sat over the fire in a great-coat, listening to the deep booming in the chimney. It was like being in a ship at sea, and I almost looked for the floor to rise in undulations and rock to and fro.

Oct. 12.—I wish I were not quite so lonely—and so poor. And yet I love both my loneliness and my poverty. The former makes me appreciate the companionship of the wind and rain, while the latter preserves my liver and prevents me wasting time in dancing attendance upon women. Poor, ill-dressed men are not acceptable "attendants."

My parents are dead, and my only sister is—no, not dead exactly, but married to a very rich man. They travel most of the time, he to find his health, she to lose herself. Through sheer neglect on her part she has long passed out of my life. The door closed when, after an absolute silence of five years, she sent me a cheque for £50 at Christmas. It was signed by her husband! I returned it to her in a thousand pieces and in an unstamped envelope. So at least I had the satisfaction of knowing that it cost her something! She wrote back with a broad quill pen that covered a whole page with three lines, "You are evidently as cracked as ever, and rude and ungrateful into the bargain." It had always been my special terror lest the insanity in my father's family should leap across the generations and appear in me. This thought haunted me, and she knew it.

So after this little exchange of civilities the door slammed, never to open again. I heard the crash it made, and, with it, the falling from the walls of my heart of many little bits of china with their own peculiar value—rare china, some of it, that only needed dusting. The same walls, too, carried mirrors in which I used sometimes to see reflected the misty lawns of childhood, the daisy chains, the wind-torn blossoms scattered through the orchard by warm rains, the robbers' cave in the long walk, and the hidden store of apples in the hay-loft. She was my inseparable companion then—but, when the door slammed, the mirrors cracked across their entire length, and the visions they held vanished forever. Now I am quite alone. At forty one cannot begin all over again to build up careful friendships, and all others are comparatively worthless.

Oct. 14.—My bedroom is 10 by 10. It is below the level of the front room, and a step leads down into it. Both rooms are very quiet on calm nights, for there is no traffic down this forsaken alley-way. In spite of the occasional larks of the wind, it is a most sheltered strip. At its upper end, below my windows, all the cats of the neighbourhood congregate as soon as darkness gathers. They lie undisturbed on the long ledge of a blind window of the opposite building, for after the postman has come and gone at 9:30, no footsteps ever dare to interrupt their sinister conclave, no step but my own, or sometimes the unsteady footfall of the son who "is somethink on a homnibus."

Oct. 15.—I dined at an "A. B. C." shop on poached eggs and coffee, and then went for a stroll round the outer edge of Regent's Park. It was ten o'clock when I got home. I counted no less than thirteen cats, all of a dark colour, crouching under the lee side of the alley walls. It was a cold night, and the stars shone like points of ice in a blue-black sky. The cats turned their heads and stared at me in silence as I passed. An odd sensation of shyness took possession of me under the glare of so many pairs of unblinking eyes. As I fumbled with the latch-key they jumped noiselessly down and pressed against my legs, as if anxious to be let in. But I slammed the door in their faces and ran quickly upstairs. The front room, as I entered to grope for the matches, felt as cold as a stone vault, and the air held an unusual dampness.

Oct. 17.—For several days I have been working on a ponderous article that allows no play for the fancy. My imagination requires a judicious rein; I am afraid to let it loose, for it carries me sometimes into appalling places beyond the stars and beneath the world. No one realizes the danger more than I do. But what a foolish thing to write here—for there is no one to know, no one to realize! My mind of late has held unusual thoughts, thoughts I have never had before, about medicines and drugs and the treatment of strange illnesses. I cannot imagine their source. At no time in my life have I dwelt upon such ideas as now constantly throng my brain. I have had no exercise lately, for the weather has been shocking; and all my afternoons have been spent in the reading-room of the British Museum, where I have a reader's ticket.

I have made an unpleasant discovery: there are rats in the house. At night from my bed I have heard them scampering across the hills and valleys of the front room, and my sleep has been a good deal disturbed in consequence.

Oct. 24.—Last night the son who is "somethink on a homnibus" came in. He had evidently been drinking, for I heard loud and angry voices below in the kitchen long after I had gone to bed. Once, too, I caught the singular words rising up to me through the floor, "Burning from top to bottom is the only thing that'll ever make this 'ouse right." I knocked on the floor, and the voices ceased suddenly, though later I again heard their clamour in my dreams.

These rooms are very quiet, almost too quiet sometimes. On windless nights they are silent as the grave, and the house might be miles in the country. The roar of London's traffic reaches me only in heavy, distant vibrations. It holds an ominous note sometimes, like that of an approaching army, or an immense tidal-wave very far away thundering in the night.

Oct. 27.—Mrs. Monson, though admirably silent, is a foolish, fussy woman. She does such stupid things. In dusting the room she puts all my things in the wrong places. The ash-trays, which should be on the writing-table she sets in a silly row on the mantelpiece. The pen-tray, which should be beside the inkstand, she hides away cleverly among the books on my reading-desk. My gloves she arranges daily in idiotic array upon a half-filled bookshelf, and I always have to rearrange them on the low table by the door. She places my armchair at impossible angles between the fire and the light, and the tablecloth—the one with Trinity Hall stains—she puts on the table in such a fashion that when I look at it I feel as if my tie and all my clothes were on crooked and awry. She exasperates me. Her very silence and meekness are irritating. Sometimes I feel inclined to throw the inkstand at her, just to bring an expression into her watery eyes and a squeak from those colourless lips. Dear me! What violent expressions I am making use of! How very foolish of me! And yet it almost seems as if the words were not my own, but had been spoken into my ear—I mean, I never make use of such terms naturally.

Oct. 30.—I have been here a month. The place does not agree with me, I think. My headaches are more frequent and violent, and my nerves are a perpetual source of discomfort and annoyance.

I have conceived a great dislike for Mrs. Monson, a feeling I am certain she reciprocates. Somehow, the impression comes frequently to me that there are goings on in this house of which I know nothing, and which she is careful to hide from me.

Last night her son slept in the house, and this morning as I was standing at the window I saw him go out. He glanced up and caught my eye. It was a loutish figure and a singularly repulsive face that I saw, and he gave me the benefit of a very unpleasant leer. At least, so I imagined.

Nov. 2.—The utter stillness of this house is beginning to oppress me. I wish there were other fellows living upstairs. No footsteps ever sound overhead, and no tread ever passes my door to go up the next flight of stairs. I am beginning to feel some curiosity to go up myself and see what the upper rooms are like. I feel lonely here and isolated, swept into a deserted corner of the world and forgotten. . . . Once I actually caught myself gazing into the long, cracked mirrors, trying to see the sunlight dancing beneath the trees in the orchard. But only deep shadows seemed to congregate there now, and I soon desisted.

It has been very dark all day, and no wind stirring. The fogs have begun. I had to use a reading-lamp all this morning. There was no cart to be heard today. I actually missed it. This morning, in the gloom and silence, I think I could almost have welcomed it. After all, the sound is a very human one, and this empty house at the end of the alley holds other noises that are not quite so satisfactory.

I have never once seen a policeman in the lane, and the postmen always hurry out with no evidence of a desire to loiter.

10 p.m.—As I write this I hear no sound but the deep murmur of the distant traffic and the low of the wind. The two sounds melt into one another. Now and again a cat raises its shrill, uncanny cry upon the darkness. The cats are always there under my windows when the darkness falls. The wind is dropping into the funnel with a noise like the sudden sweeping of immense distant wings. It is a dreary night. I feel lost and forgotten.

Nov. 3.—From my windows I can see arrivals. When anyone comes to the door I can just see the hat and shoulders and the hand on the bell. Only two fellows have been to see me since I came here two months ago. Both of them I saw from the window before they came up, and heard their voices asking if I was in. Neither of them ever came back.

I have finished the ponderous article. On reading it through, however, I was dissatisfied with it, and drew my pencil through almost every page. There were strange expressions and ideas in it that I could not explain, and viewed with amazement, not to say alarm. They did not sound like my *very own*, and I could not remember having written them. Can it be that my memory is beginning to be affected?

My pens are never to be found. That stupid old woman puts them in a different place each day. I must give her due credit for finding so many new hiding places; such ingenuity is wonderful. I have told her repeatedly, but she always says, "I'll speak to Emily, sir." Emily always says, "I'll tell Mrs. Monson, sir." Their foolishness makes me irritable and scatters all my thoughts. I should like to stick the lost pens into them and turn them out, blind-eyed, to be scratched and mauled by those thousand hungry cats. Whew! What a ghastly thought! Where in the world did it come from? Such an idea is no more my own than it is the policeman's. Yet I felt I *had* to write it. It was like a voice singing in my head, and my pen wouldn't stop till the last word was finished. What ridiculous nonsense! I must and will restrain myself. I must take more regular exercise; my nerves and liver plague me horribly.

Nov. 4.—I attended a curious lecture in the French quarter on "Death," but the room was so hot and I was so weary that I fell asleep. The only part I heard, however, touched my imagination vividly. Speaking of suicides, the lecturer said that self-murder was no escape from the miseries of the present, but only a preparation of greater sorrow for the future. Suicides, he declared, cannot shirk their responsibilities so easily. They must return to take up life exactly where they laid it so violently down, but with the added pain and punishment of their weakness. Many of them wander the earth in unspeakable misery till they can *reclothe* themselves in the body of someone else— generally a lunatic or weak-minded person, who cannot resist the hideous obsession. This is their only means of escape. Surely a weird and horrible idea! I wish I had slept all the time and not heard it at all. My mind is morbid enough without such ghastly fancies. Such mischievous propaganda should be stopped by the police. I'll write to the *Times* and suggest it. Good idea!

I walked home through Greek Street, Soho, and imagined that a hundred years had slipped back into place and De Quincey was still there, haunting the night with invocations to his "just, subtle, and mighty" drug. His vast dreams seemed to hover not very far away. Once started in my brain, the pictures refused to go away; and I saw him sleeping in that cold, tenantless mansion with the strange little waif who was afraid of its ghosts, both together in the shadows under a single horseman's cloak; or wandering in the companionship of the spectral Anne; or, later still, on his way to the eternal rendezvous she never was able to keep. What an unutterable gloom, what an untold horror of sorrow and suffering comes over me as I try to realize something of what that man—boy he then was—must have taken into his lonely heart.

As I came up the alley I saw a light in the top window, and a head and shoulders thrown in an exaggerated shadow upon the blind. I wondered what the son could be doing up there at such an hour.

Nov. 5.—This morning, while writing, someone came up the creaking stairs and knocked cautiously at my door. Thinking it was the landlady, I said, "Come in!" The knock was repeated, and I cried louder, "Come in, come in!" But no one turned the handle, and I continued my writing with a vexed "Well, stay out, then!" under my breath. Went on writing. I tried to, but my thoughts had suddenly dried up at their source. I could not set down a single word. It was a dark, yellow-fog morning, and there was little enough inspiration in the air as it was, but that stupid woman standing just outside my door waiting to be told again to come in roused a spirit of vexation that filled my head to the exclusion of all else. At last I jumped up and opened the door myself.

"What do you want, and why in the world don't you come in?" I cried out. But the words dropped into empty air. There was no one there. The fog poured up the dingy staircase in deep yellow coils, but there was no sign of a human being anywhere.

I slammed the door, with imprecations upon the house and its noises, and went back to my work. A few minutes later Emily came in with a letter.

"Were you or Mrs. Monson outside a few minutes ago knocking at my door?"

"No, sir."

"Are you sure?"

"Mrs. Monson's gone to market, and there's no one but me and the child in the 'ole 'ouse, and I've been washing the dishes for the last hour, sir."

I fancied the girl's face turned a shade paler. She fidgeted toward the door with a glance over her shoulder.

"Wait, Emily," I said, and then told her what I had heard. She stared stupidly at me, though her eyes shifted now and then over the articles in the room.

"Who was it?" I asked when I had come to the end.

"Mrs. Monson says it's honly mice," she said, as if repeating a learned lesson.

"Mice!" I exclaimed; "it's nothing of the sort. Someone was feeling about outside my door. Who was it? Is the son in the house?"

Her whole manner changed suddenly, and she became earnest instead of evasive. She seemed anxious to tell the truth.

"Oh, no, sir; there's no one in the house at all but you and me and the child, and there couldn't have been nobody at your door. As for them knocks—" She stopped abruptly, as though she had said too much.

"Well, what about the knocks?" I said more gently.

"Of course," she stammered, "the knocks isn't mice, nor the footsteps neither, but then—" Again she came to a full halt.

"Anything wrong with the house?"

"Lor', no, sir; the drains is splendid."

"I don't mean drains, girl. I mean, did anything—anything bad ever happen here?"

She flushed up to the roots of her hair, and then turned suddenly pale again. She was obviously in considerable distress, and there was something she was anxious, yet afraid to tell—some forbidden thing she was not allowed to mention.

"I don't mind what it was, only I should like to know," I said encouragingly.

Raising her frightened eyes to my face, she began to blurt out something about "that which 'appened once to a gentleman that lived hupstairs," when a shrill voice calling her name sounded below.

"Emily, Emily!" It was the returning landlady, and the girl tumbled downstairs as if pulled backward by a rope, leaving me full of conjectures as to what in the world could have happened to a gentleman *upstairs* that could in so curious a manner affect my ears *downstairs*.

Nov. 10.—I have done capital work; have finished the ponderous article and had it accepted for the —— *Review,* and another one ordered. I feel well and cheerful, and have had regular exercise and good sleep; no headaches, no nerves, no liver! Those pills the chemist recommended are wonderful. Even the gray-faced landlady rouses pity in me; I am sorry for her: so worn, so weary, so oddly put together, just like the building. She looks as if she had once suffered some shock of terror, and was momentarily dreading another. When I spoke to her today very gently about not putting the pens in the ash-tray and the gloves on the book-shelf she raised her faint eyes to mine for the first time, and said with the ghost of a smile, "I'll try and remember, sir," I felt inclined to pat her on the back and say, "Come, cheer up and be jolly. Life's not so bad after all."

Oh! I am much better. There's nothing like open air and success and good sleep. They build up as if by magic the portions of the heart eaten down by despair and unsatisfied yearnings. Even to the cats I feel friendly. When I came in at eleven o'clock tonight they followed me to the door in a stream, and I stooped down to stroke the one nearest to me. Bah! The brute hissed and spat, and struck at me with her paws. The claw caught my hand and drew blood in a thin line. The others danced sideways into the darkness, screeching, as though I had done them an injury. I believe these cats really hate me. Perhaps they are only waiting to be reinforced. Then they will attack me. Ha, ha! In spite of the momentary annoyance, this fancy sent me laughing upstairs to my room.

The fire was out, and the room seemed unusually cold. As I groped my way over to the mantelpiece to find the matches I realized all at once that there was another person standing beside me in the darkness. I could, of course, see nothing, but my fingers, feeling along the

16

ledge, came into forcible contact with something that was at once withdrawn. It was cold and moist. I could have sworn it was somebody's hand. My flesh began to creep instantly.

"Who's that?" I exclaimed in a loud voice.

My voice dropped into the silence like a pebble into a deep well. There was no answer, but at the same moment I heard someone moving away from me across the room in the direction of the door. It was a confused sort of footstep, and the sound of garments brushing the furniture on the way. The same second my hand stumbled upon the matchbox, and I struck a light. I expected to see Mrs. Monson, or Emily, or perhaps the son who is something on an omnibus. But the flare of the gas jet illumined an empty room; there was not a sign of a person anywhere. I felt the hair stir upon my head, and instinctively I backed up against the wall, lest something should approach me from behind. I was distinctly alarmed. But the next minute I recovered myself. The door was open on to the landing, and I crossed the room, not without some inward trepidation, and went out. The light from the room fell upon the stairs, but there was no one to be seen anywhere, nor was there any sound on the creaking wooden staircase to indicate a departing creature.

I was in the act of turning to go in again when a sound overhead caught my ear. It was a very faint sound, not unlike the sigh of wind; yet it could not have been the wind, for the night was still as the grave. Though it was not repeated, I resolved to go upstairs and see for myself what it all meant. Two senses had been affected—touch and hearing—and I could not believe that I had been deceived. So, with a lighted candle, I went stealthily forth on my unpleasant journey into the upper regions of this queer little old house.

On the first landing there was only one door, and it was locked. On the second there was also only one door, but when I turned the handle it opened. There came forth to meet me the chill musty air that is characteristic of a long unoccupied room. With it there came an indescribable odour. I use the adjective advisedly. Though very faint, diluted as it were, it was nevertheless an odour that made my gorge rise. I had never smelt anything like it before, and I cannot describe it.

The room was small and square, close under the roof, with a sloping ceiling and two tiny windows. It was cold as the grave, without a shred of carpet or a stick of furniture. The icy atmosphere and the nameless odour combined to make the room abominable to me, and, after lingering a moment to see that it contained no cupboards or corners into which a person might have crept for concealment, I made haste to shut the door, and went downstairs again to bed. Evidently I had been deceived after all as to the noise.

In the night I had a foolish but very vivid dream. I dreamed that the landlady and another person, dark and not properly visible, entered my room on all fours, followed by a horde of immense cats. They attacked me as I lay in bed, and murdered me, and then dragged my body upstairs and deposited it on the floor of that cold little square room under the roof.

Nov. 11.—Since my talk with Emily—the unfinished talk—I have hardly once set eyes on her. Mrs. Monson now attends wholly to my wants. As usual, she does everything exactly as I don't like it done. It is all too utterly trivial to mention, but it is exceedingly irritating. Like small doses of morphine often repeated she has finally a cumulative effect.

Nov. 12.—This morning I woke early, and came into the front room to get a book, meaning to read in bed till it was time to get up. Emily was laying the fire.

"Good morning!" I said cheerfully. "Mind you make a good fire. It's very cold."

The girl turned and showed me a startled face. It was not Emily at all!

"Where's Emily?" I exclaimed.

"You mean the girl as was 'ere before me?"

"Has Emily left?"

"I came on the 6th," she replied sullenly, "and she'd gone then." I got my book and went back to bed. Emily must have been sent away almost immediately after our conversation. This reflection kept coming between me and the printed page. I was glad when it was time to get up. Such prompt energy, such merciless decision, seemed to argue something of importance—to somebody.

Nov. 13.—The wound inflicted by the cat's claw has swollen, and causes me annoyance and some pain. It throbs and itches. I'm afraid my blood must be in poor condition, or it would have healed by now. I opened it with a penknife soaked in an antiseptic solution, and cleaned it thoroughly. I have heard unpleasant stories of the results of wounds inflicted by cats.

Nov. 14.—In spite of the curious effect this house certainly exercises upon my nerves, I like it. It is lonely and deserted in the very heart of London, but it is also for that reason quiet to work in. I wonder why it is so cheap. Some people might be suspicious, but I did not even ask the reason. No answer is better than a lie. If only I could remove the cats from the outside and the rats from the inside. I feel that I shall grow accustomed more and more to its peculiarities, and shall die here. Ah, that expression reads queerly and gives a wrong impression: I meant *live and die* here. I shall renew the lease from year to year till one of us crumbles to pieces. From present indications the building will be the first to go.

Nov. 16.—This morning I woke to find my clothes scattered about the room, and a cane chair overturned beside the bed. My coat and waistcoat looked just as if they had been *tried on* by someone in the night. I had horribly vivid dreams, too, in which someone covering his face with his hands kept coming close up to me, crying out as if in pain, "Where can I find covering? Oh, who will clothe me?" How silly, and yet it frightened me a little. It was so dreadfully real. It is now over a year since I last walked in my sleep and woke up with such a shock on the cold pavement of Earl's Court Road, where I then lived. I thought I was cured, but evidently not. This discovery has rather a disquieting effect upon me. Tonight I shall resort to the old trick of tying my toe to the bed-post.

Nov. 17.—Last night I was again troubled by most oppressive dreams. Someone seemed to be moving in the night up and down my room, sometimes passing into the front room, and then returning to stand beside the bed and stare intently down upon me. I was being watched by this person all night long. I never actually awoke, though I was often very near it. I suppose it was a nightmare from indigestion, for this morning I have one of my old vile headaches. Yet all my clothes lay about the floor when I awoke, where they had evidently been flung (had I tossed them?) during the dark hours, and my trousers trailed over the step into the front room.

Worse than this, though—I fancied I noticed about the room in the morning that strange, fetid odour. Though very faint, its mere suggestion is foul and nauseating. What in the world can it be, I wonder?. . . In future I shall lock my door.

Nov. 26.—I have accomplished a lot of good work during this past week, and have also managed to get regular exercise. I have felt well and in an equable state of mind. Only two things have occurred to disturb my equanimity. The first is trivial in itself, and no doubt to be easily explained. The upper window where I saw the light on the night of November 4, with the shadow of a large head and shoulder upon the blind, is one of the windows in the square room under the roof. In reality it has *no blind at all!*

Here is the other thing. I was coming home last night in a fresh fall of snow about eleven o'clock, my umbrella low down over my head. Half-way up the alley, where the snow was wholly untrodden, I saw a man's legs in front of me. The umbrella hid the rest of his figure, but on raising it I saw that he was tall and broad and was walking, as I was, towards the door of my house. He could not have been four feet ahead of me. I had thought the alley was empty when I entered it, but might of course been mistaken very easily.

A sudden gust of wind compelled me to lower the umbrella, and when I raised it again, not half a minute later, there was no longer any man to be seen. With a few more steps I reached the door. It was closed as usual. I then noticed with a sudden sensation of dismay that the surface of the freshly fallen snow was *unbroken.* My own footmarks were the only ones to be seen anywhere, and though I retraced my way to the point where I had first seen the man, I could find no slightest impression of any other boots. Feeling creepy and uncomfortable, I went upstairs, and was glad to get into bed.

Nov. 28.—With the fastening of my bedroom door the disturbances ceased. I am convinced that I walked in my sleep. Probably I untied my toe and then tied it up again. The fancied security of the locked door would alone have been enough to restore sleep to my troubled spirit and enable me to rest quietly.

Last night, however, the annoyance was suddenly renewed in another and more aggressive form. I woke in the darkness with the impression that someone was standing outside my bedroom door *listening.* As I became more awake the impression grew into positive knowledge. Though there was no appreciable sound of moving or breathing, I was so convinced of the propinquity of a listener that I crept out of bed and approached the door. As I did so there came faintly from the next room the unmistakable sound of someone retreating stealthily across the floor. Yet, as I heard it, it was neither the tread of a man nor a regular footstep, but rather, it seemed to me, a confused sort of crawling, almost as of someone on his hands and knees.

I unlocked the door in less than a second, and passed quickly into the front room, and I could feel, as by the subtlest imaginable vibrations upon my nerves, that the spot I was standing in had just that instant been vacated! The Listener had moved; he was now behind the other door, standing in the passage. Yet this door was also closed. I moved swiftly, and as silently as possible, across the floor, and turned the handle. A cold rush of air met me from the passage and sent shiver after shiver down my back. There was no one in the doorway; there was no one on the little landing; there was no one moving down the staircase.

Yet I had been so quick that this midnight Listener could not be very far away, and I felt that if I persevered I should eventually come face to face with him. And the courage that came so opportunely to overcome my nervousness and horror seemed born of the unwilling conviction that it was somehow necessary for my safety as well as my sanity that I should find this intruder and force his secret from him. For was it not the intent action of his mind upon my own, in concentrated listening, that had awakened me with such a vivid realisation of his presence?

Advancing across the narrow landing, I peered down into the well of the little house. There was nothing to be seen; no one was moving in the darkness. How cold the oilcloth was to my bare feet.

I cannot say what it was that suddenly drew my eyes upward. I only know that, without apparent reason, I looked up and saw a person about half-way up the next turn of the stairs, leaning forward over the balustrade and staring straight into my face. It was a man. He appeared to be clinging to the rail rather than standing on the stairs. The gloom made it impossible to see much beyond the general outline, but the head and shoulders were seemingly enormous, and stood sharply silhouetted against the skylight in the roof immediately above.

The idea flashed into my brain in a moment that I was looking into the visage of something monstrous. The huge skull, the mane-like hair, the wide-humped shoulders, suggested, in a way I did not pause to analyse, that which was scarcely human; and for some seconds, fascinated by horror, I returned the gaze and stared into the dark, inscrutable countenance above me, without knowing exactly where I was or what I was doing. Then I realized in quite a new way that I was face to face with the secret midnight Listener, and I steeled myself as best I could for what was about to come.

The source of the rash courage that came to me at this awful moment will ever be to me an inexplicable mystery. Though shivering with fear, and my forehead wet with an unholy dew, I resolved to advance. Twenty questions leaped to my lips: What are you? What do you want? Why do you listen and watch? Why do you come into my room? But none of them found articulate utterance.

I began forthwith to climb the stairs, and with the first signs of my advance *he* drew himself back into the shadows and began to move too. He retreated as swiftly as I advanced. I heard the sound of his crawling motion a few steps ahead of me, ever maintaining the same distance. When I reached the landing he was halfway up the next flight, and when I was halfway up the next flight he had already arrived at the top landing. And then I heard him open the door of the little square room under the roof and go in. Immediately, though the door did not close after him, the sound of his moving entirely ceased.

At this moment I longed for a light, or a stick, or any weapon whatsoever; but I had none of these things, and it was impossible to go back. So I marched steadily up the rest of the stairs, and in less than a minute found myself standing in the gloom face to face with the door through which this creature had just entered.

For a moment I hesitated. The door was about halfway open, and the Listener was standing evidently in his favourite attitude just be-hind it—listening. To search through that dark room for him seemed hopeless; to enter the same small space where he was seemed horrible. The very idea filled me with loathing, and I almost decided to turn back.

It is strange at such times how trivial things impinge on the con-sciousness with a shock as of something important and immense. Something—it might have been a beetle or a mouse—scuttled over the bare boards behind me. The door moved a quarter of an inch, clos-ing. My decision came back with a sudden rush, as it were, and thrust-ing out a foot, I kicked the door so that it swung sharply back to its full extent, and permitted me to walk forward slowly into the aperture of profound blackness beyond. What a queer soft sound my bare feet made on the boards! How the blood sang and buzzed in my head!

I was inside. The darkness closed over me, hiding even the win-dows. I groped my way round the walls in a thorough search; but in order to prevent all possibility of the other's escape, I first of all *closed the door.*

There we were, we two, shut in together between four walls, with-in a few feet of one another. But with what, with whom, was I thus momentarily imprisoned? A new light flashed suddenly over the affair with a swift, illuminating brilliance—and I knew I was a fool, an utter fool! I was wide awake at last, and the horror was evaporating. My cursed nerves again; a dream, a nightmare, and the old result—walking in my sleep. The figure was a dream-figure. Many a time before had the actors in my dreams stood before me for some moments after I was awake. . . . There was a chance match in my pyjamas' pocket, and I struck it on the wall.

The room was utterly empty. It held not even a shadow. I went quickly down to bed, cursing my wretched nerves and my foolish, vivid dreams. But as soon as ever I was asleep again, the same uncouth figure of a man crept back to my bedside, and bending over me with his immense head close to my ear whispered repeatedly in my dreams, "I want your body; I want its covering. I'm waiting for it, and listening always." Words scarcely less foolish than the dream.

But I wonder what that queer odour was up in the square room. I noticed it again, and stronger than ever before and it seemed to be also in my bedroom when I woke this morning.

Nov. 29.—Slowly, as moonbeams rise over a misty sea in June, the thought is entering my mind that my nerves and somnambulistic dreams do not adequately account for the influence this house exercises upon me. It holds me as with a fine, invisible net. I cannot escape if I would. It draws me, and it means to keep me.

Nov. 30.—The post this morning brought me a letter from Aden, forwarded from my old rooms in Earl's Court. It was from Chapter, my former Trinity chum, who is on his way home from the East, and asks for my address. I sent it to him at the hotel he mentioned, "to await arrival."

As I have already said, my windows command a view of the alley, and I can see an arrival without difficulty. This morning, while I was busy writing, the sound of footsteps coming up the alley filled me with a sense of vague alarm that I could in no way account for. I went over to the window, and saw a man standing below waiting for the door to be opened. His shoulders were broad, his top-hat glossy, and his overcoat fitted beautifully round the collar. All this I could see, but no more. Presently the door opened, and the shock to my nerves was unmistakable when I heard a man's voice ask, "Is Mr. —— still here?" mentioning my name.

I could not catch the answer, but it could only have been in the affirmative, for the man entered the hall and the door shut to behind him. But I waited in vain for the sound of his steps on the stairs. There was no sound of any kind. It seemed to me so strange that I opened my door and looked out. No one was anywhere to be seen. I walked across the narrow landing, and looked through the window that commands the whole length of the alley. There was no sign of a human being, coming or going. The lane was deserted. Then I deliberately walked downstairs into the kitchen, and asked the gray-faced landlady if a gentleman had just that minute called for me.

The answer, given with an odd, weary sort of smile, was "No!"

Dec. 1.—I feel genuinely alarmed and uneasy over the state of my nerves. Dreams are dreams, but never before have I had dreams in broad daylight.

I am looking forward very much to Chapter's arrival. He is a capital fellow, vigorous, healthy, with no nerves, and even less imagination; and he has £2000 a year into the bargain. Periodically he makes me offers—the last was to travel round the world with him as secretary, which was a delicate way of paying my expenses and giving me some pocket-money—offers, however, which I invariably decline. I prefer to keep his friendship. Women could not come between us; money might—therefore I give it no opportunity. Chapter always laughed at what he called my "fancies," being himself possessed only of that thin-blooded quality of imagination which is ever associated with the prosaic-minded man. Yet, if taunted with this obvious lack, his wrath is deeply stirred. His psychology is that of the cross materialist—always a rather funny article. It will afford me genuine relief, none the less, to hear the cold judgment his mind will have to pass upon the story of this house as I shall have it to tell.

Dec. 2.—The strangest part of it all I have not referred to in this brief diary. Truth to tell, I have been afraid to set it down in black and white. I have kept it in the background of my thoughts, preventing it as far as possible from taking shape. In spite of my efforts, however, it has continued to grow stronger.

Now that I come to face the issue squarely, it is harder to express than I imagined. Like a half-remembered melody that trips in the head but vanishes the moment you try to sing it, these thoughts form a group in the background of my mind, *behind* my mind, as it were, and refuse to come forward. They are crouching ready to spring, but the actual leap never takes place.

In these rooms, except when my mind is strongly concentrated on my own work, I find myself suddenly dealing in thoughts and ideas that are not my own! New, strange conceptions, wholly foreign to my temperament, are forever cropping up in my head. What precisely they are is of no particular importance. The point is that they are entirely apart from the channel in which my thoughts have hitherto been accustomed to flow. Especially they come when my mind is at rest, unoccupied; when I'm dreaming over the fire, or sitting with a book which fails to hold my attention. Then these thoughts which are not mine spring into life and make me feel exceedingly uncomfortable. Sometimes they are so strong that I almost feel as if someone were in the room beside me, thinking aloud.

Evidently my nerves and liver are shockingly out of order. I must work harder and take more vigorous exercise. The horrid thoughts never come when my mind is much occupied. But they are always there—waiting and as it were *alive*.

What I have attempted to describe above came first upon me gradually after I had been some days in the house, and then grew steadily in strength. The other strange thing has come to me only twice in all these weeks. *It appals me.* It is the consciousness of the propinquity of some deadly and loathsome disease. It comes over me like a wave of fever heat, and then passes off, leaving me cold and trembling. The air seems for a few seconds to become tainted. So penetrating and convincing is the thought of this sickness, that on both occasions my brain has turned momentarily dizzy, and through my mind, like flames of white heat, have flashed the ominous names of all the dangerous illnesses I know. I can no more explain these visitations than I can fly, yet I know there is no dreaming about the clammy skin and palpitating heart which they always leave as witnesses of their brief visit.

Most strongly of all was I aware of this nearness of a mortal sickness when, on the night of the 28th, I went upstairs in pursuit of the listening figure. When we were shut in together in that little square room under the roof, I felt that I was face to face with the actual essence of this invisible and malignant disease. Such a feeling never entered my heart before, and I pray to God it never may again.

There! Now I have confessed. I have given some expression at least to the feelings that so far I have been afraid to see in my own writing. For—since I can no longer deceive myself—the experiences of that night (28th) were no more a dream than my daily breakfast is a dream; and the trivial entry in this diary by which I sought to explain away an occurrence that caused me unutterable horror was due solely to my desire not to acknowledge in words what I really felt and believed to be true. The increase that would have accrued to my horror by so doing might have been more than I could stand.

Dec. 3.—I wish Chapter would come. My facts are all ready marshalled, and I can see his cool, gray eyes fixed incredulously on my face as I relate them: the knocking at my door, the well-dressed caller, the light in the upper window and the shadow upon the blind, the man who preceded me in the snow, the scattering of my clothes at night, Emily's arrested confession, the landlady's suspicious reticence, the midnight listener on the stairs, and those awful subsequent words in my sleep; and above all, and hardest to tell, the presence of the abominable sickness, and the stream of thoughts and ideas that are not my own.

I can see Chapter's face, and I can almost hear his deliberate words, "You've been at the tea again, and underfeeding, I expect, as usual. Better see my nerve doctor, and then come with me to the south of France." For this fellow, who knows nothing of disordered liver or high-strung nerves, goes regularly to a great nerve specialist with the periodical belief that his nervous system is beginning to decay.

Dec. 5.—Ever since the incident of the Listener, I have kept a night-light burning in my bedroom, and my sleep has been undisturbed. Last night, however, I was subjected to a far worse annoyance. I woke suddenly, and saw a man in front of the dressing-table regarding himself in the mirror. The door was locked, as usual. I knew at once it was the Listener, and the blood turned to ice in my veins. Such a wave of horror and dread swept over me that it seemed to turn me rigid in the bed, and I could neither move nor speak. I noted, however, that the odour I so abhorred was strong in the room.

The man seemed to be tall and broad. He was stooping forward over the mirror. His back was turned to me, but in the glass I saw the reflection of a huge head and face illumined fitfully by the flicker of the night-light. The spectral gray of very early morning stealing in round the edges of the curtains lent an additional horror to the picture, for it fell upon the hair that was tawny and mane-like, hanging about a face whose swollen, rugose features bore the once seen never forgotten leonine expression of—I dare not write down that awful word. But, by way of corroborative proof, I saw in the faint mingling of the two lights that there were several bronze-coloured blotches on the cheeks which the man was evidently examining with great care in the glass. The lips were pale and very thick and large. One hand I could not see, but the other rested on the ivory back of my hair-brush. Its muscles were strangely contracted, the fingers thin to emaciation, the back of the hand closely puckered up. It was like a big gray spider crouching to spring, or the claw of a great bird.

The full realisation that I was alone in the room with this nameless creature, almost within arm's reach of him, overcame me to such a degree that, when he suddenly turned and regarded me with small beady eyes, wholly out of proportion to the grandeur of their massive setting, I sat bolt upright in bed, uttered a loud cry, and then fell back in a dead swoon of terror upon the bed.

Dec. 6.—. . . When I came to this morning, the first thing I noticed was that my clothes were strewn all over the floor. . . . I find it difficult to put my thoughts together, and have sudden accesses of violent trembling. I determined that I would go at once to Chapter's hotel and find out when he is expected. I cannot refer to what happened in the night; it is too awful, and I have to keep my thoughts rigorously away from it. I feel lightheaded and queer, couldn't eat any breakfast, and have twice vomited with blood. While dressing to go out, a hansom rattled up noisily over the cobbles, and a minute later the door opened, and to my great joy in walked the very subject of my thoughts.

The sight of his strong face and quiet eyes had an immediate effect upon me, and I grew calmer again. His very handshake was a sort of tonic. But, as I listened eagerly to the deep tones of his reassuring voice, and the visions of the night time paled a little, I began to realize how very hard it was going to be to tell him my wild, intangible tale. Some men radiate an animal vigour that destroys the delicate woof of a vision and effectually prevents its reconstruction. Chapter was one of these men.

We talked of incidents that had filled the interval since we last met, and he told me something of his travels. He talked and I listened. But, so full was I of the horrid thing I had to tell that I made a poor listener. I was forever watching my opportunity to leap in and explode it all under his nose.

Before very long, however, it was borne in upon me that he too was merely talking for time. He too held something of importance in the background of his mind, something too weighty to let fall till the right moment presented itself. So that during the whole of the first half-hour we were both waiting for the psychological moment in which properly to release our respective bombs; and the intensity of our minds' action set up opposing forces that merely sufficed to hold one another in check—and nothing more.

As soon as I realized this, therefore, I resolved to yield. I renounced for the time my purpose of telling my story, and had the satisfaction of seeing that his mind, released from the restraint of my own, at once began to make preparations for the discharge of its momentous burden. The talk grew less and less magnetic; the interest waned; the descriptions of his travels became less alive. There were pauses between his sentences. Presently he repeated himself. His words clothed no living thoughts. The pauses grew longer. Then the interest dwindled altogether and went out like a candle in the wind. His voice ceased, and he looked up squarely into my face with serious and anxious eyes.

The psychological moment had come at last!

"I say—" he began, and then stopped short.

I made an unconscious gesture of encouragement, but said no word. I dreaded the impending disclosure exceedingly. A dark shadow seemed to precede it.

"I say," he blurted out at last, "what in the world made you ever come to this place—to these rooms, I mean?"

"They're cheap, for one thing," I began, "and central and—"

"They're too cheap," he interrupted. "Didn't you ask what made 'em so cheap?"

"It never occurred to me at the time."

There was a pause in which he avoided my eyes.

"For God's sake, go on, man, and tell it!" I cried, for the suspense was getting more than I could stand in my nervous condition.

"This was where Blount lived so long," he said quietly, "and where he—died. You know, in the old days I often used to come here and see him and do what I could to alleviate his—" He stuck fast again.

"Well!" I said with a great effort. "*Please* go on—faster."

"But," Chapter went on, turning his face to the window with a perceptible shiver, "he finally got so terrible I simply couldn't stand it, though I always thought I could stand anything. It got on my nerves and made me dream, and haunted me day and night."

I stared at him, and said nothing. I had never heard of Blount in my life, and didn't know what he was talking about. But all the same, I was trembling, and my mouth had become strangely dry.

"This is the first time I've been back here since," he said almost in a whisper, "and, 'pon my word, it gives me the creeps. I swear it isn't fit for a man to live in. I never saw you look so bad, old man."

"I've got it for a year," I jerked out, with a forced laugh; "signed the lease and all. I thought it was rather a bargain."

Chapter shuddered, and buttoned his overcoat up to his neck. Then he spoke in a low voice, looking occasionally behind him as though he thought someone was listening. I too could have sworn someone else was in the room with us.

"He did it himself, you know, and no one blamed him a bit; his sufferings were awful. For the last two years he used to wear a veil when he went out, and even then it was always in a closed carriage. Even the attendant who had nursed him for so long was at length obliged to leave. The extremities of both the lower limbs were gone, dropped off, and he moved about the ground on all fours with a sort of crawling motion. The odour, too, was—"

I was obliged to interrupt him here. I could hear no more details of that sort. My skin was moist, I felt hot and cold by turns, for at last I was beginning to understand.

"Poor devil," Chapter went on; "I used to keep my eyes closed as much as possible. He always begged to be allowed to take his veil off, and asked if I minded very much. I used to stand by the open window. He never touched me, though. He rented the whole house. Nothing would induce him to leave it."

"Did he occupy—these very rooms?"

"No. He had the little room on the top floor, the square one just under the roof. He preferred it because it was dark. These rooms were too near the ground, and he was afraid people might see him through the windows. A crowd had been known to follow him up to the very door, and then stand below the windows in the hope of catching a glimpse of his face."

"But there were hospitals."

"He wouldn't go near one, and they didn't like to force him. You know, they say it's *not* contagious, so there was nothing to prevent his staying here if he wanted to. He spent all his time reading medical books, about drugs and so on. His head and face were something appalling, just like a lion's."

I held up my hand to arrest further description.

"He was a burden to the world, and he knew it. One night I suppose he realized it too keenly to wish to live. He had the free use of drugs—and in the morning he was found dead on the floor. Two years ago, that was, and they said then he had still several years to live."

"Then, in Heaven's name!" I cried, unable to bear the suspense any longer, "tell me what it was he had, and be quick about it."

"I thought you knew!" he exclaimed, with genuine surprise. "I thought you knew!"

He leaned forward and our eyes met. In a scarcely audible whisper I caught the words his lip seemed almost afraid to utter:

"He was a leper!"

The Yellow Cat

By Wilbur Daniel Steele

At least once in my life I have had the good fortune to board a deserted vessel at sea. I say "good fortune" because it has left me the memory of a singular impression. I have felt a ghost of the same thing two or three times since then, when peeping through the doorway of an abandoned house.

Now that vessel was not dead. She was a good vessel, a sound vessel, even a handsome vessel, in her blunt-bowed, coastwise way. She sailed under four lowers across as blue and glittering a sea as I have ever known, and there was not a point in her sailing that one could lay a finger upon as wrong. And yet, passing that schooner at two miles, one knew, somehow, that no hand was on her wheel. Sometimes I can imagine a vessel, stricken like that, moving over the empty spaces of the sea, carrying it off quite well were it not for that indefinable suggestion of a stagger; and I can think of all those ocean gods, in whom no landsman will ever believe, looking at one another and tapping their foreheads with just the shadow of a smile.

I wonder if they all scream—these ships that have lost their souls? Mine screamed. We heard her voice, like nothing I have ever heard before, when we rowed under her counter to read her name—the *Marionnette* it was, of Halifax. I remember how it made me shiver, there in the full blaze of the sun, to hear her going on so, railing and screaming in that stark fashion. And I remember, too, how our footsteps, pattering through the vacant internals in search of that haggard utterance, made me think of the footsteps of hurrying warders roused in the night.

And we found a parrot in a cage; that was all. It wanted water. We gave it water and went away to look things over, keeping pretty close together, all of us. In the quarters the table was set for four. Two men had begun to eat, by the evidences of the plates. Nowhere in the vessel was there any sign of disorder, except one sea-chest broken out, evidently in haste. Her papers were gone and the stern davits were empty. That is how the case stood that day, and that is how it has stood to this. I saw this same *Marionnette* a week later, tied up to a Hoboken dock, where she awaited news from her owners; but even there, in the midst of all the water-front bustle, I could not get rid of the feeling that she was still very far away—in a sort of shippish other-world.

The thing happens now and then. Sometimes half a dozen years will go by without a solitary wanderer of this sort crossing the ocean paths, and then in a single season perhaps several of them will turn up: vacant waifs, impassive and mysterious—a quarter-column of tidings tucked away on the second page of the evening paper.

That is where I read the story about the *Abbie Rose.* I recollect how painfully awkward and out-of-place it looked there, cramped between ruled black edges and smelling of landsman's ink—this thing that had to do essentially with air and vast coloured spaces. I forget the exact words of the heading—something like "Abandoned Craft Picked Up At Sea"—but I still have the clipping itself, couched in the formal patter of the marine-news writer:

The first hint of another mystery of the sea came in to-day when the schooner *Abbie Rose* dropped anchor in the upper river, manned only by a crew of one. It appears that the outbound freighter *Mercury* sighted the *Abbie Rose* off Block Island on Thursday last, acting in a suspicious manner. A boat-party sent aboard found the schooner in perfect order and condition, sailing under four lower sails, the topsails being pursed up to the mastheads but not stowed. With the exception of a yellow cat, the vessel was found to be utterly deserted, though her small boat still hung in the davits. No evidences of disorder were visible in any part of the craft. The dishes were washed up, the stove in the galley was still slightly warm to the touch, everything in its proper place with the exception of the vessel's papers, which were not to be found.

All indications being for fair weather, Captain Rohmer of the *Mercury* detailed two of his company to bring the find back to this port, a distance of one hundred and fifteen miles. The only man available with a knowledge of the fore-and-aft rig was Stewart McCord, the second engineer. A seaman by the name of Björnsen was sent with him. McCord arrived this noon, after a very heavy voyage of five days, reporting that Björnsen had fallen overboard while shaking out the foretopsail. McCord himself showed evidence of the hardships he has passed through, being almost a nervous wreck.

Stewart McCord! Yes, Stewart McCord would have a knowledge of the fore-and-aft rig, or of almost anything else connected with the affairs of the sea. It happened that I used to know this fellow. I had even been quite chummy with him in the old days—that is, to the extent of drinking too many beers with him in certain hot-country ports. I remembered him as a stolid and deliberate sort of a person, with an amazing hodgepodge of learning, a stamp collection, and a theory about the effects of tropical sunshine on the Caucasian race, to which I have listened half of more than one night, stretched out naked on a freighter's deck. He had not impressed me as a fellow who would be bothered by his nerves.

And there was another thing about the story which struck me as rather queer. Perhaps it is a relic of my seafaring days, but I have always been a conscientious reader of the weather reports; and I could remember no weather in the past week sufficient to shake a man out of a top, especially a man by the name of Björnsen—a thoroughgoing seafaring name.

I was destined to hear more of this in the evening, from the ancient boatman who rowed me out on the upper river. He had been to sea in his day. He knew enough to wonder about this thing, even to indulge in a little superstitious awe about it.

"No sir-ee. Something *happened* to them four chaps. And another thing—"

I fancied I heard a sea-bird whining in the darkness overhead. A shape moved out of the gloom ahead, passed to the left, lofty and silent, and merged once more with the gloom behind—a barge at anchor, with the sea-grass clinging around her water-line.

"Funny about that other chap," the old fellow speculated. "Björnsen—I b'lieve he called 'im. Now that story sounds to me kind of—" He feathered his oars with a suspicious jerk and peered at me. "This McCord a friend of yourn?" he inquired.

"In a way," I said.

"Hm-m—well—" He turned on his thwart to squint ahead. "There she is," he announced, with something of relief, I thought.

It was hard at that time of night to make anything but a black blotch out of the *Abbie Rose*. Of course I could see that she was pot-bellied, like the rest of the coastwise sisterhood. And that McCord had not stowed his topsails. I could make them out, pursed at the mast-

33

heads and hanging down as far as the cross-trees, like huge, over-ripe pears. Then I recollected that he had found them so—probably had not touched them since; a queer way to leave tops, it seemed to me. I could see also the glowing tip of a cigar floating restlessly along the farther rail. I called: "McCord! Oh, McCord!"

The spark came swimming across the deck. "Hello! Hello, there—ah—" There was a note of querulous uneasiness there that somehow jarred with my remembrance of this man.

"Ridgeway," I explained.

He echoed the name uncertainly, still with that suggestion of peevishness, hanging over the rail and peering down at us. "Oh! By gracious!" he exclaimed, abruptly. "I'm glad to see you, Ridgeway. I had a boatman coming out before this, but I guess—well, I guess he'll be along. By gracious! I'm glad—"

"I'll not keep you," I told the gnome, putting the money in his palm and reaching for the rail. McCord lent me a hand on my wrist. Then when I stood squarely on the deck beside him he appeared to forget my presence, leaned forward heavily on the rail, and squinted after my waning boatman.

"Ahoy—boat!" he called out, sharply, shielding his lips with his hand. His violence seemed to bring him out of the blank, for he fell immediately to puffing strongly at his cigar and explaining in rather a shame-voiced way that he was beginning to think his own boatman had "passed him up."

"Come in and have a nip," he urged with an abrupt heartiness, clapping me on the shoulder.

"So you've—" I did not say what I had intended. I was thinking that in the old days McCord had made rather a fetish of touching nothing stronger than beer. Neither had he been of the shoulder-clapping sort. "So you've got something aboard?" I shifted.

"Dead men's liquor," he chuckled. It gave me a queer feeling in the pit of my stomach to hear him. I began to wish I had not come, but there was nothing for it now but to follow him into the after-house. The cabin itself might have been nine feet square, with three bunks occupying the port side. To the right opened the master's stateroom, and a door in the forward bulkhead led to the galley.

I took in these features at a casual glance. Then, hardly knowing why I did it, I began to examine them with greater care.

"Have you a match?" I asked. My voice sounded very small, as though something unheard of had happened to all the air.

"Smoke?" he asked. "I'll get you a cigar."

"No." I took the proffered match, scratched it on the side of the galley door, and passed out. There seemed to be a thousand pans there, throwing my match back at me from every wall of the box-like compartment. Even McCord's eyes, in the doorway, were large and round and shining. He probably thought me crazy. Perhaps I was, a little. I ran the match along close to the ceiling and came upon a rusty hook a little aport of the centre.

"There," I said. "Was there anything hanging from this—er—say a parrot—or something, McCord?" The match burned my fingers and went out.

"What do you mean?" McCord demanded from the doorway. I got myself back into the comfortable yellow glow of the cabin before I answered, and then it was a question.

"Do you happen to know anything about this craft's personal history?"

"No. What are you talking about! Why?"

"Well, I do," I offered. "For one thing, she's changed her name. And it happens this isn't the first time she's—Well, damn it all, fourteen years ago I helped pick up this whatever-she-is off the Virginia Capes—in the same sort of condition. There you are!" I was yapping like a nerve-strung puppy.

McCord leaned forward with his hands on the table, bringing his face beneath the fan of the hanging-lamp. For the first time I could mark how shockingly it had changed. It was almost colourless. The jaw had somehow lost its old-time security and the eyes seemed to be loose in their sockets. I had expected him to start at my announcement; he only blinked at the light.

"I am not surprised," he remarked at length. "After what I've seen and heard—" He lifted his fist and brought it down with a sudden crash on the table. "Man—let's have a nip!"

He was off before I could say a word, fumbling out of sight in the narrow stateroom. Presently he reappeared, holding a glass in either hand and a dark bottle hugged between his elbows. Putting the glasses down, he held up the bottle between his eyes and the lamp, and its shadow, falling across his face, green and luminous at the core, gave him a ghastly look—like a mutilation or an unspeakable birthmark. He shook the bottle gently and chuckled his "Dead men's liquor" again. Then he poured two half-glasses of the clear gin, swallowed his portion, and sat down.

35

"A parrot," he mused, a little of the liquor's colour creeping into his cheeks. "No, this time it was a cat, Ridgeway. A yellow cat. She was—"

"*Was?*" I caught him up. "What's happened—what's become of her?"

"Vanished. Evaporated. I haven't seen her since night before last, when I caught her trying to lower the boat—"

"*Stop it!*" It was I who banged the table now, without any of the reserve of decency. "McCord, you're drunk—*drunk*, I tell you. A *cat*! Let a *cat* throw you off your head like this! She's probably hiding out below this minute, on affairs of her own."

"Hiding?" He regarded me for a moment with the queer superiority of the damned. "I guess you don't realize how many times I've been over this hulk, from decks to keelson, with a mallet and a foot-rule."

"Or fallen overboard," I shifted, with less assurance. "Like this fellow Björnsen. By the way, McCord—" I stopped there on account of the look in his eyes.

He reached out, poured himself a shot, swallowed it, and got up to shuffle about the confined quarters. I watched their restless circuit—my friend and his jumping shadow. He stopped and bent forward to examine a Sunday-supplement chromo tacked on the wall, and the two heads drew together, as though there were something to whisper. Of a sudden I seemed to hear the old gnome croaking, "Now that story sounds to me kind of—"

McCord straightened up and turned to face me.

"What do you know about Björnsen?" he demanded.

"Well—only what they had you saying in the papers," I told him.

"Pshaw!" He snapped his fingers, tossing the affair aside. "I found her log," he announced in quite another voice.

"You did, eh? I judged, from what I read in the paper, that there wasn't a sign."

"No, no; I happened on this the other night, under the mattress in there." He jerked his head toward the stateroom. "Wait!" I heard him knocking things over in the dark and mumbling at them. After a moment he came out and threw on the table a long, cloth-covered ledger, of the common commercial sort. It lay open at about the middle, showing close script running indiscriminately across the column ruling.

"When I said 'log,'" he went on, "I guess I was going it a little strong. At least, I wouldn't want that sort of log found around *my* vessel. Let's call it a personal record. Here's his picture, somewhere—" He shook the book by its back and a common Kodak blue-print fluttered to the table. It was the likeness of a solid man with a paunch, a huge square beard, small squinting eyes, and a bald head. "What do you make of him—a writing chap?"

"From the nose down, yes," I estimated. "From the nose up, he will 'tend to his own business if you will 'tend to yours, strictly."

McCord slapped his thigh. "By gracious! that's the fellow! He hates the Chinaman. He knows as well as anything he ought not to put down in black and white how intolerably he hates the Chinaman, and yet he must sneak off to his cubby-hole and suck his pencil, and—how is it Stevenson has it?—the 'agony of composition,' you remember. Can you imagine the fellow, Ridgeway, bundling down here with the fever on him—"

"About the Chinaman," I broke in. "I think you said something about a Chinaman?"

"Yes. The cook, he must have been. I gather he wasn't the master's pick, by the reading-matter here. Probably clapped on to him by the owners—shifted from one of their others at the last moment; a queer trick. Listen." He picked up the book and, running over the pages with a selective thumb, read:

"*August second.*—First part, moderate southwesterly breeze—and so forth—er—but here he comes to it:

"Anything can happen to a man at sea, even a funeral. In special to a Chinyman, who is of no account to social welfare, being a barbarian as I look at it.

"Something of a philosopher, you see. And did you get the reserve in that 'even a funeral'? An artist, I tell you. But wait: let me catch him a bit wilder. Here:

"I'll get that mustard-coloured —— [This is back a couple of days.] Never can hear the —— coming, in them carpet slippers. Turned round and found him standing right to my back this morning. Could have stuck a knife into me easy. 'Look here!' says I, and fetched him a tap on the ear that will make him walk louder next time, I warrant. He could have stuck a knife into me easy.

"A clear case of moral funk, I should say. Can you imagine the fellow, Ridgeway—"

"Yes; oh, yes." I was ready with a phrase of my own. "A man handicapped with an imagination. You see he can't quite understand this

37

'barbarian,' who has him beaten by about thirty centuries of civiliza-
tion—and his imagination has to have something to chew on, something to hit—a 'tap on the ear,' you know."

"By gracious! that's the ticket!" McCord pounded his knee. "And
now we've got another chap going to pieces—Peters, he calls him.
Refuses to eat dinner on August the third, claiming he caught the
Chink making passes over the chowder-pot with his thumb. Can you
believe it, Ridgeway—in this very cabin here?" Then he went on with
a suggestion of haste, as though he had somehow made a slip. "Well,
at any rate, the disease seems to be catching. Next day it's Bach, the
second seaman, who begins to feel the gaff. Listen:

"Bach he comes to me to-night, complaining he's being watched.
He claims the ―― has got the evil eye. Says he can see you through
a two-inch bulkhead, and the like. The Chink's laying in his bunk,
turned the other way. 'Why don't you go aboard of him?' says I. The
Dutcher says nothing, but goes over to his own bunk and feels under
the straw. When he comes back he's looking queer. 'By God!' says he,
'the devil has swiped my gun!' . . . Now if that's true there is going to
be hell to pay in this vessel very quick. I figure I'm still master of this
vessel."

"The evil eye," I grunted. "Consciences gone wrong there somewhere."

"Not altogether, Ridgeway. I can see that yellow man peeking.
Now just figure yourself, say, eight thousand miles from home, out on
the water alone with a crowd of heathen fanatics crazy from fright,
looking around for guns and so on. Don't you believe you'd keep an
eye around the corners, kind of—eh? I'll bet a hat he was taking it all
in, lying there in his bunk, 'turned the other way.' Eh? I pity the poor
cuss—Well, there's only one more entry after that. He's good and mad.
Here:

"Now, by God! this is the end. My gun's gone, too; right out from
under lock and key, by God! I been talking with Bach this morning.
Not to let on, I had him in to clean my lamp. There's more ways than
one, he says, and so do I."

McCord closed the book and dropped it on the table. "*Finis*," he
said. "The rest is blank paper."

"Well!" I will confess I felt much better than I had for some time
past. "There's one 'mystery of the sea' gone to pot, at any rate. And now,
if you don't mind, I think I'll have another of your nips, McCord."

He pushed my glass across the table and got up, and behind his back his shadow rose to scour the corners of the room, like an incorruptible sentinel. I forgot to take up my gin, watching him. After an uneasy minute or so he came back to the table and pressed the tip of a forefinger on the book.

"Ridgeway," he said, "you don't seem to understand. This particular 'mystery of the sea' hasn't been scratched yet—not even *scratched*, Ridgeway." He sat down and leaned forward, fixing me with a didactic finger. "What happened?"

"Well, I have an idea the 'barbarian' got them, when it came to the pinch."

"And let the—remains over the side?"

"I should say."

"And they came back and got the 'barbarian' and let *him* over the side, eh? There were none left, you remember."

"Oh, good Lord, I don't know!" I flared with a childish resentment at this catechizing of his. But his finger remained there, challenging.

"I do," he announced. "The Chinaman put them over the side, as we have said. And then, after that, he died—of wounds about the head."

"So?" I had still sarcasm.

"You will remember," he went on, "that the skipper did not happen to mention a cat, a *yellow* cat, in his confessions."

"McCord," I begged him, "please drop it. Why in thunder *should* he mention a cat?"

"True. Why *should* he mention a cat? I think one of the reasons why he should *not* mention a cat is because there did not happen to be a cat aboard at that time."

"Oh, all right!" I reached out and pulled the bottle to my side of the table. Then I took out my watch. "If you don't mind," I suggested, "I think we'd better be going ashore. I've got to get to my office rather early in the morning. What do you say?"

He said nothing for the moment, but his finger had dropped. He leaned back and stared straight into the core of the light above, his eyes squinting.

"He would have been from the south of China, probably." He seemed to be talking to himself. "There's a considerable sprinkling of the belief down there, I've heard. It's an uncanny business—this transmigration of souls—"

Personally, I had had enough of it. McCord's fingers came groping across the table for the bottle. I picked it up hastily and let it go through the open companionway, where it died with a faint gurgle, out somewhere on the river.

"Now," I said to him, shaking the vagrant wrist, "either you come ashore with me or you go in there and get under the blankets. You're drunk, McCord—*drunk*. Do you hear me?"

"Ridgeway," he pronounced, bringing his eyes down to me and speaking very slowly. "You're a fool, if you can't see better than that. I'm not drunk. I'm sick. I haven't slept for three nights—and now I can't. And you say—you—" He went to pieces very suddenly, jumped up, pounded the legs of his chair on the decking, and shouted at me: "And you say that, you—you landlubber, you office coddler! You're so comfortably sure that everything in the world is cut and dried. Come back to the water again and learn how to wonder—and stop talking like a damn fool. Do you know where—Is there anything in your municipal budget to tell me where Björnsen went? Listen!" He sat down, waving me to do the same, and went on with a sort of desperate repression.

"It happened on the first night after we took this hellion. I'd stood the wheel most of the afternoon—off and on, that is, because she sails herself uncommonly well. Just put her on a reach, you know, and she carries it off pretty well—"

"I know," I nodded.

"Well, we mugged up about seven o'clock. There was a good deal of canned stuff in the galley, and Björnsen wasn't a bad hand with a kettle—a thoroughgoing Square-head he was—tall and lean and yellow-haired, with little fat, round cheeks and a white moustache. Not a bad chap at all. He took the wheel to stand till midnight, and I turned in, but I didn't drop off for quite a spell. I could hear his boots wandering around over my head, padding off forward, coming back again. I heard him whistling now and then—an outlandish air. Occasionally I could see the shadow of his head waving in a block of moonlight that lay on the decking right down there in front of the stateroom door. It came from the companion; the cabin was dark because we were going easy on the oil. They hadn't left a great deal, for some reason or other."

McCord leaned back and described with his finger where the illumination had cut the decking.

"There! I could see it from my bunk, as I lay, you understand. I must have almost dropped off once when I heard him fiddling around out here in the cabin, and then he said something in a whisper, just

40

to find out if I was still awake, I suppose. I asked him what the matter was. He came and poked his head in the door."

"'The breeze is going out,' says he. 'I was wondering if we couldn't get a little more sail on her.' Only I can't give you his fierce Square-head tang. 'How about the tops?' he suggested.

"I was so sleepy I didn't care, and I told him so. 'All right,' he says, 'but I thought I might shake out one of them tops.' Then I heard him blow at something outside. 'Scat, you ——!' Then: 'This cat's going to set me crazy, Mr. McCord,' he says, 'following me around everywhere.' He gave a kick, and I saw something yellow floating across the moon-light. It never made a sound—just floated. You wouldn't have known it ever lit anywhere, just like——"

McCord stopped and drummed a few beats on the table with his fist, as though to bring himself back to the straight narrative.

"I went to sleep," he began again. "I dreamed about a lot of things. I woke up sweating. You know how glad you are to wake up after a dream like that and find none of it is so? Well, I turned over and set-tled to go off again, and then I got a little more awake and thought to myself it must be pretty near time for me to go on deck. I scratched a match and looked at my watch. 'That fellow must be either a good chap or asleep,' I said to myself. And I rolled out quick and went above-decks. He wasn't at the wheel. I called him: 'Björnsen! Björnsen!' No answer."

McCord was really telling a story now. He paused for a long mo-ment, one hand shielding an ear and his eyeballs turned far up.

"That was the first time I really went over the hulk," he ran on. "I got out a lantern and started at the forward end of the hold, and I worked aft, and there was nothing there. Not a sign, or a stain, or a scrap of clothing, or anything. You may believe that I began to feel funny inside. I went over the decks and the rails and the house itself— inch by inch. Not a trace. I went out aft again. The cat sat on the wheel-box, washing her face. I hadn't noticed the scar on her head before, running down between her ears—rather a new scar—three or four days old, I should say. It looked ghastly and blue-white in the flat moonlight. I ran over and grabbed her up to heave her over the side—you understand how upset I was. Now you know a cat will squirm around and grab something when you hold it like that, gener-ally speaking. This one didn't. She just drooped and began to purr and looked up at me out of her moonlit eyes under that scar. I dropped her on the deck and backed off. You remember Björnsen had *kicked* her—and I didn't want anything like that happening to—"

The narrator turned upon me with a sudden heat, leaned over and shook his finger before my face.

"There you go!" he cried. "You, with your stout stone buildings and your policemen and your neighbourhood church—you're so damn sure. But I'd just like to see you out there, alone, with the moon setting, and all the lights gone tall and queer, and a shipmate—" He lifted his hand overhead, the finger-tips pressed together and then suddenly separated as though he had released an impalpable something into the air.

"Go on," I told him.

"I felt more like you do, when it got light again, and warm and sunshiny. I said 'Bah!' to the whole business. I even fed the cat, and I slept awhile on the roof of the house—I was so sure. We lay dead most of the day, without a streak of air. But that night—! Well, that night I hadn't got over being sure yet. It takes quite a jolt, you know, to shake loose several dozen generations. A fair, steady breeze had come along, the glass was high, she was staying herself like a doll, and so I figured I could get a little rest, lying below in the bunk, even if I didn't sleep.

"I tried not to sleep, in case something should come up—a squall or the like. But I think I must have dropped off once or twice. I remember I heard something fiddling around in the galley, and I hollered 'Scat!' and everything was quiet again. I rolled over and lay on my left side, staring at that square of moonlight outside my door for a long time. You'll think it was a dream—what I saw there."

"Go on," I said.

"Call this table-top the spot of light, roughly," he said. He placed a finger-tip at about the middle of the forward edge and drew it slowly toward the centre. "Here, what would correspond with the upper side of the companionway, there came down very gradually the shadow of a tail. I watched it streaking out there across the deck, wiggling the slightest bit now and then. When it had come down about half-way across the light, the solid part of the animal—its shadow, you understand—began to appear, quite big and round. But how could she hang there, done up in a ball, from the hatch?"

He shifted his finger back to the edge of the table and puddled it around to signify the shadowed body.

"I fished my gun out from behind my back. You see, I was feeling funny again. Then I started to slide one foot over the edge of the bunk, always with my eyes on that shadow. Now I swear I didn't make

42

the sound of a pin dropping, but I had no more than moved a muscle when that shadowed thing twisted itself around in a flash—and there on the floor before me was the profile of a man's head, upside down, listening—a man's head with a tail of hair."

McCord got up hastily and stepped over in front of the stateroom door, where he bent down and scratched a match.

"See," he said, holding the tiny flame above a splintered scar on the boards. "You wouldn't think a man would be fool enough to shoot at a shadow?"

He came back and sat down.

"It seemed to me all hell had shaken loose. You've no idea, Ridgeway, the rumpus a gun raises in a box like this. I found out afterward the slug ricocheted into the galley, bringing down a couple of pans—and that helped. Oh, yes, I got out of here quick enough. I stood there, half out of the companion, with my hands on the hatch and the gun between them, and my shadow running off across the top of the house shivering before my eyes like a dry leaf. There wasn't a whisper of sound in the world—just the pale water floating past and the sails towering up like a pair of twittering ghosts. And everything that crazy colour—

"Well, in a minute I saw it, just abreast of the mainmast, crouched down in the shadow of the weather rail, sneaking off forward very slowly. This time I took a good long sight before I let go. Did you ever happen to see black-powder smoke in the moonlight? It puffed out perfectly round, like a big, pale balloon, this did, and for a second something was bounding through it—without a sound, you understand—something a shade solider than the smoke and big as a cow, it looked to me. It passed from the weather side to the lee and ducked behind the sweep of the mainsail like *that*—" McCord snapped his thumb and forefinger under the light.

"Go on," I said. "What did you do then?"

McCord regarded me for an instant from beneath his lids, uncertain. His fist hung above the table. "You're—" He hesitated, his lips working vacantly. A forefinger came out of the fist and gesticulated before my face. "If you're laughing, why, damn me, I'll—"

"Go on," I repeated. "What did you do then?"

"I followed the thing." He was still watching me sullenly. "I got up and went forward along the roof of the house, so as to have an eye on either rail. You understand, this business had to be done with. I kept straight along. Every shadow I wasn't absolutely sure of I *made* sure of—point-blank. And I rounded the thing up at the very stern—sitting on the butt of the bowsprit, Ridgeway, washing her yellow face under the moon. I didn't make any bones about it this time. I put the bad end of that gun against the scar on her head and squeezed the trigger. It snicked on an empty shell. I tell you a fact; I was almost deafened by the report that didn't come.

"She followed me aft. I couldn't get away from her. I went and sat on the wheel-box and she came and sat on the edge of the house, facing me. And there we stayed for upward of an hour, without moving. Finally she went over and stuck her paw in the water-pan I'd set out for her; then she raised her head and looked at me and yawled. At sundown there'd been two quarts of water in that pan. You wouldn't think a cat could get away with two quarts of water in—"

He broke off again and considered me with a sort of weary defiance.

"What's the use?" He spread out his hands in a gesture of hopelessness. "I knew you wouldn't believe it when I started. You *couldn't*. It would be a kind of blasphemy against the sacred institution of pavements. You're too damn smug, Ridgeway. I can't shake you. You haven't sat two days and two nights, keeping your eyes open by sheer teeth-gritting, until they got used to it and wouldn't shut any more. When I tell you I found that yellow thing snooping around the davits, and three bights off the boat-fall loosened out, plain on deck—you grin behind your collar. When I tell you she padded off forward and evaporated—flickered back to hell and hasn't been seen since, then—why, you explain to yourself that I'm drunk. I tell you—" He jerked his head back abruptly and turned to face the companionway, his lips still apart. He listened so for a moment, then he shook himself out of it and went on:

"I tell you, Ridgeway, I've been over this hulk with a foot-rule. There's not a cubic inch I haven't accounted for, not a plank I—"

This time he got up and moved a step toward the companion, where he stood with his head bent forward and slightly to the side. After what might have been twenty seconds of this he whispered, "Do you hear?"

Far and far away down the reach a ferry-boat lifted its infinitesimal wail, and then the silence of the night river came down once more, profound and inscrutable. A corner of the wick above my head sputtered a little—that was all.

"Hear what?" I whispered back. He lifted a cautious finger toward

44

the opening.

"Somebody. Listen."

The man's faculties must have been keyed up to the pitch of his nerves, for to me the night remained as voiceless as a subterranean cavern. I became intensely irritated with him; within my mind I cried out against this infatuated pantomime of his. And then, of a sudden, there was a sound—the dying rumour of a ripple, somewhere in the outside darkness, as though an object had been let into the water with extreme care.

"You heard?"

I nodded. The ticking of the watch in my vest pocket came to my ears, shucking off the leisurely seconds, while McCord's fingernails gnawed at the palms of his hands. The man was really sick. He wheeled on me and cried out, "My God! Ridgeway—why don't we go out?"

I, for one, refused to be a fool. I passed him and climbed out of the opening; he followed far enough to lean his elbows on the hatch, his feet and legs still within the secure glow of the cabin.

"You see, there's nothing." My wave of assurance was possibly a little overdone.

"Over there," he muttered, jerking his head toward the shore lights. "Something swimming."

I moved to the corner of the house and listened.

"River thieves," I argued. "The place is full of—"

"*Ridgeway. Look behind you!*"

Perhaps it is the pavements—but no matter; I am not ordinarily a jumping sort. And yet there was something in the quality of that voice beyond my shoulder that brought the sweat stinging through the pores of my scalp even while I was in the act of turning.

A cat sat there on the hatch, expressionless and immobile in the gloom.

I did not say anything. I turned and went below. McCord was there already, standing on the farther side of the table. After a moment or so the cat followed and sat on her haunches at the foot of the ladder and stared at us without winking.

"I think she wants something to eat," I said to McCord.

He lit a lantern and went out into the galley. Returning with a chunk of salt beef, he threw it into the farther corner. The cat went over and began to tear at it, her muscles playing with convulsive shadow-lines under the sagging yellow hide.

45

And now it was she who listened, to something beyond the reach of even McCord's faculties, her neck stiff and her ears flattened. I looked at McCord and found him brooding at the animal with a sort of listless malevolence. "*Quick!* She has kittens somewhere about." I shook his elbow sharply. "When she starts, now—"

"You don't seem to understand," he mumbled. "It wouldn't be any use."

She had turned now and was making for the ladder with the soundless agility of her race. I grasped McCord's wrist and dragged him after me, the lantern banging against his knees. When we came up the cat was already amidships, a scarcely discernible shadow at the margin of our lantern's ring. She stopped and looked back at us with her luminous eyes, appeared to hesitate, uneasy at our pursuit of her, shifted here and there with quick, soft bounds, and stopped to fawn with her back arched at the foot of the mast. Then she was off with an amazing suddenness into the shadows forward.

"Lively now!" I yelled at McCord. He came pounding along behind me, still protesting that it was of no use. Abreast of the foremast I took the lantern from him to hold above my head.

"You see," he complained, peering here and there over the illuminated deck. "I tell you, Ridgeway, this thing—" But my eyes were in another quarter, and I slapped him on the shoulder.

"An engineer—an engineer to the core," I cried at him. "Look aloft, man."

Our quarry was almost to the cross-trees, clambering up the shrouds with a smartness no sailor has ever come to, her yellow body, cut by the moving shadows of the ratlines, a queer sight against the mat of the night. McCord closed his mouth and opened it again for two words: "By gracious!" The following instant he had the lantern and was after her. I watched him go up above my head—a ponderous, swaying climber into the sky—come to the cross-trees, and squat there with his knees clamped around the mast. The clear star of the lantern shot this way and that for a moment, then it disappeared, and in its place there sprang out a bag of yellow light, like a fire-balloon at anchor in the heavens. I could see the shadows of his head and hands moving monstrously over the inner surface of the sail, and muffled exclamations without meaning came down to me. After a moment he drew out his head and called: "All right—they're here. Heads! there below!"

I ducked at his warning, and something spanked on the planking

46

a yard from my feet. I stepped over to the vague blur on the deck and picked up a slipper—a slipper covered with some woven straw stuff and soled with a matted felt, perhaps a half-inch thick. Another struck somewhere abaft the mast, and then McCord reappeared above and began to stagger down the shrouds. Under his left arm he hugged a curious assortment of litter, a sheaf of papers, a brace of revolvers, a gray *kimono*, and a soiled apron.

"Well," he said when he had come to deck, "I feel like a man who has gone to hell and come back again. You know I'd come to the place where I really believed that about the cat. When you think of it—By gracious! we haven't come so far from the jungle, after all."

We went aft and below and sat down at the table as we had been. McCord broke a prolonged silence.

"I'm sort of glad he got away—poor cuss! He's probably climbing up a wharf this minute, shivering and scared to death. Over toward the gas-tanks, by the way he was swimming. By gracious! now that the world's turned over straight again, I feel I could sleep a solid week. Poor cuss! can you imagine him, Ridgeway—"

"Yes," I broke in. "I think I can. He must have lost his nerve when he made out your smoke and shinnied up there to stow away, taking the ship's papers with him. He would have attached some profound importance to them—remember, the 'barbarian,' eight thousand miles from home. Probably couldn't read a word. I suppose the cat followed him—the traditional source of food. He must have wanted water badly."

"I should say! He wouldn't have taken the chances he did."

"Well," I announced, "at any rate, I can say it now—there's another 'mystery of the sea' gone to pot."

McCord lifted his heavy lids.

"No," he mumbled. "The mystery is that a man who has been to sea all his life could sail around for three days with a man bundled up in his top and not know it. When I think of him peeking down at me—and playing off that damn cat—probably without realizing it—scared to death—by gracious! Ridgeway, there was a pair of funks aboard this craft, eh? Wow—yow—I could sleep—"

"I should think you could."

McCord did not answer.

"By the way," I speculated. "I guess you were right about Björnsen, McCord—that is, his fooling with the foretop. He must have been caught all of a bunch, eh?"

Again McCord failed to answer. I looked up mildly surprised, and found his head hanging back over his chair and his mouth opened wide. He was asleep.

Thrawn Janet

By Robert Louis Stevenson

The Reverend Murdoch Soulis was long minister of the moorland parish of Balweary, in the vale of Dule. A severe, bleak-faced old man, dreadful to his hearers, he dwelt in the last years of his life, without relative or servant or any human company, in the small and lonely manse under the Hanging Shaw. In spite of the iron composure of his features, his eye was wild, scared, and uncertain; and when he dwelt, in private admonitions, on the future of the impenitent, it seemed as if his eye pierced through the storms of time to the terrors of eternity. Many young persons, coming to prepare themselves against the season of the holy communion, were dreadfully affected by his talk. He had a sermon on 1st Peter, v and 8th, "The devil as a roaring lion," on the Sunday after every 17th of August, and he was accustomed to surpass himself upon that text both by the appalling nature of the matter and the terror of his bearing in the pulpit.

The children were frightened into fits, and the old looked more than usually oracular, and were, all that day, full of those hints that Hamlet deprecated. The manse itself, where it stood by the water of Dule among some thick trees, with the Shaw overhanging it on the one side, and on the other many cold, moorish hilltops rising toward the sky, had begun, at a very early period of Mr. Soulis's ministry, to be avoided in the dusk hours by all who valued themselves upon their prudence; and guidmen sitting at the clachan alehouse shook their heads together at the thought of passing late by that uncanny neighbourhood. There was one spot, to be more particular, which was regarded with especial awe. The manse stood between the highroad and the water of Dule, with a gable to each; its bank was toward the kirktown of Balweary, nearly half a mile away; in front of it, a bare garden, hedged with thorn, occupied the land between the river and the road.

The house was two storeys high, with two large rooms on each. It opened not directly on the garden, but on a causewayed path, or passage, giving on the road on the one hand, and closed on the other by the tall willows and elders that bordered on the stream. And it was this strip of causeway that enjoyed among the young parishioners of Balweary so infamous a reputation. The minister walked there often after dark, sometimes groaning aloud in the instancy of his unspoken prayers; and when he was from home, and the manse door was locked, the more daring schoolboys ventured, with beating hearts, to "follow my leader" across that legendary spot.

This atmosphere of terror, surrounding, as it did, a man of God of spotless character and orthodoxy, was a common cause of wonder and subject of inquiry among the few strangers who were led by chance or business into that unknown, outlying country. But many even of the people of the parish were ignorant of the strange events which had marked the first year of Mr. Soulis's ministrations; and among those who were better informed, some were naturally reticent, and others shy of that particular topic. Now and again, only, one of the older folk would warm into courage over his third tumbler, and recount the cause of the minister's strange looks and solitary life.

Fifty years syne, when Mr. Soulis cam' first into Ba'weary, he was still a young man,—a callant, the folk said,—fu' o' book-learnin' and grand at the exposition, but, as was natural in sae young a man, wi' nae leevin' experience in religion. The younger sort were greatly taken wi' his gifts and his gab; but auld, concerned, serious men and women were moved even to prayer for the young man, whom they took to be a self-deceiver, and the parish that was like to be sae ill supplied. It was before the days o' the Moderates—weary fa' them; but ill things are like guid—they baith come bit by bit, a pickle at a time; and there were folk even then that said the Lord had left the college professors to their ain devices, an' the lads that went to study wi' them wad hae done mair and better sittin' in a peat-bog, like their forebears of the persecution, wi' a Bible under their oxter and a speerit o' prayer in their heart.

There was nae doubt, onyway, but that Mr. Soulis had been ow-er-lang at the college. He was careful and troubled for many things besides the ae thing needful. He had a feck o' books wi' him—mair than had ever been seen before in a' that presbytery; and a sair wark the carrier had wi' them, for they were a' like to have smoored in the

50

Deil's Hag between this and Kilmackerlie. They were books o' divinity, to be sure, or so they ca'd them; but the serious were o' opinion there was little service for sae mony, when the hail o' God's Word would gang in the neuk of a plaid. Then he wad sit half the day and half the nicht forby, which was scant decent—writin', nae less; and first they were feard he wad read his sermons; and syne it proved he was writin' a book himsel', which was surely no fittin' for ane of his years an' sma' experience.

Onyway, it behooved him to get an auld, decent wife to keep the manse for him an' see to his bit denners; and he was recommended to an auld limmer,—Janet M'Clour, they ca'd her,—and sae far left to himsel' as to be ower-persuaded. There was mony advised him to the contrar', for Janet was mair than suspeckit by the best folk in Ba'weary. Lang or that, she had had a wean to a dragoon; she hadnae come forrit for maybe thretty year; and bairns had seen her mumblin' to hersel' up on Key's Loan in the gloamin', whilk was an unco time an' place for a God-fearin' woman. Howsoever, it was the laird himsel' that had first tauld the minister o' Janet; and in thae days he wad have gane a far gate to pleesure the laird. When folk tauld him that Janet was sib to the deil, it was a' superstition by his way of it; and when they cast up the Bible to him, an' the witch of Endor, he wad threep it doun their thrapples that thir days were a' gane by, and the deil was mercifully restrained.

Weel, when it got about the clachan that Janet M'Clour was to be servant at the manse, the folk were fair mad wi' her an' him thegether; and some o' the guidwives had nae better to dae than get round her door-cheeks and chairge her wi' a' that was kent again' her, frae the sodger's bairn to John Tamson's twa kye. She was nae great speaker; folk usually let her gang her ain gait, an' she let them gang theirs, wi' neither fair guid-e'en nor fair guid-day; but when she buckled to, she had a tongue to deave the miller.

Up she got, an' there wasnae an auld story in Ba'weary but she gart somebody lowp for it that day; they couldnae say ae thing but she could say twa to it; till, at the hinder end, the guidwives up and claught haud of her, and clawed the coats aff her back, and pu'd her doun the clachan to the water o' Dule, to see if she were a witch or no, soum or droun. The carline skirled till ye could hear her at the Hangin' Shaw, and she focht like ten; there was mony a guid wife bure the mark of her neist day an' mony a lang day after; and just in the hettest o' the collieshangie, wha suld come up (for his sins) but the new minister.

"Women," said he (and he had a grand voice), "I charge you in the

Lord's name to let her go."

Janet ran to him—she was fair wud wi' terror—an' clang to him, an' prayed him, for Christ's sake, save her frae the cummers; an' they, for their pairt, tauld him a' that was kent, and maybe mair.

"Woman," says he to Janet, "is this true?"

"As the Lord sees me," says she, "as the Lord made me, no a word o' 't. Forby the bairn," says she, "I've been a decent woman a' my days."

"Will you," says Mr. Soulis, "in the name of God, and before me, His unworthy minister, renounce the devil and his works?"

Weel, it wad appear that, when he askit that, she gave a girn that fairly frichtit them that saw her, an' they could hear her teeth play dirl thegether in her chafts; but there was naething for it but the ae way or the ither; an' Janet lifted up her hand and renounced the deil before them a'.

"And now," says Mr. Soulis to the guidwives, "home with ye, one and all, and pray to God for His forgiveness."

And he gied Janet his arm, though she had little on her but a sark, and took her up the clachan to her ain door like a leddy of the land, an' her scrieghin' and laughin' as was a scandal to be heard.

There were mony grave folk lang ower their prayers that nicht; but when the morn cam' there was sic a fear fell upon a' Ba'weary that the bairns hid theirsel's, and even the men folk stood and keekit frae their doors. For there was Janet comin' doun the clachan,—her or her likeness, nane could tell,—wi' her neck thrawn, and her heid on ae side, like a body that has been hangit, and a girn on her face like an unstreakit corp. By-an'-by they got used wi' it, and even speered at her to ken what was wrang; but frae that day forth she couldnae speak like a Christian woman, but slavered and played click wi' her teeth like a pair o' shears; and frae that day forth the name o' God cam' never on her lips.

Whiles she wad try to say it, but it michtnae be. Them that kenned best said least; but they never gied that Thing the name o' Janet M'Clour; for the auld Janet, by their way o' 't, was in muckle hell that day. But the minister was neither to haud nor to bind; he preached about naething but the folk's cruelty that had gien her a stroke of the palsy; he skelpt the bairns that meddled her; and he had her up to the manse that same nicht, and dwalled there a' his lane wi' her under the Hangin' Shaw.

Weel, time gaed by, and the idler sort commenced to think mair lichtly o' that black business. The minister was weel thocht o'; he was aye late at the writing—folk wad see his can'le doon by the Dule Water after twal' at e'en; and he seemed pleased wi' himsel' and upsitten as at first, though a' body could see that he was dwining. As for Janet, she cam' an' she gaed; if she didnae speak muckle afore, it was reason she should speak less then; she meddled naebody; but she was an eldritch thing to see, an' nane wad hae mistrysted wi' her for Ba'weary glebe.

About the end o' July there cam' a spell o' weather, the like o' 't never was in that countryside; it was lown an' het an' heartless; the herds couldnae win up the Black Hill, the bairns were ower-weariet to play; an' yet it was gousty too, wi claps o' het wund that rummled in the glens, and bits o' shouers that slockened naething. We aye thocht it but to thun'er on the morn; but the morn cam', an' the morn's morning, and it was aye the same uncanny weather; sair on folks and bestial. Of a' that were the waur, nane suffered like Mr. Soulis; he could neither sleep nor eat, he tauld his elders; an' when he wasnae writin' at his weary book, he wad be stravaguin' ower a' the countryside like a man possessed, when a' body else was blithe to keep caller ben the house.

Abune Hangin' Shaw, in the bield o' the Black Hill, there's a bit enclosed grund wi' an iron yert; and it seems, in the auld days, that was the kirkyaird o' Ba'weary, and consecrated by the papists before the blessed licht shone upon the kingdom. It was a great howff, o' Mr. Soulis's onyway; there he would sit an' consider his sermons' and inded it's a bieldy bit. Weel, as he came ower the wast end o' the Black Hill, ae day, he saw first twa, an' syne fower, an' syne seeven corbie craws fleein' round an' round abune the auld kirkyaird. They flew laigh and heavy, an' squawked to ither as they gaed; and it was clear to Mr. Soulis that something had put them frae their ordinar. He wasna easy fleyed, an' gaed straucht up to the wa's; and what suld he find there but a man, or the appearance of a man, sittin' in the inside upon a grave. He was of a great stature, an' black as hell, and his een were singular to see. Mr. Soulis had heard tell o' black men, mony's the time; but there was something unco abut this black man that daunted him.

Het as he was, he took a kind o' cauld grue in the marrow o' his banes; but up he spak' for a' that; an' says he, "My friend, are you a stranger in this place?" The black man answered never a word; he got upon his feet, an' begude to hirsel to the wa' on the far side; but he aye lookit at the minister; an' the minister stood an' lookit back; till a' in a meenute the black man was ower the wa' an' rinnin' for the bield o' the trees. Mr. Soulis, he hardly kenned why, ran after him; but he was sair forjaskit wi' his walk an' the het, unhalesome weather; and rin as he likit, he got nae mair than a glisk o' the black man amang the birks, till he won doun to the foot o' the hillside, an' there he saw him ance mair, gaun, hap, step, an' lowp, ower Dule Water to the manse.

Mr. Soulis wasna weel pleased that this fearsome gangrel suld mak' sae free wi' Ba'weary manse; an' he ran the harder, an' wet shoon, ower the burn, an' up the walk; but the deil a black man was there to see. He stepped out upon the road, but there was naebody there; he gaed a' ower the gairden, but na, nae black man. At the hinder end, and a bit feard as was but natural, he lifted the hasp and into the manse; and there was Janet M'Clour before his een, wi' her thrawn craig, and nane sae pleased to see him. And he aye minded sinsyne, when first he set his een upon her, he had the same cauld and deidy grue.

"Janet," says he, "have you seen a black man?"

"A black man?" quo' she. "Save us a'! Ye 're no wise, minister. There's nae black man in a' Ba'weary."

But she didna speak plain, ye maun understand; but yam-yam-mered, like a powny wi' the bit in its moo.

"Weel," says he, "Janet, if there was nae black man, I have spoken with the Accuser of the Brethren."

And he sat down like ane wi' a fever, an' his teeth chittered in his heid.

"Hoots!" says she, "think shame to yoursel', minister," an' gied him a drap brandy that she keept aye by her.

Syne Mr. Soulis gaed into his study amang a' his books. It's a lang, laigh, mirk chalmer, perishin' cauld in winter, an' no very dry even in the top o' the simmer, for the manse stands near the burn. Sae doun he sat, and thocht of a' that had come an' gane since he was in Ba'weary, an' his hame, an' the days when he was a bairn an' ran daffin' on the braes; and that black man aye ran in his heid like the owercome of a sang. Aye the mair he thocht, the mair he thocht o' the black man. He tried the prayer, an' the words wouldnae come to him; an' he tried, they say, to write at his book, but he couldnae mak' nae mair o' that. There was whiles he thocht the black man was at his oxter, an' the swat stood upon him cauld as well-water; and there was other whiles when he cam' to himsel' like a christened bairn and minded naething.

The upshot was that he gaed to the window an' stood glowrin' at Dule Water. The trees are unco thick, an' the water lies deep an' black under the manse; and there was Janet washing' the cla'es wi' her coats kilted. She had her back to the minister, an' he for his pairt, hardly kenned what he was lookin' at. Syne she turned round, an' shawed her face; Mr. Soulis had the same cauld grue as twice that day afore, an' it was borne in upon him what folk said, that Janet was deid lang syne, an' this was a bogle in her clay-cauld flesh. He drew back a pickle and he scanned her narrowly. She was tramp-trampin' in the cla'es, croonin' to hersel'; and eh! Gude guide us, but it was a fearsome face.

Whiles she sang louder, but there was nae man born o' woman that could tell the words o' her sang; an' whiles she lookit sidelang doun, but there was naething there for her to look at. There gaed a scunner through the flesh upon his banes; and that was Heeven's advertisement. But Mr. Soulis just blamed himsel', he said, to think sae ill of a puir auld afflicted wife that hadnae a freend forby himsel'; an' he put up a bit prayer for him an' her, an' drank a little caller water,—for his heart rose again' the meat,—an' gaed up to his naked bed in the gloaming.

That was a nicht that has never been forgotten in Ba'weary, the nicht o' the seeventeenth of August, seventeen hun'er' an' twal'. It had been het afore, as I hae said, but that nicht it was hetter than ever. The sun gaed doun amang unco-lookin' clouds; it fell as mirk as the pit; no a star, no a breath o' wund; ye couldnae see your han' afore your face, and even the auld folk cuist the covers frae their beds and lay pechin' for their breath. Wi' a' that he had upon his mind, it was gey and un-likely Mr. Soulis wad get muckle sleep. He lay an' he tummled; the gude, caller bed that he got into brunt his very banes; whiles he slept, and whiles he waukened; whiles he heard the time o' nicht, and whiles a tike yowlin' up the muir, as if somebody was deid; whiles he thocht he heard bogles claverin' in his lug, an' whiles he saw spunkies in the room. He behooved, he judged, to be sick; an' sick he was—little he jaloosed the sickness.

At the hinder end, he got a clearness in his mind, sat up in his sark on the bedside, and fell thinkin' ance mair o' the black man an' Janet. He couldnae weel tell how,—maybe it was the cauld to his feet,—but it cam' in upon him wi' a spate that there was some connection be-tween thir twa, an' that either or baith o' them were bogles. And just at that moment, in Janet's room, which was neist to his, there cam' a stamp o' feet as if men were wars'lin', an' then a loud bang; an' then a wund gaed reishling round the fower quarters of the house; an' then a' was ance mair as seelent as the grave.

Mr. Soulis was feard for neither man nor deevil. He got his tinder-box, an' lit a can'le, an' made three steps o' 't ower to Janet's door. It was on the hasp, an' he pushed it open, an' keeked bauldly in. It was a big room, as big as the minister's ain, an' plenished wi' grand, auld, solid gear, for he had naething else. There was a fower-posted bed wi' auld tapestry; and a braw cabinet of aik, that was fu' o' the minister's divinity books, an' put there to be out o' the gate; an' a wheen duds o' Janet's lying here and there about the floor. But nae Janet could Mr. Soulis see, nor ony sign of a contention. In he gaed (an' there's few that wad hae followed him), an' lookit a' round, an' listened.

But there was naethin' to be heard neither inside the manse nor in a' Ba'weary parish, an' naethin' to be seen but the muckle shadows turnin' round the can'le. An' then a' at aince the minister's heart played dunt an' stood stock-still, an' a cauld wund blew amang the hairs o' his heid. Whaten a weary sicht was that for the puir man's een! For there was Janet hangin' frae a nail beside the auld aik cabinet; her heid aye lay on her shouther, her een were steeked, the tongue projecket frae her mouth, and her heels were twa feet clear abune the floor.

"God forgive us all!" thocht Mr. Soulis, "poor Janet's dead."

He cam' a step nearer to the corp; an' then his heart fair whammled in his inside. For—by what cantrip it wad ill beseem a man to judge— she was hingin' frae a single nail an' by a single wursted thread for darnin' hose.

It's an awfu' thing to be your lane at nicht wi' siccan prodigies o' darkness; but Mr. Soulis was strong in the Lord. He turned an' gaed his ways oot o' that room, and locket the door ahint him; and step by step doon the stairs, as heavy as leed; and set doon the can'le on the table at the stair-foot. He couldnae pray, he couldnae think, he was dreepin' wi' caul' swat, an' naething could he hear but the dunt-dunt-duntin' o' his ain heart. He micht maybe have stood there an hour, or maybe twa, he minded sae little; when a' o' a sudden he heard a laigh, uncanny steer upstairs; a foot gaed to an' fro in the cham'er whair the corp was hingin'; syne the door was opened, though he minded weel that he had lockit it; an' syne there was a step upon the landin', an' it seemed to him as if the corp was lookin' ower the tail and doun upon him whaur he stood.

He took up the can'le again (for he couldnae want the licht), and, as saftly as ever he could, gaed straucht out o' the manse an' to the far end o' the causeway. It was aye pit-mirk; the flame o' the can'le, when he set it on the grund, brunt steedy and clear as in a room; naething moved, but the Dule Water seepin' and sabbin' doon the glen, an' yon unhaly footstep that cam' plodding' doun the stairs inside the manse. He kenned the foot ower-weel, for it was Janet's; and at ilka step that cam' a wee thing nearer, the cauld got deeper in his vitals. He commended his soul to Him that made an' keepit him; "and, O Lord," said he, "give me strength this night to war against the powers of evil."

By this time the foot was comin' through the passage for the door; he could hear a hand skirt alang the wa', as if the fearsome thing was feelin' for its way. The saughs tossed an' maned thegether, a long sigh cam' ower the hills, the flame o' the can'le was blawn aboot; an' there stood the corp of Thrawn Janet, wi' her grogram goun an' her black mutch, wi' the heid aye upon the shouther, an' the girn still upon the face o' 't,—leevin', ye wad hae said—deid, as Mr. Soulis weel kenned,—upon the threshold o' the manse.

It's a strange thing that the saul of man should be thirled into his perishable body; but the minister saw that, an' his heart didnae break.

She didnae stand there lang; she began to move again, an' cam' slowly toward Mr. Soulis whaur he stood under the saughs. A' the life o' his body, a' the strength o' his speerit, were glowerin' frae his een. It seemed she was gaun to speak, but wanted words, an' made a sign wi' the left hand. There cam' a clap o' wund, like a cat's fuff; oot gaed the can'le, the saughs skrieghed like folk' an' Mr. Soulis kenned that, live or die, this was the end o' 't.

"Witch, beldam, devil!" he cried, "I charge you, by the power of God, begone—if you be dead, to the grave; if you be damned, to hell."

An' at that moment the Lord's ain hand out o' the heevens struck the Horror whaur it stood; the auld, deid, desecrated corp o' the witch-wife, sae lang keepit frae the grave and hirselled round by deils, lowed up like a brunstane spunk and fell in ashes to the grund; the thunder followed, peal on dirling peal, the rairing rain upon the back o' that; and Mr. Soulis lowped through the garden hedge, and ran, wi' skelloch upon skelloch, for the clachan.

That same mornin' John Christie saw the black man pass the Muckle Cairn as it was chappin' six; before eicht, he gaed by the change-house at Knockdow; an' no lang after, Sandy M'Lellan saw him gaun linkin' doun the braes frae Kilmackerlie. There's little doubt but it was him that dwalled sae lang in Janet's body; but he was awa' at last; and sinsyne the deil has never fashed us in Ba'weary.

But it was a sair dispensation for the minister; lang, lang he lay ravin' in his bed; and frae that hour to this, he was the man ye ken the day.

A Terribly Strange Bed

By Wilkie Collins

Shortly after my education at college was finished, I happened to be staying at Paris with an English friend. We were both young men then, and lived, I am afraid, rather a wild life, in the delightful city of our sojourn. One night we were idling about the neighbourhood of the Palais Royal, doubtful to what amusement we should next betake ourselves. My friend proposed a visit to Frascati's; but his suggestion was not to my taste.

I knew Frascati's, as the French saying is, by heart; had lost and won plenty of five-*franc* pieces there, merely for amusement's sake, until it was amusement no longer, and was thoroughly tired, in fact, of all the ghastly respectabilities of such a social anomaly as a respectable gambling-house. "For Heaven's sake," said I to my friend, "let us go somewhere where we can see a little genuine, blackguard, poverty-stricken gaming with no false gingerbread glitter thrown over it all. Let us get away from fashionable Frascati's, to a house where they don't mind letting in a man with a ragged coat, or a man with no coat, ragged or otherwise."

"Very well," said my friend, "we needn't go out of the Palais Royal to find the sort of company you want. Here's the place just before us; as blackguard a place, by all report, as you could possibly wish to see." In another minute we arrived at the door, and entered the house, the back of which you have drawn in your sketch.

When we got upstairs, and had left our hats and sticks with the doorkeeper, we were admitted into the chief gambling-room. We did not find many people assembled there. But, few as the men were who looked up at us on our entrance, they were all types—lamentably true types—of their respective classes.

We had come to see blackguards; but these men were something worse. There is a comic side, more or less appreciable, in all black-guardism—here there was nothing but tragedy—mute, weird tragedy. The quiet in the room was horrible. The thin, haggard, long-haired young man, whose sunken eyes fiercely watched the turning up of the cards, never spoke; the flabby, fat-faced, pimply player, who pricked his piece of pasteboard perseveringly, to register how often black won, and how often red—never spoke; the dirty, wrinkled old man, with the vulture eyes and the darned great-coat, who had lost his last *sou*, and still looked on desperately, after he could play no longer—never spoke.

Even the voice of the croupier sounded as if it were strangely dulled and thickened in the atmosphere of the room. I had entered the place to laugh, but the spectacle before me was something to weep over. I soon found it necessary to take refuge in excitement from the depression of spirits which was fast stealing on me. Unfortunately I sought the nearest excitement, by going to the table and beginning to play.

Still more unfortunately, as the event will show, I won—won prodigiously; won incredibly; won at such a rate that the regular players at the table crowded round me; and staring at my stakes with hungry, superstitious eyes, whispered to one another that the English stranger was going to break the bank.

The game was *Rouge et Noir*. I had played at it in every city in Europe, without, however, the care or the wish to study the Theory of Chances—that philosopher's stone of all gamblers! And a gambler, in the strict sense of the word, I had never been. I was heart-whole from the corroding passion for play. My gaming was a mere idle amusement. I never resorted to it by necessity, because I never knew what it was to want money. I never practiced it so incessantly as to lose more than I could afford, or to gain more than I could coolly pocket without being thrown off my balance by my good luck. In short, I had hitherto frequented gambling-tables—just as I frequented ball-rooms and opera-houses—because they amused me, and because I had nothing better to do with my leisure hours.

But on this occasion it was very different—now, for the first time in my life, I felt what the passion for play really was. My success first bewildered, and then, in the most literal meaning of the word, intoxicated me. Incredible as it may appear, it is nevertheless true, that I only lost when I attempted to estimate chances, and played according to previous calculation.

If I left everything to luck, and staked without any care or consideration, I was sure to win—to win in the face of every recognized probability in favour of the bank. At first some of the men present ventured their money safely enough on my colour; but I speedily increased my stakes to sums which they dared not risk. One after another they left off playing, and breathlessly looked on at my game.

Still, time after time, I staked higher and higher, and still won. The excitement in the room rose to fever pitch. The silence was interrupted by a deep-muttered chorus of oaths and exclamations in different languages, every time the gold was shovelled across to my side of the table—even the imperturbable croupier dashed his rake on the floor in a (French) fury of astonishment at my success.

But one man present preserved his self-possession, and that man was my friend. He came to my side, and whispering in English, begged me to leave the place, satisfied with what I had already gained. I must do him the justice to say that he repeated his warnings and entreaties several times, and only left me and went away after I had rejected his advice (I was to all intents and purposes gambling drunk) in terms which rendered it impossible for him to address me again that night.

Shortly after he had gone, a hoarse voice behind me cried: "Permit me, my dear sir—permit me to restore to their proper place two *napoleons* which you have dropped. Wonderful luck, sir! I pledge you my word of honour, as an old soldier, in the course of my long experience in this sort of thing, I never saw such luck as yours—never! Go on, sir—*Sacré mille bombes!* Go on boldly, and break the bank!"

I turned round and saw, nodding and smiling at me with inveterate civility, a tall man, dressed in a frogged and braided surtout.

If I had been in my senses, I should have considered him, personally, as being rather a suspicious specimen of an old soldier. He had goggling, bloodshot eyes, mangy moustaches, and a broken nose. His voice betrayed a barrack-room intonation of the worst order, and he had the dirtiest pair of hands I ever saw—even in France. These little personal peculiarities exercised, however, no repelling influence on me.

In the mad excitement, the reckless triumph of that moment, I was ready to "fraternize" with anybody who encouraged me in my game. I accepted the old soldier's offered pinch of snuff; clapped him on the back, and swore he was the honestest fellow in the world—the most glorious relic of the Grand Army that I had ever met with. "Go on!" cried my military friend, snapping his fingers in ecstasy—"

Go on, and win! Break the bank—*Mille tonnerres!* my gallant English comrade, break the bank!"

And I *did* go on"went on at such a rate, that in another quarter of an hour the croupier called out, "Gentlemen, the bank has discontinued for tonight." All the notes, and all the gold in that "bank," now lay in a heap under my hands; the whole floating capital of the gambling-house was waiting to pour into my pockets!

"Tie up the money in your pocket-handkerchief, my worthy sir," said the old soldier, as I wildly plunged my hands into my heap of gold. "Tie it up, as we used to tie up a bit of dinner in the Grand Army; your winnings are too heavy for any breeches-pockets that ever were sewed. There! that's it—shovel them in, notes and all! *Credié!* what luck! Stop! another *napoleon* on the floor! *Ah! sacré petit polisson de Napoleon!* have I found thee at last? Now then, sir—two tight double knots each way with your honourable permission, and the money's safe. Feel it! feel it, fortunate sir! hard and round as a cannon-ball—*Ah, bah!* if they had only fired such cannon-balls at us at Austerlitz—*nom d'une pipe!* if they only had!

"And now, as an ancient grenadier, as an ex-brave of the French army, what remains for me to do? I ask what? Simply this: to entreat my valued English friend to drink a bottle of Champagne with me, and toast the goddess Fortune in foaming goblets before we part!"

Excellent ex-brave! Convivial ancient grenadier! Champagne by all means! An English cheer for an old soldier! Hurrah! hurrah! Another English cheer for the goddess Fortune! Hurrah! hurrah! hurrah!

"Bravo! the Englishman; the amiable, gracious Englishman, in whose veins circulates the vivacious blood of France! Another glass? *Ah, bah!*—the bottle is empty! Never mind! *Vive le vin!* I, the old soldier, order another bottle, and half a pound of bonbons with it!"

"No, no, ex-brave; never—ancient grenadier! *Your* bottle last time; *my* bottle this. Behold it! Toast away! The French Army! the great Napoleon! the present company! the croupier! the honest croupier's wife and daughters—if he has any! the Ladies generally! everybody in the world!"

By the time the second bottle of Champagne was emptied, I felt as if I had been drinking liquid fire—my brain seemed all aflame. No excess in wine had ever had this effect on me before in my life. Was it the result of a stimulant acting upon my system when I was in a highly excited state? Was my stomach in a particularly disordered condition? Or was the Champagne amazingly strong?

"Ex-brave of the French Army!" cried I, in a mad state of exhilaration, "*I* am on fire! how are *you?* You have set me on fire! Do you hear, my hero of Austerlitz? Let us have a third bottle of Champagne to put the flame out!"

The old soldier wagged his head, rolled his goggle-eyes, until I expected to see them slip out of their sockets; placed his dirty forefinger by the side of his broken nose; solemnly ejaculated "Coffee!" and immediately ran off into an inner room.

The word pronounced by the eccentric veteran seemed to have a magical effect on the rest of the company present. With one accord they all rose to depart. Probably they had expected to profit by my intoxication; but finding that my new friend was benevolently bent on preventing me from getting dead drunk, had now abandoned all hope of thriving pleasantly on my winnings.

Whatever their motive might be, at any rate they went away in a body. When the old soldier returned, and sat down again opposite to me at the table, we had the room to ourselves. I could see the croupier, in a sort of vestibule which opened out of it, eating his supper in solitude. The silence was now deeper than ever.

A sudden change, too, had come over the "ex-brave." He assumed a portentously solemn look; and when he spoke to me again, his speech was ornamented by no oaths, enforced by no finger-snapping, enlivened by no apostrophes or exclamations.

"Listen, my dear sir," said he, in mysteriously confidential tones—"listen to an old soldier's advice. I have been to the mistress of the house (a very charming woman, with a genius for cookery!) to impress on her the necessity of making us some particularly strong and good coffee. You must drink this coffee in order to get rid of your little amiable exaltation of spirits before you think of going home—you *must,* my good and gracious friend!

"With all that money to take home tonight, it is a sacred duty to yourself to have your wits about you. You are known to be a winner to an enormous extent by several gentlemen present tonight, who, in a certain point of view, are very worthy and excellent fellows; but they are mortal men, my dear sir, and they have their amiable weaknesses. Need I say more? Ah, no, no! you understand me!

"Now, this is what you must do—send for a cabriolet when you feel quite well again—draw up all the windows when you get into it—and tell the driver to take you home only through the large and well-lighted thoroughfares. Do this; and you and your money will be safe. Do this; and tomorrow you will thank an old soldier for giving you a word of honest advice."

Just as the ex-brave ended his oration in very lachrymose tones, the coffee came in, ready poured out in two cups. My attentive friend handed me one of the cups with a bow. I was parched with thirst, and drank it off at a draught. Almost instantly afterwards, I was seized with a fit of giddiness, and felt more completely intoxicated than ever. The room whirled round and round furiously; the old soldier seemed to be regularly bobbing up and down before me like the piston of a steam-engine.

I was half deafened by a violent singing in my ears; a feeling of utter bewilderment, helplessness, idiocy, overcame me. I rose from my chair, holding on by the table to keep my balance; and stammered out that I felt dreadfully unwell—so unwell that I did not know how I was to get home.

"My dear friend," answered the old soldier—and even his voice seemed to be bobbing up and down as he spoke—"my dear friend, it would be madness to go home in *your* state; you would be sure to lose your money; you might be robbed and murdered with the greatest ease. *I* am going to sleep here; do *you* sleep here, too—they make up capital beds in this house—take one; sleep off the effects of the wine, and go home safely with your winnings tomorrow—tomorrow, in broad daylight."

I had but two ideas left: one, that I must never let go hold of my handkerchief full of money; the other, that I must lie down some-where immediately, and fall off into a comfortable sleep. So I agreed to the proposal about the bed, and took the offered arm of the old soldier, carrying my money with my disengaged hand. Preceded by the croupier, we passed along some passages and up a flight of stairs into the bedroom which I was to occupy. The ex-brave shook me warmly by the hand, proposed that we should breakfast together, and then, followed by the croupier, left me for the night.

I ran to the wash-hand stand; drank some of the water in my jug; poured the rest out, and plunged my face into it; then sat down in a chair and tried to compose myself. I soon felt better. The change for my lungs, from the fetid atmosphere of the gambling-room to the cool air of the apartment I now occupied, the almost equally refresh-ing change for my eyes, from the glaring gaslights of the "salon" to the dim, quiet flicker of one bedroom-candle, aided wonderfully the restorative effects of cold water.

The giddiness left me, and I began to feel a little like a reasonable being again. My first thought was of the risk of sleeping all night in a gambling-house; my second, of the still greater risk of trying to get out after the house was closed, and of going home alone at night through the streets of Paris with a large sum of money about me. I had slept in worse places than this on my travels; so I determined to lock, bolt, and barricade my door, and take my chance till the next morning.

Accordingly, I secured myself against all intrusion; looked under the bed, and into the cupboard; tried the fastening of the window; and then, satisfied that I had taken every proper precaution, pulled off my upper clothing, put my light, which was a dim one, on the hearth among a feathery litter of wood-ashes, and got into bed, with the handkerchief full of money under my pillow.

I soon felt not only that I could not go to sleep, but that I could not even close my eyes. I was wide awake, and in a high fever. Every nerve in my body trembled—every one of my senses seemed to be preternaturally sharpened. I tossed and rolled, and tried every kind of position, and perseveringly sought out the cold corners of the bed, and all to no purpose.

Now I thrust my arms over the clothes; now I poked them under the clothes; now I violently shot my legs straight out down to the bottom of the bed; now I convulsively coiled them up as near my chin as they would go; now I shook out my crumpled pillow, changed it to the cool side, patted it flat, and lay down quietly on my back; now I fiercely doubled it in two, set it up on end, thrust it against the board of the bed, and tried a sitting posture. Every effort was in vain; I groaned with vexation as I felt that I was in for a sleepless night.

What could I do? I had no book to read. And yet, unless I found out some method of diverting my mind, I felt certain that I was in the condition to imagine all sorts of horrors; to rack my brain with forebodings of every possible and impossible danger; in short, to pass the night in suffering all conceivable varieties of nervous terror.

I raised myself on my elbow, and looked about the room☐which was brightened by a lovely moonlight pouring straight through the window—to see if it contained any pictures or ornaments that I could at all clearly distinguish. While my eyes wandered from wall to wall, a remembrance of Le Maistre's delightful little book, *Voyage autour de ma Chambre*, occurred to me. I resolved to imitate the French author, and find occupation and amusement enough to relieve the tedium of my wakefulness, by making a mental inventory of every article of furniture I could see, and by following up to their sources the multitude of associations which even a chair, a table, or a wash-hand stand may be made to call forth.

In the nervous unsettled state of my mind at that moment, I found it much easier to make my inventory than to make my reflections, and thereupon soon gave up all hope of thinking in Le Maistre's fanciful track—or, indeed, of thinking at all. I looked about the room at the different articles of furniture, and did nothing more.

There was, first, the bed I was lying in; a four-post bed, of all things in the world to meet with in Paris—yes, a thorough clumsy British four-poster, with the regular top lined with chintz□the regular fringed valance all round—the regular stifling, unwholesome curtains, which I remembered having mechanically drawn back against the posts without particularly noticing the bed when I first got into the room.

Then there was the marble-topped wash-hand stand, from which the water I had spilled, in my hurry to pour it out, was still dripping, slowly and more slowly, on to the brick floor. Then two small chairs, with my coat, waistcoat, and trousers flung on them. Then a large elbow-chair covered with dirty-white dimity, with my cravat and shirt collar thrown over the back. Then a chest of drawers with two of the brass handles off, and a tawdry, broken china inkstand placed on it by way of ornament for the top.

Then the dressing-table, adorned by a very small looking-glass, and a very large pincushion. Then the window—an unusually large window. Then a dark old picture, which the feeble candle dimly showed me. It was a picture of a fellow in a high Spanish hat, crowned with a plume of towering feathers. A swarthy, sinister ruffian, looking upward, shading his eyes with his hand, and looking intently upward—it might be at some tall gallows at which he was going to be hanged. At any rate, he had the appearance of thoroughly deserving it.

This picture put a kind of constraint upon me to look upward too—at the top of the bed. It was a gloomy and not an interesting object, and I looked back at the picture. I counted the feathers in the man's hat—they stood out in relief—three white, two green. I observed the crown of his hat, which was of conical shape, according to the fashion supposed to have been favoured by Guido Fawkes.

I wondered what he was looking up at. It couldn't be at the stars; such a *desperado* was neither astrologer nor astronomer. It must be at the high gallows, and he was going to be hanged presently. Would the executioner come into possession of his conical crowned hat and plume of feathers? I counted the feathers again—three white, two green.

While I still lingered over this very improving and intellectual employment, my thoughts insensibly began to wander. The moonlight shining into the room reminded me of a certain moonlight night in England—the night after a picnic party in a Welsh valley. Every incident of the drive homeward, through lovely scenery, which the moonlight made lovelier than ever, came back to my remembrance, though I had never given the picnic a thought for years; though, if I had *tried* to recollect it, I could certainly have recalled little or nothing of that scene long past.

Of all the wonderful faculties that help to tell us we are immortal, which speaks the sublime truth more eloquently than memory? Here was I, in a strange house of the most suspicious character, in a situation of uncertainty, and even of peril, which might seem to make the cool exercise of my recollection almost out of the question; nevertheless, remembering, quite involuntarily, places, people, conversations, minute circumstances of every kind, which I had thought forgotten forever; which I could not possibly have recalled at will, even under the most favourable auspices. And what cause had produced in a moment the whole of this strange, complicated, mysterious effect? Nothing but some rays of moonlight shining in at my bedroom window.

I was still thinking of the picnic—of our merriment on the drive home—of the sentimental young lady who *would* quote *Childe Harold* because it was moonlight. I was absorbed by these past scenes and past amusements, when, in an instant, the thread on which my memories hung snapped asunder; my attention immediately came back to present things more vividly than ever, and I found myself, I neither knew why nor wherefore, looking hard at the picture again.

Looking for what?

Good God! the man had pulled his hat down on his brows! No! the hat itself was gone! Where was the conical crown? Where the feathers—three white, two green? Not there! In place of the hat and feathers, what dusky object was it that now hid his forehead, his eyes, his shading hand?

Was the bed moving?

I turned on my back and looked up. Was I mad? drunk? dreaming? giddy again? or was the top of the bed really moving down—sinking slowly, regularly, silently, horribly, right down throughout the whole of its length and breadth—right down upon me, as I lay underneath?

My blood seemed to stand still. A deadly paralysing coldness stole all over me as I turned my head round on the pillow and determined to test whether the bed-top was really moving or not, by keeping my eye on the man in the picture.

The next look in that direction was enough. The dull, black, frowzy outline of the valance above me was within an inch of being parallel with his waist. I still looked breathlessly. And steadily and slowly—very slowly—I saw the figure, and the line of frame below the figure, vanish, as the valance moved down before it.

I am, constitutionally, anything but timid. I have been on more than one occasion in peril of my life, and have not lost my self-possession for an instant; but when the conviction first settled on my mind that the bed-top was really moving, was steadily and continuously sinking down upon me, I looked up shuddering, helpless, panic-stricken, beneath the hideous machinery for murder, which was advancing closer and closer to suffocate me where I lay.

I looked up, motionless, speechless, breathless. The candle, fully spent, went out; but the moonlight still brightened the room. Down and down, without pausing and without sounding, came the bed-top, and still my panic-terror seemed to bind me faster and faster to the mattress on which I lay—down and down it sank, till the dusty odour from the lining of the canopy came stealing into my nostrils.

At that final moment the instinct of self-preservation startled me out of my trance, and I moved at last. There was just room for me to roll myself sidewise off the bed. As I dropped noiselessly to the floor, the edge of the murderous canopy touched me on the shoulder.

Without stopping to draw my breath, without wiping the cold sweat from my face, I rose instantly on my knees to watch the bed-top. I was literally spellbound by it. If I had heard footsteps behind me, I could not have turned round; if a means of escape had been miraculously provided for me, I could not have moved to take advantage of it. The whole life in me was, at that moment, concentrated in my eyes.

It descended—the whole canopy, with the fringe round it, came down—down—close down; so close that there was not room now to squeeze my finger between the bed-top and the bed. I felt at the sides, and discovered that what had appeared to me from beneath to be the ordinary light canopy of a four-post bed was in reality a thick, broad mattress, the substance of which was concealed by the valance and its fringe.

I looked up and saw the four posts rising hideously bare. In the middle of the bed-top was a huge wooden screw that had evidently worked it down through a hole in the ceiling, just as ordinary presses are worked down on the substance selected for compression. The frightful apparatus moved without making the faintest noise. There had been no creaking as it came down; there was now not the faintest sound from the room above.

Amid a dead and awful silence I beheld before me—in the nineteenth century, and in the civilized capital of France—such a machine for secret murder by suffocation as might have existed in the worst days of the Inquisition, in the lonely inns among the Hartz Mountains, in the mysterious tribunals of Westphalia! Still, as I looked on it, I could not move, I could hardly breathe, but I began to recover the power of thinking, and in a moment I discovered the murderous conspiracy framed against me in all its horror.

My cup of coffee had been drugged, and drugged too strongly. I had been saved from being smothered by having taken an overdose of some narcotic. How I had chafed and fretted at the fever fit which had preserved my life by keeping me awake! How recklessly I had confided myself to the two wretches who had led me into this room, determined, for the sake of my winnings, to kill me in my sleep by the surest and most horrible contrivance for secretly accomplishing my destruction! How many men, winners like me, had slept, as I had proposed to sleep, in that bed, and had never been seen or heard of more! I shuddered at the bare idea of it.

But, ere long, all thought was again suspended by the sight of the murderous canopy moving once more. After it had remained on the bed—as nearly as I could guess—about ten minutes, it began to move up again. The villains who worked it from above evidently believed that their purpose was now accomplished. Slowly and silently, as it had descended, that horrible bed-top rose towards its former place. When it reached the upper extremities of the four posts, it reached the ceiling, too. Neither hole nor screw could be seen; the bed became in appearance an ordinary bed again—the canopy an ordinary canopy— even to the most suspicious eyes.

Now, for the first time, I was able to move—to rise from my knees—to dress myself in my upper clothing—and to consider of how I should escape. If I betrayed by the smallest noise that the attempt to suffocate me had failed, I was certain to be murdered. Had I made any noise already? I listened intently, looking towards the door.

No! no footsteps in the passage outside—no sound of a tread, light or heavy, in the room above—absolute silence everywhere. Besides locking and bolting my door, I had moved an old wooden chest against it, which I had found under the bed. To remove this chest (my blood ran cold as I thought of what its contents *might* be!) without making some disturbance was impossible; and, moreover, to think of escaping through the house, now barred up for the night, was sheer insanity. Only one chance was left me—the window. I stole to it on tiptoe.

My bedroom was on the first floor, above an *entresol,* and looked into a back street, which you have sketched in your view. I raised my hand to open the window, knowing that on that action hung, by the merest hair-breadth, my chance of safety. They keep vigilant watch in a House of Murder. If any part of the frame cracked, if the hinge creaked, I was a lost man! It must have occupied me at least five minutes, reckoning by time—five *hours,* reckoning by suspense—to open that window.

I succeeded in doing it silently—in doing it with all the dexterity of a house-breaker—and then looked down into the street. To leap the distance beneath me would be almost certain destruction! Next, I looked round at the sides of the house. Down the left side ran a thick water-pipe which you have drawn—it passed close by the outer edge of the window. The moment I saw the pipe I knew I was saved. My breath came and went freely for the first time since I had seen the canopy of the bed moving down upon me!

To some men the means of escape which I had discovered might have seemed difficult and dangerous enough—to *me* the prospect of slipping down the pipe into the street did not suggest even a thought of peril. I had always been accustomed, by the practice of gymnastics, to keep up my schoolboy powers as a daring and expert climber; and knew that my head, hands, and feet would serve me faithfully in any hazards of ascent or descent. I had already got one leg over the window-sill, when I remembered the handkerchief filled with money under my pillow. I could well have afforded to leave it behind me, but I was revengefully determined that the miscreants of the gambling-house should miss their plunder as well as their victim. So I went back to the bed and tied the heavy handkerchief at my back by my cravat.

Just as I had made it tight and fixed it in a comfortable place, I thought I heard a sound of breathing outside the door. The chill feeling of horror ran through me again as I listened. No! dead silence still in the passage—I had only heard the night air blowing softly into the room. The next moment I was on the windowsill—and the next I had a firm grip on the water-pipe with my hands and knees.

I slid down into the street easily and quietly, as I thought I should, and immediately set off at the top of my speed to a branch *Prefecture* of Police, which I knew was situated in the immediate neighbourhood. A "Sub-prefect," and several picked men among his subordinates, happened to be up, maturing, I believe, some scheme for discovering the perpetrator of a mysterious murder which all Paris was talking of just then.

When I began my story, in a breathless hurry and in very bad French, I could see that the sub-prefect suspected me of being a drunken Englishman who had robbed somebody; but he soon altered his opinion as I went on, and before I had anything like concluded, he shoved all the papers before him into a drawer, put on his hat, supplied me with another (for I was bareheaded), ordered a file of soldiers, desired his expert followers to get ready all sorts of tools for breaking open doors and ripping up brick flooring, and took my arm, in the most friendly and familiar manner possible, to lead me with him out of the house. I will venture to say that when the sub-prefect was a little boy, and was taken for the first time to the play, he was not half as much pleased as he was now at the job in prospect for him at the gambling-house!

Away we went through the streets, the sub-prefect cross-examining and congratulating me in the same breath as we marched at the head of our formidable *posse comitatus*. Sentinels were placed at the back and front of the house the moment we got to it; a tremendous battery of knocks was directed against the door; a light appeared at a window; I was told to conceal myself behind the police—then came more knocks and a cry of "Open in the name of the law!"

At that terrible summons bolts and locks gave way before an invisible hand, and the moment after the sub-prefect was in the passage, confronting a waiter half-dressed and ghastly pale. This was the short dialogue which immediately took place:

"We want to see the Englishman who is sleeping in this house?"

"He went away hours ago."

"He did no such thing. His friend went away; *he* remained. Show us to his bedroom!"

"I swear to you, *Monsieur le Sous-prefect,* he is not here! he—"

"I swear to you, *Monsieur le Garçon,* he is. He slept here—he didn't find your bed comfortable—he came to us to complain of it—here he is among my men—and here am I ready to look for a flea or two in his bedstead. Renaudin! (calling to one of the subordinates, and pointing to the waiter) collar that man and tie his hands behind him. Now, then, gentlemen, let us walk upstairs!"

Every man and woman in the house was secured—the "Old Soldier" the first. Then I identified the bed in which I had slept, and then we went into the room above.

No object that was at all extraordinary appeared in any part of it. The sub-prefect looked round the place, commanded everybody to be silent, stamped twice on the floor, called for a candle, looked attentively at the spot he had stamped on, and ordered the flooring there to be carefully taken up. This was done in no time. Lights were produced, and we saw a deep raftered cavity between the floor of this room and the ceiling of the room beneath. Through this cavity there ran perpendicularly a sort of case of iron thickly greased; and inside the case appeared the screw, which communicated with the bed-top below.

Extra lengths of screw, freshly oiled; levers covered with felt; all the complete upper works of a heavy press—constructed with infernal ingenuity so as to join the fixtures below, and when taken to pieces again, to go into the smallest possible compass—were next discovered and pulled out on the floor. After some little difficulty the sub-prefect succeeded in putting the machinery together, and, leaving his men to work it, descended with me to the bedroom. The smothering canopy was then lowered, but not so noiselessly as I had seen it lowered. When I mentioned this to the sub-prefect, his answer, simple as it was, had a terrible significance. "My men," said he, "are working down the bed-top for the first time—the men whose money you won were in better practice."

We left the house in the sole possession of two police agents-every one of the inmates being removed to prison on the spot. The sub-prefect, after taking down my *"procés verbal"* in his office, returned with me to my hotel to get my passport. "Do you think," I asked, as I gave it to him, "that any men have really been smothered in that bed, as they tried to smother *me?*"

"I have seen dozens of drowned men laid out at the Morgue," answered the sub-prefect, "in whose pocketbooks were found letters stating that they had committed suicide in the Seine, because they had lost everything at the gaming table. Do I know how many of those men entered the same gambling-house that *you* entered? won as *you* won? took that bed as *you* took it? slept in it? were smothered in it?

and were privately thrown into the river, with a letter of explanation written by the murderers and placed in their pocket-books?

"No man can say how many or how few have suffered the fate from which you have escaped. The people of the gambling-house kept their bedstead machinery a secret from *us*—even from the police! The dead kept the rest of the secret for them. Goodnight, or rather good-morning, Monsieur Faulkner! Be at my office again at nine o'clock—in the meantime, *au revoir!*"

The rest of my story is soon told. I was examined and re-examined; the gambling-house was strictly searched all through from top to bottom; the prisoners were separately interrogated; and two of the less guilty among them made a confession.

I discovered that the Old Soldier was the master of the gambling-house—*justice* discovered that he had been drummed out of the army as a vagabond years ago; that he had been guilty of all sorts of villainies since; that he was in possession of stolen property, which the owners identified; and that he, the croupier, another accomplice, and the woman who had made my cup of coffee, were all in the secret of the bedstead. There appeared some reason to doubt whether the inferior persons attached to the house knew anything of the suffocating machinery; and they received the benefit of that doubt, by being treated simply as thieves and vagabonds.

As for the Old Soldier and his two head myrmidons, they went to the galleys; the woman who had drugged my coffee was imprisoned for I forget how many years; the regular attendants at the gambling-house were considered "suspicious" and placed under "surveillance"; and I became, for one whole week (which is a long time) the head "lion" in Parisian society.

My adventure was dramatized by three illustrious play-makers, but never saw theatrical daylight; for the censorship forbade the introduction on the stage of a correct copy of the gambling-house bedstead.

One good result was produced by my adventure, which any censorship must have approved: it cured me of ever again trying *"Rouge et Noir"* as an amusement. The sight of a green cloth, with packs of cards and heaps of money on it, will henceforth be forever associated in my mind with the sight of a bed canopy descending to suffocate me in the silence and darkness of the night.

Just as Mr. Faulkner pronounced these words he started in his chair, and resumed his stiff, dignified position in a great hurry. "Bless my soul!" cried he, with a comic look of astonishment and vexation, "while I have been telling you what is the real secret of my interest in the sketch you have so kindly given to me, I have altogether forgotten that I came here to sit for my portrait. For the last hour or more I must have been the worst model you ever had to draw from!"

"On the contrary, you have been the best," said I. "I have been trying to catch your likeness; and, while telling your story, you have unconsciously shown me the natural expression I wanted to insure my success."

The Man With the Pale Eyes

By Guy de Maupassant

A.k.a. The Man With the Blue Eyes

Monsieur Pierre Agénor de Vargnes, the Examining Magistrate, was the exact opposite of a practical joker. He was dignity, staidness, correctness personified. As a sedate man, he was quite incapable of being guilty, even in his dreams, of anything resembling a practical joke, however remotely. I know nobody to whom he could be compared, unless it be the present president (Jules Grévy) of the French Republic. I think it is useless to carry the analogy any further, and having said thus much, it will be easily understood that a cold shiver passed through me when I heard the following.

At about eight o'clock, one morning last winter, as he was leaving the house to go to the *Palais de Justice,* his footman handed him a card, on which was printed:

> *Doctor James Ferdinand,*
> *Member of the Academy of Medicine,*
> *Port-au-Prince,*
> *Chevalier of the Legion of Honour.*

At the bottom of the card, there was written in pencil: *From Lady Frogère*

Monsieur de Vargnes knew the lady very well. She was a very agreeable Creole from Haiti, whom he had met in many drawing-rooms, and, on the other hand, though the doctor's name did not awaken any recollections in him, his quality and titles alone demanded the courtesy of an interview, however short it might be. Therefore, although he was in a hurry to get out, Monsieur de Vargnes told the footman to show in his early visitor, but to tell him beforehand that his master was much pressed for time, as he had to go to the Law Courts.

When the doctor came in, in spite of his usual imperturbability, the magistrate could not restrain a movement of surprise, for the doctor presented that strange anomaly of being a negro of the purest, blackest type, with the eyes of a white man—of a man from the North—pale, cold, clear, blue eyes, and his surprise increased when, after a few words of excuse for his untimely visit, he added, with an enigmatical smile:

"My eyes surprise you, do they not? I was sure that they would, and, to tell you the truth, I came here in order that you might look at them well, and never forget them."

His smile, and his words, even more than his smile, seemed to be those of a madman. He spoke very softly, with that childish, lisping voice, which is peculiar to negroes, and his mysterious, almost menacing words, consequently, sounded all the more as if they were uttered at random by a man bereft of his reason. But the doctor's looks, the looks of those pale, cold, clear, blue eyes, were certainly not those of a madman. They clearly expressed menace, yes, menace, as well as irony, and, above all, implacable ferocity, and their glance was like a flash of lightning, which one could never forget.

"I have seen," Monsieur de Vargnes used to say, when speaking about it, "the looks of many murderers, but in none of them have I ever observed such a depth of crime, and of impudent security in crime."

And this impression was so strong, that Monsieur de Vargnes thought that he was the victim of some hallucination, especially as when he spoke about his eyes, the doctor continued with a smile, and in his most childish accents:

"Of course, *Monsieur*, you cannot understand what I am saying to you, and I must beg your pardon for it. Tomorrow, you will receive a letter which will explain it at all to you, but, first all, it was necessary that I should let you have a good, a careful look at my eyes, my eyes which are myself, my only and true self, as you will see."

With these words, and with a polite bow, the doctor went out, leaving Monsieur de Vargnes extremely surprised, and a prey to this doubt, as he said to himself:

"Is he merely a madman? The fierce expression, and the criminal depths of his looks are perhaps caused merely by the extraordinary contrast between his fierce looks and his pale eyes."

And absorbed in these thoughts, Monsieur de Vargnes unfortunately allowed several minutes to elapse, and then he thought to himself suddenly:

"No, I am not the sport of any hallucination, and this is no case of an optical phenomenon. This man is evidently some terrible criminal, and I have altogether failed in my duty in not arresting him myself at once, illegally, even at the risk of my life."

The judge ran downstairs in pursuit of the doctor, but it was too late; he had disappeared. In the afternoon, he called on Madame Frogère, to ask her whether she could tell him anything about the matter. She, however, did not know the negro doctor in the least, and was even able to assure him that he was a fictitious personage, for, as she was well acquainted with the upper classes in Haiti, she knew that the Academy of Medicine at Port-au-Prince had no doctor of that name among its members. As Monsieur de Vargnes persisted, and gave descriptions of the doctor, especially mentioning his extraordinary eyes, Madame Frogère began to laugh, and said:

"You have certainly had to do with a hoaxer, my dear *Monsieur.* The eyes which you have described, are certainly those of a white man, and the individual must have been painted."

On thinking it over, Monsieur de Vargnes remembered that the doctor had nothing of the negro about him, but his black skin, his woolly hair and beard, and his way of speaking, which was easily imitated. He had not the characteristic, undulating walk. Perhaps, after all, he was only a practical joker, and during the whole day, Monsieur de Vargnes took refuge in that view, which rather wounded his dignity as a man of consequence, but which appeased his scruples as a magistrate.

The next day, he received the promised letter, which was written, as well as addressed, in characters cut out of the newspapers. It was as follows:

Monsieur,—

Doctor James Ferdinand does not exist, but the man whose eyes you saw does, and you will certainly recognize his eyes. This man has committed two crimes, for which he does not feel any remorse, but, as he is a psychologist, he is afraid of some day yielding to the irresistible temptation of confessing his crimes. You know better than anyone (and that is your most powerful aid), with what imperious force criminals, especially intellectual ones, feel this temptation.

That great Poet, Edgar Poe, has written masterpieces on this subject, which express the truth exactly, but he has omitted to mention the last phenomenon, which I will tell you. Yes, I, a criminal, feel a terrible wish for somebody to know of my crimes, and, when this requirement is satisfied, my secret has been revealed to a confidant, I shall be tranquil for the future, and be freed from this demon of perversity, which only tempts us once.

Well! Now that is accomplished. You shall have my secret; from the day that you recognize me by my eyes, you will try and find out what I am guilty of, and how I was guilty, and you will discover it, being a master of your profession, which, by-the-bye, has procured you the honour of having been chosen by me to bear the weight of this secret, which now is shared by us, and by us two alone. I say, advisedly, *by us two alone.* You could not, as a matter of fact, prove the reality of this secret to anyone, unless I were to confess it, and I defy you to obtain my public confession, as I have confessed it to you, *and without danger to myself.*

Three months later, Monsieur de Vargnes met Monsieur X—— at an evening party and at first sight, and without the slightest hesitation, he recognized in him those very pale, very cold, and very clear blue eyes, eyes which it was impossible to forget.

The man himself remained perfect impassive, so that Monsieur de Vargnes was forced to say to himself:

"Probably I am the sport of a hallucination at this moment, or else there are two pairs of eyes that are perfectly similar, in the world. And what eyes! Can it be possible?"

The magistrate instituted inquiries into his life, and he discovered this, which removed all his doubts.

Five years previously, Monsieur X—— had been a very poor, but very brilliant medical student, who, although he never took his doctor's degree, had already made himself remarkable by his microbiological researches.

A young and very rich widow had fallen in love with him and married him. She had one child by her first marriage, and in the space of six months, first the child and then the mother died of typhoid fever, and thus Monsieur X—— had inherited a large fortune, in due form, and without any possible dispute. Everybody said that he had attended to the two patients with the utmost devotion. Now, were these two deaths the two crimes mentioned in his letter?

But then, Monsieur X—— must have poisoned his two victims with the microbes of typhoid fever, which he had skilfully cultivated in them, so as to make the disease incurable, even by the most devoted care and attention. Why not?

"Do you believe it?" I asked Monsieur de Vargnes.

"Absolutely," he replied. "And the most terrible thing about it is, that the villain is right when he defies me to force him to confess his crime publicly for I see no means of obtaining a confession, none whatever. For a moment, I thought of magnetism, but who could magnetize that man with those pale, cold, bright eyes? With such eyes, he would force the magnetizer to denounce himself as the culprit."

And then he said, with a deep sigh:

"Ah! Formerly there was something good about justice!"

And when he saw my inquiring looks, he added in a firm and perfectly convinced voice:

"Formerly, justice had torture at its command."

"Upon my word," I replied, with all an author's unconscious and simple egotism, "it is quite certain that without the torture, this strange tale would have no conclusion, and that is very unfortunate, as far as regards the story I intended to make of it."

The Birthmark
By Nathaniel Hawthorne

In the latter part of the last century there lived a man of science, an eminent proficient in every branch of natural philosophy, who not long before our story opens had made experience of a spiritual affinity more attractive than any chemical one. He had left his laboratory to the care of an assistant, cleared his fine countenance from the furnace smoke, washed the stain of acids from his fingers, and persuaded a beautiful woman to become his wife. In those days when the comparatively recent discovery of electricity and other kindred mysteries of Nature seemed to open paths into the region of miracle, it was not unusual for the love of science to rival the love of woman in its depth and absorbing energy.

The higher intellect, the imagination, the spirit, and even the heart might all find their congenial aliment in pursuits which, as some of their ardent votaries believed, would ascend from one step of powerful intelligence to another, until the philosopher should lay his hand on the secret of creative force and perhaps make new worlds for himself. We know not whether Aylmer possessed this degree of faith in man's ultimate control over Nature. He had devoted himself, however, too unreservedly to scientific studies ever to be weaned from them by any second passion. His love for his young wife might prove the stronger of the two; but it could only be by intertwining itself with his love of science, and uniting the strength of the latter to his own.

Such a union accordingly took place, and was attended with truly remarkable consequences and a deeply impressive moral. One day, very soon after their marriage, Aylmer sat gazing at his wife with a trouble in his countenance that grew stronger until he spoke.

"Georgiana," said he, "has it never occurred to you that the mark upon your cheek might be removed?"

"No, indeed," said she, smiling; but perceiving the seriousness of his manner, she blushed deeply. "To tell you the truth it has been so often called a charm that I was simple enough to imagine it might be so."

"Ah, upon another face perhaps it might," replied her husband; "but never on yours. No, dearest Georgiana, you came so nearly perfect from the hand of Nature that this slightest possible defect, which we hesitate whether to term a defect or a beauty, shocks me, as being the visible mark of earthly imperfection."

"Shocks you, my husband!" cried Georgiana, deeply hurt; at first reddening with momentary anger, but then bursting into tears. "Then why did you take me from my mother's side? You cannot love what shocks you!"

To explain this conversation it must be mentioned that in the centre of Georgiana's left cheek there was a singular mark, deeply interwoven, as it were, with the texture and substance of her face. In the usual state of her complexion—a healthy though delicate bloom—the mark wore a tint of deeper crimson, which imperfectly defined its shape amid the surrounding rosiness. When she blushed it gradually became more indistinct, and finally vanished amid the triumphant rush of blood that bathed the whole cheek with its brilliant glow.

But if any shifting motion caused her to turn pale there was the mark again, a crimson stain upon the snow, in what Aylmer sometimes deemed an almost fearful distinctness. Its shape bore not a little similarity to the human hand, though of the smallest pygmy size. Georgiana's lovers were wont to say that some fairy at her birth hour had laid her tiny hand upon the infant's cheek, and left this impress there in token of the magic endowments that were to give her such sway over all hearts. Many a desperate swain would have risked life for the privilege of pressing his lips to the mysterious hand. It must not be concealed, however, that the impression wrought by this fairy sign manual varied exceedingly, according to the difference of temperament in the beholders.

Some fastidious persons—but they were exclusively of her own sex—affirmed that the bloody hand, as they chose to call it, quite destroyed the effect of Georgiana's beauty, and rendered her countenance even hideous. But it would be as reasonable to say that one of those small blue stains which sometimes occur in the purest statuary marble would convert the Eve of Powers to a monster. Masculine observers, if the birthmark did not heighten their admiration, contented themselves with wishing it away, that the world might possess one living specimen of ideal loveliness without the semblance of a flaw. After his marriage,—for he thought little or nothing of the matter before,—Aylmer discovered that this was the case with himself.

Had she been less beautiful,—if Envy's self could have found aught else to sneer at,—he might have felt his affection heightened by the prettiness of this mimic hand, now vaguely portrayed, now lost, now stealing forth again and glimmering to and fro with every pulse of emotion that throbbed within her heart; but seeing her otherwise so perfect, he found this one defect grow more and more intolerable with every moment of their united lives. It was the fatal flaw of humanity which Nature, in one shape or another, stamps ineffaceably on all her productions, either to imply that they are temporary and finite, or that their perfection must be wrought by toil and pain.

The crimson hand expressed the ineludible gripe in which mortality clutches the highest and purest of earthly mould, degrading them into kindred with the lowest, and even with the very brutes, like whom their visible frames return to dust. In this manner, selecting it as the symbol of his wife's liability to sin, sorrow, decay, and death, Aylmer's sombre imagination was not long in rendering the birthmark a frightful object, causing him more trouble and horror than ever Georgiana's beauty, whether of soul or sense, had given him delight.

At all the seasons which should have been their happiest, he invariably and without intending it, nay, in spite of a purpose to the contrary, reverted to this one disastrous topic. Trifling as it at first appeared, it so connected itself with innumerable trains of thought and modes of feeling that it became the central point of all. With the morning twilight Aylmer opened his eyes upon his wife's face and recognized the symbol of imperfection; and when they sat together at the evening hearth his eyes wandered stealthily to her cheek, and beheld, flickering with the blaze of the wood fire, the spectral hand that wrote mortality where he would fain have worshipped.

Georgiana soon learned to shudder at his gaze. It needed but a glance with the peculiar expression that his face often wore to change the roses of her cheek into a deathlike paleness, amid which the crimson hand was brought strongly out, like a bass-relief of ruby on the whitest marble.

Late one night when the lights were growing dim, so as hardly to betray the stain on the poor wife's cheek, she herself, for the first time, voluntarily took up the subject.

"Do you remember, my dear Aylmer," said she, with a feeble attempt at a smile, "have you any recollection of a dream last night about this odious hand?"

"None! none whatever!" replied Aylmer, starting; but then he added, in a dry, cold tone, affected for the sake of concealing the real depth of his emotion, "I might well dream of it; for before I fell asleep it had taken a pretty firm hold of my fancy."

"And you did dream of it?" continued Georgiana, hastily; for she dreaded lest a gush of tears should interrupt what she had to say. "A terrible dream! I wonder that you can forget it. Is it possible to forget this one expression?—'It is in her heart now; we must have it out!' Reflect, my husband; for by all means I would have you recall that dream."

The mind is in a sad state when Sleep, the all-involving, cannot confine her spectres within the dim region of her sway, but suffers them to break forth, affrighting this actual life with secrets that perchance belong to a deeper one. Aylmer now remembered his dream. He had fancied himself with his servant Aminadab, attempting an operation for the removal of the birthmark; but the deeper went the knife, the deeper sank the hand, until at length its tiny grasp appeared to have caught hold of Georgiana's heart; whence, however, her husband was inexorably resolved to cut or wrench it away.

When the dream had shaped itself perfectly in his memory, Aylmer sat in his wife's presence with a guilty feeling. Truth often finds its way to the mind close muffled in robes of sleep, and then speaks with uncompromising directness of matters in regard to which we practise an unconscious self-deception during our waking moments. Until now he had not been aware of the tyrannizing influence acquired by one idea over his mind, and of the lengths which he might find in his heart to go for the sake of giving himself peace.

"Aylmer," resumed Georgiana, solemnly, "I know not what may be the cost to both of us to rid me of this fatal birthmark. Perhaps its removal may cause cureless deformity; or it may be the stain goes as deep as life itself. Again: do we know that there is a possibility, on any terms, of unclasping the firm gripe of this little hand which was laid upon me before I came into the world?"

"Dearest Georgiana, I have spent much thought upon the subject," hastily interrupted Aylmer. "I am convinced of the perfect practicability of its removal."

"If there be the remotest possibility of it," continued Georgiana, "let the attempt be made at whatever risk. Danger is nothing to me; for life, while this hateful mark makes me the object of your horror and disgust,—life is a burden which I would fling down with joy. Either remove this dreadful hand, or take my wretched life! You have deep science. All the world bears witness of it. You have achieved great wonders. Cannot you remove this little, little mark, which I cover with the tips of two small fingers? Is this beyond your power, for the sake of your own peace, and to save your poor wife from madness?"

"Noblest, dearest, tenderest wife," cried Aylmer, rapturously, "doubt not my power. I have already given this matter the deepest thought— thought which might almost have enlightened me to create a being less perfect than yourself. Georgiana, you have led me deeper than ever into the heart of science. I feel myself fully competent to render this dear cheek as faultless as its fellow; and then, most beloved, what will be my triumph when I shall have corrected what Nature left imperfect in her fairest work! Even Pygmalion, when his sculptured woman assumed life, felt not greater ecstasy than mine will be."

"It is resolved, then," said Georgiana, faintly smiling. "And, Aylmer, spare me not, though you should find the birthmark take refuge in my heart at last."

Her husband tenderly kissed her cheek—her right cheek—not that which bore the impress of the crimson hand.

The next day Aylmer apprised his wife of a plan that he had formed whereby he might have opportunity for the intense thought and constant watchfulness which the proposed operation would require; while Georgiana, likewise, would enjoy the perfect repose essential to its success. They were to seclude themselves in the extensive apartments occupied by Aylmer as a laboratory, and where, during his toilsome youth, he had made discoveries in the elemental powers of Nature that had roused the admiration of all the learned societies in Europe.

Seated calmly in this laboratory, the pale philosopher had investigated the secrets of the highest cloud region and of the profoundest mines; he had satisfied himself of the causes that kindled and kept alive the fires of the volcano; and had explained the mystery of fountains, and how it is that they gush forth, some so bright and pure, and others with such rich medicinal virtues, from the dark bosom of the earth. Here, too, at an earlier period, he had studied the wonders of the human frame, and attempted to fathom the very process by which Nature assimilates all her precious influences from earth and air, and from the spiritual world, to create and foster man, her masterpiece.

The latter pursuit, however, Aylmer had long laid aside in unwilling recognition of the truth—against which all seekers sooner or later stumble—that our great creative Mother, while she amuses us with apparently working in the broadest sunshine, is yet severely careful to keep her own secrets, and, in spite of her pretended openness, shows us nothing but results. She permits us, indeed, to mar, but seldom to mend, and, like a jealous patentee, on no account to make. Now, however, Aylmer resumed these half-forgotten investigations; not, of course, with such hopes or wishes as first suggested them; but because they involved much physiological truth and lay in the path of his proposed scheme for the treatment of Georgiana.

As he led her over the threshold of the laboratory, Georgiana was cold and tremulous. Aylmer looked cheerfully into her face, with intent to reassure her, but was so startled with the intense glow of the birthmark upon the whiteness of her cheek that he could not restrain a strong convulsive shudder. His wife fainted.

"Aminadab! Aminadab!" shouted Aylmer, stamping violently on the floor.

Forthwith there issued from an inner apartment a man of low stature, but bulky frame, with shaggy hair hanging about his visage, which was grimed with the vapors of the furnace. This personage had been Aylmer's underworker during his whole scientific career, and was admirably fitted for that office by his great mechanical readiness, and the skill with which, while incapable of comprehending a single principle, he executed all the details of his master's experiments. With his vast strength, his shaggy hair, his smoky aspect, and the indescribable earthiness that incrusted him, he seemed to represent man's physical nature; while Aylmer's slender figure, and pale, intellectual face, were no less apt a type of the spiritual element.

"Throw open the door of the *boudoir*, Aminadab," said Aylmer, "and burn a *pastil*."

"Yes, master," answered Aminadab, looking intently at the lifeless form of Georgiana; and then he muttered to himself, "If she were my wife, I'd never part with that birthmark."

When Georgiana recovered consciousness she found herself breathing an atmosphere of penetrating fragrance, the gentle potency of which had recalled her from her deathlike faintness. The scene around her looked like enchantment. Aylmer had converted those smoky, dingy, sombre rooms, where he had spent his brightest years in recondite pursuits, into a series of beautiful apartments not unfit to be the secluded abode of a lovely woman. The walls were hung with gorgeous curtains, which imparted the combination of grandeur and grace that no other species of adornment can achieve; and as they fell from the ceiling to the floor, their rich and ponderous folds, concealing all angles and straight lines, appeared to shut in the scene from infinite space.

For aught Georgiana knew, it might be a pavilion among the clouds. And Aylmer, excluding the sunshine, which would have interfered with his chemical processes, had supplied its place with perfumed lamps, emitting flames of various hue, but all uniting in a soft, empurpled radiance. He now knelt by his wife's side, watching her earnestly, but without alarm; for he was confident in his science, and felt that he could draw a magic circle round her within which no evil might intrude.

"Where am I? Ah, I remember," said Georgiana, faintly; and she placed her hand over her cheek to hide the terrible mark from her husband's eyes.

"Fear not, dearest!" exclaimed he. "Do not shrink from me! Believe me, Georgiana, I even rejoice in this single imperfection, since it will be such a rapture to remove it."

"Oh, spare me!" sadly replied his wife. "Pray do not look at it again. I never can forget that convulsive shudder."

In order to soothe Georgiana, and, as it were, to release her mind from the burden of actual things, Aylmer now put in practice some of the light and playful secrets which science had taught him among its profounder lore. Airy figures, absolutely bodiless ideas, and forms of unsubstantial beauty came and danced before her, imprinting their momentary footsteps on beams of light. Though she had some indistinct idea of the method of these optical phenomena, still the illusion was almost perfect enough to warrant the belief that her husband possessed sway over the spiritual world.

Then again, when she felt a wish to look forth from her seclusion, immediately, as if her thoughts were answered, the procession of external existence flitted across a screen. The scenery and the figures of actual life were perfectly represented, but with that bewitching, yet indescribable difference which always makes a picture, an image, or a shadow so much more attractive than the original. When wearied of this, Aylmer bade her cast her eyes upon a vessel containing a quantity of earth. She did so, with little interest at first; but was soon startled to perceive the germ of a plant shooting upward from the soil. Then came the slender stalk; the leaves gradually unfolded themselves; and amid them was a perfect and lovely flower.

"It is magical!" cried Georgiana. "I dare not touch it."

"Nay, pluck it," answered Aylmer,—"pluck it, and inhale its brief perfume while you may. The flower will wither in a few moments and leave nothing save its brown seed vessels; but thence may be perpetuated a race as ephemeral as itself."

But Georgiana had no sooner touched the flower than the whole plant suffered a blight, its leaves turning coal-black as if by the agency of fire.

"There was too powerful a stimulus," said Aylmer, thoughtfully.

To make up for this abortive experiment, he proposed to take her portrait by a scientific process of his own invention. It was to be effected by rays of light striking upon a polished plate of metal. Georgiana assented; but, on looking at the result, was affrighted to find the features of the portrait blurred and indefinable; while the minute figure of a hand appeared where the cheek should have been. Aylmer snatched the metallic plate and threw it into a jar of corrosive acid.

Soon, however, he forgot these mortifying failures. In the intervals of study and chemical experiment he came to her flushed and exhausted, but seemed invigorated by her presence, and spoke in glowing language of the resources of his art. He gave a history of the long dynasty of the alchemists, who spent so many ages in quest of the universal solvent by which the golden principle might be elicited from all things vile and base.

Aylmer appeared to believe that, by the plainest scientific logic, it was altogether within the limits of possibility to discover this long-sought medium; "but," he added, "a philosopher who should go deep enough to acquire the power would attain too lofty a wisdom to stoop to the exercise of it." Not less singular were his opinions in regard to the elixir vitae. He more than intimated that it was at his option to concoct a liquid that should prolong life for years, perhaps interminably; but that it would produce a discord in Nature which all the world, and chiefly the quaffer of the immortal nostrum, would find cause to curse.

"Aylmer, are you in earnest?" asked Georgiana, looking at him with amazement and fear. "It is terrible to possess such power, or even to dream of possessing it."

"Oh, do not tremble, my love," said her husband. "I would not wrong either you or myself by working such inharmonious effects upon our lives; but I would have you consider how trifling, in comparison, is the skill requisite to remove this little hand."

At the mention of the birthmark, Georgiana, as usual, shrank as if a red-hot iron had touched her cheek.

Again Aylmer applied himself to his labours. She could hear his voice in the distant furnace room giving directions to Aminadab, whose harsh, uncouth, misshapen tones were audible in response, more like the grunt or growl of a brute than human speech. After hours of absence, Aylmer reappeared and proposed that she should now examine his cabinet of chemical products and natural treasures of the earth. Among the former he showed her a small vial, in which, he remarked, was contained a gentle yet most powerful fragrance, capable of impregnating all the breezes that blow across a kingdom. They were of inestimable value, the contents of that little vial; and, as he said so, he threw some of the perfume into the air and filled the room with piercing and invigorating delight.

"And what is this?" asked Georgiana, pointing to a small crystal globe containing a gold-coloured liquid. "It is so beautiful to the eye that I could imagine it the elixir of life."

"In one sense it is," replied Aylmer; "or, rather, the elixir of immortality. It is the most precious poison that ever was concocted in this world. By its aid I could apportion the lifetime of any mortal at whom you might point your finger. The strength of the dose would determine whether he were to linger out years, or drop dead in the midst of a breath. No king on his guarded throne could keep his life if I, in my private station, should deem that the welfare of millions justified me in depriving him of it."

"Why do you keep such a terrific drug?" inquired Georgiana in horror.

"Do not mistrust me, dearest," said her husband, smiling; "its virtuous potency is yet greater than its harmful one. But see! here is a powerful cosmetic. With a few drops of this in a vase of water, freckles may be washed away as easily as the hands are cleansed. A stronger infusion would take the blood out of the cheek, and leave the rosiest beauty a pale ghost."

"Is it with this lotion that you intend to bathe my cheek?" asked Georgiana, anxiously.

"Oh, no," hastily replied her husband; "this is merely superficial. Your case demands a remedy that shall go deeper."

In his interviews with Georgiana, Aylmer generally made minute inquiries as to her sensations and whether the confinement of the rooms and the temperature of the atmosphere agreed with her. These questions had such a particular drift that Georgiana began to conjecture that she was already subjected to certain physical influences, either breathed in with the fragrant air or taken with her food. She fancied likewise, but it might be altogether fancy, that there was a stirring up of her system—a strange, indefinite sensation creeping through her veins, and tingling, half painfully, half pleasurably, at her heart. Still, whenever she dared to look into the mirror, there she beheld herself pale as a white rose and with the crimson birthmark stamped upon her cheek. Not even Aylmer now hated it so much as she.

To dispel the tedium of the hours which her husband found it necessary to devote to the processes of combination and analysis, Georgiana turned over the volumes of his scientific library. In many dark old tomes she met with chapters full of romance and poetry. They were the works of philosophers of the middle ages, such as Albertus Magnus, Cornelius Agrippa, Paracelsus, and the famous friar who created the prophetic Brazen Head. All these antique naturalists stood in advance of their centuries, yet were imbued with some of their credulity, and therefore were believed, and perhaps imagined themselves to have acquired from the investigation of Nature a power above Nature, and from physics a sway over the spiritual world. Hardly less curious and imaginative were the early volumes of the Transactions of the Royal Society, in which the members, knowing little of the limits of natural possibility, were continually recording wonders or proposing methods whereby wonders might be wrought.

But to Georgiana the most engrossing volume was a large folio from her husband's own hand, in which he had recorded every experiment of his scientific career, its original aim, the methods adopted for its development, and its final success or failure, with the circumstances to which either event was attributable. The book, in truth, was both the history and emblem of his ardent, ambitious, imaginative, yet practical and laborious life. He handled physical details as if there were nothing beyond them; yet spiritualized them all, and redeemed himself from materialism by his strong and eager aspiration towards the infinite. In his grasp the veriest clod of earth assumed a soul.

Georgiana, as she read, reverenced Aylmer and loved him more profoundly than ever, but with a less entire dependence on his judgment than heretofore. Much as he had accomplished, she could not but observe that his most splendid successes were almost invariably failures, if compared with the ideal at which he aimed. His brightest diamonds were the merest pebbles, and felt to be so by himself, in comparison with the inestimable gems which lay hidden beyond his reach. The volume, rich with achievements that had won renown for its author, was yet as melancholy a record as ever mortal hand had penned. It was the sad confession and continual exemplification of the shortcomings of the composite man, the spirit burdened with clay and working in matter, and of the despair that assails the higher nature at finding itself so miserably thwarted by the earthly part. Perhaps every man of genius in whatever sphere might recognize the image of his own experience in Aylmer's journal.

So deeply did these reflections affect Georgiana that she laid her face upon the open volume and burst into tears. In this situation she was found by her husband.

"It is dangerous to read in a sorcerer's books," said he with a smile, though his countenance was uneasy and displeased. "Georgiana, there are pages in that volume which I can scarcely glance over and keep my senses. Take heed lest it prove as detrimental to you."

"It has made me worship you more than ever," said she.

"Ah, wait for this one success," rejoined he, "then worship me if you will. I shall deem myself hardly unworthy of it. But come, I have sought you for the luxury of your voice. Sing to me, dearest."

So she poured out the liquid music of her voice to quench the thirst of his spirit. He then took his leave with a boyish exuberance of gayety, assuring her that her seclusion would endure but a little longer, and that the result was already certain. Scarcely had he departed when Georgiana felt irresistibly impelled to follow him. She had forgotten to inform Aylmer of a symptom which for two or three hours past had begun to excite her attention. It was a sensation in the fatal birthmark, not painful, but which induced a restlessness throughout her system. Hastening after her husband, she intruded for the first time into the laboratory.

The first thing that struck her eye was the furnace, that hot and feverish worker, with the intense glow of its fire, which by the quantities of soot clustered above it seemed to have been burning for ages. There was a distilling apparatus in full operation. Around the room were retorts, tubes, cylinders, crucibles, and other apparatus of chemical research. An electrical machine stood ready for immediate use. The atmosphere felt oppressively close, and was tainted with gaseous odours which had been tormented forth by the processes of science.

The severe and homely simplicity of the apartment, with its naked walls and brick pavement, looked strange, accustomed as Georgiana had become to the fantastic elegance of her boudoir. But what chiefly, indeed almost solely, drew her attention, was the aspect of Aylmer himself.

He was pale as death, anxious and absorbed, and hung over the furnace as if it depended upon his utmost watchfulness whether the liquid which it was distilling should be the draught of immortal happiness or misery. How different from the sanguine and joyous mien that he had assumed for Georgiana's encouragement!

"Carefully now, Aminadab; carefully, thou human machine; carefully, thou man of clay!" muttered Aylmer, more to himself than his assistant. "Now, if there be a thought too much or too little, it is all over."

"Ho! ho!" mumbled Aminadab. "Look, master! look!"

Aylmer raised his eyes hastily, and at first reddened, then grew paler than ever, on beholding Georgiana. He rushed towards her and seized her arm with a gripe that left the print of his fingers upon it.

"Why do you come hither? Have you no trust in your husband?" cried he, impetuously. "Would you throw the blight of that fatal birthmark over my labors? It is not well done. Go, prying woman, go!"

"Nay, Aylmer," said Georgiana with the firmness of which she possessed no stinted endowment, "it is not you that have a right to complain. You mistrust your wife; you have concealed the anxiety with which you watch the development of this experiment. Think not so unworthily of me, my husband. Tell me all the risk we run, and fear not that I shall shrink; for my share in it is far less than your own."

"No, no, Georgiana!" said Aylmer, impatiently; "it must not be."

"I submit," replied she calmly. "And, Aylmer, I shall quaff whatever draught you bring me; but it will be on the same principle that would induce me to take a dose of poison if offered by your hand."

"My noble wife," said Aylmer, deeply moved, "I knew not the height and depth of your nature until now. Nothing shall be concealed. Know, then, that this crimson hand, superficial as it seems, has clutched its grasp into your being with a strength of which I had no previous conception. I have already administered agents powerful enough to do aught except to change your entire physical system. Only one thing remains to be tried. If that fail us we are ruined."

"Why did you hesitate to tell me this?" asked she.

"Because, Georgiana," said Aylmer, in a low voice, "there is danger."

"Danger? There is but one danger—that this horrible stigma shall be left upon my cheek!" cried Georgiana. "Remove it, remove it, whatever be the cost, or we shall both go mad!"

"Heaven knows your words are too true," said Aylmer, sadly. "And now, dearest, return to your *boudoir*. In a little while all will be tested."

He conducted her back and took leave of her with a solemn tenderness which spoke far more than his words how much was now at stake. After his departure Georgiana became rapt in musings. She considered the character of Aylmer, and did it completer justice than at any previous moment. Her heart exulted, while it trembled, at his honourable love—so pure and lofty that it would accept nothing less than perfection nor miserably make itself contented with an earthlier nature than he had dreamed of. She felt how much more precious was such a sentiment than that meaner kind which would have borne with the imperfection for her sake, and have been guilty of treason to holy love by degrading its perfect idea to the level of the actual; and with her whole spirit she prayed that, for a single moment, she might satisfy his highest and deepest conception. Longer than one moment she well knew it could not be; for his spirit was ever on the march, ever ascending, and each instant required something that was beyond the scope of the instant before.

The sound of her husband's footsteps aroused her. He bore a crystal goblet containing a liquor colourless as water, but bright enough to be the draught of immortality. Aylmer was pale; but it seemed rather the consequence of a highly-wrought state of mind and tension of spirit than of fear or doubt.

"The concoction of the draught has been perfect," said he, in answer to Georgiana's look. "Unless all my science have deceived me, it cannot fail."

"Save on your account, my dearest Aylmer," observed his wife, "I might wish to put off this birthmark of mortality by relinquishing mortality itself in preference to any other mode. Life is but a sad possession to those who have attained precisely the degree of moral advancement at which I stand. Were I weaker and blinder it might be happiness. Were I stronger, it might be endured hopefully. But, being what I find myself, methinks I am of all mortals the most fit to die."

"You are fit for heaven without tasting death!" replied her husband "But why do we speak of dying? The draught cannot fail. Behold its effect upon this plant."

On the window seat there stood a geranium diseased with yellow blotches, which had overspread all its leaves. Aylmer poured a small quantity of the liquid upon the soil in which it grew. In a little time, when the roots of the plant had taken up the moisture, the unsightly blotches began to be extinguished in a living verdure.

"There needed no proof," said Georgiana, quietly. "Give me the goblet I joyfully stake all upon your word."

"Drink, then, thou lofty creature!" exclaimed Aylmer, with fervid admiration. "There is no taint of imperfection on thy spirit. Thy sensible frame, too, shall soon be all perfect."

She quaffed the liquid and returned the goblet to his hand.

"It is grateful," said she with a placid smile. "Methinks it is like water from a heavenly fountain; for it contains I know not what of unobtrusive fragrance and deliciousness. It allays a feverish thirst that had parched me for many days. Now, dearest, let me sleep. My earthly senses are closing over my spirit like the leaves around the heart of a rose at sunset."

She spoke the last words with a gentle reluctance, as if it required almost more energy than she could command to pronounce the faint and lingering syllables. Scarcely had they loitered through her lips ere she was lost in slumber. Aylmer sat by her side, watching her aspect with the emotions proper to a man the whole value of whose existence was involved in the process now to be tested. Mingled with this mood, however, was the philosophic investigation characteristic of the man of science.

Not the minutest symptom escaped him. A heightened flush of the cheek, a slight irregularity of breath, a quiver of the eyelid, a hardly perceptible tremor through the frame,—such were the details which, as the moments passed, he wrote down in his folio volume. Intense thought had set its stamp upon every previous page of that volume, but the thoughts of years were all concentrated upon the last.

While thus employed, he failed not to gaze often at the fatal hand, and not without a shudder. Yet once, by a strange and unaccountable impulse he pressed it with his lips. His spirit recoiled, however, in the very act, and Georgiana, out of the midst of her deep sleep, moved uneasily and murmured as if in remonstrance. Again Aylmer resumed his watch. Nor was it without avail. The crimson hand, which at first had been strongly visible upon the marble paleness of Georgiana's cheek, now grew more faintly outlined. She remained not less pale than ever; but the birthmark with every breath that came and went, lost somewhat of its former distinctness. Its presence had been awful; its departure was more awful still. Watch the stain of the rainbow fading out the sky, and you will know how that mysterious symbol passed away.

"By Heaven! it is well-nigh gone!" said Aylmer to himself, in almost irrepressible ecstasy. "I can scarcely trace it now. Success! success! And now it is like the faintest rose colour. The lightest flush of blood across her cheek would overcome it. But she is so pale!"

He drew aside the window curtain and suffered the light of natural day to fall into the room and rest upon her cheek. At the same time he heard a gross, hoarse chuckle, which he had long known as his servant Aminadab's expression of delight.

"Ah, clod! ah, earthly mass!" cried Aylmer, laughing in a sort of frenzy, "you have served me well! Matter and spirit—earth and heaven—have both done their part in this! Laugh, thing of the senses! You have earned the right to laugh."

These exclamations broke Georgiana's sleep. She slowly unclosed her eyes and gazed into the mirror which her husband had arranged for that purpose. A faint smile flitted over her lips when she recognized how barely perceptible was now that crimson hand which had once blazed forth with such disastrous brilliancy as to scare away all their happiness. But then her eyes sought Aylmer's face with a trouble and anxiety that he could by no means account for.

"My poor Aylmer!" murmured she.

"Poor? Nay, richest, happiest, most favoured!" exclaimed he. "My peerless bride, it is successful! You are perfect!"

"My poor Aylmer," she repeated, with a more than human tenderness, "you have aimed loftily; you have done nobly. Do not repent that with so high and pure a feeling, you have rejected the best the earth could offer. Aylmer, dearest Aylmer, I am dying!"

Alas! it was too true! The fatal hand had grappled with the mystery of life, and was the bond by which an angelic spirit kept itself in union with a mortal frame. As the last crimson tint of the birthmark—that sole token of human imperfection—faded from her cheek, the parting breath of the now perfect woman passed into the atmosphere, and her soul, lingering a moment near her husband, took its heavenward flight. Then a hoarse, chuckling laugh was heard again! Thus ever does the gross fatality of earth exult in its invariable triumph over the immortal essence which, in this dim sphere of half development, demands the completeness of a higher state.

Yet, had Alymer reached a profounder wisdom, he need not thus have flung away the happiness which would have woven his mortal life of the selfsame texture with the celestial. The momentary circumstance was too strong for him; he failed to look beyond the shadowy scope of time, and, living once for all in eternity, to find the perfect future in the present.

The Biter Bit

By Wilkie Collins

From Chief Inspector Theakstone, of the Detective Police, to Sergeant Bulmer, of the Same Force.

London, 4th July, 18—.

Sergeant Bulmer—This is to inform you that you are wanted to assist in looking up a case of importance, which will require all the attention of an experienced member of the force. The matter of the robbery on which you are now engaged you will please to shift over to the young man who brings you this letter. You will tell him all the circumstances of the case, just as they stand; you will put him up to the progress you have made (if any) toward detecting the person or persons by whom the money has been stolen; and you will leave him to make the best he can of the matter now in your hands. He is to have the whole responsibility of the case, and the whole credit of his success if he brings it to a proper issue.

So much for the orders that I am desired to communicate to you.

A word in your ear, next, about this new man who is to take your place. His name is Matthew Sharpin, and he is to have the chance given him of dashing into our office at one jump— supposing he turns out strong enough to take it. You will naturally ask me how he comes by this privilege. I can only tell you that he has some uncommonly strong interest to back him in certain high quarters, which you and I had better not mention except under our breaths. He has been a lawyer's clerk, and he is wonderfully conceited in his opinion of himself, as well as mean and underhand, to look at. According to his own account, he leaves his old trade and joins ours of his own free will and preference.

You will no more believe that than I do. My notion is, that he has managed to ferret out some private information in connection with the affairs of one of his master's clients, which makes him rather an awkward customer to keep in the office for the future, and which, at the same time, gives him hold enough over his employer to make it dangerous to drive him into a corner by turning him away. I think the giving him this unheard-of chance among us is, in plain words, pretty much like giving him hush money to keep him quiet.

However that may be, Mr. Matthew Sharpin is to have the case now in your hands, and if he succeeds with it he pokes his ugly nose into our office as sure as fate. I put you up to this, sergeant, so that you may not stand in your own light by giving the new man any cause to complain of you at headquarters, and remain yours,

Francis Theakstone.

From Mr. Matthew Sharpin to Chief Inspector Theakstone.

London, 5th July, 18—.

Dear Sir—Having now been favoured with the necessary instructions from Sergeant Bulmer, I beg to remind you of certain directions which I have received relating to the report of my future proceedings which I am to prepare for examination at headquarters.

The object of my writing, and of your examining what I have written before you send it to the higher authorities, is, I am informed, to give me, as an untried hand, the benefit of your advice in case I want it (which I venture to think I shall not) at any stage of my proceedings. As the extraordinary circumstances of the case on which I am now engaged make it impossible for me to absent myself from the place where the robbery was committed until I have made some progress toward discovering the thief, I am necessarily precluded from consulting you personally. Hence the necessity of my writing down the various details, which might perhaps be better communicated by word of mouth.

This, if I am not mistaken, is the position in which we are now placed. I state my own impressions on the subject in writing, in order that we may clearly understand each other at the outset;

and have the honour to remain your obedient servant,

Matthew Sharpin.

From Chief Inspector Theakstone to Mr. Matthew Sharpin.

London, 5th July, 18—.

Sir—You have begun by wasting time, ink, and paper. We both of us perfectly well knew the position we stood in toward each other when I sent you with my letter to Sergeant Bulmer. There was not the least need to repeat it in writing. Be so good as to employ your pen in future on the business actually in hand.

You have now three separate matters on which to write me. First, you have to draw up a statement of your instructions received from Sergeant Bulmer, in order to show us that nothing has escaped your memory, and that you are thoroughly acquainted with all the circumstances of the case which has been intrusted to you.

Secondly, you are to inform me what it is you propose to do. Thirdly, you are to report every inch of your progress (if you make any) from day to day, and, if need be, from hour to hour as well. This is your duty. As to what my duty may be, when I want you to remind me of it, I will write and tell you so.

In the meantime, I remain yours,   Francis Theakstone.

From Mr. Matthew Sharpin to Chief Inspector Theakstone.

London, 6th July, 18—.

Sir—You are rather an elderly person, and as such, naturally inclined to be a little jealous of men like me, who are in the prime of their lives and their faculties. Under these circumstances, it is my duty to be considerate toward you, and not to bear too hardly on your small failings. I decline, therefore, altogether to take offense at the tone of your letter; I give you the full benefit of the natural generosity of my nature; I sponge the very existence of your surly communication out of my memory—in short, Chief Inspector Theakstone, I forgive you, and proceed to business.

My first duty is to draw up a full statement of the instructions I have received from Sergeant Bulmer. Here they are at your service, according to my version of them.

At Number Thirteen Rutherford Street, Soho, there is a stationer's shop. It is kept by one Mr. Yatman. He is a married man, but has no family. Besides Mr. and Mrs. Yatman, the other inmates in the house are a lodger, a young single man named Jay, who occupies the front room on the second floor—a shopman, who sleeps in one of the attics, and a servant-of-all-work, whose bed is in the back kitchen. Once a week a charwoman comes to help this servant. These are all the persons who, on ordinary occasions, have means of access to the interior of the house, placed, as a matter of course, at their disposal.

Mr. Yatman has been in business for many years, carrying on his affairs prosperously enough to realize a handsome independence for a person in his position. Unfortunately for himself, he endeavoured to increase the amount of his property by speculating. He ventured boldly in his investments; luck went against him; and rather less than two years ago he found himself a poor man again. All that was saved out of the wreck of his property was the sum of two hundred pounds.

Although Mr. Yatman did his best to meet his altered circumstances, by giving up many of the luxuries and comforts to which he and his wife had been accustomed, he found it impossible to retrench so far as to allow of putting by any money from the income produced by his shop. The business has been declining of late years, the cheap advertising stationers having done it injury with the public. Consequently, up to the last week, the only surplus property possessed by Mr. Yatman consisted of the two hundred pounds which had been recovered from the wreck of his fortune. This sum was placed as a deposit in a joint-stock bank of the highest possible character.

Eight days ago Mr. Yatman and his lodger, Mr. Jay, held a conversation on the subject of the commercial difficulties which are hampering trade in all directions at the present time. Mr. Jay (who lives by supplying the newspapers with short paragraphs relating to accidents, offenses, and brief records of remarkable occurrences in general—who is, in short, what they call a penny-a-liner) told his landlord that he had been in the city that day and heard unfavourable rumours on the subject of the joint-stock banks. The rumours to which he alluded had already reached the ears of Mr. Yatman from other quarters, and the confirmation of them by his lodger had such an effect on his mind—predisposed as it was to alarm by the experience of his former losses—that he resolved to go at once to the bank and withdraw his deposit. It was then getting on toward the end of the afternoon, and he arrived just in time to receive his money before the bank closed.

He received the deposit in bank-notes of the following amounts: one fifty-pound note, three twenty-pound notes, six ten-pound notes, and six five-pound notes. His object in drawing the money in this form was to have it ready to lay out immediately in trifling loans, on good security, among the small trades-people of his district, some of whom are sorely pressed for the very means of existence at the present time. Investments of this kind seemed to Mr. Yatman to be the most safe and the most profitable on which he could now venture.

He brought the money back in an envelope placed in his breast pocket, and asked his shopman, on getting home, to look for a small, flat, tin cash-box, which had not been used for years, and which, as Mr. Yatman remembered it, was exactly of the right size to hold the bank-notes. For some time the cash-box was searched for in vain. Mr. Yatman called to his wife to know if she had any idea where it was. The question was overheard by the servant-of-all-work, who was taking up the tea-tray at the time, and by Mr. Jay, who was coming downstairs on his way out to the theatre. Ultimately the cash-box was found by the shopman. Mr. Yatman placed the banknotes in it, secured them by a padlock, and put the box in his coat pocket. It stuck out of the coat pocket a very little, but enough to be seen. Mr. Yatman remained at home, upstairs, all that evening. No visitors called. At eleven o'clock he went to bed, and put the cash-box under his pillow.

When he and his wife woke the next morning the box was gone. Payment of the notes was immediately stopped at the Bank of England, but no news of the money has been heard of since that time.

So far the circumstances of the case are perfectly clear. They point unmistakably to the conclusion that the robbery must have been committed by some person living in the house. Suspicion falls, therefore, upon the servant-of-all-work, upon the shopman, and upon Mr. Jay. The two first knew that the cash-box was being inquired for by their master, but did not know what it was he wanted to put into it. They would assume, of course, that it was money. They both had opportunities (the servant when she took away the tea, and the shopman when he came, after shutting up, to give the keys of the till to his master) of seeing the cash-box in Mr. Yatman's pocket, and of inferring naturally, from its position there, that he intended to take it into his bedroom with him at night.

Mr. Jay, on the other hand, had been told, during the afternoon's conversation on the subject of joint-stock banks, that his landlord had a deposit of two hundred pounds in one of them. He also knew that Mr. Yatman left him with the intention of drawing that money out; and he heard the inquiry for the cash-box afterward, when he was coming downstairs. He must, therefore, have inferred that the money was in the house, and that the cash-box was the receptacle intended to contain it. That he could have had any idea, however, of the place in which Mr. Yatman intended to keep it for the night is impossible, seeing that he went out before the box was found, and did not return till his landlord was in bed. Consequently, if he committed the robbery, he must have gone into the bedroom purely on speculation.

Speaking of the bedroom reminds me of the necessity of noticing the situation of it in the house, and the means that exist of gaining easy access to it at any hour of the night.

The room in question is the back room on the first floor. In consequence of Mrs. Yatman's constitutional nervousness on the subject of fire, which makes her apprehend being burned alive in her room, in case of accident, by the hampering of the lock if the key is turned in it, her husband has never been accustomed to lock the bedroom door. Both he and his wife are, by their own admission, heavy sleepers; consequently, the risk to be run by any evil-disposed persons wishing to plunder the bedroom was of the most trifling kind. They could enter the room by merely turning the handle of the door; and, if they moved with ordinary caution, there was no fear of their waking the sleepers inside. This fact is of importance. It strengthens our conviction that the money must have been taken by one of the inmates of the house, because it tends to show that the robbery, in this case, might have been committed by persons not possessed of the superior vigilance and cunning of the experienced thief.

Such are the circumstances, as they were related to Sergeant Bulmer, when he was first called in to discover the guilty parties, and, if possible, to recover the lost bank-notes. The strictest inquiry which he could institute failed of producing the smallest fragment of evidence against any of the persons on whom suspicion naturally fell. Their language and behaviour on being informed of the robbery was perfectly consistent with the language and behaviour of innocent people. Sergeant Bulmer felt from the first that this was a case for private inquiry and secret observation. He began by recommending Mr. and Mrs. Yatman to affect a feeling of perfect confidence in the innocence of the persons living under their roof, and he then opened the campaign by employing himself in following the goings and comings, and in discovering the friends, the habits, and the secrets of the maid-of-all-work.

Three days and nights of exertion on his own part, and on that of others who were competent to assist his investigations, were enough to satisfy him that there was no sound cause for suspicion against the girl.

He next practiced the same precaution in relation to the shopman. There was more difficulty and uncertainty in privately clearing up this person's character without his knowledge, but the obstacles were at last smoothed away with tolerable success; and, though there is not the same amount of certainty in this case which there was in the case of the girl, there is still fair reason for supposing that the shopman has had nothing to do with the robbery of the cash-box.

As a necessary consequence of these proceedings, the range of suspicion now becomes limited to the lodger, Mr. Jay.

When I presented your letter of introduction to Sergeant Bulmer, he had already made some inquiries on the subject of this young man. The result, so far, has not been at all favourable. Mr. Jay's habits are irregular; he frequents public houses, and seems to be familiarly acquainted with a great many dissolute characters; he is in debt to most of the trades-people whom he employs; he has not paid his rent to Mr. Yatman for the last month; yesterday evening he came home excited by liquor, and last week he was seen talking to a prize-fighter; in short, though Mr. Jay does call himself a journalist, in virtue of his penny-a-line contributions to the newspapers, he is a young man of low tastes, vulgar manners, and bad habits. Nothing has yet been discovered in relation to him which redounds to his credit in the smallest degree.

I have now reported, down to the very last details, all the particulars communicated to me by Sergeant Bulmer. I believe you will not find an omission anywhere; and I think you will admit, though you are prejudiced against me, that a clearer statement of facts was never laid before you than the statement I have now made. My next duty is to tell you what I propose to do now that the case is confided to my hands.

In the first place, it is clearly my business to take up the case at the point where Sergeant Bulmer has left it. On his authority, I am justified in assuming that I have no need to trouble myself about the maid-of-all-work and the shopman. Their characters are now to be considered as cleared up. What remains to be privately investigated is the question of the guilt or innocence of Mr. Jay. Before we give up the notes for lost, we must make sure, if we can, that he knows nothing about them.

This is the plan that I have adopted, with the full approval of Mr. and Mrs. Yatman, for discovering whether Mr. Jay is or is not the person who has stolen the cash-box:

I propose today to present myself at the house in the character of a young man who is looking for lodgings. The back room on the second floor will be shown to me as the room to let, and I shall establish myself there tonight as a person from the country who has come to London to look for a situation in a respectable shop or office.

By this means I shall be living next to the room occupied by Mr. Jay. The partition between us is mere lath and plaster. I shall make a small hole in it, near the cornice, through which I can see what Mr. Jay does in his room, and hear every word that is said when any friend happens to call on him. Whenever he is at home, I shall be at my post of observation; whenever he goes out, I shall be after him. By employing these means of watching him, I believe I may look forward to the discovery of his secret—if he knows anything about the lost bank-notes—as to a dead certainty.

What you may think of my plan of observation I cannot undertake to say. It appears to me to unite the invaluable merits of boldness and simplicity.

Fortified by this conviction, I close the present communication with feelings of the most sanguine description in regard to the future, and remain your obedient servant,

Matthew Sharpin.

From the Same to the Same.

7th July.

Sir—As you have not honoured me with any answer to my last communication, I assume that, in spite of your prejudices against me, it has produced the favourable impression on your mind which I ventured to anticipate. Gratified and encouraged beyond measure by the token of approval which your eloquent silence conveys to me, I proceed to report the progress that has been made in the course of the last twenty-four hours.

I am now comfortably established next door to Mr. Jay, and I am delighted to say that I have two holes in the partition instead of one. My natural sense of humour has led me into the pardonable extravagance of giving them both appropriate names. One I call my peep-hole, and the other my pipe-hole. The name of the first explains itself; the name of the second refers to a small tin pipe or tube inserted in the hole, and twisted so that the mouth of it comes close to my ear while I am standing at my post of observation. Thus, while I am looking at Mr. Jay through my peep-hole, I can hear every word that may be spoken in his room through my pipe-hole.

Perfect candour—a virtue which I have possessed from my childhood—compels me to acknowledge, before I go any further, that the ingenious notion of adding a pipe-hole to my proposed peep-hole originated with Mrs. Yatman. This lady—a most intelligent and accomplished person, simple, and yet distinguished in her manners, has entered into all my little plans with an enthusiasm and intelligence which I cannot too highly praise.

Mr. Yatman is so cast down by his loss that he is quite incapable of affording me any assistance. Mrs. Yatman, who is evidently most tenderly attached to him, feels her husband's sad condition of mind even more acutely than she feels the loss of the money, and is mainly stimulated to exertion by her desire to assist in raising him from the miserable state of prostration into which he has now fallen.

"The money, Mr. Sharpin," she said to me yesterday evening, with tears in her eyes, "the money may be regained by rigid economy and strict attention to business. It is my husband's wretched state of mind that makes me so anxious for the discovery of the thief. I may be wrong, but I felt hopeful of success as soon as you entered the house; and I believe that, if the wretch who robbed us is to be found, you are the man to discover him." I accepted this gratifying compliment in the spirit in which it was offered, firmly believing that I shall be found, sooner or later, to have thoroughly deserved it.

Let me now return to business—that is to say, to my peep-hole and my pipe-hole.

I have enjoyed some hours of calm observation of Mr. Jay. Though rarely at home, as I understand from Mrs. Yatman, on ordinary occasions, he has been indoors the whole of this day. That is suspicious, to begin with. I have to report, further, that he rose at a late hour this morning (always a bad sign in a young man), and that he lost a great deal of time, after he was up, in yawning and complaining to himself of headache. Like other debauched characters, he ate little or nothing for breakfast. His next proceeding was to smoke a pipe—a dirty clay pipe, which a gentleman would have been ashamed to put between his lips.

When he had done smoking he took out pen, ink and paper, and sat down to write with a groan—whether of remorse for having taken the banknotes, or of disgust at the task before him, I am unable to say. After writing a few lines (too far away from my peep-hole to give me a chance of reading over his shoulder), he leaned back in his chair, and amused himself by humming the tunes of popular songs. I recognized "My Mary Anne," "Bobbin' Around," and "Old Dog Tray," among other melodies. Whether these do or do not represent secret signals by which he communicates with his accomplices remains to be seen.

After he had amused himself for some time by humming, he got up and began to walk about the room, occasionally stopping to add a sentence to the paper on his desk. Before long he went to a locked cupboard and opened it. I strained my eyes eagerly, in expectation of making a discovery. I saw him take something carefully out of the cupboard—he turned round— and it was only a pint bottle of brandy! Having drunk some of the liquor, this extremely indolent reprobate lay down on his bed again, and in five minutes was fast asleep.

After hearing him snoring for at least two hours, I was recalled to my peep-hole by a knock at his door. He jumped up and opened it with suspicious activity.

A very small boy, with a very dirty face, walked in, said: "Please, sir, they're waiting for you," sat down on a chair with his legs a long way from the ground, and instantly fell asleep! Mr. Jay swore an oath, tied a wet towel round his head, and, going back to his paper, began to cover it with writing as fast as his fingers could move the pen.

Occasionally getting up to dip the towel in water and tie it on again, he continued at this employment for nearly three hours; then folded up the leaves of writing, woke the boy, and gave them to him, with this remarkable expression: "Now, then, young sleepy-head, quick march! If you see the governor, tell him to have the money ready for me when I call for it." The boy grinned and disappeared. I was sorely tempted to follow "sleepy-head," but, on reflection, considered it safest still to keep my eye on the proceedings of Mr. Jay.

In half an hour's time he put on his hat and walked out. Of course I put on my hat and walked out also. As I went downstairs I passed Mrs. Yatman going up. The lady has been kind enough to undertake, by previous arrangement between us, to search Mr. Jay's room while he is out of the way, and while I am necessarily engaged in the pleasing duty of following him wherever he goes.

On the occasion to which I now refer, he walked straight to the nearest tavern and ordered a couple of mutton-chops for his dinner. I placed myself in the next box to him, and ordered a couple of mutton-chops for my dinner. Before I had been in the room a minute, a young man of highly suspicious manners and appearance, sitting at a table opposite, took his glass of porter in his hand and joined Mr. Jay. I pretended to be reading the newspaper, and listened, as in duty bound, with all my might.

"Jack has been here inquiring after you," says the young man.

"Did he leave any message?" asks Mr. Jay.

"Yes," says the other. "He told me, if I met with you, to say that he wished very particularly to see you tonight, and that he would give you a look in at Rutherford Street at seven o'clock."

"All right," says Mr. Jay. "I'll get back in time to see him."

Upon this, the suspicious-looking young man finished his porter, and saying that he was rather in a hurry, took leave of his friend (perhaps I should not be wrong if I said his accomplice?), and left the room.

At twenty-five minutes and a half past six—in these serious cases it is important to be particular about time—Mr. Jay finished his chops and paid his bill. At twenty-six minutes and three-quarters I finished my chops and paid mine. In ten minutes more I was inside the house in Rutherford Street, and was received by Mrs. Yatman in the passage. That charming woman's face exhibited an expression of melancholy and disappointment which it quite grieved me to see.

"I am afraid, ma'am," says I, "that you have not hit on any little criminating discovery in the lodger's room?"

She shook her head and sighed. It was a soft, languid, fluttering sigh—and, upon my life, it quite upset me. For the moment I forgot business, and burned with envy of Mr. Yatman.

"Don't despair, ma'am," I said, with an insinuating mildness which seemed to touch her. "I have heard a mysterious conversation—I know of a guilty appointment—and I expect great things from my peep-hole and my pipe-hole tonight. Pray don't be alarmed, but I think we are on the brink of a discovery."

Here my enthusiastic devotion to business got the better part of my tender feelings. I looked—winked—nodded—left her.

When I got back to my observatory, I found Mr. Jay digesting his mutton-chops in an armchair, with his pipe in his mouth. On his table were two tumblers, a jug of water, and the pint bottle of brandy. It was then close upon seven o'clock. As the hour struck the person described as "Jack" walked in.

He looked agitated—I am happy to say he looked violently agitated. The cheerful glow of anticipated success diffused itself (to use a strong expression) all over me, from head to foot. With breathless interest I looked through my peep-hole, and saw the visitor—the "Jack" of this delightful case—sit down, facing me, at the opposite side of the table to Mr. Jay. Making allowance for the difference in expression which their countenances just now happened to exhibit, these two abandoned villains were so much alike in other respects as to lead at once to the conclusion that they were brothers.

Jack was the cleaner man and the better dressed of the two. I admit that, at the outset. It is, perhaps, one of my failings to push justice and impartiality to their utmost limits. I am no Pharisee; and where Vice has its redeeming point, I say, let Vice have its due—yes, yes, by all manner of means, let Vice have its due.

"What's the matter now, Jack?" says Mr. Jay.

"Can't you see it in my face?" says Jack. "My dear fellow, delays are dangerous. Let us have done with suspense, and risk it, the day after tomorrow."

"So soon as that?" cries Mr. Jay, looking very much astonished. "Well, I'm ready, if you are. But, I say, Jack, is somebody else ready, too? Are you quite sure of that?"

He smiled as he spoke—a frightful smile—and laid a very strong emphasis on those two words, "Somebody else." There is evidently a third ruffian, a nameless desperado, concerned in the business.

"Meet us tomorrow," says Jack, "and judge for yourself. Be in the Regent's Park at eleven in the morning, and look out for us at the turning that leads to the Avenue Road."

"I'll be there," says Mr. Jay. "Have a drop of brandy-and-water? What are you getting up for? You're not going already?"

"Yes, I am," says Jack. "The fact is, I'm so excited and agitated that I can't sit still anywhere for five minutes together. Ridiculous as it may appear to you, I'm in a perpetual state of nervous flutter. I can't, for the life of me, help fearing that we shall be found out. I fancy that every man who looks twice at me in the street is a spy—"

At these words I thought my legs would have given way under me. Nothing but strength of mind kept me at my peep-hole—nothing else, I give you my word of honour.

"Stuff and nonsense!" cries Mr. Jay, with all the effrontery of a veteran in crime. "We have kept the secret up to this time, and we will manage cleverly to the end. Have a drop of brandy and water, and you will feel as certain about it as I do."

Jack steadily refused the brandy-and-water, and steadily persisted in taking his leave.

"I must try if I can't walk it off," he said. "Remember tomorrow morning—eleven o'clock, Avenue Road, side of the Regent's Park."

With those words he went out. His hardened relative laughed

desperately and resumed the dirty clay pipe.

I sat down on the side of my bed, actually quivering with excitement.

It is clear to me that no attempt has yet been made to change the stolen banknotes, and I may add that Sergeant Bulmer was of that opinion also when he left the case in my hands. What is the natural conclusion to draw from the conversation which I have just set down? Evidently that the confederates meet tomorrow to take their respective shares in the stolen money, and to decide on the safest means of getting the notes changed the day after.

Mr. Jay is, beyond a doubt, the leading criminal in this business, and he will probably run the chief risk—that of changing the fifty-pound note. I shall, therefore, still make it my business to follow him—attending at the Regent's Park tomorrow, and doing my best to hear what is said there. If another appointment is made for the day after, I shall, of course, go to it. In the meantime, I shall want the immediate assistance of two competent persons (supposing the rascals separate after their meeting) to follow the two minor criminals. It is only fair to add that, if the rogues all retire together, I shall probably keep my subordinates in reserve. Being naturally ambitious, I desire, if possible, to have the whole credit of discovering this robbery to myself.

8th July.

I have to acknowledge, with thanks, the speedy arrival of my two subordinates—men of very average abilities, I am afraid; but, fortunately, I shall always be on the spot to direct them.

My first business this morning was necessarily to prevent possible mistakes by accounting to Mr. and Mrs. Yatman for the presence of two strangers on the scene. Mr. Yatman (between ourselves, a poor, feeble man) only shook his head and groaned. Mrs. Yatman (that superior woman) favoured me with a charming look of intelligence.

"Oh, Mr. Sharpin!" she said, "I am so sorry to see those two men! Your sending for their assistance looks as if you were beginning to be doubtful of success."

I privately winked at her (she is very good in allowing me to do so without taking offense), and told her, in my facetious way, that she laboured under a slight mistake.

"It is because I am sure of success, ma'am, that I send for them. I am determined to recover the money, not for my own sake only, but for Mr. Yatman's sake—and for yours."

I laid a considerable amount of stress on those last three words. She said: "Oh, Mr. Sharpin!" again, and blushed of a heavenly red, and looked down at her work. I could go to the world's end with that woman if Mr. Yatman would only die.

I sent off the two subordinates to wait until I wanted them at the Avenue Road gate of the Regent's Park. Half-an-hour afterward I was following the same direction myself at the heels of Mr. Jay.

The two confederates were punctual to the appointed time. I blush to record it, but it is nevertheless necessary to state that the third rogue—the nameless desperado of my report, or, if you prefer it, the mysterious "somebody else" of the conversation between the two brothers—is—a woman! and, what is worse, a young woman! and, what is more lamentable still, a nice-looking woman! I have long resisted a growing conviction that, wherever there is mischief in this world, an individual of the fair sex is inevitably certain to be mixed up in it. After the experience of this morning, I can struggle against that sad conclusion no longer. I give up the sex—excepting Mrs. Yatman, I give up the sex.

The man named "Jack" offered the woman his arm. Mr. Jay placed himself on the other side of her. The three then walked away slowly among the trees. I followed them at a respectful distance. My two subordinates, at a respectful distance, also, followed me.

It was, I deeply regret to say, impossible to get near enough to them to overhear their conversation without running too great a risk of being discovered. I could only infer from their gestures and actions that they were all three talking with extraordinary earnestness on some subject which deeply interested them. After having been engaged in this way a full quarter of an hour, they suddenly turned round to retrace their steps.

My presence of mind did not forsake me in this emergency. I signed to the two subordinates to walk on carelessly and pass them, while I myself slipped dexterously behind a tree. As they came by me, I heard "Jack" address these words to Mr. Jay:

"Let us say half-past ten tomorrow morning. And mind you

come in a cab. We had better not risk taking one in this neighbourhood."

Mr. Jay made some brief reply which I could not overhear. They walked back to the place at which they had met, shaking hands there with an audacious cordiality which it quite sickened me to see. They then separated. I followed Mr. Jay. My subordinates paid the same delicate attention to the other two.

Instead of taking me back to Rutherford Street, Mr. Jay led me to the Strand. He stopped at a dingy, disreputable-looking house, which, according to the inscription over the door, was a newspaper office, but which, in my judgment, had all the external appearance of a place devoted to the reception of stolen goods.

After remaining inside for a few minutes, he came out whistling, with his finger and thumb in his waistcoat pocket. Some men would now have arrested him on the spot. I remembered the necessity of catching the two confederates, and the importance of not interfering with the appointment that had been made for the next morning. Such coolness as this, under trying circumstances, is rarely to be found, I should imagine, in a young beginner, whose reputation as a detective policeman is still to make.

From the house of suspicious appearance Mr. Jay betook himself to a cigar-divan, and read the magazines over a cheroot. From the divan he strolled to the tavern and had his chops. I strolled to the tavern and had my chops. When he had done he went back to his lodging. When I had done I went back to mine. He was overcome with drowsiness early in the evening, and went to bed. As soon as I heard him snoring, I was overcome with drowsiness and went to bed also.

Early in the morning my two subordinates came to make their report.

They had seen the man named "Jack" leave the woman at the gate of an apparently respectable villa residence not far from the Regent's Park. Left to himself, he took a turning to the right, which led to a sort of suburban street, principally inhabited by shopkeepers. He stopped at the private door of one of the houses, and let himself in with his own key—looking about him as he opened the door, and staring suspiciously at my men as they lounged along on the opposite side of the way. These were all the particulars which the subordinates had to communicate. I kept them in my room to attend on me, if needful, and mounted to my peep-hole to have a look at Mr. Jay.

He was occupied in dressing himself, and was taking extraordinary pains to destroy all traces of the natural slovenliness of his appearance. This was precisely what I expected. A vagabond like Mr. Jay knows the importance of giving himself a respectable look when he is going to run the risk of changing a stolen banknote. At five minutes past ten o'clock he had given the last brush to his shabby hat and the last scouring with bread-crumb to his dirty gloves. At ten minutes past ten he was in the street, on his way to the nearest cab-stand, and I and my subordinates were close on his heels.

He took a cab and we took a cab. I had not overheard them appoint a place of meeting when following them in the Park on the previous day, but I soon found that we were proceeding in the old direction of the Avenue Road gate. The cab in which Mr. Jay was riding turned into the Park slowly. We stopped outside, to avoid exciting suspicion. I got out to follow the cab on foot. Just as I did so, I saw it stop, and detected the two confederates approaching it from among the trees. They got in, and the cab was turned about directly. I ran back to my own cab and told the driver to let them pass him, and then to follow as before.

The man obeyed my directions, but so clumsily as to excite their suspicions. We had been driving after them about three minutes (returning along the road by which we had advanced) when I looked out of the window to see how far they might be ahead of us. As I did this, I saw two hats popped out of the windows of their cab, and two faces looking back at me. I sank into my place in a cold sweat; the expression is coarse, but no other form of words can describe my condition at that trying moment.

"We are found out!" I said, faintly, to my two subordinates. They stared at me in astonishment. My feelings changed instantly from the depth of despair to the height of indignation.

"It is the cabman's fault. Get out, one of you," I said, with dignity—"get out, and punch his head."

Instead of following my directions (I should wish this act of disobedience to be reported at headquarters) they both looked out of the window. Before I could pull them back they both sat down again. Before I could express my just indignation, they both grinned, and said to me: "Please to look out, sir!"

I did look out. Their cab had stopped.

Where?

At a church door!

What effect this discovery might have had upon the ordinary run of men I don't know. Being of a strong religious turn myself, it filled me with horror. I have often read of the unprincipled cunning of criminal persons, but I never before heard of three thieves attempting to double on their pursuers by entering a church! The sacrilegious audacity of that proceeding is, I should think, unparalleled in the annals of crime.

I checked my grinning subordinates by a frown. It was easy to see what was passing in their superficial minds. If I had not been able to look below the surface, I might, on observing two nicely dressed men and one nicely dressed woman enter a church before eleven in the morning on a week day, have come to the same hasty conclusion at which my inferiors had evidently arrived. As it was, appearances had no power to impose on me. I got out, and, followed by one of my men, entered the church. The other man I sent round to watch the vestry door. You may catch a weasel asleep, but not your humble servant, Matthew Sharpin!

We stole up the gallery stairs, diverged to the organ-loft, and peered through the curtains in front. There they were, all three, sitting in a pew below—yes, incredible as it may appear, sitting in a pew below!

Before I could determine what to do, a clergyman made his appearance in full canonicals from the vestry door, followed by a clerk. My brain whirled and my eyesight grew dim. Dark remembrances of robberies committed in vestries floated through my mind. I trembled for the excellent man in full canonicals—I even trembled for the clerk.

The clergyman placed himself inside the altar rails. The three desperadoes approached him. He opened his book and began to read. What? you will ask.

I answer, without the slightest hesitation, the first lines of the Marriage Service.

My subordinate had the audacity to look at me, and then to

stuff his pocket-handkerchief into his mouth. I scorned to pay any attention to him. After I had discovered that the man "Jack" was the bridegroom, and that the man Jay acted the part of father, and gave away the bride, I left the church, followed by my men, and joined the other subordinate outside the vestry door. Some people in my position would now have felt rather crestfallen, and would have begun to think that they had made a very foolish mistake. Not the faintest misgiving of any kind troubled me. I did not feel in the slightest degree depreciated in my own estimation. And even now, after a lapse of three hours, my mind remains, I am happy to say, in the same calm and hopeful condition.

As soon as I and my subordinates were assembled together out-side the church, I intimated my intention of still following the other cab in spite of what had occurred. My reason for deciding on this course will appear presently. The two subordinates appeared to be astonished at my resolution. One of them had the impertinence to say to me:

"If you please, sir, who is it that we are after? A man who has stolen money, or a man who has stolen a wife?"

The other low person encouraged him by laughing. Both have deserved an official reprimand, and both, I sincerely trust, will be sure to get it.

When the marriage ceremony was over, the three got into their cab and once more our vehicle (neatly hidden round the cor-ner of the church, so that they could not suspect it to be near them) started to follow theirs.

We traced them to the terminus of the South-western Railway. The newly-married couple took tickets for Richmond, pay-ing their fare with a half sovereign, and so depriving me of the pleasure of arresting them, which I should certainly have done if they had offered a bank-note. They parted from Mr. Jay, saying: "Remember the address—14 Babylon Terrace. You dine with us tomorrow week."

Mr. Jay accepted the invitation, and added, jocosely, that he was going home at once to get off his clean clothes, and to be com-fortable and dirty again for the rest of the day. I have to report that I saw him home safely, and that he is comfortable and dirty again (to use his own disgraceful language) at the present mo-ment.

Here the affair rests, having by this time reached what I may call its first stage.

I know very well what persons of hasty judgment will be inclined to say of my proceedings thus far. They will assert that I have been deceiving myself all through in the most absurd way; they will declare that the suspicious conversations which I have reported referred solely to the difficulties and dangers of successfully carrying out a runaway match; and they will appeal to the scene in the church as offering undeniable proof of the correctness of their assertions. So let it be. I dispute nothing up to this point. But I ask a question, out of the depths of my own sagacity as a man of the world, which the bitterest of my enemies will not, I think, find it particularly easy to answer.

Granted the fact of the marriage, what proof does it afford me of the innocence of the three persons concerned in that clandestine transaction? It gives me none. On the contrary, it strengthens my suspicions against Mr. Jay and his confederates, because it suggests a distinct motive for their stealing the money. A gentleman who is going to spend his honeymoon at Richmond wants money; and a gentleman who is in debt to all his trades-people wants money. Is this an unjustifiable imputation of bad motives? In the name of outraged Morality, I deny it. These men have combined together, and have stolen a woman. Why should they not combine together and steal a cash-box? I take my stand on the logic of rigid Virtue, and I defy all the sophistry of Vice to move me an inch out of my position.

Speaking of virtue, I may add that I have put this view of the case to Mr. and Mrs. Yatman. That accomplished and charming woman found it difficult at first to follow the close chain of my reasoning. I am free to confess that she shook her head, and shed tears, and joined her husband in premature lamentation over the loss of the two hundred pounds. But a little careful explanation on my part, and a little attentive listening on hers, ultimately changed her opinion.

She now agrees with me that there is nothing in this unexpected circumstance of the clandestine marriage which absolutely tends to divert suspicion from Mr. Jay, or Mr. "Jack," or the runaway lady. "Audacious hussy" was the term my fair friend used in speaking of her; but let that pass. It is more to the purpose to record that Mrs. Yatman has not lost confidence in me, and that

Mr. Yatman promises to follow her example, and do his best to look hopefully for future results.

I have now, in the new turn that circumstances have taken, to await advice from your office. I pause for fresh orders with all the composure of a man who has got two strings to his bow. When I traced the three confederates from the church door to the railway terminus, I had two motives for doing so. First, I followed them as a matter of official business, believing them still to have been guilty of the robbery.

Secondly, I followed them as a matter of private speculation, with a view of discovering the place of refuge to which the runaway couple intended to retreat, and of making my information a marketable commodity to offer to the young lady's family and friends. Thus, whatever happens, I may congratulate myself beforehand on not having wasted my time. If the office approves of my conduct, I have my plan ready for further proceedings.

If the office blames me, I shall take myself off, with my marketable information, to the genteel villa residence in the neighbourhood of the Regent's Park. Anyway, the affair puts money into my pocket, and does credit to my penetration as an uncommonly sharp man.

I have only one word more to add, and it is this: If any individual ventures to assert that Mr. Jay and his confederates are innocent of all share in the stealing of the cash-box, I, in return, defy that individual—though he may even be Chief Inspector Theakstone himself—to tell me who has committed the robbery at Rutherford Street, Soho.

Strong in that conviction, I have the honour to be your very obedient servant,   Matthew Sharpin.

From Chief Inspector Theakstone to Sergeant Bulmer.

Birmingham, July 9th.

Sergeant Bulmer—That empty-headed puppy, Mr. Matthew Sharpin, has made a mess of the case at Rutherford Street, exactly as I expected he would. Business keeps me in this town, so I write to you to set the matter straight. I inclose with this the pages of feeble scribble-scrabble which the creature Sharpin calls a report.

Look them over; and when you have made your way through

all the gabble, I think you will agree with me that the conceited booby has looked for the thief in every direction but the right one. You can lay your hand on the guilty person in five minutes, now. Settle the case at once; forward your report to me at this place, and tell Mr. Sharpin that he is suspended till further notice.

Yours,   Francis Theakstone.

From Sergeant Bulmer to Chief Inspector Theakstone.

London, July 10th.

Inspector Theakstone—Your letter and inclosure came safe to hand. Wise men, they say, may always learn something even from a fool. By the time I had got through Sharpin's maundering report of his own folly, I saw my way clear enough to the end of the Rutherford Street case, just as you thought I should. In half an hour's time I was at the house. The first person I saw there was Mr. Sharpin himself.

"Have you come to help me?" says he.

"Not exactly," says I. "I've come to tell you that you are suspended till further notice."

"Very good," says he, not taken down by so much as a single peg in his own estimation. "I thought you would be jealous of me. It's very natural and I don't blame you. Walk in, pray, and make yourself at home. I'm off to do a little detective business on my own account, in the neighbourhood of the Regent's Park. Ta-ta, sergeant, ta-ta!"

With those words he took himself out of the way, which was exactly what I wanted him to do.

As soon as the maid-servant had shut the door, I told her to inform her master that I wanted to say a word to him in private. She showed me into the parlour behind the shop, and there was Mr. Yatman all alone, reading the newspaper.

"About this matter of the robbery, sir," says I.

He cut me short, peevishly enough, being naturally a poor, weak, womanish sort of man.

"Yes, yes, I know," says he. "You have come to tell me that your wonderfully clever man, who has bored holes in my second floor partition, has made a mistake, and is off the scent of the scoundrel who has stolen my money."

"Yes, sir," says I. "That is one of the things I came to tell you.

But I have got something else to say besides that."

"Can you tell me who the thief is?" says he, more pettish than ever.

"Yes, sir," says I, "I think I can."

He put down the newspaper, and began to look rather anxious and frightened.

"Not my shopman?" says he. "I hope, for the man's own sake, it's not my shopman."

"Guess again, sir," says I.

"That idle slut, the maid?" says he.

"She is idle, sir," says I, "and she is also a slut; my first inquiries about her proved as much as that. But she's not the thief."

"Then, in the name of Heaven, who is?" says he.

"Will you please to prepare yourself for a very disagreeable surprise, sir?" says I. "And, in case you lose your temper, will you excuse my remarking that I am the stronger man of the two, and that if you allow yourself to lay hands on me, I may unintentionally hurt you, in pure self-defence."

He turned as pale as ashes, and pushed his chair two or three feet away from me.

"You have asked me to tell you, sir, who has taken your money," I went on. "If you insist on my giving you an answer—"

"I do insist," he said, faintly. "Who has taken it?"

"Your wife has taken it," I said, very quietly, and very positively at the same time.

He jumped out of the chair as if I had put a knife into him, and struck his fist on the table so heavily that the wood cracked again.

"Steady, sir," says I. "Flying into a passion won't help you to the truth."

"It's a lie!" says he, with another smack of his fist on the table— "a base, vile, infamous lie! How dare you——"

He stopped, and fell back into the chair again, looked about him in a bewildered way, and ended by bursting out crying.

"When your better sense comes back to you, sir," says I, "I am sure you will be gentleman enough to make an apology for the language you have just used. In the meantime, please to listen, if you can, to a word of explanation. Mr. Sharpin has sent in a report to our inspector of the most irregular and ridiculous kind, setting down not only all his own foolish doings and sayings, but the doings and sayings of Mrs. Yatman as well. In most cases, such a document would have been fit only for the waste paper basket; but in this particular case it so happens that Mr. Sharpin's budget of nonsense leads to a certain conclusion, which the simpleton of a writer has been quite innocent of suspecting from the beginning to the end.

"Of that conclusion I am so sure that I will forfeit my place if it does not turn out that Mrs. Yatman has been practicing upon the folly and conceit of this young man, and that she has tried to shield herself from discovery by purposely encouraging him to suspect the wrong persons. I tell you that confidently; and I will even go further. I will undertake to give a decided opinion as to why Mrs. Yatman took the money, and what she has done with it, or with a part of it. Nobody can look at that lady, sir, without being struck by the great taste and beauty of her dress—"

As I said those last words, the poor man seemed to find his powers of speech again. He cut me short directly as haughtily as if he had been a duke instead of a stationer.

"Try some other means of justifying your vile calumny against my wife," says he. "Her milliner's bill for the past year is on my file of receipted accounts at this moment."

"Excuse me, sir," says I, "but that proves nothing. Milliners, I must tell you, have a certain rascally custom which comes within the daily experience of our office.

"A married lady who wishes it can keep two accounts at her dressmaker's; one is the account which her husband sees and pays; the other is the private account, which contains all the extravagant items, and which the wife pays secretly, by instalments, whenever she can. According to our usual experience, these instalments are mostly squeezed out of the housekeeping money. In your case, I suspect, no instalments have been paid; proceedings have been threatened; Mrs. Yatman, knowing your altered circumstances, has felt herself driven into a corner, and she has paid her private account out of your cash-box."

"I won't believe it," says he. "Every word you speak is an abominable insult to me and to my wife."

"Are you man enough, sir," says I, taking him up short, in order to save time and words, "to get that receipted bill you spoke of just now off the file, and come with me at once to the milliner's shop where Mrs. Yatman deals?"

He turned red in the face at that, got the bill directly, and put on his hat. I took out of my pocket-book the list containing the numbers of the lost notes, and we left the house together immediately.

Arrived at the milliner's (one of the expensive West-end houses, as I expected), I asked for a private interview, on important business, with the mistress of the concern. It was not the first time that she and I had met over the same delicate investigation. The moment she set eyes on me she sent for her husband. I mentioned who Mr. Yatman was, and what we wanted.

"This is strictly private?" inquires the husband. I nodded my head.

"And confidential?" says the wife. I nodded again.

"Do you see any objection, dear, to obliging the sergeant with a sight of the books?" says the husband.

"None in the world, love, if you approve of it," says the wife.

All this while poor Mr. Yatman sat looking the picture of astonishment and distress, quite out of place at our polite conference. The books were brought, and one minute's look at the pages in which Mrs. Yatman's name figured was enough, and more than enough, to prove the truth of every word that I had spoken.

There, in one book, was the husband's account which Mr. Yatman had settled; and there, in the other, was the private account, crossed off also, the date of settlement being the very day after the loss of the cash-box. This said private account amounted to the sum of a hundred and seventy-five pounds, odd shillings, and it extended over a period of three years. Not a single instalment had been paid on it. Under the last line was an entry to this effect:

"Written to for the third time, June 23rd."

I pointed to it, and asked the milliner if that meant "last June." Yes, it did mean last June; and she now deeply regretted to say that it had been accompanied by a threat of legal proceedings.

"I thought you gave good customers more than three years' credit?" says I.

The milliner looks at Mr. Yatman, and whispers to me, "Not when a lady's husband gets into difficulties."

She pointed to the account as she spoke. The entries after the time when Mr. Yatman's circumstances became involved were just as extravagant, for a person in his wife's situation, as the entries for the year before that period. If the lady had economized in other things, she had certainly not economized in the matter of dress.

There was nothing left now but to examine the cash-book, for form's sake. The money had been paid in notes, the amounts and numbers of which exactly tallied with the figures set down in my list.

After that, I thought it best to get Mr. Yatman out of the house immediately. He was in such a pitiable condition that I called a cab and accompanied him home in it. At first he cried and raved like a child; but I soon quieted him; and I must add, to his credit, that he made me a most handsome apology for his language as the cab drew up at his house door. In return, I tried to give him some advice about how to set matters right for the future with his wife. He paid very little attention to me, and went upstairs muttering to himself about a separation.

Whether Mrs. Yatman will come cleverly out of the scrape or not seems doubtful. I should say myself that she would go into screeching hysterics, and so frighten the poor man into forgiving her. But this is no business of ours. So far as we are concerned, the case is now at an end, and the present report may come to a conclusion along with it.

I remain, accordingly, yours to command,

Thomas Bulmer.

P.S. "I have to add that, on leaving Rutherford Street, I met Mr. Matthew Sharpin coming to pack up his things.

"Only think!" says he, rubbing his hands in great spirits, "I've been to the genteel villa residence, and the moment I mentioned my business they kicked me out directly. There were two witnesses of the assault, and it's worth a hundred pounds to me if it's worth a farthing."

"I wish you joy of your luck," says I.

"Thank you," says he. "When may I pay you the same compliment on finding the thief?"

"Whenever you like," says I, "for the thief is found."

"Just what I expected," says he. "I've done all the work, and now you cut in and claim all the credit "Mr. Jay, of course."

"No," says I.

"Who is it then?" says he.

"Ask Mrs. Yatman," says I. "She's waiting to tell you."

"All right! I'd much rather hear it from that charming woman than from you," says he, and goes into the house in a mighty hurry.

What do you think of that, Inspector Theakstone? Would you like to stand in Mr. Sharpin's shoes? I shouldn't, I can promise you.

From Chief Inspector Theakstone to Mr. Matthew Sharpin.

July 12th.

Sir—Sergeant Bulmer has already told you to consider yourself suspended until further notice. I have now authority to add that your services as a member of the Detective police are positively declined. You will please to take this letter as notifying officially your dismissal from the force.

I may inform you, privately, that your rejection is not intended to cast any reflections on your character. It merely implies that you are not quite sharp enough for our purposes. If we are to have a new recruit among us, we should infinitely prefer Mrs. Yatman.

Your obedient servant,   Francis Theakstone.

Note on the Preceding Correspondence, Added by Mr. Theakstone.

The inspector is not in a position to append any explanations of importance to the last of the letters. It has been discovered that Mr. Matthew Sharpin left the house in Rutherford Street five minutes after his interview outside of it with Sergeant Bulmer, his manner expressing the liveliest emotions of terror and astonishment, and his left cheek displaying a bright patch of red, which looked as if it might have been the result of what is popularly termed a smart box on the ear.

He was also heard by the shopman at Rutherford Street to use a very shocking expression in reference to Mrs. Yatman, and was seen to clinch his fist vindictively as he ran round the corner of the street. Nothing more has been heard of him; and it is conjectured that he has left London with the intention of offering his valuable services to the provincial police.

On the interesting domestic subject of Mr. and Mrs. Yatman still less is known. It has, however, been positively ascertained that the medical attendant of the family was sent for in a great hurry on the day when Mr. Yatman returned from the milliner's shop. The neighbouring chemist received, soon afterward, a prescription of a soothing nature to make up for Mrs. Yatman.

The day after, Mr. Yatman purchased some smelling-salts at the shop, and afterward appeared at the circulating library to ask for a novel descriptive of high life that would amuse an invalid lady. It has been inferred from these circumstances that he has not thought it desirable to carry out his threat of separating from his wife, at least in the present (presumed) condition of that lady's sensitive nervous system.

A Witch's Den

By Mme. Helena Blavatsky

Our kind host Sham Rao was very gay during the remaining hours of our visit. He did his best to entertain us, and would not hear of our leaving the neighbourhood without having seen its greatest celebrity, its most interesting sight. A *jadu wâlâ*—sorceress—well known in the district, was just at this time under the influence of seven sister-goddesses, who took possession of her by turns, and spoke their oracles through her lips. Sham Rao said we must not fail to see her, be it only in the interests of science.

The evening closes in, and we once more get ready for an excursion. It is only five miles to the cavern of the Pythia of Hindostan; the road runs through a jungle, but it is level and smooth. Besides, the jungle and its ferocious inhabitants have ceased to frighten us. The timid elephants we had in the "dead city" are sent home, and we are to mount new behemoths belonging to a neighbouring *râjâ*. The pair that stand before the verandah like two dark hillocks are steady and trustworthy. Many a time these two have hunted the royal tiger, and no wild shrieking or thunderous roaring can frighten them. And so, let us start!

The ruddy flames of the torches dazzle our eyes and increase the forest gloom. Our surroundings seem so dark, so mysterious. There is something indescribably fascinating, almost solemn, in these night-journeys in the out-of-the-way corners of India. Everything is silent and deserted around you, everything is dozing on the earth and overhead. Only the heavy, regular tread of the elephants breaks the stillness of the night, like the sound of falling hammers in the underground smithy of Vulcan. From time to time uncanny voices and murmurs are heard in the black forest.

"The wind sings its strange song amongst the ruins," says one of us, "what a wonderful acoustic phenomenon!"

"*Bhûta, bhûta!*" whisper the awestruck torch-bearers. They brandish their torches and swiftly spin on one leg, and snap their fingers to chase away the aggressive spirits.

The plaintive murmur is lost in the distance. The forest is once more filled with the cadences of its invisible nocturnal life—the metallic whirr of the crickets, the feeble, monotonous croak of the tree-frog, the rustle of the leaves. From time to time all this suddenly stops short and then begins again, gradually increasing and increasing.

Heavens! What teeming life, what stores of vital energy are hidden under the smallest leaf, the most imperceptible blades of grass, in this tropical forest! Myriads of stars shine in the dark blue of the sky, and myriads of fireflies twinkle at us from every bush, moving sparks, like a pale reflection of the far-away stars.

We left the thick forest behind us, and reached a deep glen, on three sides bordered with the thick forest, where even by day the shadows are as dark as by night. We were about two thousand feet above the foot of the Vindhya ridge, judging by the ruined wall of Mandu, straight above our heads.

Suddenly a very chilly wind rose that nearly blew our torches out. Caught in the labyrinth of bushes and rocks, the wind angrily shook the branches of the blossoming syringas, then, shaking itself free, it turned back along the glen and flew down the valley, howling, whistling and shrieking, as if all the fiends of the forest together were joining in a funeral song.

"Here we are," said Sham Rao, dismounting. "Here is the village; the elephants cannot go any further."

"The village? Surely you are mistaken. I don't see anything but trees."

"It is too dark to see the village. Besides, the huts are so small, and so hidden by the bushes, that even by daytime you could hardly find them. And there is no light in the houses, for fear of the spirits."

"And where is your witch? Do you mean we are to watch her performance in complete darkness?"

Sham Rao cast a furtive, timid look round him; and his voice, when he answered our questions, was somewhat tremulous.

"I implore you not to call her a witch! She may hear you. . . . It is not far off, it is not more than half a mile. Do not allow this short distance to shake your decision. No elephant, and not even a horse, could make its way there. We must walk. . . . But we shall find plenty of light there. . . ."

This was unexpected, and far from agreeable. To walk in this gloomy Indian night; to scramble through thickets of cactuses; to venture in a dark forest, full of wild animals—this was too much for Miss X—. She declared that she would go no further. She would wait for us in the *howdah* on the elephant's back, and perhaps would go to sleep.

Narayan was against this *parti de plaisir* from the very beginning, and now, without explaining his reasons, he said she was the only sensible one among us.

"You won't lose anything," he remarked, "by staying where you are. And I only wish everyone would follow your example."

"What ground have you for saying so, I wonder?" remonstrated Sham Rao, and a slight note of disappointment rang in his voice, when he saw that the excursion, proposed and organized by himself, threatened to come to nothing. "What harm could be done by it? I won't insist any more that the 'incarnation of gods' is a rare sight, and that the Europeans hardly ever have an opportunity of witnessing it; but, besides, the Kangalim in question is no ordinary woman. She leads a holy life; she is a prophetess, and her blessing could not prove harmful to anyone. I insisted on this excursion out of pure patriotism."

"*Sahib*, if your patriotism consists in displaying before foreigners the worst of our plagues, then why did you not order all the lepers of your district to assemble and parade before the eyes of our guests? You are a *patèl*, you have the power to do it."

How bitterly Narayan's voice sounded to our unaccustomed ears. Usually he was so even-tempered, so indifferent to everything belonging to the exterior world.

Fearing a quarrel between the Hindus, the colonel remarked, in a conciliatory tone, that it was too late for us to reconsider our expedition. Besides, without being a believer in the "incarnation of gods," he was personally firmly convinced that demoniacs existed even in the West. He was eager to study every psychological phenomenon, wherever he met with it, and whatever shape it might assume.

It would have been a striking sight for our European and American friends if they had beheld our procession on that dark night. Our way lay along a narrow winding path up the mountain. Not more than two people could walk together—and we were thirty, including the torch-bearers. Surely some reminiscence of night sallies against the Confederate Southerners had revived in the colonel's breast, judging by the readiness with which he took upon himself the leadership of our small expedition. He ordered all the rifles and revolvers to be loaded, despatched three torch-bearers to march ahead of us, and arranged us in pairs. Under such a skilled chieftain we had nothing to fear from tigers; and so our procession started, and slowly crawled up the winding path.

It cannot be said that the inquisitive travellers, who appeared later on, in the den of the prophetess of Mandu, shone through the freshness and elegance of their costumes. My gown, as well as the travelling suits of the colonel and of Mr. Y— were nearly torn to pieces. The cactuses gathered from us whatever tribute they could, and the Babu's dishevelled hair swarmed with a whole colony of grasshoppers and fireflies, which probably, were attracted thither by the smell of cocoanut oil. The stout Sham Rao panted like a steam engine. Narayan alone was like his usual self—that is to say, like a bronze Hercules, armed with a club. At the last abrupt turn of the path, after having surmounted the difficulty of climbing over huge, scattered stones, we suddenly found ourselves on a perfectly smooth place; our eyes, in spite of our many torches, were dazzled with light, and our ears were struck by a medley of unusual sounds.

A new glen opened before us, the entrance of which, from the valley, was well masked by thick trees. We understood how easily we might have wandered round it, without ever suspecting its existence. At the bottom of the glen we discovered the abode of the celebrated Kangalim.

The den, as it turned out, was situated in the ruin of an old Hindu temple in tolerably good preservation. In all probability it was built long before the "Dead City," because during the epoch of the latter, the heathen were not allowed to have their own places of worship; and the temple stood quite close to the wall of the town, in fact, right under it. The cupolas of the two smaller lateral pagodas had fallen long ago, and huge bushes grew out of their altars. This evening their branches were hidden under a mass of bright-coloured rags, bits of ribbon, little pots, and various other talismans, because, even in them, popular superstition sees something sacred.

"And are not these poor people right? Did not these bushes grow on sacred ground? Is not their sap impregnated with the incense of offerings, and the exhalations of holy anchorites, who once lived and breathed here?"

The learned but superstitious Sham Rao would only answer our questions by new questions.

But the central temple, built of red granite, stood unharmed by time, and, as we learned afterwards, a deep tunnel opened just behind its closely-shut door. What was beyond it no one knew. Sham Rao assured us that no man of the last three generations had ever stepped over the threshold of this thick iron door; no one had seen the subterranean passage for many years. Kangalim lived there in perfect isolation, and, according to the oldest people in the neighbourhood, she had always lived there. Some people said she was three hundred years old; others alleged that a certain old man on his death-bed had revealed to his son that this old woman was no one else than *his own uncle*. This fabulous uncle had settled in the cave in the times when the "Dead City" still counted several hundreds of inhabitants. The hermit, busy paving his road to Moksha, had no intercourse with the rest of the world, and nobody knew how he lived and what he ate. But a good while ago, in the days when the *bellati* (foreigners) had not yet taken possession of this mountain, the old hermit suddenly was transformed into a hermitess. She continues his pursuits and speaks with his voice, and often in his name; but she receives worshippers, which was not the practice of her predecessor.

We had come too early, and the Pythia did not at first appear. But the square before the temple was full of people, and a wild though picturesque scene it was. An enormous bonfire blazed in the centre, and round it crowded the naked savages like so many black gnomes, adding whole branches of trees sacred to the seven sister-goddesses. Slowly and evenly they all jumped from one leg to another to a tune of a single monotonous musical phrase, which they repeated in chorus, accompanied by several local drums and tambourines. The hushed trill of the latter mingled with the forest echoes and the hysterical moans of two little girls, who lay under a heap of leaves by the fire. The poor children were brought here by their mothers, in the hope that the goddesses would take pity upon them and banish the two evil spirits under whose obsession they were. Both mothers were quite young, and sat on their heels blankly and sadly staring at the flames. No one paid us the slightest attention when we appeared, and afterwards during all our stay these people acted as if we were invisible. Had we worn a cap of darkness they could not have behaved more strangely.

"They feel the approach of the gods! The atmosphere is full of their sacred emanations!" mysteriously explained Sham Rao, contemplating with reverence the natives, whom his beloved Haeckel might have easily mistaken for his "missing link," the brood of his *Bathybius*

Haeckelii.

"They are simply under the influence of toddy and opium!" retorted the irreverent *babu*.

The lookers-on moved as in a dream, as if they all were only half-awakened somnambulists, but the actors were simply victims of St. Vitus's dance. One of them, a tall old man, a mere skeleton with a long white beard, left the ring and begun whirling vertiginously, with his arms spread like wings, and loudly grinding his long, wolf-like teeth. He was painful and disgusting to look at. He soon fell down, and was carelessly, almost mechanically pushed aside by the feet of the others still engaged in their demoniac performance.

All this was frightful enough, but many more horrors were in store for us.

Waiting for the appearance of the *prima donna* of this forest opera company, we sat down on the trunk of a fallen tree, ready to ask innumerable questions of our condescending host. But I was hardly seated when a feeling of indescribable astonishment and horror made me shrink back.

I beheld the skull of a monstrous animal, the like of which I could not find in my zoological reminiscences.

This head was much larger than the head of an elephant skeleton. And still it could not be anything but an elephant, judging by the skilfully restored trunk, which wound down to my feet like a gigantic black leech. But an elephant has no horns, whereas this one had four of them! The front pair stuck from the flat forehead slightly bending forward and then spreading out; and the others had a wide base, like the root of a deer's horn, that gradually decreased almost up to the middle, and bore long branches enough to decorate a dozen ordinary elks. Pieces of the transparent amber-yellow rhinoceros skin were strained over the empty eye-holes of the skull, and small lamps burning behind them only added to the horror, the devilish appearance of this head.

"What can this be?" was our unanimous question. None of us had ever met anything like it, and even the colonel looked aghast.

"It is a Sivatherium," said Narayan. "Is it possible you never came across these fossils in European museums? Their remains are common enough in the Himalayas, though, of course, in fragments. They were called after Shiva."

"If the collector of this district ever hears that this antediluvian relic adorns the den of your—ahem!—witch," remarked the *babu*, "it won't adorn it many days longer."

All around the skull and on the floor of the portico there were heaps of white flowers, which, though not quite antediluvian, were totally unknown to us. They were as large as a big rose, and their white petals were covered with a red powder, the inevitable concomitant of every Indian religious ceremony. Further on there were groups of co-coanuts, and large brass dishes filled with rice, each adorned with a red or green taper. In the centre of the portico there stood a queer-shaped censer, surrounded with chandeliers. A little boy, dressed from head to foot in white, threw into it handfuls of aromatic powders.

"These people, who assemble here to worship Kangalim," said Sham Rao, "do not actually belong either to her sect or to any other. They are devil-worshippers. They do not believe in Hindu gods; they live in small communities; they belong to one of the many Indian races which usually are called the hill-tribes. Unlike the Shanars of Southern Travancore, they do not use the blood of sacrificial animals; they do not build separate temples to their *bhutas*. But they are pos-sessed by the strange fancy that the goddess Kâli, the wife of Shiva, from time immemorial has had a grudge against them, and sends her favourite evil spirits to torture them. Save this little difference, they have the same beliefs as the Shanars. God does not exist for them; and even Shiva is considered by them as an ordinary spirit. Their chief worship is offered to the souls of the dead.

"These souls, however righteous and kind they may be in their lifetime, become after death as wicked as can be; they are happy only when they are torturing living men and cattle. As the opportunities of doing so are the only reward for the virtues they possessed when in-carnated, a very wicked man is punished by becoming after his death a very soft-hearted ghost; he loathes his loss of daring, and is altogether miserable. The results of this strange logic are not bad, nevertheless. These savages and devil-worshippers are the kindest and the most truth-loving of all the hill-tribes. They do whatever they can to be worthy of their ultimate reward; because, don't you see, they all long to become the wickedest of devils!"

And put in good humour by his own wittiness, Sham Rao laughed till his hilarity became offensive, considering the sacredness of the place.

"A year ago some business matters sent me to Tinevelli," contin-ued he. "Staying with a friend of mine, who is a Shanar, I was allowed to be present at one of the ceremonies in the honour of devils. No

European has as yet witnessed this worship, whatever the missionaries may say; but there are many converts amongst the Shanars, who willingly describe them to the *padres*. My friend is a wealthy man, which is probably the reason why the devils are especially vicious to him. They poison his cattle, spoil his crops and his coffee plants, and persecute his numerous relations, sending them sunstrokes, madness and epilepsy, over which illnesses they especially preside. These wicked demons have settled in every corner of his spacious landed property—in the woods, the ruins, and even in his stables.

"To avert all this, my friend covered his land with *stucco* pyramids, and prayed humbly, asking the demons to draw their portraits on each of them, so that he may recognize them and worship each of them separately, as the rightful owner of this, or that, particular pyramid. And what do you think?... Next morning all the pyramids were found covered with drawings. Each of them bore an incredibly good likeness of the dead of the neighbourhood. My friend had known personally almost all of them. He found also a portrait of his own late father amongst the lot."

"Well? And was he satisfied?"

"Oh, he was very glad, very satisfied. It enabled him to choose the right thing to gratify the personal tastes of each demon, don't you see? He was not vexed at finding his father's portrait. His father was somewhat irascible; once he nearly broke both his son's legs, administering to him fatherly punishment with an iron bar, so that he could not possibly be very dangerous after his death. But another portrait, found on the best and the prettiest of the pyramids, amazed my friend a good deal, and put him in a blue funk. The whole district recognized an English officer, a certain Captain Pole, who in his lifetime was as kind a gentleman as ever lived."

"Indeed? But do you mean to say that this strange people worshipped Captain Pole also?"

"Of course they did! Captain Pole was such a worthy man, such an honest officer, that, after his death, he could not help being promoted to the highest rank of Shanar devils. The Pe-Kovil, demon's-house, sacred to his memory, stands side by side with the Pe-Kovil Bhadrakâlî, which was recently conferred on the wife of a certain German missionary, who also was a most charitable lady and so is very dangerous now."

"But what are their ceremonies? Tell us something about their rites."

"Their rites consist chiefly of dancing, singing, and killing sacrificial animals. The Shanars have no castes, and eat all kinds of meat. The crowd assembles about the Pe-Kovil, previously designated by the priest; there is a general beating of drums, and slaughtering of fowls, sheep and goats. When Captain Pole's turn came an ox was killed, as a thoughtful attention to the peculiar tastes of his nation. The priest appeared, covered with bangles, and holding a wand on which tinkled numberless little bells, and wearing garlands of red and white flowers round his neck, and a black mantle, on which were embroidered the ugliest fiends you can imagine. Horns were blown and drums rolled incessantly. And oh, I forgot to tell you there was also a kind of fiddle, the secret of which is known only to the Shanar priesthood. Its bow is ordinary enough, made of bamboo; but it is whispered that the strings are human veins. . . . When Captain Pole took possession of the priest's body, the priest leaped high in the air, and then rushed on the ox and killed him. He drank off the hot blood, and then began his dance. But what a fright he was when dancing! You know, I am not superstitious. . . . Am I?. . ."

Sham Rao looked at us inquiringly, and I, for one, was glad at this moment that Miss X— was half a mile off, asleep in the *howdah*.

"He turned, and turned, as if possessed by all the demons of Nâraka. The enraged crowd hooted and howled when the priest begun to inflict deep wounds all over his body with the bloody sacrificial knife. To see him, with his hair waving in the wind and his mouth covered with foam; to see him bathing in the blood of the sacrificed animal, mixing it with his own, was more than I could bear. I felt as if hallucinated, I fancied I also was spinning round. . . ."

Sham Rao stopped abruptly, struck dumb. Kangalim stood before us!

Her appearance was so unexpected that we all felt embarrassed. Carried away by Sham Rao's description, we had noticed neither how nor whence she came. Had she appeared from beneath the earth we could not have been more astonished. Narayan stared at her, opening wide his big jet-black eyes; the Babu clicked his tongue in utter confusion.

Imagine a skeleton seven feet high, covered with brown leather, with a dead child's tiny head stuck on its bony shoulders; the eyes set so deep and at the same time flashing such fiendish flames all through your body that you begin to feel your brain stop working, your thoughts become entangled and your blood freeze in your veins.

131

I describe my personal impressions, and no words of mine can do them justice. My description is too weak. Mr. Y— and the colonel both grew pale under her stare and Mr. Y— made a movement as if about to rise.

Needless to say that such an impression could not last. As soon as the witch had turned her gleaming eyes to the kneeling crowd, it vanished as swiftly as it had come. But still all our attention was fixed on this remarkable creature.

Three hundred years old! Who can tell? Judging by her appearance, we might as well conjecture her to be a thousand. We beheld a genuine living mummy, or rather a mummy endowed with motion. She seemed to have been withering since the creation. Neither time, nor the ills of life, nor the elements could ever affect this living statue of death. The all-destroying hand of time had touched her and stopped short. Time could do no more, and so had left her. And with all this, not a single gray hair. Her long black locks shone with a greenish sheen, and fell in heavy masses down to her knees.

To my great shame, I must confess that a disgusting reminiscence flashed into my memory. I thought about the hair and the nails of corpses growing in the graves, and tried to examine the nails of the old woman.

Meanwhile, she stood motionless as if suddenly transformed into an ugly idol. In one hand she held a dish with a piece of burning camphor, in the other a handful of rice, and she never removed her burning eyes from the crowd. The pale yellow flame of the camphor flickered in the wind, and lit up her death-like head, almost touching her chin; but she paid no heed to it. Her neck, as wrinkled as a mushroom, as thin as a stick, was surrounded by three rows of golden medallions. Her head was adorned with a golden snake. Her grotesque, hardly human body was covered by a piece of saffron-yellow muslin.

The demoniac little girls raised their heads from beneath the leaves, and set up a prolonged animal-like howl. Their example was followed by the old man, who lay exhausted by his frantic dance.

The witch tossed her head convulsively, and began her invocations, rising on tiptoe, as if moved by some external force.

"The goddess, one of the seven sisters, begins to take possession of her," whispered Sham Rao, not even thinking of wiping away the big drops of sweat that streamed from his brow. "Look, look at her!"

This advice was quite superfluous. We *were* looking at her, and at nothing else.

At first, the movements of the witch were slow, unequal, somewhat convulsive; then, gradually, they became less angular; at last, as if catching the cadence of the drums, leaning all her long body forward, and writhing like an eel, she rushed round and round the blazing bonfire. A dry leaf caught in a hurricane could not fly swifter. Her bare bony feet trod noiselessly on the rocky ground. The long locks of her hair flew round her like snakes, lashing the spectators, who knelt, stretching their trembling arms towards her, and writhing as if they were alive. Whoever was touched by one of this Fury's black curls, fell down on the ground, overcome with happiness, shouting thanks to the goddess, and considering himself blessed forever. It was not human hair that touched the happy elect, it was the goddess herself, one of the seven.

Swifter and swifter fly her decrepit legs; the young, vigorous hands of the drummer can hardly follow her. But she does not think of catching the measure of his music; she rushes, she flies forward. Staring with her expressionless, motionless orbs at something before her, at something that is not visible to our mortal eyes, she hardly glances at her worshippers; then her look becomes full of fire, and whoever she looks at feels burned through to the marrow of his bones. At every glance she throws a few grains of rice. The small handful seems inexhaustible, as if the wrinkled palm contained the bottomless bag of Prince Fortunatus.

Suddenly she stops as if thunderstruck.

The mad race round the bonfire had lasted twelve minutes, but we looked in vain for a trace of fatigue on the death-like face of the witch. She stopped only for a moment, just the necessary time for the goddess to release her. As soon as she felt free, by a single effort she jumped over the fire and plunged into the deep tank by the *portico*. This time she plunged only once, and whilst she stayed under the water the second sister-goddess entered her body. The little boy in white produced another dish, with a new piece of burning camphor, just in time for the witch to take it up, and to rush again on her headlong way.

The colonel sat with his watch in his hand. During the second obsession the witch ran, leaped, and raced for exactly fourteen minutes. After this, she plunged twice in the tank, in honor of the second sister; and with every new obsession the number of her plunges increased, till it became six.

It was already an hour and a half since the race began. All this time the witch never rested, stopping only for a few seconds, to disappear under the water.

"She is a fiend, she cannot be a woman!" exclaimed the colonel, seeing the head of the witch immersed for the sixth time in the water.

"Hang me if I know!" grumbled Mr. Y—, nervously pulling his beard. "The only thing I know is that a grain of her cursed rice entered my throat, and I can't get it out!"

"Hush, hush! Please, do be quiet!" implored Sham Rao. "By talking you will spoil the whole business!"

I glanced at Narayan and lost myself in conjectures.

His features, which usually were so calm and serene, were quite altered at this moment by a deep shadow of suffering. His lips trembled, and the pupils of his eyes were dilated, as if by a dose of *belladonna*. His eyes were lifted over the heads of the crowd, as if in his disgust he tried not to see what was before him, and at the same time could not see it, engaged in a deep reverie which carried him away from us and from the whole performance.

"What is the matter with him?" was my thought, but I had no time to ask him, because the witch was again in full swing, chasing her own shadow.

But with the seventh goddess the program was slightly changed. The running of the old woman changed to leaping. Sometimes bending down to the ground, like a black panther, she leaped up to some worshipper, and halting before him touched his forehead with her finger, while her long, thin body shook with inaudible laughter. Then, again, as if shrinking back playfully from her shadow, and chased by it, in some uncanny game, the witch appeared to us like a horrid caricature of Dinorah, dancing her mad dance. Suddenly she straightened herself to her full height, darted to the *portico* and crouched before the smoking censer, beating her forehead against the granite steps. Another jump, and she was quite close to us, before the head of the monstrous Sivatherium. She knelt down again and bowed her head to the ground several times, with the sound of an empty barrel knocked against something hard.

We had hardly the time to spring to our feet and shrink back when she appeared on the top of the Sivatherium's head, standing there amongst the horns.

Narayan alone did not stir, and fearlessly looked straight in the eyes of the frightful sorceress.

But what was this? Who spoke in those deep manly tones? Her lips

134

were moving, from her breast were issuing those quick, abrupt phrases, but the voice sounded hollow as if coming from beneath the ground.

"Hush, hush!" whispered Sham Rao, his whole body trembling. "She is going to prophesy! . . ."

"She?" incredulously inquired Mr. Y—. "This a woman's voice? I don't believe it for a moment. Someone's uncle must be stowed away somewhere about the place. Not the fabulous uncle she inherited from, but a real live one!. . ."

Sham Rao winced under the irony of this supposition, and cast an imploring look at the speaker.

"Woe to you! woe to you!" echoed the voice. "Woe to you, children of the impure Jaya and Vijaya! of the mocking, unbelieving lingerers round great Shiva's door! Ye, who are cursed by eighty thousand sages Woe to you who believe not in the goddess Kâli, and you who deny us, her seven divine sisters! Flesh-eating, yellow-legged vultures! friends of the oppressors of our land! dogs who are not ashamed to eat from the same trough with the *Bellati!*" (foreigners).

"It seems to me that your prophetess only foretells the past," said Mr. Y—, philosophically putting his hands in his pockets. "I should say that she is hinting at you, my dear Sham Rao."

"Yes! and at us also," murmured the colonel, who was evidently beginning to feel uneasy.

As to the unlucky Sham Rao, he broke out in a cold sweat, and tried to assure us that we were mistaken, that we did not fully understand her language.

"It is not about you, it is not about you! It is of me she speaks, because I am in government service. Oh, she is inexorable!"

"*Râkshasas! Asuras!*" thundered the voice. "How dare you appear before us? how dare you to stand on this holy ground in boots made of a cow's sacred skin? Be cursed for etern——"

But her curse was not destined to be finished. In an instant the Hercules-like Narayan had fallen on the Sivatherium, and upset the whole pile, the skull, the horns and the demoniac Pythia included. A second more, and we thought we saw the witch flying in the air towards the *portico.* A confused vision of a stout, shaven Brahman, suddenly emerging from under the Sivatherium and instantly disappearing in the hollow beneath it, flashed before my dilated eyes.

But, alas! after the third second had passed, we all came to the embarrassing conclusion that, judging from the loud clang of the door of the cave, the representative of the Seven Sisters had ignominiously fled. The moment she had disappeared from our inquisitive eyes to her subterranean domain, we all realized that the unearthly hollow voice we had heard had nothing supernatural about it and belonged to the Brahman hidden under the Sivatherium—to someone's live uncle, as Mr. Y— had rightly supposed.

★★★★★★

Oh, Narayan! how carelessly, how disorderly the worlds rotate around us. I begin to seriously doubt their reality. From this moment I shall earnestly believe that all things in the universe are nothing but illusion, a mere *Mâyâ*. I am becoming a Vedantin. . . . I doubt that in the whole universe there may be found anything more objective than a Hindu witch flying up the spout.

★★★★★★

Miss X— woke up, and asked what was the meaning of all this noise. The noise of many voices and the sounds of the many retreating footsteps, the general rush of the crowd, had frightened her. She listened to us with a condescending smile, and a few yawns, and went to sleep again.

Next morning, at daybreak, we very reluctantly, it must be owned, bade goodbye to the kind-hearted, good-natured Sham Rao. The confoundingly easy victory of Narayan hung heavily on his mind. His faith in the holy hermitess and the seven goddesses was a good deal shaken by the shameful capitulation of the sisters, who had surrendered at the first blow from a mere mortal. But during the dark hours of the night he had had time to think it over, and to shake off the uneasy feeling of having unwillingly misled and disappointed his European friends.

Sham Rao still looked confused when he shook hands with us at parting, and expressed to us the best wishes of his family and himself.

As to the heroes of this truthful narrative, they mounted their elephants once more, and directed their heavy steps towards the high road and Jubbulpore.

Ligeia

By Edgar Allan Poe

And the will therein lieth, which dieth not. Who knoweth the mysteries of the will, with its vigour? For God is but a great will prevading all things by nature of its intentness. Man doth not yield himself to the angels, nor unto death utterly, save only through the weakness of his feeble will.—Joseph Glanvill.

I cannot, for my soul, remember how, when, or even precisely where, I first became acquainted with the lady Ligeia. Long years have since elapsed, and my memory is feeble through much suffering. Or, perhaps, I cannot *now* bring these points to mind, because, in truth, the character of my beloved, her rare learning, her singular yet placid caste of beauty, and the thrilling and enthralling eloquence of her low musical language, made their way into my heart by paces so steadily and stealthily progressive, that they have been unnoticed and unknown. Yet I believe that I met her first and most frequently in some large, old, decaying city near the Rhine. Of her family I have surely heard her speak. That it is of a remotely ancient date cannot be doubted. Ligeia! Ligeia! Buried in studies of a nature more than all else adapted to deaden impressions of the outward world, it is by that sweet word alone—by Ligeia—that I bring before mine eyes in fancy the image of her who is no more.

And now, while I write, a recollection flashes upon me that I have *never known* the paternal name of her who was my friend and my betrothed, and who became the partner of my studies, and finally the wife of my bosom. Was it a playful charge on the part of my Ligeia? Or was it a test of my strength of affection, that I should institute no inquiries upon this point? Or was it rather a caprice of my own—a wildly romantic offering on the shrine of the most passionate devotion? I but indistinctly recall the fact itself—what wonder that I have utterly forgotten the circumstances which originated or attended it? And, indeed, if ever that spirit which is entitled Romance—if ever she, the wan and the misty-winged Ashtophet of idolatrous Egypt—presided, as they tell, over marriages ill-omened, then most surely she presided over mine.

There is one dear topic, however, on which my memory fails me not. It is the *person* of Ligeia. In stature she was tall, somewhat slender, and, in her latter days, even emaciated. I would in vain attempt to portray the majesty, the quiet ease of her demeanour, or the incomprehensible lightness and elasticity of her footfall. She came and departed as a shadow. I was never made aware of her entrance into my closed study, save by the dear music of her low sweet voice, as she placed her marble hand upon my shoulder. In beauty of face no maiden ever equalled her. It was the radiance of an opium-dream—an airy and spirit-lifting vision more wildly divine than the fantasies which hovered about the slumbering souls of the daughters of Delos. Yet her features were not of that regular mould which we have been falsely taught to worship in the classical labours of the heathen. "There is no exquisite beauty," says Bacon, Lord Verulam, speaking truly of all the forms and *genera* of beauty, "without some strangeness in the proportion."

Yet, although I saw that the features of Ligeia were not of a classic regularity—although I perceived that her loveliness was indeed exquisite and felt that there was much of strangeness pervading it—yet I have tried in vain to detect the irregularity and to trace home my own perception of "the strange." I examined the contour of the lofty and pale forehead; it was faultless—how cold indeed that word when applied to a majesty so divine—the skin rivalling the purest ivory; the commanding extent and repose, the gentle prominence of the regions above the temples; and then the raven-black, the glossy, the luxuriant and naturally-curling tresses, setting forth the full force of the Homeric epithet, "hyacinthine"! I looked at the delicate outlines of the nose, and nowhere but in the graceful medallions of the Hebrews had I beheld a similar perfection. There were the same luxurious smoothness of surface, the same scarcely perceptible tendency to the aquiline, the same harmoniously curved nostrils speaking the free spirit.

I regarded the sweet mouth. Here was indeed the triumph of all things heavenly—the magnificent turn of the short upper lip, the soft, voluptuous slumber of the under, the dimples which sported, and the colour which spoke, the teeth glancing back, with a brilliancy almost startling, every ray of the holy light which fell upon them in her serene and placid, yet most exultingly radiant of all smiles. I scrutinized the formation of the chin, and here, too, I found the gentleness of breadth, the softness and the majesty, the fullness and the spirituality of the Greek—the contour which the god Apollo revealed but in a dream, to Cleomenes, the son of the Athenian. And then I peered into the large eyes of Ligeia.

For eyes we have no models in the remotely antique. It might have been, too, that in these eyes of my beloved lay the secret to which Lord Verulam alludes. They were, I must believe, far larger than the ordinary eyes of our own race. They were even fuller than the fullest of the gazelle eyes of the tribe of the valley of Nourjahad. Yet it was only at intervals—in moments of intense excitement—that this peculiarity became more than slightly noticeable in Ligeia. And at such moments was her beauty—in my heated fancy thus it appeared perhaps—the beauty of beings either above or apart from the earth—the beauty of the fabulous *houri* of the Turk. The hue of the orbs was the most brilliant of black, and far over them hung jetty lashes of great length. The brows, slightly irregular in outline, had the same tint.

The "strangeness," however, which I found in the eyes, was of a nature distinct from the formation, or the colour, or the brilliancy of the features, and must, after all, be referred to the expression. Ah, word of no meaning, behind whose vast latitude of mere sound we intrench our ignorance of so much of the spiritual! The expression of the eyes of Ligeia! How for long hours have I pondered upon it! How have I, through the whole of a midsummer night, struggled to fathom it! What was it—that something more profound than the well of Democritus—which lay far within the pupils of my beloved? What *was* it? I was possessed with a passion to discover. Those eyes, those large, those shining, those divine orbs—they became to me twin stars of Leda, and I to them devoutest of astrologers.

There is no point, among the many incomprehensible anomalies of the science of mind, more thrillingly exciting than the fact—never, I believe, noticed in the schools—that in our endeavours to recall to memory something long forgotten, we often find ourselves upon the very verge of remembrance, without being able, in the end, to remember. And thus how frequently, in my intense scrutiny of Ligeia's eyes, have I felt approaching the full knowledge of their expression—felt it approaching, yet not quite be mine—and so at length entirely depart! And (strange, oh strangest mystery of all!) I found in the commonest objects of the universe, a circle of analogies to that expression. I mean to say that, subsequently to the period when Ligeia's beauty passed into my spirit, there dwelling as in a shrine, I derived from many existences in the material world a sentiment such as I felt always around, within me, by her large and luminous orbs.

Yet not the more could I define that sentiment, or analyze, or even steadily view it. I recognized it, let me repeat, sometimes in the survey of a rapidly-growing vine, in the contemplation of a moth, a butterfly, a chrysalis, a stream of running water. I have felt it in the ocean, in the falling of a meteor. I have felt it in the glances of unusually aged people. And there are one or two stars in heaven, (one especially, a star of the sixth magnitude, double and changeable, to be found near the large star in Lyra) in a telescopic scrutiny of which I have been made aware of the feeling. I have been filled with it by certain sounds from stringed instruments, and not unfrequently by passages from books. Among innumerable other instances, I well remember something in a volume of Joseph Glanvill, which (perhaps merely from its quaintness—who shall say?) never failed to inspire me with the sentiment:

And the will therein lieth, which dieth not. Who knoweth the mysteries of the will, with its vigour? For God is but a great will pervading all things by nature of its intentness. Man doth not yield him to the angels, nor unto death utterly, save only through the weakness of his feeble will.

Length of years and subsequent reflection have enabled me to trace, indeed, some remote connection between this passage in the English moralist and a portion of the character of Ligeia. An intensity in thought, action, or speech was possibly, in her, a result or at least an index of that gigantic volition which, during our long intercourse, failed to give other and more immediate evidence of its existence. Of all the women whom I have ever known, she—the outwardly calm, the ever-placid Ligeia—was the most violently a prey to the tumultuous vultures of stern passion. And of such passion I could form no estimate, save by the miraculous expansion of those eyes which at once so delighted and appalled me, by the almost magical melody, modulation, distinctness, and placidity of her very low voice, and by the fierce energy (rendered doubly effective by contrast with her manner of utterance) of the wild words which she habitually uttered.

I have spoken of the learning of Ligeia; it was immense, such as I have never known in woman. In the classical tongues was she deeply proficient, and as far as my own acquaintance extended in regard to the modern dialects of Europe, I have never known her at fault. Indeed upon any theme of the most admired, because simply the most abstruse of the boasted erudition of the academy, have I ever found Ligeia at fault? How singularly, how thrillingly, this one point in the nature of my wife has forced itself, at this late period only, upon my attention! I said her knowledge was such as I have never known in woman—but where breathes the man who has traversed, and successfully, all the wide areas of moral, physical, and mathematical science?

I saw not then what I now clearly perceive, that the acquisitions of Ligeia were gigantic, were astounding; yet I was sufficiently aware of her infinite supremacy to resign myself, with a child-like confidence, to her guidance through the chaotic world of metaphysical investigation at which I was most busily occupied during the earlier years of our marriage. With how vast a triumph, with how vivid a delight, with how much of all that is ethereal in hope, did I feel, as she bent over me in studies but little sought—but less known—that delicious vista by slow degrees expanding before me, down whose long, gorgeous, and all untrodden path I might at length pass onward to the goal of a wisdom too divinely precious not to be forbidden!

How poignant, then, must have been the grief with which, after some years, I beheld my well-grounded expectations take wings to themselves and fly away! Without Ligeia I was but as a child groping benighted. Her presence, her readings alone, rendered vividly luminous the many mysteries of the transcendentalism in which we were immersed. Wanting the radiant lustre of her eyes, letters, lambent and golden, grew duller than Saturnian lead. And now those eyes shone less and less frequently upon the pages over which I pored. Ligeia grew ill. The wild eyes blazed with a too, too glorious effulgence; the pale fingers became of the transparent waxen hue of the grave; and the blue veins upon the lofty forehead swelled and sank impetuously with the tides of the most gentle emotion. I saw that she must die—and I struggled desperately in spirit with the grim Azrael. And the struggles of the passionate wife were, to my astonishment, even more energetic than my own. There had been much in her stern nature to impress me with the belief that, to her, death would have come without its terrors; but not so.

Words are impotent to convey any just idea of the fierceness of resistance with which she wrestled with the Shadow. I groaned in anguish at the pitiable spectacle. I would have soothed, I would have reasoned, but, in the intensity of her wild desire for life—for life—*but* for life—solace and reason were alike the uttermost of folly. Yet not until the last instance, amid the most convulsive writhings of her fierce spirit, was shaken the external placidity of her demeanour. Her voice grew more gentle—grew more low—yet I would not wish to dwell upon the wild meaning of the quietly uttered words. My brain reeled as I hearkened, entranced, to a melody more than mortal, to assumptions and aspirations which mortality had never before known.

That she loved me I should not have doubted, and I might have been easily aware that, in a bosom such as hers, love would have reigned no ordinary passion. But in death only was I fully impressed with the strength of her affection. For long hours, detaining my hand, would she pour out before me the overflowing of a heart whose more than passionate devotion amounted to idolatry. How had I deserved to be so blessed by such confessions? How had I deserved to be so cursed with the removal of my beloved in the hour of her making them? But upon this subject I cannot bear to dilate. Let me say only, that in Ligeia's more than womanly abandonment to a love, alas! all unmerited, all unworthily bestowed, I at length recognized the principle of her longing, with so wildly earnest a desire, for the life which was now fleeing so rapidly away. It is this wild longing—it is this eager vehemence of desire for life—but for life—that I have no power to portray, no utterance capable of expressing.

At high noon of the night in which she departed, beckoning me peremptorily to her side, she bade me repeat certain verses composed by herself not many days before. I obeyed her. They were these:

Lo! 'tis a gala night
Within the lonesome latter years!
An angel throng, bewinged, bedight
In veils, and drowned in tears,
Sit in a theatre, to see
A play of hopes and fears,
While the orchestra breathes fitfully
The music of the spheres.

Mimes, in the form of God on high,
Mutter and mumble low,
And hither and thither fly;
Mere puppets they, who come and go
At bidding of vast formless things

That shift the scenery to and fro,
Flapping from out their condor wings

Invisible Woe!
That motley drama!—oh, be sure
It shall not be forgot!
With its Phantom chased for evermore,
By a crowd that seize it not,
Through a circle that ever returneth in
To the self-same spot;
And much of Madness, and more of Sin

And Horror, the soul of the plot!
But see, amid the mimic rout
A crawling shape intrude!
A blood-red thing that writhes from out
The scenic solitude!
It writhes!—it writhes!—with mortal
The mimes become its food,
And the seraphs sob at vermin fangs

In human gore imbued.
Out—out are the lights—out all!
And over each quivering form,
The curtain, a funeral pall,
Comes down with the rush of a storm—
And the angels, all pallid and wan,
Uprising, unveiling, affirm
That the play is the tragedy, "Man,"
And its hero, the Conqueror Worm.

"O God!" half-shrieked Ligeia, leaping to her feet and extending her arms aloft with a spasmodic movement, as I made an end of these lines, "O God! O Divine Father! Shall these things be undeviatingly so? Shall this conqueror be not once conquered? Are we not part and parcel in Thee? Who—who knoweth the mysteries of the will with its vigour? Man doth not yield him to the angels, *nor unto death utterly,* save only through the weakness of his feeble will."

And now, as if exhausted with emotion, she suffered her white arms to fall, and returned solemnly to her bed of death. And as she breathed her last sighs, there came mingled with them a low murmur from her lips. I bent to them my ear, and distinguished again, the concluding words of the passage in Glanvill: "*Man doth not yield him to the angels, nor unto death utterly, save only through the weakness of his feeble will."*

She died, and I, crushed into the very dust with sorrow, could no longer endure the lonely desolation of my dwelling in the dim and decaying city by the Rhine. I had no lack of what the world calls wealth. Ligeia had brought me far more, very far more than ordinarily falls to the lot of mortals. After a few months, therefore, of weary and aimless wandering, I purchased and put in some repair an abbey which I shall not name in one of the wildest and least frequented portions of fair England. The gloomy and dreary grandeur of the building, the almost savage aspect of the domain, the many melancholy and time-honoured memories connected with both, had much in unison with the feelings of utter abandonment which had driven me into that remote and unsocial region of the country.

Yet, although the external abbey with its verdant decay hanging about it suffered but little alteration, I gave way with a child-like perversity, and perchance with a faint hope of alleviating my sorrows, to a display of more than regal magnificence within. For such follies, even in childhood, I had imbibed a taste, and now they came back to me as if in the dotage of grief. Alas, I feel how much even of incipient madness might have been discovered in the gorgeous and fantastic draperies, in the solemn carvings of Egypt, in the wild cornices and furniture, in the Bedlam patterns of the carpets of tufted gold! I had become a bounden slave in the trammels of opium, and my labours and my orders had taken a colouring from my dreams. But these absurdities I must not pause to detail. Let me speak only of that one chamber, ever accursed, whither in a moment of mental alienation, I led from the altar as my bride—as the successor of the unforgotten Ligeia—the fair-haired and blue-eyed Lady Rowena Trevanion, of Tremaine.

There is no individual portion of the architecture and decoration of that bridal chamber which is not now visibly before me. Where were the souls of the haughty family of the bride, when, through thirst of gold, they permitted to pass the threshold of an apartment *so* bedecked, a maiden and a daughter so beloved? I have said that I minutely remember the details of the chamber, yet I am sadly forgetful on topics of deep moment; and here there was no system, no keeping, in the fantastic display, to take hold upon the memory. The room lay in a high turret of the castellated abbey, was pentagonal in shape, and of capacious size.

Occupying the whole southern face of the pentagon was the sole window—an immense sheet of unbroken glass from Venice—a single pane, and tinted of a leaden hue, so that the rays of either the sun or moon passing through it fell with a ghastly lustre on the objects within. Over the upper portion of this huge window extended the trellis-work of an aged vine which clambered up the massy walls of the turret. The ceiling, of gloomy-looking oak, was excessively lofty, vaulted, and elaborately fretted with the wildest and most grotesque specimens of a semi-Gothic, semi-Druidical device. From out the most central recess of this melancholy vaulting depended, by a single chain of gold with long links, a huge censer of the same metal, Saracenic in pattern, and with many perforations so contrived that there writhed in and out of them, as if endued with a serpent vitality, a continual succession of parti-coloured fires.

Some few ottomans and golden candelabra of Eastern figure were in various stations about; and there was the couch, too—the bridal couch—of an Indian model, and low, and sculptured of solid ebony, with a pall-like canopy above. In each of the angles of the chamber stood on end a gigantic sarcophagus of black granite, from the tombs of the kings over against Luxor, with their aged lids full of immemorial sculpture. But in the draping of the apartment lay, alas! the chief fantasy of all. The lofty walls, gigantic in height—even unproportion-ably so—were hung from summit to foot in vast folds with a heavy and massive-looking tapestry—tapestry of a material which was found alike as a carpet on the floor, as a covering for the ottomans and the ebony bed, as a canopy for the bed, and as the gorgeous volutes of the curtains which partially shaded the window.

The material was the richest cloth of gold. It was spotted all over, at irregular intervals, with arabesque figures, about a foot in diameter, and wrought upon the cloth in patterns of the most jetty black. But these figures partook of the true character of the arabesque only when regarded from a single point of view. By a contrivance now common, and indeed traceable to a very remote period of antiquity, they were made changeable in aspect. To one entering the room they bore the appearance of simple monstrosities, but upon a farther advance this appearance gradually departed; and, step by step as the visitor moved his station in the chamber he saw himself surrounded by an endless succession of the ghastly forms which belong to the superstition of the Norman, or arise in the guilty slumbers of the monk. The phan-tasmagoric effect was vastly heightened by the artificial introduction of a strong continual current of wind behind the draperies—giving a hideous and uneasy animation to the whole.

In halls such as these—in a bridal chamber such as this—I passed, with the Lady of Tremaine, the unhallowed hours of the first month of our marriage—passed them with but little disquietude. That my wife dreaded the fierce moodiness of my temper, that she shunned me, and loved me but little, I could not help perceiving; but it gave me rather pleasure than otherwise. I loathed her with a hatred belonging more to demon than to man.

My memory flew back—oh, with what intensity of regret!—to Ligeia, the beloved, the august, the beautiful, the entombed. I revelled in recollections of her purity, of her wisdom, of her lofty, her ethereal nature, of her passionate, her idolatrous love. Now, then, did my spirit fully and freely burn with more than all the fires of her own. In the excitement of my opium dreams (for I was habitually fettered in the shackles of the drug) I would call aloud upon her name, during the silence of the night, or among the sheltered recesses of the glens by day, as if, through the wild eagerness, the solemn passion, the consuming ardour of my longing for the departed, I could restore her to the pathway she had abandoned—ah, could it be forever?—upon the earth.

About the commencement of the second month of the marriage the Lady Rowena was attacked with sudden illness, from which her recovery was slow. The fever which consumed her rendered her nights uneasy; and in her perturbed state of half-slumber she spoke of sounds and of motions in and about the chamber of the turret which I concluded had no origin save in the distemper of her fancy, or perhaps in the phantasmagoric influences of the chamber itself. She became at length convalescent—finally, well. Yet but a brief period elapsed ere a second more violent disorder again threw her upon a bed of suffering, and from this attack her frame, at all times feeble, never altogether recovered. Her illnesses were, after this epoch, of alarming character and of more alarming recurrence, defying alike the knowledge and the great exertions of her physicians. With the increase of the chronic disease, which had thus, apparently, taken too sure hold upon her constitution to be eradicated by human means, I could not fail to observe a similar increase in the nervous irritation of her temperament, and in her excitability by trivial causes of fear. She spoke again, and now more frequently and pertinaciously, of the sounds—of the slight sounds—and of the unusual motions among the tapestries, to which she had formerly alluded.

One night near the closing in of September she pressed this distressing subject with more than usual emphasis upon my attention. She had just awakened from an unquiet slumber, and I had been watching, with feelings half of anxiety, half of vague terror, the workings of her emaciated countenance. I sat by the side of her ebony bed, upon one of the ottomans of India. She partly arose, and spoke, in an earnest low whisper, of sounds which she then heard, but which I could not hear, of motions which she then saw, but which I could not perceive. The wind was rushing hurriedly behind the tapestries, and I wished to show her (what, let me confess it, I could not all believe) that those almost inarticulate breathings, and those very gentle variations of the figures upon the wall, were but the natural effects of that customary rushing of the wind.

But a deadly pallor overspreading her face had proved to me that my exertions to reassure her would be fruitless. She appeared to be fainting, and no attendants were within call. I remembered where was deposited a decanter of light wine which had been ordered by her physicians, and hastened across the chamber to procure it. But as I stepped beneath the light of the censer, two circumstances of a startling nature attracted my attention. I had felt that some palpable although invisible object had passed lightly by my person; and I saw that there lay upon the golden carpet, in the very middle of the rich lustre thrown from the censer, a shadow—a faint, indefinite shadow of angelic aspect, such as might be fancied for the shadow of a shade. But I was wild with the excitement of an immoderate dose of opium, and heeded these things but little, nor spoke of them to Rowena. Having found the wine, I recrossed the chamber and poured out a gobletful which I held to the lips of the fainting lady.

She had now partially recovered, however, and took the vessel herself, while I sank upon an ottoman near me, with my eyes fastened upon her person. It was then that I became distinctly aware of a gentle footfall upon the carpet and near the couch; and in a second after as Rowena was in the act of raising the wine to her lips I saw, or may have dreamed that I saw, fall within the goblet, as if from some invisible spring in the atmosphere of the room, three or four large drops of a brilliant and ruby-coloured fluid. If this I saw—not so Rowena. She swallowed the wine unhesitatingly, and I forbore to speak to her of a circumstance which must, after all, I considered, have been but the suggestion of a vivid imagination, rendered morbidly active by the terror of the lady, by the opium, and by the hour.

Yet I cannot conceal it from my own perception that, immediately subsequent to the fall of the ruby-drops, a rapid change for the worse took place in the disorder of my wife, so that, on the third subsequent night the hands of her menials prepared her for the tomb, and on the fourth I sat alone with her shrouded body in that fantastic chamber which had received her as my bride. Wild visions, opium-engendered, fluttered, shadow-like, before me. I gazed with unquiet eye upon the *sarcophagi* in the angles of the room, upon the varying figures of the drapery, and upon the writhing of the parti-coloured fires in the censer overhead. My eyes then fell, as I called to mind the circumstances of a former night to the spot beneath the glare of the censer where I had seen the faint traces of the shadow.

It was there, however, no longer; and breathing with greater freedom, I turned my glances to the pallid and rigid figure upon the bed. Then rushed upon me a thousand memories of Ligeia—and then came back upon my heart with the turbulent violence of a flood the whole of that unutterable woe with which I had regarded *her* thus enshrouded. The night waned; and still, with a bosom full of bitter thoughts of the one only and supremely beloved, I remained gazing upon the body of Rowena.

It might have been midnight, or perhaps earlier, or later—for I had taken no note of time—when a sob, low, gentle, but very distinct, startled me from my reverie. I *felt* that it came from the bed of ebony—the bed of death. I listened in an agony of superstitious terror—but there was no repetition of the sound. I strained my vision to detect any motion in the corpse—but there was not the slightest perceptible. Yet I could not have been deceived. I *had* heard the noise, however faint, and my soul was awakened within me. I resolutely and perseveringly kept my attention riveted upon the body. Many minutes elapsed before any circumstance occurred tending to throw light upon the mystery.

At length it became evident that a slight, a very feeble and barely noticeable tinge of colour had flushed up within the cheeks, and along the sunken small veins of the eyelids. Through a species of unutterable horror and awe, for which the language of mortality has no sufficiently energetic expression, I felt my heart cease to beat, my limbs grow rigid where I sat. Yet a sense of duty finally operated to restore my self-possession. I could no longer doubt that we had been precipitate in our preparations—that Rowena still lived. It was necessary that some immediate exertion be made, yet the turret was altogether apart from the portion of the abbey tenanted by the servants—there were none within call, and I had no means of summoning them to my aid without leaving the room for many minutes—and this I could not venture to do. I therefore struggled alone in my endeavours to call back the spirit still hovering. In a short period it was certain, however, that a relapse had taken place, the colour disappeared from both eyelid and cheek, leaving a wanness even more than that of marble; the lips became doubly shrivelled and pinched up in the ghastly expression of death; a repulsive clamminess and coldness overspread rapidly the surface of the body; and all the usual rigorous stiffness immediately supervened. I fell back with a shudder upon the couch from which I had been so startlingly aroused, and again gave myself up to passionate waking visions of Ligeia.

An hour thus elapsed, when—could it be possible?—I was a second time aware of some vague sound issuing from the region of the bed. I listened—in extremity of horror. The sound came again—it was a sigh. Rushing to the corpse, I saw—distinctly saw—a tremor upon the lips. In a minute afterward they relaxed, disclosing a bright line of the pearly teeth. Amazement now struggled in my bosom with the profound awe which had hitherto reigned there alone. I felt that my vision grew dim, that my reason wandered, and it was only by a violent effort that I at length succeeded in nerving myself to the task which duty thus once more had pointed out.

There was now a partial glow upon the forehead and upon the cheek and throat, a perceptible warmth pervaded the whole frame, there was even a slight pulsation at the heart. The lady *lived*; and with redoubled ardour I betook myself to the task of restoration. I chafed and bathed the temples and the hands and used every exertion which experience and no little medical reading could suggest. But in vain. Suddenly, the color fled, the pulsation ceased, the lips resumed the expression of the dead, and, in an instant afterward, the whole body took upon itself the icy chilliness, the livid hue, the intense rigidity, the sunken outline, and all the loathsome peculiarities of that which has been, for many days, a tenant of the tomb.

And again I sunk into visions of Ligeia—and again, (what marvel that I shudder while I write?) *again* there reached my ears a low sob from the region of the ebony bed. But why should I minutely detail the unspeakable horrors of that night? Why should I pause to relate how, time after time, until near the period of the gray dawn, this hideous drama of revivification was repeated; how each terrific relapse was only into a sterner and apparently more irredeemable death; how each agony wore the aspect of a struggle with some invisible foe; and how each struggle was succeeded by I know not what of wild change in the personal appearance of the corpse? Let me hurry to a conclusion.

The greater part of the fearful night had worn away, and she who had been dead, once again stirred—and now more vigorously than hitherto, although arousing from a dissolution more appalling in its utter hopelessness than any. I had long ceased to struggle or to move, and remained sitting rigidly upon the ottoman, a helpless prey to a whirl of violent emotions, of which extreme awe was perhaps the least terrible, the least consuming. The corpse, I repeat, stirred, and now more vigorously than before. The hues of life flushed up with unwonted energy into the countenance, the limbs relaxed, and, save that the eyelids were yet pressed heavily together and that the bandages and draperies of the grave still imparted their charnel character to the figure, I might have dreamed that Rowena had indeed shaken off utterly the fetters of Death. But if this idea was not even then altogether adopted, I could at least doubt no longer, when arising from the bed, tottering, with feeble steps, with closed eyes, and with the manner of one bewildered in a dream, the thing that was enshrouded advanced boldly and palpably into the middle of the apartment.

I trembled not—I stirred not—for a crowd of unutterable fancies connected with the air, the stature, the demeanour of the figure, rushing hurriedly through my brain, had paralyzed—had chilled me into stone. I stirred not—but gazed upon the apparition. There was a mad disorder in my thoughts—a tumult unappeasable. Could it, indeed, be the living Rowena who confronted me? Could it indeed be Rowena at all—the fair-haired, the blue-eyed Lady Rowena Trevanion of Tremaine? Why, *why* should I doubt it? The bandage lay heavily about the mouth—but then might it not be the mouth of the breathing Lady of Tremaine? And the cheeks—there were the roses as in her noon of life—yes, these might indeed be the fair cheeks of the living Lady of Tremaine. And the chin, with its dimples, as in health, might it not be hers?—but *had she then grown taller since her malady?* What inexpressible madness seized me with that thought!

One bound, and I had reached her feet. Shrinking from my touch she let fall from her head, unloosened, the ghastly cerements which had confined it, and there streamed forth into the rushing atmosphere of the chamber huge masses of long and dishevelled hair; *it was blacker than the raven wings of midnight!* And now slowly opened the eyes of the figure which stood before me. "Here then, at least," I shrieked aloud, "can I never—can I never be mistaken—these are the full and the black, and the wild eyes of my lost love—of the Lady—of the Lady Ligeia."

Chan Tow the Highrob

By Chester Bailey Fernald

Before me sits the Chinese—my friend who, when the hurly-burly's done, spins me out the hours with narratives of ancient Yellowland. His name is Fuey Fong, and he speaks to me thus:

"Missa Gordon, whatta is Chrisinjin Indevil Shoshiety?"

I explain to him as best a journalist may the purpose of the Society for Christian Endeavour.

"We', dissa morning I go down to lailload station. Shee vay many peoples getta on tlain. Assa conductor, 'Whatta is?' Conductor tole me: 'You can't go. You a *heeffen*. Dissa *Chrisinjin* Indevil Shoshiety.'

"Dissa mek me vay tire. 'Me'ican peoples fink ole China heeffen. Fink doan' know about Gaw of heffen. Dissa 'Me'icans doan' know whatta is. China peoples benieve Olemighty Gaw semma lika you."

Fuey endures in meditation several moments. Then he says:

"Missa Gordon, I tay you how about Gaw convert China clilimal?"

"How God converted a Chinese criminal?"

"Yeh. I tay you. Dissa case somma lika dis:

"One tem was China highrob. His nem was Chan Tow. Live by rob on pubnic highway evely one he can. Dissa highrob live in place call Kan Suh. We', one tem was merchan', nem Jan Han Sun, getta lich in Kan Suh; say hisse'f: 'I getta lich; now mus' go home Tsan Ran Foo, shee my de-ah fadder-mudder-in-'aw an' my de-ah wife.' So med determine to go home nex' day.

"Kan Suh to Tsan Ran Foo about dousands miles distant, and dissa parts China no lailload, no canal. So dissa trivveler declude to ride in horse-carry-chair."

"What is a horse-carry-chair?"

"We', I tay you. Somma lika dis: Two horse—one befront, one inhine. Two long stick, and carry-chair in minnle. Usa roop somma lika harness. Dissa way trivvle long distance ole ove' China.

"We', nex' day Missa Jan start out faw Tsan Ran Foo in horse-carry-chair. Hed big backage of go' an' sivver. Bye-bye—trivvle long tem—was pass high tree. Up high tree was Chan Tow—dissa highrob—was vay bad man! Chan Tow up tree to watch to stea' whatta he can, semma lika vutture."

"Like a *vulture*."

"Like a vutture—big bird—eat dead beas' ole he can.

"Chan Tow look down on load, and shee horse-carry-chair wif Missa Jan feet stick out. Nen dissa highrob say hisse'f: 'Vay nice feet; lich man. I go fonnow him. Maybe can stea' from him.' So fonnow 'long Missa Jan by day, by night, severow day—doan' lose sight ole dissa tem. Bye-bye Missa Jan was trivvle ole night, and leach hotel early morning. He tole hotel-kipper: 'You giva me loom. I slip ole day.' Nen tek his backage go' an' sivver, an' tek to bed wif him. Chan Tow come 'long; say: 'Giva me loom nex' my de-ah frien' jussa come in horse-carry-chair.' Hotelkipper look him, an' say, 'Whatta your nem is?' Chan Tow say, 'My nem Chow Ying Hoo.' Dissa nem, transnate Ingernish, mean Brev Tiger."

"And what does Chan Tow mean?"

"Oh, Chan Tow mean ole semma bad faminy.

"We', dissa highrob slip nex' loom Missa Jan; but no can fine how to rob him ole dissa tem. Getta vay much disgussion; but nex' day he fonnow long inhine dissa lich man jussa semma befaw. Somma tem eat at semma tabuh wif Jan; but Jan getta begin to suspicious, an' ole tem getta his go' an' sivver unnerneaf him when he shet down to tabuh. Chan Tow say hisse'f: 'You fink I doan' know how to shucshess to stea' yo' money. Maybe I big foo' you.'

"We', bye-bye was mont' go by. Dissa merchan' reach his netive sheety. Firs' he go immedinity to respec' his fadder-mudder-in-'aw, becose his fadder-mudder dead. Dey vay gnad to shee him—vay denight. Dey assa him vay many quishuns; but he tole dem: 'I mus' go to my de-ah wife. I not sheen her so long tem.' Nen he smi' hisse'f, an' tole horse-carry-chair-man run wif him quick to fine his de-ah wife. When he allive ne' his house, say to man: 'Goo'by! I go ressa way on footstep.' Nen go vay quier on his tiptoe, and lock vay soft at his daw."

Here pauses the Chinese, and looks at me. Shortly he says:

"We'?"

153

"Well?" I echo.

"We', dissa last tem dissa merchan' Jan Han Sun was sheen annibe!"

"Does the highrob follow him and kill him?"

"No one shee any highrob. No one shee any horse-carry-chairman. No one shee any Jan. No maw!

"Nex' morning come fadder-mudder-in-'aw to congratchnate dissa daughter. Said, 'We vay denight, vay gnad, yo' husban' come home. Where he is dissa morning? Daughter look vay supp'ise.' Said, 'When you shee my husban' come home?' Parents said: 'Why, my de-ah daughter, yo' husban' pass by my daw las' night. We hev vay short convisition beggedder, an' he say bling home glate many go' an' sivver—mek you habby. Nen left us come shee you.'

"Nen, vay suddenity, dissa daughter say: 'I fink you ki' my husban', so you can rob! I hev you arres'.'

"An' she go to magistrate an' mek petition. Say her fadder-mudder to ki' her husban'. Her fadder-mudder bofe vay indignant; but was putta in jai'.

"Magistrate examine case, assa many quishuns, search bofe dissa house—but can't fine who mudder dissa merchan'. Fadder-mudder-in'-aw say, 'We innocent.' Daughter say, 'You liars!' Her parents med declaration, 'I doan' hed mudder to any person.' Two mont's go by. Can't fine who mudder. Nen daughter petition to supere court; say dissa magistrate doan' know how fine who mudder. Supere court send word, 'You doan' fine who mudder in six mont's—deglade yo' lank.' Dissa China way to mek law.

"We', dissa magistrate, whatta he do? Doan' like getta deglade; dissa spoi' his whole life. Say hisse'f: 'I vay detest to get deglade. Mus' go mek detectif—fine who mudder.' Nex' day left his court, and go mek long trivvle—ole dress up like a fortune-tayer."

"Like a fortune-teller?"

"Yeh; fortune-tayer. Vay low common in China. Go roun' wif ole kine bad peoples.

"Magistrate look jussa somma poh fortune-taye. Nen go on load an' trivvle—trivvle vay far. Eve'y tem shee a man look lika somma bad man, try mek frien's wif him. But no can fine who mudder. Long tem trivvle—'way intehuh China; but no can fine anyone knows about dissa case. Say hisse'f: 'Pitty soon I getta discoulagement. Two mont's maw getta deglade, getta disglace! I doan' know I ki' hisse'f!'

"One day was stag' 'long load; getta 'mos' exhaus'. Bofe sides load

154

was high heels, no house. Kep' on, on; semma heels; semma no house; mus' lie down in load wifout any subber, wifout any dlink. Dissa magistrate begin getta desplate. Nen he finks, 'I play to Gaw an' my ancestors.' So begin play lika diss: 'O Gaw, O my ancestors, givva me res'; givva me foo'; givva me wadder! Nen I kip on fawever fine who ki' Jan Han Sun.' Nen magistrate stag' 'long few steps, an' dlop down on big lock. No*can*any fudder.

"Pitty soon look roun'; shee litty light shine from winnidow. Dissa was littyoshantyhouse—vay poh look——"

"Littyoshantyhouse?"

"Litty—ole—shanty—house!

"We', magistrate to lock at daw. Come to daw littyoneddy——"

"Little old what?"

"Litty—ole—neddy!

"Dissa oneddy she was vay ole, vay feeble. He tole her: 'Please, oneddy, you givva me kunderness let me go slip in yo' house tonight! I 'mos' died. No subber, no wadder—'mos' exhaus'!' Oneddy tole him: 'Walks in; walks in! But you mus' kip vay quier, my de-ah sir; as quier as can be! My son is dreffel differcut man. His profussion was highrob. He getta home minnernight; an' you doan' kip quier, I fred he to strike you!' But magistrate say: 'I too tire' to getta scare'. You nedda me stay wif you.'

"So oneddy giva him to eat, an' show him to go slip unner tabuh in katchen. Nen he lie down, an' play once more his ancestors an' Gaw: 'You he'p me oleleddy; I kip plomise. Nou he'p me somma maw—I fine who mudder.' Nen go slip.

"Bye-bye was dleam 'bout gleen moudens, gleen wadder. Hear' spi'its say, 'I wi' assist you.' Ole dissa vay good sign. Suddinity was wek up from his slip, and shaw oneddy stand befaw him—ole in dark. She say: 'My son come home in vay good humours. Say lak mek yo' acquaintenance.' Dissa tem was minnernight. Magistrate craw' out from unner tabuh, an' fonnow oneddy in nex' loom. Heah was Chan Tow, dissa highrob. Was fee' in vay good tempiniment to-night—hedda jus' rob litty gir' her earlings."

"It made him very happy to have stolen earrings from a little girl?"

"Oh, yeh. Earlings med jay-stone.

"We', Chan Tow he vay denight to shee dissa fortune-tayer. Mek put hisse'f down to tabuh, eat subbah wif him, an' mek oneddy hop 'long getta ole bes' was in oshantyhouse. Chan Tow say: 'My de-ah sir,

I am exceediny denight to shee you. We bofe about sem profussions: you fortune-tayer; I was highrob.' Nen bofe eat, dlink long tem, an' Chan Tow tay ole about his shucshess in binniziz."

"You mean business?"

"Yeh; binniziz.

"Tay ole about his binniziz. Tay how stea' watch from 'Me'ican missiolary man. Tay how——"

"How did he steal the watch from the American missionary?"

"We', somma lika dis: Chan Tow was vay stlong man, but vay litty meat on his boles. One day shee missiolary man come 'long load. Hedda watch-chain hang out. Chan Tow lie down in load, an' begin kick an' scleam ole semma sick white woman. Missiolary man was vay sympafy, an' tole him, 'Whatta is?' Chan Tow say: 'Much vay sick! Much vay sick! You no he'p me home I getta died! You tekka me home I mek good Chrisinjin boy!' Missiolary man vay good man; say hisse'f: 'Gaw sen' me dissa man mek convict to Chrisinjanity. I he'p him!' So tek up Chan Tow in his arm to tek home. Chan Tow kep' gloan, gloan,—an' ole dissa tem was put his han' in missiolary his pocket an' stea' dissa watch! Nen Chan Tow kep' hang on missiolary his neck an' say hisse'f: 'I lika dissa to ride better I lika to walk. I letta dissa missiolary man ca'y me jusso far he can.' So missiolary man stag' long tem 'ong load, an' kep' sweat, sweat—semma lika glass ice-wadder; an' Chan Tow kep' gloan semma like ole barn daw."

"Chan Tow kept groaning like an old barn door, and the missionary man kept perspiring like a glass of ice-water?"

"Oh, no! Missiolary man sweat. Bye-bye, hedda ca'y dissa highrob two miles—'way down vanney, 'way up heel. Nen missiolary man lose ole his breffs, an' begin to gaps. He say, 'Mus' res'; mus' putta you down!' Chan Tow kep' gloan, an' say: 'You putta me down I doan' know I die. Mus' getta home!' Missiolary man say: 'Can't he'p—I 'mos' exhaus'.' Nen dissa highrob jump down vay well, an' say: 'We', I mus' getta home. I walk ressa way—leave you to res'. Goo'by!' Nen run fas' he can down dissa heel.

"Missiolary man stay look him run, an' kep' fink ole tem. Nen say hisse'f: 'I fink dissa man inshinsherity. I lose ole dissa tem wif him! Whatta tem it is?' Nen he search his watch. 'Oh, my! No watch; no convict! Dissa vay bad day!'"

The Chinese grins with the greatest pleasure.

"We', magistrate an' highrob kep' tay ole 'bout expelunces in binniziz."

"*Business!*"

"Yeh; *binniziz.*

"Kep' tay ole about binniziz. Bye-bye pea-oil light go out. Oneddy craw' up on bed an' go slip. Nen two men stay an' smoke pipe—ole dark. Magistrate closs his legs an' say, ole lika he doan' care: 'Missa Highrob, dissa light go out mek me remin' whatta habben Tsan Ran Foo. You heard about dissa case? Man nem Jan Han Sun go home his wife—no can fine who mudder.' Chan Tow smi' vay plou',[1] an' say: 'Oh, my de-ah brudder, I know ole 'bout dissa case. I was to shee dissa man getta ki' in his own houses.'

"Magistrate dlaw glate big breff frough his pipe. Swallow smoke clea' down his stomach! Mek big cough—nearny cough his top head off!—an' wek oneddy! Nen he say: 'We', we'! You good dea' maw wise dissa magistrate Tsan Ran Foo. I hea' he was deglade his rank. Cannot fine who mudder!'

"Chan Tow say: 'Dissa magistrate mus' come fine me. No one ess can tay him. I tay you ole about dissa mudder. You lika hea'?' Magistrate say: 'We', I vay tire'. But lika hea' you talk better I lika go slip, my de-ah sir!' Dissa mek highrob vay plou', an' he begin lika dis:

"'One day shaw horse-carry-chair trivvle 'long load. Shaw feet stick out—vay nice feet; mus' be lich man. So fonnow him. He hev big backage go' an' sivver, but eve'y tem go subbah mus' oleways shet hisse'f on top dissa backage. Fonnow him long tem—severow weeks. But cannot stea' from him. Bye-bye he reach his home Tsan Ran Foo, an' go to respec' his mudder-fadder-in-'aw; nen go fine his wife. Dissa tem was minnernight—vay dark. Fink was good tem to stea' from him, an' getta his go' an' sivver. So kep' fonnow 'long load. When he getta his house he lock long tem at his daw, but was no answer. Nen say, vay loud: "De-ah wife, letta me in! I am yo' de-ah husban' come home." So bye-bye was daw open, an' his wife come say: "O my de-ah husban'! so denight to shee you!" Nen ole dark.

"'Nen I go roun' back his house. Getta long bamboo po', an' putta dissa po' up 'gainst house to shin up dissa loof. Nen cut with knife a litty roun' ho' frough loof, an' look down into dissa house. Can look down into loom, an' shee ole whatta was habben.

"'Vay soon Jan examine tabuh; say: "O my de-ah wife, whatta faw you setta dissa tabuh for two peoples? You have compaly?" Wife say: "O my de-ah husban', eve'y tem since you go 'way I setta dissa tabuh faw two peoples—you and me—jussa semma you heah!" Jan smi' vay

_____
1. Proud.

157

plou,' an' say, "You are shinsherny[2] my de-ah wife!"—was mak fee' vay good.

"'Nen his wife tole him: "Now we hev jubinee; eat, dlink—mek me'y tem!" So I lie on top dissa loof, vay dly, vay hunger; an' ole tem shee her husban' eat subbah an' kip dlink, dlink, an' kiss his wife, an' dlink, an' getta maw an' maw intoshcate. Bye-bye was so intoshcate mus' go slip. Nen his wife he'p him go bed, an' he begin snow.'"

"How's that?"

"Begin snow—snowul—snole! Begin snole!"

"It began to snow?"

"On, no; I tay you. Dissa merchan' begin mekka lika dis." Fuey makes a sound that is unmistakable.

"'We', nen look shee whatta dissa woman go do. She go to hooks on wa', an' tek down lot her dresses. Nen I shee man step out. Dissa woman whisper to him: "Shee my husban' slip. He bling back glate many go' and sivver! You love me, you tekka dissa sharp knife and ki' him. Nen we getta marry begedder tomorrow, an' mek habby tem."

"'Her *beau* say: "Oh, no. I fred ki' him. Fred I get behead." An' nen dissa woman getta vay mad wif him, an' say: "You doan' ki' him, I tekka dissa knife an' chot op yo' head op, instamentty!" Nen he begin tek off his mine——'"

"Took off his mind?"

"Yeh," says Fuey; "I do' know dissa word—semma you tek off yo' clo's."

"Changed his mind?"

"Yeh."

"'Begin to tek off—chenge his mine—an' say: "How I ki' him?" Woman say: "You tekka dissa sharp knife."

"'Nen he clep up to dissa bed, his eye ole stick from his head. When he getta where dissa mer-out chan' slip, an' snow, snow, ole semma hev good dleam, dissa beau mek like was to chenge his mine 'gain; but dissa woman whisper: "Quick! Quick!"—an' nen ole sudden dissa beau stlike. Nen Jan Han Sun was died—instamentty!

"'Dissa woman begin rip up flaw. Her *beau* he'p her ole he can, an' work vay hard, fas'—fred somebody come. Kep' look roun'. An' eve'y tem pea-oil light flicker, look roun' to shee who was. Ole tem stop to hol' his ear on flaw—shee who come. Flaw rip up; nen go getta shover an' dig long ho' in earf, unnerneaf dissa bed. Nen vay quick shover back ole dissa earf, fix flaw, an' blow out light.

2. Sincerely.

"'Ole tem I stay up dissa loof. Vay hunger—no wadder; an' cannot rob dissa merchan' becose he dead! Getta vay disgussion. Light go out, I hang foot over' side dissa loof, an' begin fink. Maw I fink, maw getta disgussion. Bye-bye getta *vay, vay* disgussion. Nen tek dissa bamboo po' to shove frough dissa ho' in loof—vay quier. When he shove frough, nen I ole suddenity begin push, jab, shove—quick—ole semma churn budder. Down below woman an' her *beau* begin squea', squea', ole semma rat! 'Most scare' to def! Nen I shin down loof—run 'way.'"

Fuey draws a long breath, and smiles at me his calm, celestial smile.

"We', Chan Tow finis' his sto'y. Magistrate was ole tem smoke big clou's smoke, an' mek loom look lika was on fire. Mek oneddy wek up an' open daw. When Chan Tow finis', magistrate say: 'My de-ah brudder de highrob, yo' sto'y vay intinesse, vay intinesse! I fink I go slip.' So ole thlee was lie down to go slip, an' Chan Tow was tek his op' pipe an' begin smoke opi'. Whatta you say—hurt de pipe?"

"Hit the pipe."

"Oh, yeh; hit pipe. I doan' spe'k Ingernish vay we'."

"Magistrate wet long tem. Bye-bye oneddy begin to snow, an' nen bye-bye Chan Tow getta doan' know."

"Chan Tow got *don't know?*"

"Getta ole semma was died. Doan' know."

"Unconscious?"

"Yeh; uh-uh-coshious!" sneezes Fuey.

"Nen magistrate begin craw' 'long on his stoamch—inchy—inchy—cross flaw—out daw. Nen run fas' he can towards Tsan Ran Foo.

"One mont' go by, an' magistrate sit up in his high chair in his court. Befron him dissa woman an' her beau,—ole cover wif mark dissa bamboo po',—an' dissa fadder-mudder-in-'aw, an' dissa highrob. Magistrate say, vay slow—ole semma idol talk: '*Dissa—woman—her lover—are convert—to behead—by hev dey heads cut off—till dey dead!* What you fink, woman?' Woman say: 'Yo' Excennency, I vay gnad to be behead wif my de-ah lover. I vay satisfaction we behead begedder. Our spi'its begedder habby fo'ever.' Nen she turn kiss her *beau*; but he too scare to spe'k. An' bofe was tek out to behead—dissa woman ole tem to mek to kiss her *beau*.

"Magistrate say to highrob: 'You know me? Who eata subbah wif you sucha-sucha night?' Chan Tow say, 'O yo' Excennency, I doan' know who was!' Magistrate say: 'I was dissa man. I glate t'anks faw you.

159

Awso dissa fadder-mudder-in-'aw dissa dead man. Gaw sen' me to yo' house to mek you instlument to convert dissa mudderers. I give you good position; awso money."

"And that was how these criminals were *converted*?" I say, remembering the promise of the story.

"Yeh; convert to behead. Dissa case," concluded Fuey, "show how Gaw can convert cliliman when he wish; show how Gaw is glate. I tay you China peoples not heeffen. China 'ligion teach to try to affection one anudder; respec' yo' parents; an' charity an' pure moral. If people do right I fink he shall be saved."

May Day Eve

By Algernon Blackwood

1

It was in the spring when I at last found time from the hospital work to visit my friend, the old folk-lorist, in his country isolation, and I rather chuckled to myself, because in my bag I was taking down a book that utterly refuted all his tiresome pet theories of magic and the powers of the soul.

These theories were many and various, and had often troubled me. In the first place, I scorned them for professional reasons, and, in the second, because I had never been able to argue quite well enough to convince or to shake his faith, in even the smallest details, and any scientific knowledge I brought to bear only fed him with confirmatory data. To find such a book, therefore, and to know that it was safely in my bag, wrapped up in brown paper and addressed to him, was a deep and satisfactory joy, and I speculated a good deal during the journey how he would deal with the overwhelming arguments it contained against the existence of any important region outside the world of sensory perceptions.

Speculative, too, I was whether his visionary habits and absorbing experiments would permit him to remember my arrival at all, and I was accordingly relieved to hear from the solitary porter that the "professor" had sent a "veeckle" to meet me, and that I was thus free to send my bag and walk the four miles to the house across the hills.

It was a calm, windless evening, just after sunset, the air warm and scented, and delightfully still. The train, already sinking into distance, carried away with it the noise of crowds and cities and the last suggestions of the stressful life behind me, and from the little station on the moorland I stepped at once into the world of silent, growing things, tinkling sheep-bells, shepherds, and wild, desolate spaces.

My path lay diagonally across the turfy hills. It slanted a mile or so to the summit, wandered vaguely another two miles among gorse-bushes along the crest, passed Tom Bassett's cottage by the pines, and then dropped sharply down on the other side through rather thin woods to the ancient house where the old folk-lorist lived and dreamed himself into his impossible world of theory and fantasy. I fell to thinking busily about him during the first part of the ascent, and convinced myself, as usual, that, but for his generosity to the poor, and his benign aspect, the peasantry must undoubtedly have regarded him as a wizard who speculated in souls and had dark dealings with the world of faery.

The path I knew tolerably well. I had already walked it once before—a winter's day some years ago—and from the cottage onward felt sure of my way; but for the first mile or so there were so many cross cattle-tracks, and the light had become so dim that I felt it wise to inquire more particularly. And this I was fortunately able to do of a man who with astonishing suddenness rose from the grass where he had been lying behind a clump of bushes, and passed a few yards in front of me at a high pace downhill toward the darkening valley.

He was in such a state of hurry that I called out loudly to him, fearing to be too late, but on hearing my voice he turned sharply, and seemed to arrive almost at once beside me. In a single instant he was standing there, quite close, looking, with a smile and a certain expression of curiosity, I thought, into my face. I remember thinking that his features, pale and wholly untanned, were rather wonderful for a countryman, and that the eyes were those of a foreigner; his great swiftness, too, gave me a distinct sensation—something almost of a start—though I knew my vision was at fault at the best of times, and of course especially so in the deceptive twilight of the open hillside.

Moreover—as the way often is with such instructions—the words did not stay in my mind very clearly after he had uttered them, and the rapid, panther-like movements of the man as he quickly vanished down the hill again left me with little more than a sweeping gesture indicating the line I was to follow. No doubt his sudden rising from behind the gorse-bush, his curious swiftness, and the way he peered into my face, and even touched me on the shoulder, all combined to distract my attention somewhat from the actual words he used; and the fact that I was travelling at a wrong angle, and should have come out a mile too far to the right, helped to complete my feeling that his gesture, pointing the way, was sufficient.

On the crest of the ridge, panting a little with the unwonted exertion, I lay down to rest a moment on the grass beside a flaming yellow gorse-bush. There was still a good hour before I should be looked for at the house; the grass was very soft, the peace and silence soothing. I lingered, and lit a cigarette. And it was just then, I think, that my subconscious memory gave back the words, the actual words, the man had spoken, and the heavy significance of the personal pronoun, as he had emphasised it in his odd foreign voice, touched me with a sense of vague amusement: "The safest way *for you* now," he had said, as though I was so obviously a townsman and might be in danger on the lonely hills after dark. And the quick way he had reached my side, and then slipped off again like a shadow down the steep slope, completed a definite little picture in my mind. Then other thoughts and memories rose up and formed a series of pictures, following each other in rapid succession, and forming a chain of reflections undirected by the will and without purpose or meaning. I fell, that is, into a pleasant reverie.

Below me, and infinitely far away, it seemed, the valley lay silent under a veil of blue evening haze, the lower end losing itself among darkening hills whose peaks rose here and there like giant plumes that would surely nod their great heads and call to one another once the final shadows were down. The village lay, a misty patch, in which lights already twinkled. A sound of rooks faintly cawing, of sea-gulls crying far up in the sky, and of dogs barking at a great distance rose up out of the general murmur of evening voices. Odours of farm and field and open spaces stole to my nostrils, and everything contributed to the feeling that I lay on the top of the world, nothing between me and the stars, and that all the huge, free things of the earth—hills, valleys, woods, and sloping fields—lay breathing deeply about me.

A few sea-gulls—in daytime hereabouts they fill the air—still circled and wheeled within range of sight, uttering from time to time sharp, petulant cries; and far in the distance there was just visible a shadowy line that showed where the sea lay.

Then, as I lay gazing dreamily into this still pool of shadows at my feet, something rose up, something sheet-like, vast, imponderable, off the whole surface of the mapped-out country, moved with incredible swiftness down the valley, and in a single instant climbed the hill where I lay and swept by me, yet without hurry, and in a sense without speed. Veils in this way rose one after another, filling the cups between the hills, shrouding alike fields, village, and hillside as they passed, and settled down somewhere into the gloom behind me over the ridge, or slipped off like vapour into the sky.

Whether it was actually mist rising from the surface of the fast-cooling ground, or merely the earth giving up her heat to the night, I could not determine. The coming of the darkness is ever a series of mysteries. I only know that this indescribable vast stirring of the landscape seemed to me as though the earth were unfolding immense sable wings from her sides, and lifting them for silent, gigantic strokes so that she might fly more swiftly from the sun into the night. The darkness, at any rate, did drop down over everything very soon afterward, and I rose up hastily to follow my pathway, realising with a degree of wonder strangely new to me the magic of twilight, the blue open depths into the valley below, and the pale yellow heights of the watery sky above.

I walked rapidly, a sense of chilliness about me, and soon lost sight of the valley altogether as I got upon the ridge proper of these lonely and desolate hills.

It could not have been more than fifteen minutes that I lay there in reverie, yet the weather, I at once noticed, had changed very abruptly, for mist was seething here and there about me, rising somewhere from smaller valleys in the hills beyond, and obscuring the path, while overhead there was plainly a sound of wind tearing past, far up, with a sound of high shouting. A moment before it had been the stillness of a warm spring night, yet now everything had changed; wet mist coated me, raindrops smartly stung my face, and a gusty wind, descending out of cool heights, began to strike and buffet me, so that I buttoned my coat and pressed my hat more firmly upon my head.

The change was really this—and it came to me for the first time in my life with the power of a real conviction—that everything about me seemed to have become suddenly *alive*.

It came oddly upon me—prosaic, matter-of-fact, materialistic doctor that I was—this realisation that the world about me had somehow stirred into life; oddly, I say, because Nature to me had always been merely a more or less definite arrangement of measurement, weight, and colour, and this new presentation of it was utterly foreign to my temperament. A valley to me was always a valley; a hill, merely a hill; a field, so many acres of flat surface, grass or ploughed, drained well or drained ill; whereas now, with startling vividness, came the strange, haunting idea that after all they could be something more than valley, hill, and field; that what I had hitherto perceived by these names were only the veils of something that lay concealed within, something alive. In a word, that the poetic sense I had always rather sneered at, in others, or explained away with some shallow physiological label, had apparently suddenly opened up in myself without any obvious cause.

And, the more I puzzled over it, the more I began to realise that its genesis dated from those few minutes of reverie lying under the gorse-bush (reverie, a thing I had never before in all my life indulged in!), or, now that I came to reflect more accurately, from my brief interview with that wild-eyed, swift-moving, shadowy man of whom I had first inquired the way.

I recalled my singular fancy that veils were lifting off the surface of the hills and fields, and a tremor of excitement accompanied the memory. Such a thing had never before been possible to my practical intelligence, and it made me feel suspicious—suspicious about myself. I stood still a moment—I looked about me into the gathering mist, above me to the vanishing stars, below me to the hidden valley, and then sent an urgent summons to my individuality, as I had always known it, to arrest and chase these undesirable fancies.

But I called in vain. No answer came. Anxiously, hurriedly, confusedly, too, I searched for my normal self, but could not find it; and this failure to respond induced in me a sense of uneasiness that touched very nearly upon the borders of alarm.

I pushed on faster and faster along the turfy track among the gorse-bushes with a dread that I might lose the way altogether, and a sudden desire to reach home as soon as might be. Then, without warning, I emerged unexpectedly into clear air again, and the vapour swept past me in a rushing wall and rose into the sky. Anew I saw the lights of the village behind me in the depths, here and there a line of smoke rising against the pale yellow sky, and stars overhead peering down through thin wispy clouds that stretched their wind-signs across the night.

After all, it had been nothing but a stray bit of sea-fog driving up from the coast, for the other side of the hills, I remembered, dipped their chalk cliffs straight into the sea, and strange lost winds must often come a-wandering this way with the sharp changes of temperature about sunset. None the less, it was disconcerting to know that mist and storm lay hiding within possible reach, and I walked on smartly for a sight of Tom Bassett's cottage and the lights of the Manor House in the valley a short mile beyond.

The clearing of the air, however, lasted but a very brief while, and vapour was soon rising about me as before, hiding the path and making bushes and stone walls look like running shadows. It came, driven apparently, by little independent winds up the many side gullies, and it was very cold, touching my skin like a wet sheet. Curious great shapes, too, it assumed as the wind worked to and fro through it: forms of men and animals; grotesque, giant outlines; ever shifting and running along the ground with silent feet, or leaping into the air with sharp cries as the gusts twisted them inwardly and lent them voice. More and more I pushed my pace, and more and more darkness and vapour obliterated the landscape.

The going was not otherwise difficult, and here and there cowslips glimmered in patches of dancing yellow, while the springy turf made it easy to keep up speed; yet in the gloom I frequently tripped and plunged into prickly gorse near the ground, so that from shin to knee was soon a-tingle with sharp pain. Odd puffs and spits of rain stung my face, and the periods of utter stillness were always followed by little shouting gusts of wind, each time from a new direction. Troubled is perhaps too strong a word, but flustered I certainly was; and though I recognised that it was due to my being in an environment so remote from the town life I was accustomed to, I found it impossible to stifle altogether the feeling of malaise that had crept into my heart, and I looked about with increasing eagerness for the lighted windows of Bassett's cottage.

More and more, little pin-pricks of distress and confusion accumulated, adding to my realisation of being away from streets and shop-windows, and things I could classify and deal with. The mist, too, distorted as well as concealed, played tricks with sounds as well as with sights. And, once or twice, when I stumbled upon some crouching sheep, they got up without the customary alarm and hurry of sheep, and moved off slowly into the darkness, but in such a singular way that I could almost have sworn they were not sheep at all, but human beings crawling on all-fours, looking back and grimacing at me over their shoulders as they went. On these occasions—for there were more than one—I never could get close enough to feel their woolly wet backs, as I should have liked to do; and the sound of their tinkling bells came faintly through the mist, sometimes from one direction, sometimes from another, sometimes all round me as though a whole flock surrounded me; and I found it impossible to analyse or explain the idea I received that they were *not* sheep-bells at all, but something quite different.

But mist and darkness, and a certain confusion of the senses caused by the excitement of an utterly strange environment, can account for a great deal. I pushed on quickly. The conviction that I had strayed from the route grew, nevertheless, for occasionally there was a great commotion of seagulls about me, as though I had disturbed them in their sleeping-places. The air filled with their plaintive cries, and I heard the rushing of multitudinous wings, sometimes very close to my head, but always invisible owing to the mist. And once, above the swishing of the wet wind through the gorse-bushes, I was sure I caught the faint thunder of the sea and the distant crashing of waves rolling up some steep-throated gully in the cliffs. I went cautiously after this, and altered my course a little away from the direction of the sound.

Yet, increasingly all the time, it came to me how the cries of the sea-birds sounded like laughter, and how the everlasting wind blew and drove about me with a purpose, and how the low bushes persistently took the shape of stooping people, moving stealthily past me, and how the mist more and more resembled huge protean figures escorting me across the desolate hills, silently, with immense footsteps. For the inanimate world now touched my awakened poetic sense in a manner hitherto unguided, and became fraught with the pregnant messages of a dimly concealed life. I readily understood, for the first time, how easily a superstitious peasantry might people their world, and how even an educated mind might favour an atmosphere of legend. I stumbled along, looking anxiously for the lights of the cottage.

Suddenly, as a shape of writhing mist whirled past, I received so direct a stroke of wind that it was palpably a blow in the face. Something swept by with a shrill cry into the darkness. It was impossible to prevent jumping to one side and raising an arm by way of protection, and I was only just quick enough to catch a glimpse of the sea-gull as it raced past, with suddenly altered flight, beating its powerful wings over my head. Its white body looked enormous as the mist swallowed it. At the same moment a gust tore my hat from my head and flung the flap of my coat across my eyes. But I was well-trained by this time, and made a quick dash after the retreating black object, only to find on overtaking it that I held a prickly branch of gorse. The wind combed my hair viciously.

Then, out of a corner of my eye, I saw my hat still rolling, and grabbed swiftly at it; but just as I closed on it, the real hat passed in front of me, turning over in the wind like a ball, and I instantly released my first capture to chase it. Before it was within reach, another one shot between my feet so that I stepped on it. The grass seemed covered with moving hats, yet each one, when I seized it, turned into a piece of wood, or a tiny gorse-bush, or a black rabbit hole, till my hands were scored with prickles and running blood. In the darkness, I reflected, all objects looked alike, as though by general conspiracy. I straightened up and took a long breath, mopping the blood with my handkerchief. Then something tapped at my feet, and on looking down, there was the hat within easy reach, and I stooped down and put it on my head again. Of course, there were a dozen ways of explaining my confusion and stupidity, and I walked along wondering which to select. My eyesight, for one thing—and under such conditions why seek further? It was nothing, after all, and the dizziness was a momentary effect caused by the effort and stooping.

But for all that, I shouted aloud, on the chance that a wandering shepherd might hear me; and of course no answer came, for it was like calling in a padded room, and the mist suffocated my voice and killed its resonance.

It was really very discouraging: I was cold and wet and hungry; my legs and clothes torn by the gorse, my hands scratched and bleeding; the wind brought water to my eyes by its constant buffeting, and my skin was numb from contact with the chill mist. Fortunately I had matches, and after some difficulty, by crouching under a wall, I caught a swift glimpse of my watch, and saw that it was but little after eight o'clock. Supper I knew was at nine, and I was surely over half-way by this time. But here again was another instance of the way everything seemed in a conspiracy against me to appear otherwise than ordinary, for in the gleam of the match my watch-glass showed as the face of a little old gray man, uncommonly like the folk-lorist himself, peering up at me with an expression of whimsical laughter. My own reflection it could not possibly have been, for I am clean-shaven, and this face looked up at me through a running tangle of gray hair. Yet a second and third match revealed only the white surface with the thin black hands moving across it.

2

And it was at this point, I well remember, that I reached what was for me the true heart of the adventure, the little fragment of real experience I learned from it and took back with me to my doctor's life in London, and that has remained with me ever since, and helped me to a new sympathetic insight into the intricacies of certain curious mental cases I had never before really understood.

For it was sufficiently obvious by now that a curious change had been going forward in me for some time, dating, so far as I could focus my thoughts sufficiently to analyse, from the moment of my speech with that hurrying man of shadow on the hillside. And the first deliberate manifestation of the change, now that I looked back, was surely the awakening in my prosaic being of the "poetic thrill"; my sudden amazing appreciation of the world around me as something alive. From that moment the change in me had worked ahead subtly, swiftly. Yet, so natural had been the beginning of it, that although it was a radically new departure for my temperament, I was hardly aware at first of what had actually come about; and it was only now, after so many encounters, that I was forced at length to acknowledge it.

It came the more forcibly too, because my very commonplace ideas of beauty had hitherto always been associated with sunshine and crude effects; yet here this new revelation leaped to me out of wind and mist and desolation on a lonely hillside, out of night, darkness, and discomfort. New values rushed upon me from all sides. Everything had changed, and the very simplicity with which the new values presented themselves proved to me how profound the change, the readjustment, had been. In such trivial things the evidence had come that I was not aware of it until repetition forced my attention: the veils rising from valley and hill; the mountain tops as personalities that shout or murmur in the darkness; the crying of the sea birds and of the living, purposeful wind; above all, the feeling that Nature about me was instinct with a life differing from my own in degree rather than in kind; everything, from the conspiracy of the gorse-bushes to the disappearing hat, showed that a fundamental attitude of mind in me had changed—and changed, too, without my knowledge or consent.

Moreover, at the same time the deep sadness of beauty had entered my heart like a stroke; for all this mystery and loveliness, I realized poignantly was utterly independent and careless of *me*, as me; and that while I must pass, decay, grow old, these manifestations would remain forever young and unalterably potent. And thus gradually had I become permeated with the recognition of a region hitherto unknown to me, and that I had always depreciated in others and especially, it now occurred to me, in my friend the old folk-lorist.

Here surely, I thought, was the beginning of conditions which, carried a little further, must become pathogenic. That the change was real and pregnant I had no doubt whatever. My consciousness was expanding and I had caught it in the very act. I had of course read much concerning the changes of personality, swift, kaleidoscopic—

had come across something of it in my practice—and had listened to the folk-lorist holding forth like a man inspired upon ways and means of reaching concealed regions of the human consciousness, and opening it to the knowledge of things called magical, so that one became free of a larger universe. But it was only now for the first time, on these bare hills, in touch with the wind and the rain, that I realized in how simple a fashion the frontiers of consciousness could shift this way and that, or with what touch of genuine awe the certainty might come that one stood on the borderland of new, untried, perhaps dangerous, experiences.

At any rate, it did now come to me that my consciousness had shifted its frontiers very considerably, and that whatever might happen must seem not abnormal, but quite simple and inevitable, and of course utterly true. This very simplicity, however, doing no violence to my being, brought with it none the less a sense of dread and discomfort; and my dim awareness that unknown possibilities were about me in the night puzzled and distressed me perhaps more than I cared to admit.

3

All this that takes so long to describe became apparent to me in a few seconds. What I had always despised ascended the throne.

But with the finding of Bassett's cottage, as a sign-post close to home, my former *sang-froid*, my stupidity, would doubtless return, and my relief was therefore considerable when at length a faint gleam of light appeared through the mist, against which the square dark shadow of the chimney-line pointed upwards. After all, I had not strayed so very far out of the way. Now I could definitely ascertain where I was wrong.

Quickening my pace, I scrambled over a broken stone wall, and almost ran across the open bit of grass to the door. One moment the black outline of the cottage was there in front of me, and the next, when I stood actually against it—there was nothing! I laughed to think how utterly I had been deceived. Yet not utterly, for as I groped back again over the wall, the cottage loomed up a little to the left, with its windows lighted and friendly, and I had only been mistaken in my angle of approach after all. Yet again, as I hurried to the door, the mist drove past and thickened a second time—and the cottage was not where I had seen it!

My confusion increased a lot after that. I scrambled about in all directions, rather foolishly hurried, and over countless stone walls it seemed, and completely dazed as to the true points of the compass. Then suddenly, just when a kind of despair came over me, the cottage stood there solidly before my eyes, and I found myself not two feet from the door. Was ever mist before so deceptive? And there, just behind it, I made out the row of pines like a dark wave breaking through the night. I sniffed the wet resinous odour with joy, and a genuine thrill ran through me as I saw the unmistakable yellow light of the windows. At last I was near home and my troubles would soon be over.

A cloud of birds rose with shrill cries off the roof and whirled into the darkness when I knocked with my stick on the door, and human voices, I was almost certain, mingled somewhere with them, though it was impossible to tell whether they were within the cottage or outside. It all sounded confusedly with a rush of air like a little whirlwind, and I stood there rather alarmed at the clamour of my knocking. By way, too, of further proof that my imagination had awakened, the significance of that knocking at the door set something vibrating within me that most surely had never vibrated before, so that I suddenly realized with what atmosphere of mystical suggestion is the mere act of knocking surrounded—*knocking at a door*—both for him who knocks, wondering what shall be revealed on opening, and for him who stands within, waiting for the summons of the knocker. I only know that I hesitated a lot before making up my mind to knock a second time.

And, anyhow, what happened subsequently came in a sort of haze. Words and memory both failed me when I try to record it truthfully, so that even the faces are difficult to visualise again, the words almost impossible to hear.

Before I knew it the door was open and before I could frame the words of my first brief question, I was within the threshold, and the door was shut behind me.

I had expected the little dark and narrow hallway of a cottage, oppressive of air and odour, but instead I came straight into a room that was full of light and full of—people. And the air tasted like the air about a mountain-top.

To the end I never saw what produced the light, nor understood how so many men and women found space to move comfortably to and fro, and pass each other as they did, within the confines of those four walls. An uncomfortable sense of having intruded upon some private gathering was, I think, my first emotion; though how the poverty-stricken country-side could have produced such an assemblage puzzled me beyond belief. And my second emotion—if there was any division at all in the wave of wonder that fairly drenched me—was feeling a sort of glory in the presence of such an atmosphere of splendid and vital *youth*. Everything vibrated, quivered, shook about me, and I almost felt myself as an aged and decrepit man by comparison.

I know my heart gave a great fiery leap as I saw them, for the faces that met me were fine, vigorous, and comely, while burning everywhere through their ripe maturity shone the ardours of youth and a kind of deathless enthusiasm. Old, yet eternally young they were, as rivers and mountains count their years by thousands, yet remain ever youthful; and the first effect of all those pairs of eyes lifted to meet my own was to send a whirlwind of unknown thrills about my heart and make me catch my breath with mingled terror and delight. A fear of death, and at the same time a sensation of touching something vast and eternal that could never die, surged through me.

A deep hush followed my entrance as all turned to look at me. They stood, men and women, grouped about a table, and something about them—not their size alone—conveyed the impression of being *gigantic*, giving me strangely novel realisations of freedom, power, and immense existence more or less than human.

I can only record my thoughts and impressions as they came to me and as I dimly now remember them. I had expected to see old Tom Bassett crouching half asleep over a peat fire, a dim lamp on the table beside him, and instead this assembly of tall and splendid men and women stood there to greet me, and stood in silence. It was little wonder that at first the ready question died upon my lips, and I almost forgot the words of my own language.

"I thought this was Tom Bassett's cottage!" I managed to ask at length, and looked straight at the man nearest me across the table. He had wild hair falling about his shoulders and a face of clear beauty. His eyes, too, like all the rest, seemed shrouded by something veil-like that reminded me of the shadowy man of whom I had first inquired the way. They were *shaded*—and for some reason I was glad they were.

At the sound of my voice, unreal and thin, there was a general movement throughout the room, as though everyone changed places, passing each other like those shapes of fluid sort I had seen outside in the mist. But no answer came. It seemed to me that the mist even penetrated into the room about me and spread inwardly over my thoughts.

"Is this the way to the Manor House?" I asked again, louder, fighting my inward confusion and weakness. "Can *no one* tell me?"

Then apparently everyone began to answer at once, or rather, not to answer directly, but to speak to each other in such a way that I could easily overhear. The voices of the men were deep, and of the women wonderfully musical, with a slow rhythm like that of the sea, or of the wind through the pine-trees outside. But the unsatisfactory nature of what they said only helped to increase my sense of confusion and dismay.

"Yes," said one; "Tom Bassett *was* here for a while with the sheep, but his home was not here."

"He asks the way to a house when he does not even know the way to his own mind!" another voice said, sounding overhead it seemed.

"And could he recognise the signs if we told him?" came in the singing tones of a woman's voice close behind me.

And then, with a noise more like running water, or wind in the wings of birds, than anything else I could liken it to, came several voices together:

"And what sort of way does he seek? The splendid way, or merely the easy?"

"Or the short way of fools!"

"But he must have *some* credentials, or he never could have got as far as this," came from another.

A laugh ran round the room at this, though what there was to laugh at I could not imagine. It sounded like wind rushing about the hills. I got the impression too that the roof was somehow open to the sky, for their laughter had such a spacious quality in it, and the air was so cool and fresh, and moving about in currents and waves.

"It was I who showed him the way," cried a voice belonging to someone who was looking straight into my face over the table. "It was the safest way for him once he had got so far——"

I looked up and met his eye, and the sentence remained unfinished. It was the hurrying, shadowy man of the hillside. He had the same shifting outline as the others now, and the same veiled and shaded eyes, and as I looked the sense of terror stirred and grew in me. I had come in to ask for help, but now I was only anxious to be free of them all and out again in the rain and darkness on the moor. Thoughts of escape filled my brain, and I searched quickly for the door through which I had entered. But nowhere could I discover it again. The walls were bare; not even the windows were visible. And the room seemed to fill and empty of these figures as the waves of the sea fill and empty a cavern, crowding one upon another, yet never occupying more space, or less. So the coming and going of these men and women always evaded me.

And my terror became simply a terror that the veils of their eyes might lift, and that they would look at me with their clear, naked sight. I became horribly aware of their eyes. It was not that I felt them evil, but that I feared the new depths in me their merciless and terrible insight would stir into life. My consciousness had expanded quite enough for one night! I must escape at all costs and claim my own self again, however limited. I must have sanity, even if with limitations, but sanity at any price.

But meanwhile, though I tried hard to find my voice again, there came nothing but a thin piping sound that was like reeds whistling where winds meet about a corner. My throat was contracted, and I could only produce the smallest and most ridiculous of noises. The power of movement, too, was far less than when I first came in, and every moment it became more difficult to use my muscles, so that I stood there, stiff and awkward, face to face with this assemblage of shifting, wonderful people.

"And now," continued the voice of the man who had last spoken, "and now the safest way for him will be through the other door, where he shall see that which he may more easily understand."

With a great effort I regained the power of movement, while at the same time a burst of anger and a determination to be done with it all and to overcome my dreadful confusion drove me forward.

He saw me coming, of course, and the others indeed opened up and made a way for me, shifting to one side or the other whenever I came too near them, and never allowing me to touch them. But at last, when I was close in front of the man, ready both to speak and act, he was no longer there. I never saw the actual change—but instead of a man it was a woman! And when I turned with amazement, I saw that the other occupants walking like figures in some ancient ceremony, were moving slowly toward the far end of the room. One by one, as they filed past, they raised their calm, passionless faces to mine, immensely vital, proud, austere, and then, without further word or gesture, they opened the door I had lost and disappeared through it one by one into the darkness of the night beyond. And as they went it seemed that the mist swallowed them up and a gust of wind caught them away, and the light also went with them, leaving me alone with the figure who had last spoken.

Moreover it was just here that a most disquieting thought flashed through my brain with unreasoning conviction, shaking my personality, as it were, to the foundations: *viz.*, that I had hitherto been spending my life in the pursuit of false knowledge, in the mere classifying and labelling of effects, the analysis of results, scientific so called; whereas it was the folk-lorist, and such like, who with their dreams and prayers were all the time on the path of real knowledge, the trail of causes; that the one was merely adding to the mechanical comfort and safety of the body, ultimately degrading the highest part of man, and never advancing the type, while the other—but then I had never yet believed in a soul—and now was no time to begin, terror or no terror. Clearly, my thoughts were wandering.

4

It was at this moment the sound of the purring first reached me—deep, guttural purring—that made me think at once of some large concealed animal. It was precisely what I had heard many a time at the Zoological Gardens, and I had visions of cows chewing the cud, or horses munching hay in a stall outside the cottage. It was certainly an animal sound, and one of pleasure and contentment.

Semi-darkness filled the room. Only a very faint moonlight, struggling through the mist, came through the window, and I moved back instinctively toward the support of the wall against my back. Somewhere, through openings, came the sound of the night driving over the roof, and far above I had visions of those everlasting winds streaming by with clouds as large as continents on their wings. Something in me wanted to sing and shout, but something else in me at the same time was in a very vivid state of unreasoning terror. I felt immense, yet tiny, confident, yet timid; a part of huge, universal forces, yet an utterly small, personal, and very limited being.

In the corner of the room on my right stood the woman. Her face was hid by a mass of tumbling hair, that made me think of living grasses on a field in June. Thus her head was partially turned from me, and the moonlight, catching her outline, just revealed it against the wall like an impressionist picture. Strange hidden memories stirred in the depths of me, and for a moment I felt that I knew all about her. I stared about me quickly, nervously, trying to take in everything at once. Then the purring sound grew much louder and closer, and I forgot my notion that this woman was no stranger to me and that

I knew her as well as I knew myself. That purring thing was in the room close beside me. Between us two, indeed, it was, for I now saw that her arm nearest to me was raised, and that she was pointing to the wall in front of us.

Following the direction of her hand, I saw that the wall was transparent, and that I could see through a portion of it into a small square space beyond, as though I was looking through gauze instead of bricks. This small inner space was lighted, and on stooping down I saw that it was a sort of cupboard or cell-like cage let into the wall. The thing that purred was there in the centre of it.

I looked closer. It was a being, apparently a *human* being, crouched down in its narrow cage, feeding. I saw the body stooping over a quantity of coarse-looking, piled-up substance that was evidently food. It was like a man huddled up. There it squatted, happy and contented, with the minimum of air, light, and space, dully satisfied with its prisoned cage behind the bars, utterly unconscious of the vast world about it, grunting with pleasure, purring like a great cat, scornfully ignorant of what might lie beyond. The cell, moreover, I saw was a perfect masterpiece of mechanical contrivance and inventive ingenuity—the very last word in comfort, safety and scientific skill.

I was in the act of trying to fit in my memory some of the details of its construction and arrangement, when I made a chance noise, and at once became too agitated to note carefully what I saw. For at the noise the creature turned, and I saw that it *was* a human being—a man. I was aware of a face close against my own as it pressed forward, but a face with embryonic features impossible to describe and utterly loathsome, with eyes, ears, nose and skin, only just sufficiently alive and developed to transfer the minimum of gross sensation to the brain. The mouth, however, was large and thick-lipped, and the jaws were still moving in the act of slow mastication.

I shrank back, shuddering with mingled pity and disgust, and at the same moment the woman beside me called me softly *by my own name*. She had moved forward a little so that she stood quite close to me, full in the thin stream of moonlight that fell across the floor, and I was conscious of a swift transition from hell to heaven as my gaze passed from that embryonic visage to a countenance so refined, so majestic, so divinely sensitive in its strength, that it was like turning from the face of a devil to look upon the features of a goddess.

At the same instant I was aware that both beings—the creature and the woman—were moving rapidly toward me.

A pain like a sharp sword dived deep down into me and twisted horribly through my heart, for as I saw them coming I realized in one swift moment of terrible intuition that they had their life in me, that they were born of my own being, and were indeed *projections of myself.* They were portions of my consciousness projected outwardly into objectivity, and their degree of reality was just as great as that of any other part of me.

With a dreadful swiftness they rushed toward me, and in a single second had merged themselves into my own being; and I understood in some marvellous manner beyond the possibility of doubt that they were symbolic of my own soul: the dull animal part of me that had hitherto acknowledged nothing beyond its cage of minute sensations, and the higher part, almost out of reach, and in touch with the stars, that for the first time had feebly awakened into life during my journey over the hill.

5

I forget altogether how it was that I escaped, whether by the window or the door. I only know I found myself a moment later making great speed over the moor, followed by screaming birds and shouting winds, straight on the track downhill toward the Manor House. Something must have guided me, for I went with the instinct of an animal, having no uncertainties as to turnings, and saw the welcome lights of windows before I had covered another mile. And all the way I felt as though a great sluice gate had been opened to let a flood of new perceptions rush like a sea over my inner being, so that I was half ashamed and half delighted, partly angry, yet partly happy.

Servants met me at the door, several of them, and I was aware at once an atmosphere of commotion in the house. I arrived breathless and hatless, wet to the skin, my hands scratched and my boots caked with mud.

"We made sure you were lost, sir," I heard the old butler say, and I heard my own reply, faintly, like the voice of someone else:

"I thought so too."

A minute later I found myself in the study, with the old folk-lorist standing opposite. In his hands he held the book I had brought down for him in my bag, ready addressed. There was a curious smile on his face.

"It never occurred to me that you would dare to *walk*—tonight of all nights," he was saying.

I stared without a word. I was bursting with the desire to tell him something of what had happened and try to be patient with his explanations, but when I sought for words and sentences my story seemed suddenly flat and pointless, and the details of my adventure began to evaporate and melt away, and seemed hard to remember.

"I had an exciting walk," I stammered, still a little breathless from running. "The weather was all right when I started from the station."

"The weather is all right still," he said, "though you may have found some evening mist on the top of the hills. But it's not that I meant."

"What then?"

"I meant," he said, still laughing quizzically, "that you were a very brave man to walk tonight over the enchanted hills, because this is May Day eve, and on May Day eve, you know, *They* have power over the minds of men, and can put glamour upon the imagination——"

"Who—'*they*?' What do you mean?"

He put my book down on the table beside him and looked quietly for a moment into my eyes, and as he did so the memory of my adventure began to revive in detail, and I thought quickly of the shadowy man who had shown me the way first. What could it have been in the face of the old folk-lorist that made me think of this man? A dozen things ran like flashes through my excited mind, and while I attempted to seize them I heard the old man's voice continue. He seemed to be talking to himself as much as to me.

"The elemental beings you have always scoffed at, of course; they who operate ceaselessly behind the screen of appearances, and who fashion and mould the moods of the mind. And an extremist like you—for extremes are always dangerously weak—is their legitimate prey."

"Pshaw!" I interrupted him, knowing that my manner betrayed me hopelessly, and that he had guessed much. "Any man may have subjective experiences, I suppose——"

Then I broke off suddenly. The change in his face made me start; it had taken on for the moment so exactly the look of the man on the hillside. The eyes gazing so steadily into mine had shadows in them, I thought.

"*Glamour!*" he was saying, "all glamour! One of them must have come very close to you, or perhaps touched you." Then he asked sharply, "Did you meet anyone? Did you speak with anyone?"

"I came by Tom Bassett's cottage," I said. "I didn't feel quite sure of my way and I went in and asked."

"All glamour," he repeated to himself, and then aloud to me, "and as for Bassett's cottage, it was burnt down three years ago, and nothing stands there now but broken, roofless walls——"

He stopped because I had seized him by the arm. In the shadows of the lamp-lit room behind him I thought I caught sight of dim forms moving past the bookshelves. But when my eye tried to focus them they faded and slipped away again into ceiling and walls. The details of the hilltop cottage, however, started into life again at the sight, and I seized my friend's arm to tell him. But instantly, when I tried, it all faded away again as though it had been a dream, and I could recall nothing intelligible to repeat to him.

He looked at me and laughed.

"They always obliterate the memory afterward," he said gently, "so that little remains beyond a mood, or an emotion, to show how profoundly deep their touch has been. Though sometimes part of the change remains and becomes permanent—as I hope in your case it may."

Then, before I had time to answer, to swear, or to remonstrate, he stepped briskly past me and closed the door into the hall, and then drew me aside farther into the room. The change that I could not understand was still working in his face and eyes.

"If you have courage enough left to come with me," he said, speaking very seriously, "we will go out again and see more. Up till midnight, you know, there is still the opportunity, and with me perhaps you won't feel so—so——"

It was impossible somehow to refuse; everything combined to make me go. We had a little food and then went out into the hall, and he clapped a wide-awake on his gray hairs. I took a cloak and seized a walking-stick from the stand. I really hardly knew what I was doing. The new world I had awakened to seemed still a-quiver about me.

As we passed out on to the gravel drive the light from the hall windows fell upon his face, and I saw that the change I had been so long observing was nearing its completeness, for there breathed about him that keen, wonderful atmosphere of eternal youth I had felt upon the inmates of the cottage. He seemed to have gone back forty years; a veil was gathering over his eyes; and I could have sworn that somehow his stature had increased, and that he moved beside me with a vigour and power I had never seen in him before.

And as we began to climb the hill together in silence I saw that the stars were clear overhead and there was no mist, that the trees stood motionless without wind, and that beyond us on the summit of the hills there were lights dancing to and fro, appearing and disappearing like the inflection of stars in water.

The Box With the Iron Clamps

By Florence Marryat

1

Molton Chase is a charming, old-fashioned country house, which
has been in the possession of the Clayton family for centuries past;
and as Harry Clayton, its present owner, has plenty of money, and
(having tasted the pleasures of matrimony for only five years) has no
knowledge (as yet) of the delights of college and school bills coming in at Christmas-time, it is his will to fill the Chase at that season
with guests, to each of whom he extends a welcome, as hearty as it is
sincere.

"Bella! are you not going to join the riding-party this afternoon?"
he said across the luncheon-table to his wife, one day in a December
not long ago.

"Bella" was a dimpled little woman, whose artless expression of
countenance would well bear comparison with the honest, genial face
opposite to her, and who replied at once—

"No! not this afternoon, Harry, dear. You know the Damers may
come at any time between this and seven o'clock, and I should not
like to be out when they arrive."

"And may I ask Mrs. Clayton who *are* the Damers," inquired a
friend of her husband, who, on account of being handsome, considered himself licensed to be pert—"that their advent should be the
cause of our losing the pleasure of your company this afternoon?"

But the last thing Bella Clayton ever did was to take offence.

"The Damers are my cousins, Captain Moss," she replied; "at least
Blanche Damer is."

At this juncture a dark-eyed man who was sitting at the other end
of the table dropped the flirting converse he had been maintaining
with a younger sister of Mrs. Clayton's, and appeared to become in-

terested in what his hostess was saying.

"Colonel Damer," he continued, "has been in India for the last twelve years, and only returned to England a month ago; therefore it would seem unkind on the first visit he has paid to his relatives that there should be no one at home to welcome him."

"Has Mrs. Damer been abroad for as long a time?" resumed her questioner, a vision arising on his mental faculties of a lemon-coloured woman with shoes down at heel.

"Oh dear no!" replied his hostess. "Blanche came to England about five years ago, but her health has been too delicate to rejoin her husband in India since. Have we all finished, Harry, dear?"—and in another minute the luncheon-table was cleared.

As Mrs. Clayton crossed the hall soon afterwards to visit her nursery, the same dark-eyed man who had regarded her fixedly when she mentioned the name of Blanche Damer followed and accosted her.

"Is it long since you have seen your cousin Mrs. Damer, Mrs. Clayton?"

"I saw her about three years ago, Mr. Laurence; but she had a severe illness soon after that, and has been living on the Continent ever since. Why do you ask?"

"For no especial reason," he answered smiling. "Perhaps I am a little jealous lest this new-comer to whose arrival you look forward with so much interest should usurp more of your time and attention than we less-favoured ones can spare."

He spoke with a degree of sarcasm, real or feigned, which Mrs. Clayton immediately resented.

"I am not aware that I have been in the habit of neglecting my guests, Mr. Laurence," she replied; "but my cousin Blanche is more likely to remind me of my duties than to tempt me to forget them."

"Forgive me," he said, earnestly. "You have mistaken my meaning altogether. But are you very intimate with this lady?"

"Very much so," was the answer. "We were brought up together, and loved each other as sisters until she married and went to India. For some years after her return home our intercourse was renewed, and only broken, on the occasion of her being ill and going abroad, as I have described to you. Her husband, I have, of course, seen less of, but I like what I know of him, and am anxious to show them both all the hospitality in my power. She is a charming creature, and I am sure you will admire her."

"Doubtless I shall," he replied; "that is if she does not lay claim to all Mrs. Clayton's interest in the affairs of Molton Chase."

"No fear of that," laughed the cheery little lady as she ascended the stairs, and left Mr. Laurence standing in the hall beneath.

"Clayton," observed that gentleman, as he re-entered the luncheon-room and drew his host into the privacy of a bay-window, "I really am afraid I shall have to leave you this evening—if you won't think it rude of me to go so suddenly."

"But *why*, my dear fellow?" exclaimed Harry Clayton, as his blue eyes searched into the other's soul. "What earthly reason can you have for going, when your fixed plan was to stay with us over Christmas Day?"

"Well! there is lots of work waiting for me to do, you know; and really the time slips away so, and time is money to a slave like myself—that—"

"Now, my dear Laurence," said Harry Clayton conclusively, "you know you are only making excuses. All the work that was absolutely necessary for you to do before Christmas was finished before you came here, and you said you felt yourself licensed to take a whole month's holiday. Now, was not that the case?"

Mr. Laurence could not deny the fact, and so he looked undecided, and was silent.

"Don't let me hear any more about your going before Christmas Day," said his host, "or I shall be offended, and so will Bella; to say nothing of Bella's sister—eh, Laurence!"

Whereupon Mr. Laurence felt himself bound to remain; and saying in his own mind that fate was against him, dropped the subject of his departure altogether.

One hour later, the riding party being then some miles from Molton Chase, a travelling carriage laden with trunks drove up to the house, and Mrs. Clayton, all blushes and smiles, stood on the hall-steps to welcome her expected guests.

Colonel Damer was the first to alight. He was a middle-aged man, but with a fine soldierly bearing, which took off from his years; and he was so eager to see to the safe exit of his wife from the carriage-door that he had not time to do more than take off his hat to blooming Bella on the steps.

"Now, my love," he exclaimed as the lady's form appeared, "pray take care; two steps: that's right—here you are, safe."

And then Mrs. Damer, being securely landed, was permitted to fly into the cousinly arms which were opened to receive her.

"My dear Bella!"

"My dearest Blanche—I am so delighted to see you again. Why, you are positively frozen! Pray come in at once to the fire. Colonel Damer, my servants will see to the luggage—do leave it to them, and come and warm yourselves."

A couple of men-servants now came forward and offered to see to the unloading of the carriage—but Mrs. Damer did not move.

"Will you not go in, my love, as your cousin proposes?" said her husband. "I can see to the boxes if you should wish me to do so."

"No, thank you," was the low reply; and there was such a ring of melancholy in the voice of Mrs. Damer that a stranger would have been attracted by it. "I prefer waiting until the carriage is unpacked."

"Never mind the luggage, Blanche," whispered Mrs. Clayton, in her coaxing manner. "Come in to the fire, dear—I have so much to tell you."

"Wait a minute, Bella," said her cousin; and the entreaty was so firm that it met with no further opposition.

"One—two—three—four," exclaimed Colonel Damer, as the boxes successively came to the ground. "I am afraid you will think we are going to take you by storm, Mrs. Clayton; but perhaps you know my wife's fancy for a large travelling *kit* of old. Is that all, Blanche?"

"That is all—thank you," in the same low melancholy tones in which she had spoken before. "Now, Bella, dear, which is to be my room?"

"You would rather go there first, Blanche?"

"Yes, please—I'm tired. Will you carry up that box for me?" she continued, pointing out one of the trunks to the servant.

"Directly, ma'am," he returned, as he was looking for change for a sovereign wherewith to accommodate Colonel Damer—but the lady lingered until he was at leisure. Then he shouldered the box next to the one she had indicated, and she directed his attention to the fact, and made him change his burden.

"They'll all go up in time, ma'am," the man remarked; but Mrs. Damer, answering nothing, did not set her foot upon the stairs until he was halfway up them, with the trunk she had desired him to take first.

Then she leaned wearily upon Bella Clayton's arm, pressing it fondly to her side, and so the two went together to the bedroom which had been appointed for the reception of the new guests. It was a large and cosily-furnished apartment, with a dressing-room opening from it. When the ladies arrived there they found the servant awaiting them with the box in question.

"Where will you have it placed, ma'am?" he demanded of Mrs. Damer.

"Under the bed, please."

But the bedstead was a French one, and the mahogany sides were so deep that nothing could get beneath them but dust; and the trunk, although small, was heavy and strong and clamped with iron, not at all the sort of trunk that would go *anywhere*.

"Nothing will go under the bed, ma'am!" said the servant in reply.

Mrs. Damer slightly changed colour.

"Never mind then: leave it there. Oh! what a comfort a good fire is," she continued, turning to the hearth-rug, and throwing herself into an arm-chair. "We have had such a cold drive from the station."

"But about your box, Blanche?" said Mrs. Clayton, who had no idea of her friends being put to any inconvenience. "It can't stand there; you'll unpack it, won't you? or shall I have it moved into the passage?"

"Oh, no, thank you, Bella—please let it stand where it is: it will do very well indeed."

"What will do very well?" exclaimed Colonel Damer, who now entered the bedroom, followed by a servant with another trunk.

"Only Blanche's box, Colonel Damer," said Bella Clayton. "She doesn't wish to unpack it, and it will be in her way here, I'm afraid. It *might* stand in your dressing-room."—This she said as a "feeler," knowing that some gentlemen do not like to be inconvenienced, even in their dressing-rooms.

But Colonel Damer was as unselfish as it was possible for an old Indian to be.

"Of course it can," he replied. "Here (to the servant), just shoulder that box, will you, and move it into the next room."

The man took up the article in question rather carelessly, and nearly let it fall again. Mrs. Damer darted forward as if to save it.

"Pray put it down," she said, nervously. "I have no wish to have it moved—I shall require it by-and-by; it will be no inconvenience—"

"Just as you like, dear," said Mrs. Clayton, who was becoming rather tired of the little discussion. "And now take off your things, dear Blanche, and let me ring for some tea."

Colonel Damer walked into his dressing-room and left the two ladies alone. The remainder of the luggage was brought upstairs; the tea was ordered and served, and whilst Mrs. Clayton busied herself in pouring it out, Mrs. Damer sank back upon a sofa which stood by the fire, and conversed with her cousin.

She had been beautiful, this woman, in her earlier youth, though no one would have thought it to see her now. As Bella handed her the tea she glanced towards the thin hand stretched out to receive it, and from thence to the worn face and hollow eyes, and could scarcely believe she saw the same person she had parted from three years before.

But she had not been so intimate with her of late, and she was almost afraid of commenting upon her cousin's altered appearance, for fear it might wound her; all she said was:

"You look very delicate still, dear Blanche; I was in hopes the change to the Continent would have set you up and made you stronger than you were when you left England."

"Oh, no; I never shall be well again," was Mrs. Damer's careless reply: "it's an old story now, Bella, and it's no use talking about it. Whom have you staying in the house at present, dear?"

"Well, we are nearly full," rejoined Mrs. Clayton. "There is my old godfather, General Knox—you remember him, I know—and his son and daughter; and the Ainsleys and their family; *ditto*, the Bayleys and the Armstrongs, and then, for single men, we have young Brooke, and Harry's old friend, Charley Moss, and Herbert Laurence, and—are you ill, Blanchey?"

An exclamation had burst from Mrs. Damer—hardly an exclamation, so much as a half-smothered cry—but whether of pain or fear, it was hard to determine.

"Are you ill?" reiterated Mrs. Clayton, full of anxiety for her fragile-looking cousin.

"No," replied Blanche Damer, pressing her hand to her side, but still deadly pale from the effect of whatever emotion she had gone through; "it is nothing; I feel faint after our long journey."

Colonel Damer had also heard the sound, and now appeared upon the threshold of his dressing-room. He was one of those well-meaning, but fussy men, who can never have two women alone for a quarter of an hour without intruding on their privacy.

"Did you call, my dearest?" he asked of his wife. "Do you want anything?"

"Nothing, thank you," replied Bella for her cousin; "Blanche is only a little tired and overcome by her travelling."

"I think, after all, that I will move that trunk away for you into my room," he said, advancing towards the box which had already been the subject of discussion. Mrs. Damer started from the sofa with a face of crimson.

"I *beg* you will leave my boxes alone," she said, with an imploring tone in her voice which was quite unfitted to the occasion. "I have not brought one more than I need, and I wish them to remain under my own eye."

"There must be something very valuable in that receptacle," said Colonel Damer, facetiously, as he beat a retreat to his own quarters.

"Is it your linen box?" demanded Mrs. Clayton of her cousin.

"Yes," in a hesitating manner; "that is, it contains several things that I have in daily use; but go on about your visitors, Bella: are there any more?"

"I don't think so: where had I got to?—oh! to the bachelors: well, there are Mr. Brooke and Captain Moss, and Mr. Laurence (the poet, you know; Harry was introduced to him last season by Captain Moss), and my brother Alfred; and that's all."

"A very respectable list," said Mrs. Damer, languidly. "What kind of a man is the—the poet you spoke of?"

"Laurence?—oh, he seems a very pleasant man; but he is very silent and abstracted, as I suppose a poet should be. My sister Carrie is here, and they have quite got up a flirtation together; however, I don't suppose it will come to anything."

"And your nursery department?"

"Thriving, thank you; I think you *will* be astonished to see my boy. Old Mrs. Clayton says he is twice the size that Harry was at that age; and the little girls can run about and talk almost as well as I can. But I must not expect you, Blanche, to take the same interest in babies that I do."

This she added, remembering that the woman before her was childless. Mrs. Damer moved uneasily on her couch, but she said nothing; and soon after the sound of a gong reverberating through the hall warned Mrs. Clayton that the dinner was not far off and the riding-party must have returned; so, leaving her friend to her toilet, she took her departure.

As she left the room, Mrs. Damer was alone. She had no maid of her own, and she had refused the offices of Mrs. Clayton, assuring her that she was used to dress herself; but she made little progress in that department, as she lay on the couch in the firelight, with her face buried in her hands, and thoughts coursing through her mind of which heaven alone knew the tendency.

"Come, my darling," said the kind, coaxing voice of her husband, as, after knocking more than once without receiving any answer, he entered her room, fully dressed, and found her still arrayed in her travelling things, and none of her boxes unpacked. "You will never be ready for dinner at this rate. Shall I make an excuse for your not appearing at table this evening? I am sure Mrs. Clayton would wish you to keep your room if you are too tired to dress."

"I am not too tired, Harry," said Mrs. Damer, rising from the couch, "and I shall be ready in ten minutes," unlocking and turning over the contents of a box as she spoke.

"Better not, perhaps, my love," interposed the colonel, in mild expostulation; "you will be better in bed, and can see your kind friends tomorrow morning."

"I am going down to dinner tonight," she answered, gently, but decisively. She was a graceful woman now she stood on her feet, and threw off the heavy wraps in which she had travelled, with a slight, willowy figure, and a complexion which was almost transparent in its delicacy; but her face was very thin, and her large blue eyes had a scared and haggard look in them, which was scarcely less painful to witness than the appearance of anxiety which was expressed by the knitted brows by which they were surmounted. As she now raised her fair attenuated hands to rearrange her hair, which had once been abundant and glossy, her husband could not avoid remarking upon the change which had passed over it.

"I had no idea you had lost your hair so much, darling," he said; "I have not seen it down before tonight. Why, where is it all gone to?" he continued, as he lifted the light mass in his hands, and remembered of what a length and weight it used to be, when he last parted from her.

"Oh, I don't know," she rejoined, sadly; "gone, with my youth, I suppose, Henry."

"My poor girl!" he said, gently, "you have suffered very much in this separation. I had no right to leave you alone for so many years. But it is all over now, dearest, and I will take such good care of you that you will be obliged to get well and strong again."

She turned round suddenly from the glass, and pressed her lips upon the hand which held her hair.

"Don't," she murmured; "pray don't speak to me so, Henry! I can't bear it; I can't indeed!"

He thought it was from excess of feeling that she spoke; and so it was, though not as he imagined. So he changed the subject lightly, and bade her be lazy no longer, but put on her dress, if she was really determined to make one of the party at dinner that evening.

In another minute, Mrs. Damer had brushed her diminished hair into the fashion in which she ordinarily wore it; thrown on an evening-robe of black, which, while it contrasted well with her fairness, showed the falling away of her figure in a painful degree; and was ready to accompany her husband downstairs.

They were met at the door of the drawing-room by their host, who was eager to show cordiality towards guests of whom his wife thought so much, and having also been acquainted himself with Mrs. Damer since her return to England. He led her up to the sofa whereon Bella sat; and, dinner being almost immediately announced, the little hostess was busy pairing off her couples.

"Mr. Laurence!" she exclaimed; and then looking around the room, "where *is* Mr. Laurence?" So that that gentleman was forced to leave the window-curtains, behind which he had ensconced himself, and advance into the centre of the room. "Oh, here you are at last; will you take Mrs. Damer down to dinner?" and proceeding immediately with the usual form of introduction—"Mr. Laurence—Mrs. Damer."

They bowed to each other; but over the lady's face, as she went through her share of the introduction, there passed so indescribable, and yet so unmistakable a change, that Mrs. Clayton, although not very quick, could not help observing it, and she said, involuntarily—

"Have you met Mr. Laurence before, Blanche?"

"I believe I have had that pleasure—in London—many years ago."

The last words came out so faintly that they were almost undistinguishable.

"Why didn't you tell me so?" said Bella Clayton, reproachfully, to Mr. Laurence.

He was beginning to stammer out some excuse about its having been so long ago, when Mrs. Damer came to his aid, in her clear, cold voice—

"It *was* very long ago: we must both be forgiven for having forgotten the circumstance."

"Well, you must renew your acquaintanceship at dinner," said Mrs. Clayton, blithely, as she trotted off to make matters pleasant between the rest of her visitors. As she did so, Mr. Laurence remained standing by the sofa, but he did not attempt to address Mrs. Damer. Only, when the room was nearly cleared, he held out his arm to her, and she rose to accept it. But the next minute she had sunk back again upon the sofa, and Mrs. Clayton was at her cousin's side. Mrs. Damer had fainted.

"Poor darling!" exclaimed Colonel Damer, as he pressed forward to the side of his wife. "I was afraid coming down tonight would be too much for her, but she would make the attempt; she has so much spirit. Pray don't delay the dinner, Mrs. Clayton; I will stay by her, if you will excuse the apparent rudeness, until she is sufficiently recovered to go to bed."

But even as he spoke his wife raised herself from the many arms which supported her, and essayed to gain her feet.

"Bella, dear! I am all right again. Pray, if you love me, don't make a scene about a little fatigue. I often faint now: let me go up to my bedroom and lie down, as I ought to have done at first, and I shall be quite well tomorrow morning."

She would accept no one's help—not even her husband's, though it distressed him greatly that she refused it—but walked out of the room of her own accord, and toiled wearily up the staircase which led her to the higher stories; whilst more than one pair of eyes watched her ascent, and more than one appetite was spoilt for the coming meal.

"Don't you think that Blanche is looking very ill?" demanded Bella Clayton of Colonel Damer, at the dinner-table. She had been much struck herself with the great alteration in her cousin's looks, and fancied that her husband was not so alarmed about it as he ought to be.

"I do, indeed," he replied; "but it is the last thing she will acknowledge herself. She has very bad spirits and appetite; appears always in a low fever, and is so nervous that the least thing will frighten her. That, to me, is the worst and most surprising change of all: such a high-couraged creature as she used to be."

"Yes, indeed," replied Mrs. Clayton; "I can hardly imagine Blanche being nervous at anything. It must have come on since her visit to the Continent, for she was not so when she stayed here last."

"When was that?" demanded the colonel, anxiously.

"Just three years ago this Christmas," was the answer. "I don't think I ever saw her look better than she did then, and she was the life of the house. But soon afterwards she went to Paris, and then we heard of her illness, and this is my first meeting with her since that time. I was very much shocked when she got out of the carriage: I should scarcely have known her again." Here Mrs. Clayton stopped, seeing that the attention of Mr. Laurence, who sat opposite to her, appeared to be riveted on her words, and Colonel Damer relapsed into thought and spoke no more.

In the meanwhile Mrs. Damer had gained her bedroom. Women had come to attend upon her, sent by their mistress, and laden with offers of refreshment and help of every kind, but she had dismissed them and chosen to be alone. She felt too weak to be very restless, but she had sat by the fire and cried, until she was so exhausted that her bed suggested itself to her, as the best place in which she could be; but rising to undress, preparatory to seeking it, she had nearly fallen, and catching feebly at the bedpost had missed it, and sunk down by the side of the solid black box, which was clamped with iron and fastened with a padlock, and respecting which she had been so particular a few hours before. She felt as if she was dying, and as if this were the fittest place for her to die on.

"There is nothing in my possession," she cried, "that really belongs to me but *this*—this which I loathe and abhor, and love and weep over at one and the same moment." And, strange to relate, Mrs. Damer turned on her side and kneeling by the iron-clamped chest pressed her lips upon its hard, unyielding surface, as if it had life wherewith to answer her embrace. And then the wearied creature dragged herself up again into an unsteady position, and managed to sustain it until she was ready to lie down upon her bed.

The next morning she was much better. Colonel Damer and Bella Clayton laid their heads together and decided that she was to remain in bed until after breakfast, therefore she was spared meeting with the assembled strangers until the dinner-hour again, for luncheon was a desultory meal at Molton Chase, and scarcely any of the gentlemen were present at it that day. After luncheon Mrs. Clayton proposed driving Mrs. Damer out in her pony-chaise.

"I don't think you will find it cold, dear, and we can come home by the lower shrubberies and meet the gentlemen as they return from shooting," Colonel Damer being one of the shooting party. But Mrs. Damer had declined the drive, and made her cousin understand so plainly that she preferred being left alone, that Mrs. Clayton felt no compunction in acceding to her wishes, and laying herself out to please the other ladies staying in the house.

And Mrs. Damer did wish to be alone. She wanted to think over the incidents of the night before, and devise some plan by which she could persuade her husband to leave the Grange as soon as possible without provoking questions which she might find it difficult to answer. When the sound of the wheels of her cousin's pony-chaise had died away, and the great stillness pervading Molton Grange proclaimed that she was the sole inmate left behind, she dressed herself in a warm cloak, and drawing the hood over her head prepared for a stroll about the grounds. A little walk she thought would do her good, and with this intention she left the house. The Grange gardens were extensive and curiously laid out, and there were many winding shrubbery paths about them, which strangers were apt to find easier to enter than to find their way out of again.

Into one of these Mrs. Damer now turned her steps for the sake of privacy and shelter; but she had not gone far before, on turning an abrupt corner, she came suddenly upon the figure of the gentleman she had been introduced to the night before, Mr. Laurence, who she had imagined to be with the shooting party. He was half lying, half sitting across a rustic seat which encircled the huge trunk of an old tree, with his eyes bent upon the ground and a cigar between his lips. He was more an intellectual and fine-looking than a handsome man, but he possessed two gifts which are much more winning than beauty, a mind of great power, and the art of fascination. As Mrs. Damer came full in view of him, too suddenly to stop herself or to retreat, he rose quickly from the attitude he had assumed when he thought himself secure from interruption and stood in her pathway. She attempted to pass him with an inclination of the head, but he put out his hand and stopped her.

"Blanche! you must speak to me; you shall not pass like this; I insist upon it!" and she tried in vain to disengage her arm from his detaining clasp.

"Mr. Laurence, what right have you to hold me thus?"

"What right, Blanche? The right of every man over the woman who loves him!"

"That is your right over me no longer. I have tried to avoid you. You have both seen and known it! No *gentleman* would force himself upon my notice in this manner."

"Your taunt fails to have any effect upon me. I have sought an explanation of your extraordinary conduct from you in vain. My letters have been unanswered, my entreaties for a last interview disregarded; and now that chance has brought us together again, I must have what I have a right to ask from your own lips. I did not devise this meeting;

I did not even know you had returned to England till yesterday, and then I sought to avoid you; but it was fated that we should meet, and it is fated that you satisfy my curiosity."

"What do you want to know?" she asked, in a low voice.

"First, have you ceased to love me?"

The angry light which had flashed across her face when he used force to detain her died away; the pallid lips commenced to tremble, and in the sunken eyes large teardrops rose and hung quivering upon the long eyelashes.

"Enough, Blanche," Mr. Laurence continued, in a softer voice. "Nature answers me. I will not give you the needless pain of speaking. Then, why did you forsake me? Why did you leave England without one line of farewell, and why have you refused to hold any communication with me since that time?"

"I *could* not," she murmured. "You do not know; you cannot feel; you could never understand my feelings on that occasion."

"That is no answer to my question, Blanche," he said firmly, "and an answer I will have. What was the immediate cause of your breaking faith with me? I loved you, you know how well. What drove you from me? Was it fear, or indifference, or a sudden remorse?"

"It was," she commenced slowly, and then as if gathering up a great resolution, she suddenly exclaimed, "Do you *really* wish to know what parted us?"

"I really intend to know," he replied, and the old power which he had held over her recommenced its sway. "Whatever it was it has not tended to your happiness," he continued, "if I may judge from your looks. You are terribly changed, Blanche! I think even I could have made you happier than you appear to have been."

"I have had enough to change me," she replied. "If you will know then, come with me, and I will show you."

"Today?"

"At once; tomorrow may be too late." She began to walk towards the house as she spoke, rapidly and irregularly, her heart beating fast, but no trace of weakness in her limbs; and Herbert Laurence followed her, he scarcely knew why, expecting that she had desired it.

Into Molton Grange she went, up the broad staircase and to her chamber door before she paused to see if he was following. When she did so she found that he stood just behind her on the wide landing.

"You can enter," she said, throwing open the door of her bedroom, "don't be afraid; there is nothing here except the cause for which I parted with you." In her agitation and excitement, scarcely pausing to fasten the door behind her, Mrs. Damer fell down on her knees before the little black box with its iron clamps and ponderous padlock; and drawing a key from her bosom, applied it to the lock, and in another minute had thrown back the heavy lid. Having displaced some linen which lay at the top, she carefully removed some lighter materials, and then calling to the man behind her, bid him look in and be satisfied. Mr. Laurence advanced to the box, quite ignorant as to the reason of her demand; but as his eye fell upon its contents, he started backwards and covered his face with his hands. As he drew them slowly away again he met the sad, earnest look with which the kneeling woman greeted him, and for a few moments they gazed at one another in complete silence. Then Mrs. Damer withdrew her eyes from his and rearranged the contents of the black box; the heavy lid shut with a clang, the padlock was fast again, the key in her bosom, and she rose to her feet and prepared to leave the room in the same unbroken silence. But he again detained her, and this time his voice was hoarse and changed.

"Blanche! tell me, is this the truth?"

"As I believe in heaven," she answered.

"And this was the reason that we parted—this the sole cause of our estrangement?"

"Was it not enough?" she said. "I erred, but it was as one in a dream. When I awoke I could no longer err and be at peace. At peace did I say? I have known no peace since I knew you; but I should have died and waked up in hell, if I had not parted with you. This is all the truth, believe it or not as you will; but there may, there can be nothing in future between you and me. Pray let me pass you."

"But that—that—box, Blanche!" exclaimed Herbert Laurence, with drops of sweat, notwithstanding the temperature of the day, upon his forehead. "It was an accident, a misfortune; *you* did not do it?"

She turned upon him eyes which were full of mingled horror and scorn.

"I *do* it!" she said; "what are you dreaming of? I was mad; but not so mad as that! How could you think it?" and the tears rose in her eyes more at the supposition which his question had raised than at the idea that he could so misjudge her.

"But why do you keep this? why do you carry it about with you, Blanche? It is pure insanity on your part. How long is it since you have travelled in company with that dreadful box?"

"More than two years," she said in a fearful whisper. "I have tried to get rid of it, but to no purpose; there was always someone in the way. I have reasoned with myself, and prayed to be delivered from it, but I have never found an opportunity. And now, what does it matter? The burden and heat of the day are past."

"Let me do it for you," said Mr. Laurence. "Whatever our future relation to one another, I cannot consent that you should run so terrible a risk through fault of mine. The strain upon your mind has been too great already. Would to heaven I could have borne it for you! but you forbid me even the privilege of knowing that you suffered. Now that I have ascertained it, it must be my care that the cause of our separation shall at least live in your memory only." And as he finished speaking he attempted to lift the box; but Mrs. Damer sprang forward and prevented him.

"Leave it!" she cried; "do not dare to touch it; it is *mine*! It has gone wherever I have gone for years. Do you think, for the little space that is left me, that I would part with the only link left between me and my dread past?" and saying this she threw herself upon the black trunk and burst into tears.

"Blanche! you love me as you ever did," exclaimed Herbert Laurence. "These tears confess it. Let me make amends to you for this; let me try to make the happiness of your future life!"

But before his sentence was concluded Mrs. Damer had risen from her drooping attitude and stood before him.

"Make amends!" she echoed scornfully. "How can you 'make amends'? Nothing can wipe out the memory of the shame and misery that I have passed through, nothing restore the quiet conscience I have lost. I do not know if I love you still or not. When I think of it, my head swims, and I only feel confused and anxious. But I am sure of one thing, that the horror of my remorse for even having listened to you has power to overwhelm any regret that may be lingering in my unworthy breast, and that the mere fact of your bodily presence is agony to me. When I met you today I was battling with my invention to devise some means of leaving the place where you are without exciting suspicion. If you ever loved, have pity on me now; take the initiative, and rid me of yourself."

"Is this your final decision, Blanche?" he asked, slowly. "Will you not regret it when too late, and you are left alone with only *that*?"

She shuddered, and he caught at the fact as a sign of relenting.

"Dearest, loveliest," he commenced.—This woman had been the

loveliest to him in days gone past, and though she was so terribly changed in eyes that regarded her less, Herbert Laurence, her once lover, could still trace above the languor and debility and distress of her present appearance, the fresh, sparkling woman who had sacrificed herself for his sake; and although his style of address signified more than he really thought for her, the knowledge of how much she had undergone since their separation had the power to make him imagine that this partial reanimation of an old flame was a proof that the fire which kindled it had never perished. Therefore it did not appear absurd in his mental eyes to preface his appeal to Mrs. Damer thus: "Dearest, loveliest—" but she turned upon him as though he had insulted her.

"Mr. Laurence!" she exclaimed, "I have told you that the past is past; be good enough to take me at my word. Do you think that I have lived over two years of solitary shame and grief, to break the heart that trusts in me *now*? If I had any wish, or any thought to the contrary, it would be impossible. I am enveloped by kind words and acts, by care and attention, which chain me as closely to my home as if I were kept a prisoner between four walls. I could not free myself if I would," she continued, throwing back her arms, as though she tried to break an invisible thrall. "I must die first; the cords of gratitude are bound about me so closely. It is killing me, as nothing else could kill," she added, in a lower voice. "I lived under your loss, and the knowledge of my own disgrace; but I cannot live under his perpetual kindness and perfect trust. It cannot last much longer: for mercy's sake, leave me in peace until the end comes!"

"And the box?" he demanded.

"I will provide for the box before that time," she answered, sadly; "but if you have any fear, keep the key yourself: the lock is not one that can be forced."

She took the key from her bosom, where it hung on a broad black ribbon, as she spoke, and handed it to him. He accepted it without demur.

"You are so rash," he said; "it will be safer with me: let me take the box also?"

"No, no!" said Mrs. Damer, hurriedly; "you shall not; and it would be no use. If it were out of my sight, I should dream that it was found, and talk of it in my sleep. I often rise in the night now to see if it is safe. Nothing could do away with it. If you buried it, someone would dig it up; if you threw it in the water, it would float. It would lie still nowhere but on my heart, where it ought to be!—it ought to be!"

Her eyes had reassumed the wild, restless expression which they took whilst speaking of the past, and her voice had sunk to a low, fearful whisper.

"This is madness," muttered Herbert Laurence; and he was right. On the subject of the black box Mrs. Damer's brain was turned.

He was just about to speak to her again, and try to reason her out of her folly, when voices were heard merrily talking together in the hall, and her face worked with the dread of discovery.

"Go!" she said; "pray, go at once. I have told you everything." And in another moment Herbert Laurence had dashed through the passage to the privacy of his own room; and Mrs. Clayton, glowing from her drive, and with a fine rosy baby in her arms, had entered the apartment of her cousin.

2

Bella found her cousin sitting in an armchair, with the cloak still over her shoulders, and a face of ashy whiteness, the reaction of her excitement.

"My dear, how ill you look!" was her first exclamation. "Have you been out?"

"I went a little way into the shrubberies," said Mrs. Damer; "but the day turned so cold."

"Do you think so? We have all been saying what a genial afternoon it is: but it certainly does not seem to have agreed with you. Look at my boy: isn't he a fine fellow?—he has been out all day in the garden. I often wish you had a child, Blanchey."

"Do you, dear? it is more than I do."

"Ah, but you can't tell, till they are really yours, how much pleasure they give you; no one knows who has not been a mother."

"No; I suppose not."

Mrs. Damer shivered as she said the words, and looked into the baby's fat, unmeaning face with eyes of sad import. Mrs. Clayton thought she had wounded her cousin, and stooped to kiss the slight offence away; but she fancied that Blanche almost shrunk from her embrace.

"She must be really ill," thought the kindly little Bella, who had no notion of such a thing as heart-sickness for an apparently happy married woman. "She ought to see a doctor: I shall tell Colonel Damer so."

In another half-hour they were at her side together, urging her to take their advice.

"Now, my darling," said the colonel, when Mrs. Damer faintly protested against being made a fuss about, "you must be good for my sake. You know how precious you are to me, and how it would grieve me to have you laid up; let me send for Dr. Barlow, as your cousin advises. You were very much overcome by the long journey here, and I am afraid the subsequent excitement of seeing your kind friends has been too much for you. You do not half know how dear you are to me, Blanche, or you would not refuse such a trifling request. Here have I been, for five years, dearest, only looking forward from day to day to meeting my dear loving little wife again; and then to have you so ill as this the first month of our reunion, is a great trial to me. Pray let me send for Dr. Barlow."

But Mrs. Damer pleaded for delay. She had become chilled through being out in the shrubberies; she had not yet got over the fatigue of her journey; she had caught a cold whilst crossing from Havre to Folkestone: it was anything and everything but an illness which required medical attendance. If she were not better in the morning, she promised to make no opposition to their wishes.

So she forced herself to rise and dress for dinner. She appeared there calm and collected, and continued so throughout the evening, talking with Mr. Laurence quite as much as with the rest of the company; and she went to bed at the same hour as the other guests of Molton Grange, receiving with her cousin's goodnight, congratulations on the evident improvement of her health.

"I cannot quite make out what has come to that cousin of yours, Bella," said Harry Clayton to his wife, as they too retired for the night; "she doesn't appear half such a jolly woman as she used to be."

"She is certainly very much altered," was Mrs. Clayton's response; "but I think it must be chiefly owing to her health; a feeling of debility is so very depressing."

"I suppose it can't be anything on her mind, Bella?" suggested the husband, after a pause.

"On her *mind*, Harry!" said Bella, sitting up in bed in her wonderment; "of course not; why, how could it be? She has everything she can wish for; and, I am sure, no woman could have a more devoted husband than Colonel Damer. He has been speaking a great deal about her to me today, and his anxiety is something enormous. On her *mind*!—what a funny idea, Harry; what could have put that in your head?"

"I am sure I don't know," was the husband's reply, rather ruefully given, as if conscious he had made a great mistake.

"You old *goose*," said his wife, with an emphatic kiss, as she composed herself to her innocent slumbers.

But before they were broken by nature, in the gray of the morning, Mrs. Clayton was roused by a tapping at the bedroom door; a tapping to which all Mr. Clayton's shouts to "come in," only served as a renewal.

"Who can it be, Harry?—do get up and see," said Bella.

So Harry got up, like a dutiful husband, and opened the door, and the figure of Colonel Damer, robed in a dressing-gown, and looking very shadowy and unreal in the dawning, presented itself on the threshold.

"Is your wife here?" demanded the colonel briefly.

"Of course she is," said Mr. Clayton, wondering what the colonel wanted with her.

"Will she come to Mrs. Damer? she is *very* ill," was the next sentence, delivered tremblingly.

"Very ill!" exclaimed Bella, jumping out of bed and wrapping herself in a dressing-gown. "How do you mean, Colonel Damer?—when did it happen?"

"God knows!" he said, in an agitated voice; "but for some time after she fell asleep she was feverish and excited, and spoke much. I woke suddenly in the night and missed her, and going in search of her with a light, found her fallen on the landing."

"Fainted?" said Bella.

"I don't know now whether it was a faint or a fit," he replied, "but I incline to the latter belief. I carried her back to her bed, and gave her some restoratives, not liking to disturb you—"

"Oh! why didn't you, Colonel Damer?" interposed his hostess.

"—and thought she was better, till just now, when she had another attack of unconsciousness, and is so weak after it she cannot move. She has fever too, I am sure, from the rapidity of her pulse, and I don't think her head is quite clear."

"Harry, dear, send for Dr. Barlow at once," thrusting her naked feet into slippers, "and come back with me, Colonel Damer; she should not be left for a minute."

And she passed swiftly along the corridor to her cousin's room. As she neared that of Mr. Laurence, the door opened a little, and a voice asked huskily—

"Is anything the matter, Mrs. Clayton? I have been listening to noises in the house for the last hour."

"My cousin, Mrs. Damer, has been taken ill, Mr. Laurence, but we have sent for the doctor; I am going to her now."

And as the door closed again she fancied that she heard a sigh.

Blanche Damer was lying on her pillows very hot and flushed, with that anxious, perturbed look which the eyes assume when the brain is only half clouded, and can feel itself to be wandering.

"Blanche, dearest," cried Bella, as she caught sight of her face, "what is the matter? How did this happen?"

"I dreamt that he had taken it," said Mrs. Damer, slowly and sadly; "but it was a mistake: he must not have it yet—not yet! only a little while to wait now!—but he has the key."

"Her mind is wandering at present," said Colonel Damer, who had followed Mrs. Clayton into the room.

"Oh, Colonel Damer," exclaimed Bella, tearfully, "how dreadful it is!—she frightens me! Could she have knocked her head in falling? Have you no idea why she got up and went into the passage?"

"Not the slightest," he returned. And now that she examined him under the morning light, which was by this time streaming through the open shutters, Bella Clayton saw how aged and haggard his night's anxiety had made him look. "My wife has been very subject to both sleeping-talking and walking since my return, and I have several times missed her, as I did last night, and found her walking about the room in her sleep, but she has never been like this before. When I first found her in the passage, I asked her why she had gone there, or what she wanted, and she said, 'the key.' When I had relifted her into bed, I found her bunch of keys as usual, on the dressing-table, therefore I imagine she could not then have known what she was talking about. I trust Dr. Barlow will not be long in coming; I am deeply anxious."

And he looked the truth of what he uttered; whilst poor little Mrs. Clayton could only press his hand and entreat him to be hopeful; and his wife lay on her pillows, and silently stared into vacancy. As soon as the doctor arrived he pronounced the patient to be suffering from an attack of pressure on the brain, and wished to know whether she had not been subjected to some great mental shock or strain.

Here Colonel Damer came forward and stoutly denied the possibility of such a thing. He had joined his wife from India a month ago, at which time she was, though in delicate, not in bad health, and he had never left her since. They had crossed from Havre to Folkestone three days before, and Mrs. Damer had not complained of any unusual sickness or fatigue. She was a person of a highly excitable and nervous temperament, and her appetite and spirit were variable; otherwise there had been nothing in her state of health to call for anxiety on the part of her friends.

Dr. Barlow listened to all these statements, and believed as much of them as he chose. However he waived the subject of the cause of the disaster; the fact that it had occurred was undeniable; and the remedies for such emergencies were immediately resorted to. But all proved alike ineffectual, for the simple reason that the irrevocable fiat had gone forth, and Blanche Damer was appointed to die.

As the day wore on, and the case assumed a darker aspect, and the doctor's prognostications became less hopeful, Colonel Damer worked himself into a perfect frenzy of fear.

"Save her, Dr. Barlow," he had said to that gentleman, in the insane manner in which people are used to address the Faculty, as if it was in their power to do more than help the efforts of nature. "Save her life, for God's sake! and there is nothing that I can do for you, of earthly good, that shall not be yours. Shall I call in other advice? Shall I telegraph to London? Is there anyone there who can save her? It is my life as well as hers that is trembling in the scale. For the love of heaven, do not stand on ceremony, but only tell me what is best to be done!"

Of course Dr. Barlow told him that if he was not perfectly satisfied, he should wish him to telegraph to town for further advice, and mentioned several names celebrated in such cases; at the same time he assured Colonel Damer that he did not believe any number of doctors could do more for the patient than he was doing, and that it was impossible to guess at the probable termination of the illness for some days to come.

Bella Clayton gave up the duty of amusing her guests, and stationed herself at the bedside of her cousin; and the unhappy husband wandered in and out of the room like a ghost; trying to think upon each fresh visit, that there was a slight improvement in the symptoms, and spending the intervening time in praying for the life which he fondly imagined had been devoted to himself. Meanwhile, whenever Mrs. Damer opened her lips, it was to ramble on in this manner:

"Dying!" her hollow voice would exclaim; "crushed to death beneath the weight of a pyramid of blessings that lies like lead upon my chest and reaches to the ceiling. Kind words—fond care, and sweet attentions—they bow me down to the earth! I am stifling beneath the burden of their silent reproaches. Two and two are four; and four and four is eight; eight times locked should be secure—but there is a worm that dieth not, and a fire that is not quenched."

"Oh! don't come in here, Colonel Damer," poor Bella would exclaim, as the unhappy man would creep to the foot of the bed and stand listening, with blanched cheeks, to the delirious ravings of his wife. "She doesn't know what she is saying, remember; and she will be better tomorrow, doubtless. Don't distress yourself more, by listening to all this nonsense."

"I don't believe she will ever be better, Mrs. Clayton," he replied, on one of these occasions. This was on the third day.

"Dearest!" the sick woman resumed, in a plaintively soft voice, without being in the least disturbed by the conversation around her, "if you have ever loved me, you will believe in this hour that I love you in return. If you have given me your love, I have given you more than my life."

"Does she speak of me?" demanded Colonel Damer.

"I think so," said Bella Clayton, sadly.

"Take it off! take it off!" cried Mrs. Damer, starting with terror—"this box—this iron-clamped box which presses on my soul. What have I done? Where shall I go? How am I to meet him again?"

"What does she say?" asked the colonel, trembling.

"Colonel Damer, I must beg you to quit the room," said Bella, weeping. "I cannot bear to stay here with both of you. Pray leave me alone with Blanche until she is quieter."

And so the husband left the chamber, with fellow tears in his eyes, and she set herself to the painful task of attempting to soothe the delirious woman.

"If he would only strike me," moaned Mrs. Damer, "or frown at me, or tell me that I lie, I could bear it better; but he is killing me with kindness. Where is the box?—open it—let him see all. I am ready to die. But I forgot—there is no key, and no one shall touch it: it is mine—mine. Hark! I hear it! I hear it! How could I put it there? Let me go—no one shall hold me! Let me go, I say—I *hear* it; and—and—the world is nothing to me!"

At last, when they had almost despaired of ever seeing her sleep again, there came an uninterrupted hour of repose from sheer weariness; and then wide-open hollow eyes—a changed voice sounding with the question—"Bella! have I been ill?" and Mrs. Damer's delirium was over.

Over with her life. For on his next visit Dr. Barlow found her sensible but cold and pulseless, and broke to her friends the news that twelve hours more would end her existence.

Colonel Damer went wild, and telegraphed at once to London for men who arrived when his wife was ready to be coffined. Bella heard the decree and wept silently; and a great gloom fell upon the guests of Molton Chase, who had been left altogether on poor Harry's hands since Mrs. Damer's illness.

The dying woman lay very silent and exhausted for some time after she had waked from that brief, memory-restoring sleep. When she next spoke, she said, observing her cousin's swollen eyes—

"Am I dying, Bella?"

Poor little Mrs. Clayton did not at all know what answer to make to such a direct question, but she managed to stammer out something which, whatever it was meant for, was taken as affirmative by the one it most concerned.

"I thought so. Shall I never be able to get out of bed again?"

"I am afraid not, darling—you are so weak!"

"Yes, I am—I can hardly raise my hand. And yet I must rise if I can. I have something so particular to do."

"Cannot I do it for you, Blanche?"

"*Will* you do it, Bella?"

"Anything—everything, love! How can you ask me?"

"And you will promise secrecy? Let me look in your face. Yes, it is a true face, as it has ever been, and I can trust you. Have the black box moved out of my room before I die, Bella—mind, *before* I die, and placed in your own dressing-room."

"What, dear, your linen box?"

"Yes, my linen box, or whatever you choose to call it. Take it away *at once*, Bella. Tell no one; and when I am dead, have it buried in my grave. Surely you could manage so much for me!"

"And Colonel Damer?"

"If you speak to him about it, Bella, or to your husband, or to any one, I'll never forgive you, and I'm dying!" cried Mrs. Damer, almost rising in her excitement. "Oh! why have I delayed it so long, why did I not see to this before? I cannot even die in peace."

"Yes, yes, dearest Blanche, I will do it, indeed I will," said Mrs. Clayton, alarmed at her emotion; "and no one shall know of it but myself. Shall I send it to my room at once? You may trust entirely to my discretion. Pray, have no fear!"

"Yes! at once—directly; it cannot be too soon!" said Mrs. Damer, falling back exhausted on her pillow. So a servant was called, and the iron-clamped box was carried away from the sick-room and secreted in Mrs. Clayton's private apartment. Mrs. Damer seemed so weak, that her cousin suggested summoning her husband to her side, but she appeared to shrink from an interview with him.

"I have nothing to say but what will make him sad to think of afterwards," she murmured. "Let me die with you alone, dear Bella. It is better so."

So Colonel Damer, although he went backwards and forwards all the night, was not called at any particular moment to see the last of his wife, and Blanche had her wish. She died alone with her faithful little cousin before the morning broke. As she was just going, she said, in a vague sort of manner—

"Tell him, Bella, that I forgive him as I hope to be forgiven. And that I have seen Heaven open tonight, and a child spirit pleading with the Woman-born for us; and that the burden is lifted off my soul at last." And then she added solemnly—"I will arise and go to my Father—," and went before she could finish the sentence.

Innocent Bella repeated her last message in perfect faith to Colonel Damer.

"She told me to tell you, that she felt herself forgiven, and that she had seen Heaven opened for her, and the weight of her sins was lifted off her soul. Oh! Colonel Damer, pray think of that, and take comfort. She is happier than you could make her."

But the poor faithful husband was, for the present, beyond all reach of comfort.

The London doctors arrived with the daylight, and had to be solemnly entertained at breakfast, and warmed and comforted before they were despatched home again. The Christmas guests were all packing up their boxes, preparatory to taking their leave of Molton Chase, for it was impossible to think of festivities with such a bereavement in the house. And Harry Clayton told his wife that he was very thankful that they thought of doing so.

"It has been a most unfortunate business altogether, Bella, and of course they all felt it, poor things; and the more so because they could take no active part in it. The house has had a pall over it the last week; and it would have been still worse if they had remained. As for Laurence, I never saw a man so cut up. He has eaten nothing since your poor cousin was taken ill. One would think she had been his sister, or his dearest friend."

"Is he going with the rest, Harry?"

"No; he will stay till after the funeral; then he is going abroad. He feels deeply with you, Bella, and desired me to tell you so."

"He is very good—thank him in my name."

★★★★★★

But released from the care of thinking for her guests, and sitting crying alone in her dressing-room, poor Mrs. Clayton could not imagine what to do with the iron-clamped black box. She had promised Blanche not to confide in her husband, or Colonel Damer. The latter, having no family vault, wished to lay the remains of his wife amongst those of the Claytons in the country churchyard of Molton; but how to get the black box conveyed to the grave without the knowledge of the chief mourners was a mystery beyond the fathoming of Bella's open heart. But in the midst of her perplexity, Fate sent her aid. On the second day of her cousin's death, a gentle tap sounded at her chamber door, and on her invitation to enter being answered, she was surprised to see Mr. Laurence on the threshold—come, as she imagined, to offer his sympathy in person.

"This is very kind of you, Mr. Laurence," she said.

"I can scarcely claim your gratitude, Mrs. Clayton. I have sought you to speak on a very important but painful subject. May I ask your attention for a few moments?"

"Of course you may!" And she motioned him to a seat.

"It concerns her whom we have lost. Mrs. Clayton, tell me truly—did you love your cousin?"

"Dearly—very dearly, Mr. Laurence. We were brought up together."

"Then I may depend on your discretion; and if you wish to save her memory you must exercise it in her behalf. There is a small iron-clamped black trunk amongst her boxes, which must not fall into Colonel Damer's hands. Will you have that box conveyed from her chamber to your own, and (if you will so far trust my honour) make it over to me?"

"To you, Mr. Laurence—the iron-bound box? What possible knowledge can you have of my cousin's secret?"

"Her secret?"

"Yes—she confided that box to my care the night she died. She made me promise to do (without question) what you have just asked me to perform, and I did it. The trunk is already here."

And throwing open a cupboard at the side of the room, she showed him the chest which he had mentioned.

"I see that it is," he answered. "How do you design disposing of it?"

"She wished it to be buried in her grave."

"That is impossible in its present state. The contents must be removed."

"But how?" Mrs. Clayton demanded, in surprise. "It is locked and double locked, and there is no key."

"*I* have the key," he answered, gravely.

"Oh! Mr. Laurence," exclaimed his hostess, trembling, "there is some dreadful mystery here. For heaven's sake tell me what it is! What connection can you possibly have with this box of my poor cousin's, if you have only met her once in your life?"

"Did she say so?" he asked.

"No; but I fancied so. Have you known her? When? where? and why did you not tell us so before?"

"How can I tell you now?" he said, gazing into the pure womanly face upraised to his own, bearing an expression which was half-surprise and half-fear but which seemed as though it could never dream of anything like shame.

"You are too good and too happy, Mrs. Clayton, to know of, or be able to sympathize with, the troubles and temptations which preceded our fatal friendship and her fall."

"Blanche's *fall!*" ejaculated Bella Clayton, in a voice of horror.

"Don't interrupt me, please, Mrs. Clayton," he said, hurriedly, covering his face with his hands, "or I shall never be able to tell you the wretched story. I knew your cousin years ago. Had you any suspicion that she was unhappy in her marriage?"

"No! none!" replied Bella, with looks of surprise.

"She *was* then, thoroughly unhappy, as scores of women are, simply because the hearts of the men they are bound to are opposed to theirs in every taste and feeling. I met her when she first returned to England, and—it is the old story, Mrs. Clayton—I loved her, and was mad enough to tell her so. When a selfish man and an unselfish woman have mutually confessed their preference for each other, the result is easily anticipated. I ruined her—forgive my plain speaking—and she still loved on, and forgave me."

"Oh, Blanche!" exclaimed Bella Clayton, hiding her hot face in her hands.

"We lived in a fool's paradise for some months, and then one day she left her house and went to the Continent, without giving me any warning of her intention. I was thunderstruck when I heard it, and deeply hurt, and as soon as I had traced her to Paris, I followed and demanded an explanation of her conduct. But she refused to see me, and when she found me pertinacious, left the city as suddenly as she had done that of London. Since which time she has answered no letters of mine, nor did we ever meet until, most unexpectedly, I met her in your house. My pride, after her first refusals to see me, was too great to permit me to renew my entreaties, and so I called her a flirt, and inconstant. I tried to banish her remembrance from my heart—and I thought I had succeeded."

"Oh, my poor darling!" exclaimed Mrs. Clayton. "This accounts then for her holding aloof from all her relations for so long a time, by which means she estranged herself from many of them. She was working out her penitence and deep remorse in solitary misery; and she would not even let me share her confidence. But about the box, Mr. Laurence; what has all this to do with the black box?"

"When I met her in your shrubbery the other day, and reproached her for her desertion of me, insisting upon her giving me the reason of her change of mind, she bade me follow her to her own apartment. There, unlocking the box before you, she showed me its contents."

"And they are—?" inquired Mrs. Clayton, breathlessly.

"Would you like to see them?" he demanded, taking a key from his pocket. "I have as much right to show them you as she would have had. But is your love for her dead memory and reputation strong enough to insure your eternal secrecy on the subject?"

"It is," said Bella Clayton, decidedly.

"This box," continued Mr. Laurence, applying the key he held to the lock of the iron-clamped black trunk, "has accompanied my poor girl on all her travels for the last two years. The dreadful secret of its contents which she bore in silent, solitary misery all that time has been, I believe, the ultimate cause of her death, by proving too heavy a burden for the sensitive and proud spirit which was forced to endure the knowledge of its shame. She was killed by her remorse. If you have courage, Mrs. Clayton, for the sight, look at *this*—and pity the feelings I must endure as I kneel here and look at it with you."

He threw back the lid and the topmost linen as he spoke, and Bella Clayton pressed eagerly forward to see, carefully laid amidst withered flowers and folds of cambric, the tiny skeleton of a new-born creature whose angel was even then beholding the face of his Father in Heaven.

She covered her eyes with her clasped hands, no less to shut out the sight than to catch the womanly tears which poured forth at it, and then she cried between her sobs—

"Oh! my poor, poor Blanche, what must she not have suffered! God have mercy on her soul!"

"Amen!" said Herbert Laurence.

"You will let me take the box away with me, Mrs. Clayton?" he asked, gently.

She looked up as he spoke, and the tears were standing in his eyes.

"Yes—yes," she said; "take it away; do what you will with it, only never speak of it to me again."

He never did but once, and that was but an allusion. On the evening of the day on which they committed the remains of Blanche Damer to the dust, he lay in wait for Mrs. Clayton on the landing.

"All has been done as she desired," he whispered; and Mrs. Clayton asked for no further explanation. The secret of which she had been made an unwilling recipient pressed so heavily on her conscience, that she was thankful when he left Molton Grange and went abroad, as he had expressed his intention of doing.

Since which time she has never seen Herbert Laurence again; and Colonel Damer, whose grief at the funeral and for some time after was nearly frenzied, having—like most men who mourn much outwardly—found a source of consolation in the shape of another wife, the story of Blanche Damer's life and death is remembered, for aught her cousin knows to the contrary, by none but herself.

I feel that an objection will be raised to this episode by some people on the score of its being *unnatural*; to whom all I can say in answer is, that the principal incident on which the interest of it turns—that of the unhappy Mrs. Damer having been made so great a coward by conscience that she carried the proof of her frailty about with her for years, too fearful of discovery to permit it to leave her sight—is *a fact*.

To vary the circumstances under which the discovery of the contents of the black box was finally made, and to alter the names of places and people so as to avoid general recognition, I have made my province: to relate the story itself, since, in the form I now present it to my readers, it can give pain to no one, I consider my privilege.

The Clavecin, Bruges

By George Wharton Edwards

A silent, grass-grown market-place, upon the uneven stones of which the *sabots* of a passing peasant clatter loudly. A group of sleepy-looking soldiers in red trousers lolling about the wide portal of the Belfry, which rears aloft against the pearly sky

All the height it has
Of ancient stone.

As the chime ceases there lingers for a space a faint musical hum in the air; the stones seem to carry and retain the melody; one is loath to move for fear of losing some part of the harmony.

I feel an indescribable impulse to climb the four hundred odd steps; incomprehensible, for I detest steeple-climbing, and have no patience with steeple-climbers.

Before I realize it, I am at the stairs. "Hold, sir!" from behind me. "It is forbidden." In wretched French a weazen-faced little soldier explains that repairs are about to be made in the tower, in consequence of which visitors are forbidden. A *franc* removes this military obstacle, and I press on.

At the top of the stairs is an old Flemish woman shelling peas, while over her shoulder peeps a tame magpie. A savoury odour of stewing vegetables fills the air.

"What do you wish, sir?" Many shrugs, gesticulations, and sighs of objurgation, which are covered by a shining new five-*franc* piece, and she produces a bunch of keys. As the door closes upon me the magpie gives a hoarse, gleeful squawk.

. . . A huge, dim room with a vaulted ceiling. Against the wall lean ancient stone statues, noseless and disfigured, crowned and sceptered effigies of forgotten lords and ladies of Flanders. High up on the wall two slitted Gothic windows, through which the violet light of day is streaming. I hear the gentle coo of pigeons. To the right a low door, some vanishing steps of stone, and a hanging hand-rope. Before I have taken a dozen steps upward I am lost in the darkness; the steps are worn hollow and sloping, the rope is slippery—seems to have been waxed, so smooth has it become by handling. Four hundred steps and over; I have lost track of the number, and stumble giddily upward round and round the slender stone shaft. I am conscious of low openings from time to time—openings to what? I do not know. A damp smell exhales from them, and the air is cold upon my face as I pass them.

At last a dim light above. With the next turn a blinding glare of light, a moment's blankness, then a vast panorama gradually dawns upon me. Through the frame of stonework is a vast reach of grayish green bounded by the horizon, an immense shield embossed with silvery lines of waterways, and studded with clustering red-tiled roofs. A rim of pale yellow appears—the sand-dunes that line the coast—and dimly beyond a grayish film, evanescent, flashing—the North Sea.

Something flies through the slit from which I am gazing, and following its flight upward, I see a long beam crossing the gallery, whereon are perched an array of jackdaws gazing down upon me in wonder.

I am conscious of a rhythmic movement about me that stirs the air, a mysterious, beating, throbbing sound, the machinery of the clock, which someone has described as a "*heart of iron beating in a breast of stone.*"

I lean idly in the narrow slit, gazing at the softened landscape, the exquisite harmony of the greens, grays, and browns, the lazily turning arms of far-off mills, reminders of Cuyp, Van der Velde, Teniers, shadowy, mysterious recollections. I am conscious of uttering aloud some commonplaces of delight. A slight and sudden movement behind me, a smothered cough. A little old man in a black velvet coat stands looking up at me, twisting and untwisting his hands. There are ruffles at his throat and wrists, and an amused smile spreads over his face, which is cleanly shaven, of the colour of wax, with a tiny network of red lines over the cheek-bones, as if the blood had been forced there by some excess of passion and had remained. He has heard my sentimental ejaculation. I am conscious of the absurdity of the situation, and move aside for him to pass. He makes a courteous gesture with one ruffled hand.

There comes a prodigious rattling and grinding noise from above—then a jangle of bells, some half-dozen notes in all. At the first stroke the old man closes his eyes, throws back his head, and follows the rhythm with his long white hands, as though playing a piano. The sound dies away; the place becomes painfully silent; still the regular motion of the old man's hands continues. A creepy, shivery feeling runs up and down my spine; a fear of which I am ashamed seizes upon me.

"Fine pells, sare," says the little old man, suddenly dropping his hands, and fixing his eyes upon me. "You sall not hear such pells in your countree. But stay not here; come wis me, and I will show you the clavecin. You sall not see the clavecin yet? No?"

I had not, of course, and thanked him.

"You sall see Melchior, *Melchior t'e Groote, t'e magnif'.*"

As he spoke we entered a room quite filled with curious machinery, a medley of levers, wires, and rope above; below, two large cylinders studded with shining brass points.

He sprang among the wires with a spidery sort of agility, caught one, pulled and hung upon it with, all his weight. There came a *r-r-r-r-r-r* of fans and wheels, followed by a shower of dust; slowly one great cylinder began to revolve; wires and ropes reaching into the gloom above began to twitch convulsively; faintly came the jangle of far-off bells. Then came a pause, then a deafening *boom*, that well nigh stunned me. As the waves of sound came and went, the little old man twisted and untwisted his hands in delight, and ejaculated, "Melchior you haf heeard, *Melchior t'e Groote—t'e bourdon.*"

I wanted to examine the machinery, but he impatiently seized my arm and almost dragged me away saying, "I will skow you—I will skow you. Come wis me."

From a pocket he produced a long brass key and unlocked a door covered with red leather, disclosing an up-leading flight of steps to which he pushed me. It gave upon an octagon-shaped room with a curious floor of sheet-lead. Around the wall ran a seat under the diamond-paned Gothic windows. From their shape I knew them to be the highest in the tower. I had seen them from the square below many times, with the framework above upon which hung row upon row of bells.

In the middle of the room was a rude sort of keyboard, with pedals below, like those of a large organ. Fronting this construction sat a long, high-backed bench. On the rack over the keyboard rested some sheets of music, which, upon examination, I found to be of parchment and written by hand. The notes were curious in shape, consisting of squares of black and diamonds of red upon the lines. Across the top of the page was written, in a straggling hand, "Van den Gheyn Nikolaas." I turned to the little old man with the ruffles. "Van den Gheyn!" I said in surprise, pointing to the parchment. "Why, that is the name of the most celebrated of *carillonneurs*, Van den Gheyn of Louvain." He untwisted his hands and bowed. "Eet ees ma name, *mynheer*—I am the *carillonneur.*"

I fancied that my face showed all too plainly the incredulity I felt, for his darkened, and he muttered, "You not belief, Engelsch? Ah, I show you; then you belief, parehap," and with astounding agility seated himself upon the bench before the clavecin, turned up the ruffles at his wrists, and literally threw himself upon the keys. A sound of thunder accompanied by a vivid flash of lightning filled the air, even as the first notes of the bells reached my ears. Involuntarily I glanced out of the diamond-leaded window—dark clouds were all about us, the housetops and surrounding country were no longer to be seen.

A blinding flash of lightning seemed to fill the room; the arms and legs of the little old man sought the keys and pedals with inconceivable rapidity; the music crashed about us with a deafening din, to the accompaniment of the thunder, which seemed to sound in unison with the boom of the bourdon. It was grandly terrible. The face of the little old man was turned upon me, but his eyes were closed. He seemed to find the pedals intuitively, and at every peal of thunder, which shook the tower to its foundations, he would open his mouth, a toothless cavern, and shout aloud. I could not hear the sounds for the crashing of the bells. Finally, with a last deafening crash of iron rods and thunderbolts, the noise of the bells gradually died away. Instinctively I had glanced above when the crash came, half expecting to see the roof torn off.

"I think we had better go down," I said. "This tower has been struck by lightning several times, and I imagine that discretion—"

I don't know what more I said, for my eyes rested upon the empty bench, and the bare rack where the music had been. The clavecin was one mass of twisted iron rods, tangled wires, and decayed, worm-eaten woodwork; the little old man had disappeared. I rushed to the red leather-covered door; it was fast. I shook it in a veritable terror; it would not yield. With a bound I reached the ruined clavecin, seized one of the pedals, and tore it away from the machine. The end was armed with an iron point. This I inserted between the lock and the door. I twisted the lock from the worm-eaten wood with one turn of the wrist, the door opened, and I almost fell down the steep steps. The second door at the bottom was also closed. I threw my weight against it once, twice; it gave, and I half slipped, half ran down the winding steps in the darkness.

Out at last into the fresh air of the lower passage! At the noise I made in closing the ponderous door came forth the old *custode*.

In my excitement I seized her by the arm, saying, "Who was the little old man in the black velvet coat with the ruffles? Where is he?"

She looked at me in a stupid manner. "Who is he," I repeated—"the little old man who played the clavecin?"

"Little old man, sir? I don't know," said the crone. "There has been no one in the tower today but yourself."

The Diamond Lens

By Fitz-James O'Brien

1

THE BENDING OF THE TWIG

From a very early period of my life the entire bent of my inclinations had been towards microscopic investigations. When I was not more than ten years old, a distant relative of our family, hoping to astonish my inexperience, constructed a simple microscope for me, by drilling in a disk of copper a small hole, in which a drop of pure water was sustained by capillary attraction. This very primitive apparatus, magnifying some fifty diameters, presented, it is true, only indistinct and imperfect forms, but still sufficiently wonderful to work up my imagination to a preternatural state of excitement.

Seeing me so interested in this rude instrument, my cousin explained to me all that he knew about the principles of the microscope, related to me a few of the wonders which had been accomplished through its agency, and ended by promising to send me one regularly constructed, immediately on his return to the city. I counted the days, the hours, the minutes, that intervened between that promise and his departure.

Meantime I was not idle. Every transparent substance that bore the remotest resemblance to a lens I eagerly seized upon, and employed in vain attempts to realize that instrument, the theory of whose construction I as yet only vaguely comprehended. All panes of glass containing those oblate spheroidal knots familiarly known as "bull's-eyes" were ruthlessly destroyed, in the hope of obtaining lenses of marvellous power. I even went so far as to extract the crystalline humour from the eyes of fishes and animals, and endeavoured to press it into the microscopic service. I plead guilty to having stolen the glasses from my Aunt Agatha's spectacles, with a dim idea of grinding them into lenses of wondrous magnifying properties,—in which attempt it is scarcely necessary to say that I totally failed.

At last the promised instrument came. It was of that order known as Field's simple microscope, and had cost perhaps about fifteen dollars. As far as educational purposes went, a better apparatus could not have been selected. Accompanying it was a small treatise on the microscope,—its history, uses, and discoveries. I comprehended then for the first time the *Arabian Nights' Entertainments*. The dull veil of ordinary existence that hung across the world seemed suddenly to roll away, and to lay bare a land of enchantments. I felt towards my companions as the seer might feel towards the ordinary masses of men. I held conversations with nature in a tongue which they could not understand. I was in daily communication with living wonders, such as they never imagined in their wildest visions.

I penetrated beyond the external portal of things, and roamed through the sanctuaries. Where they beheld only a drop of rain slowly rolling down the window-glass, I saw a universe of beings animated with all the passions common to physical life, and convulsing their minute sphere with struggles as fierce and protracted as those of men. In the common spots of mould, which my mother, good housekeeper that she was, fiercely scooped away from her jam pots, there abode for me, under the name of mildew, enchanted gardens, filled with dells and avenues of the densest foliage and most astonishing verdure, while from the fantastic boughs of these microscopic forests, hung strange fruits glittering with green, and silver, and gold.

It was no scientific thirst that at this time filled my mind. It was the pure enjoyment of a poet to whom a world of wonders has been disclosed. I talked of my solitary pleasures to none. Alone with my microscope, I dimmed my sight, day after day and night after night, poring over the marvels which it unfolded to me. I was like one who, having discovered the ancient Eden still existing in all its primitive glory, should resolve to enjoy it in solitude, and never betray to mortal the secret of its locality. The rod of my life was bent at this moment. I destined myself to be a microscopist.

Of course, like every novice, I fancied myself a discoverer. I was ignorant at the time of the thousands of acute intellects engaged in the same pursuit as myself, and with the advantage of instruments a thousand times more powerful than mine. The names of Leeuwenhoek, Williamson, Spencer, Ehrenberg, Schmaltz, Dujardin, Staccato, and Schlseiden were then entirely unknown to me, or if known, I was ignorant of their patient and wonderful researches. In every fresh specimen of cryptogamic which I placed beneath my instrument I believed that I discovered wonders of which the world was as yet ignorant. I remember well the thrill of delight and admiration that shot through me the first time that I discovered the common wheel animalcule (*Rotifera vulgaris*) expanding and contracting its flexible spokes, and seemingly rotating through the water. Alas! as I grew older, and obtained some works treating of my favourite study, I found that I was only on the threshold of a science to the investigation of which some of the greatest men of the age were devoting their lives and intellects.

As I grew up, my parents, who saw but little likelihood of anything practical resulting from the examination of bits of moss and drops of water through a brass tube and a piece of glass, were anxious that I should choose a profession. It was their desire that I should enter the counting-house of my uncle, Ethan Blake, a prosperous merchant, who carried on business in New York. This suggestion I decisively combated. I had no taste for trade; I should only make a failure; in short, I refused to become a merchant.

But it was necessary for me to select some pursuit. My parents were staid New England people, who insisted on the necessity of labour; and therefore, although, thanks to the bequest of my poor Aunt Agatha, I should, on coming of age, inherit a small fortune sufficient to place me above want, it was decided that, instead of waiting for this, I should act the nobler part, and employ the intervening years in rendering myself independent.

After much cogitation I complied with the wishes of my family, and selected a profession. I determined to study medicine at the New York Academy. This disposition of my future suited me. A removal from my relatives would enable me to dispose of my time as I pleased without fear of detection. As long as I paid my Academy fees, I might shirk attending the lectures if I chose; and, as I never had the remotest intention of standing an examination, there was no danger of my being "plucked." Besides, a metropolis was the place for me. There I could obtain excellent instruments, the newest publications, intimacy with men of pursuits kindred with my own,—in short, all things necessary to insure a profitable devotion of my life to my beloved science.

I had an abundance of money, few desires that were not bounded by my illuminating mirror on one side and my object-glass on the other; what, therefore, was to prevent my becoming an illustrious investigator of the veiled worlds? It was with the most buoyant hope that I left my New England home and established myself in New York.

2
THE LONGING OF A MAN OF SCIENCE

My first step, of course, was to find suitable apartments. These I obtained, after a couple of days' search, in Fourth Avenue; a very pretty second-floor unfurnished, containing sitting-room, bedroom, and a smaller apartment which I intended to fit up as a laboratory. I furnished my lodgings simply, but rather elegantly, and then devoted all my energies to the adornment of the temple of my worship. I visited Pike, the celebrated optician, and passed in review his splendid collection of microscopes,—Field's Compound, Hingham's, Spencer's, Nachet's Binocular (that founded on the principles of the stereoscope), and at length fixed upon that form known as Spencer's Trunnion Microscope, as combining the greatest number of improvements with an almost perfect freedom from tremor.

Along with this I purchased every possible accessory,—draw-tubes, micrometers, a *camera-lucida*, lever-stage, acromatic condensers, white cloud illuminators, prisms, parabolic condensers, polarizing apparatus, forceps, aquatic boxes, fishing-tubes, with a host of other articles, all of which would have been useful in the hands of an experienced microscopist, but, as I afterwards discovered, were not of the slightest present value to me. It takes years of practice to know how to use a complicated microscope. The optician looked suspiciously at me as I made these wholesale purchases. He evidently was uncertain whether to set me down as some scientific celebrity or a madman. I think he inclined to the latter belief. I suppose I was mad. Every great genius is mad upon the subject in which he is greatest. The unsuccessful madman is disgraced and called a lunatic.

Mad or not, I set myself to work with a zeal which few scientific students have ever equalled. I had everything to learn relative to the delicate study upon which I had embarked,—a study involving the most earnest patience, the most rigid analytic powers, the steadiest hand, the most untiring eyes, the most refined and subtle manipulation.

For a long time half my apparatus lay inactively on the shelves of my laboratory, which was now most amply furnished with every possible contrivance for facilitating my investigations. The fact was that I did not know how to use some of my scientific implements,—never having been taught microscopic,—and those whose use I understood theoretically were of little avail, until by practice I could attain the necessary delicacy of handling. Still, such was the fury of my ambition, such the untiring perseverance of my experiments, that, difficult of credit as it may be, in the course of one year I became theoretically and practically an accomplished microscopist.

During this period of my labours, in which I submitted specimens of every substance that came under my observation to the action of my lenses, I became a discoverer—in a small way, it is true, for I was very young, but still a discoverer. It was I who destroyed Ehrenberg's theory that the *Volvox globator* was an animal, and proved that his "nomads" with stomachs and eyes were merely phases of the formation of a vegetable cell, and were, when they reached their mature state, incapable of the act of conjugation, or any true generative act, without which no organism rising to any stage of life higher than vegetable can be said to be complete. It was I who resolved the singular problem of rotation in the cells and hairs of plants into ciliary attraction, in spite of the assertions of Mr. Wenham and others, that my explanation was the result of an optical illusion.

But notwithstanding these discoveries, laboriously and painfully made as they were, I felt horribly dissatisfied. At every step I found myself stopped by the imperfections of my instruments. Like all active microscopists, I gave my imagination full play. Indeed, it is a common complaint against many such, that they supply the defects of their instruments with the creations of their brains. I imagined depths beyond depths in nature which the limited power of my lenses prohibited me from exploring. I lay awake at night constructing imaginary microscopes of immeasurable power, with which I seemed to pierce through the envelopes of matter down to its original atom. How I cursed those imperfect mediums which necessity through ignorance compelled me to use!

How I longed to discover the secret of some perfect lens, whose magnifying power should be limited only by the resolvability of the object, and which at the same time should be free from spherical and chromatic aberrations, in short from all the obstacles over which the poor microscopist finds himself continually stumbling! I felt convinced that the simple microscope, composed of a single lens of such vast yet perfect power was possible of construction. To attempt to bring the compound microscope up to such a pitch would have been com-

mencing at the wrong end; this latter being simply a partially successful endeavour to remedy those very defects of the simple instrument
which, if conquered, would leave nothing to be desired.

It was in this mood of mind that I became a constructive microscopist. After another year passed in this new pursuit, experimenting
on every imaginable substance,—glass, gems, flints, crystals, artificial
crystals formed of the alloy of various vitreous materials,—in short,
having constructed as many varieties of lenses as Argus had eyes, I
found myself precisely where I started, with nothing gained save an
extensive knowledge of glass-making. I was almost dead with despair.
My parents were surprised at my apparent want of progress in my
medical studies (I had not attended one lecture since my arrival in
the city), and the expenses of my mad pursuit had been so great as to
embarrass me very seriously.

I was in this frame of mind one day, experimenting in my laboratory on a small diamond,—that stone, from its great refracting power,
having always occupied my attention more than any other,—when a
young Frenchman, who lived on the floor above me, and who was in
the habit of occasionally visiting me, entered the room.

I think that Jules Simon was a Jew. He had many traits of the He-
brew character: a love of jewellery, of dress, and of good living. There
was something mysterious about him. He always had something to
sell, and yet went into excellent society. When I say sell, I should perhaps have said peddle; for his operations were generally confined to
the disposal of single articles,—a picture, for instance, or a rare carving
in ivory, or a pair of duelling-pistols, or the dress of a Mexican *cabal-
lero*. When I was first furnishing my rooms, he paid me a visit, which
ended in my purchasing an antique silver lamp, which he assured me
was a Cellini,—it was handsome enough even for that, and some
other knickknacks for my sitting-room. Why Simon should pursue
this petty trade I never could imagine. He apparently had plenty of
money, and had the *entrée* of the best houses in the city,—taking care,
however, I suppose, to drive no bargains within the enchanted circle
of the Upper Ten. I came at length to the conclusion that this peddling
was but a mask to cover some greater object, and even went so far as
to believe my young acquaintance to be implicated in the slave-trade.
That, however, was none of my affair.

On the present occasion, Simon entered my room in a state of
considerable excitement.

"*Ah! mon ami!*" he cried, before I could even offer him the ordinary salutation, "it has occurred to me to be the witness of the most astonishing things in the world. I promenade myself to the house of Madame ———. How does the little animal—*le renard*—name himself in the Latin?"

"*Vulpes*," I answered.

"Ah! yes,—*Vulpes*. I promenade myself to the house of Madame Vulpes."

"The spirit medium?"

"Yes, the great medium. Great heavens! what a woman! I write on a slip of paper many of questions concerning affairs the most secret,—affairs that conceal themselves in the abysses of my heart the most profound; and behold! by example! what occurs? This devil of a woman makes me replies the most truthful to all of them. She talks to me of things that I do not love to talk of to myself. What am I to think? I am fixed to the earth!"

"Am I to understand you, M. Simon, that this Mrs. Vulpes replied to questions secretly written by you, which questions related to events known only to yourself?"

"Ah! more than that, more than that," he answered, with an air of some alarm. "She related to me things—But," he added, after a pause, and suddenly changing his manner, "why occupy ourselves with these follies? It was all the biology, without doubt. It goes without saying that it has not my credence.—But why are we here, *mon ami*? It has occurred to me to discover the most beautiful thing as you can imagine,—a vase with green lizards on it, composed by the great Bernard Palissy. It is in my apartment; let us mount. I go to show it to you."

I followed Simon mechanically; but my thoughts were far from Palissy and his enamelled ware, although I, like him, was seeking in the dark a great discovery. This casual mention of the spiritualist, Madame Vulpes, set me on a new track. What if this spiritualism should be really a great fact? What if, through communication with more subtile organisms than my own, I could reach at a single bound the goal, which perhaps a life of agonizing mental toil would never enable me to attain?

While purchasing the Palissy vase from my friend Simon, I was mentally arranging a visit to Madame Vulpes.

3
THE SPIRIT OF LEEUWENHOEK

Two evenings after this, thanks to an arrangement by letter and the promise of an ample fee, I found Madame Vulpes awaiting me at her residence alone. She was a coarse-featured woman, with keen and rather cruel dark eyes, and an exceedingly sensual expression about her mouth and under jaw. She received me in perfect silence, in an apartment on the ground floor, very sparely furnished. In the centre of the room, close to where Mrs. Vulpes sat, there was a common round mahogany table. If I had come for the purpose of sweeping her chimney, the woman could not have looked more indifferent to my appearance. There was no attempt to inspire the visitor with awe. Everything bore a simple and practical aspect. This intercourse with the spiritual world was evidently as familiar an occupation with Mrs. Vulpes as eating her dinner or riding in an omnibus.

"You come for a communication, Mr. Linley?" said the medium, in a dry, business-like tone of voice.

"By appointment,—yes."

"What sort of communication do you want—a written one?"

"Yes—I wish for a written one."

"From any particular spirit?"

"Yes."

"Have you ever known this spirit on this earth?"

"Never. He died long before I was born. I wish merely to obtain from him some information which he ought to be able to give better than any other."

"Will you seat yourself at the table, Mr. Linley," said the medium, "and place your hands upon it?"

I obeyed,—Mrs. Vulpes being seated opposite to me, with her hands also on the table. We remained thus for about a minute and a half, when a violent succession of raps came on the table, on the back of my chair, on the floor immediately under my feet, and even on the window-panes. Mrs. Vulpes smiled composedly.

"They are very strong tonight," she remarked. "You are fortunate." She then continued, "Will the spirits communicate with this gentleman?"

Vigorous affirmative.

"Will the particular spirit he desires to speak with communicate?"

A very confused rapping followed this question.

"I know what they mean," said Mrs. Vulpes, addressing herself to me; "they wish you to write down the name of the particular spirit that you desire to converse with. Is that so?" she added, speaking to her invisible guests.

That it was so was evident from the numerous affirmatory responses. While this was going on, I tore a slip from my pocket-book, and scribbled a name, under the table.

"Will this spirit communicate in writing with this gentleman?" asked the medium once more.

After a moment's pause, her hand seemed to be seized with a violent tremor, shaking so forcibly that the table vibrated. She said that a spirit had seized her hand and would write. I handed her some sheets of paper that were on the table, and a pencil. The latter she held loosely in her hand, which presently began to move over the paper with a singular and seemingly involuntary motion. After a few moments had elapsed, she handed me the paper, on which I found written, in a large, uncultivated hand, the words, "He is not here, but has been sent for." A pause of a minute or so now ensued, during which Mrs. Vulpes remained perfectly silent, but the raps continued at regular intervals. When the short period I mention had elapsed, the hand of the medium was again seized with its convulsive tremor, and she wrote, under this strange influence, a few words on the paper, which she handed to me. They were as follows:—

"I am here. Question me. Leeuwenhoek."

I was astounded. The name was identical with that I had written beneath the table, and carefully kept concealed. Neither was it at all probable that an uncultivated woman like Mrs. Vulpes should know even the name of the great father of microscopics. It may have been biology; but this theory was soon doomed to be destroyed. I wrote on my slip—still concealing it from Mrs. Vulpes—a series of questions, which, to avoid tediousness, I shall place with the responses, in the order in which they occurred:—

I.—Can the microscope be brought to perfection?
Spirit.—Yes.
I.—Am I destined to accomplish this great task?
Spirit.—You are.
I.—I wish to know how to proceed to attain this end. For the love which you bear to science, help me!
Spirit.—A diamond of one hundred and forty carats, submitted to electro-magnetic currents for a long period, will experience a rearrangement of its atom *sinter se*, and from that stone you will form the universal lens.

I.—Will great discoveries result from the use of such a lens?

Spirit.—So great that all that has gone before is as nothing.

I.—But the refractive power of the diamond is so immense, that the image will be formed within the lens. How is that difficulty to be surmounted?

Spirit.—Pierce the lens through its axis, and the difficulty is obviated. The image will be formed in the pierced space, which will itself serve as a tube to look through. Now I am called. Goodnight.

I cannot at all describe the effect that these extraordinary communications had upon me. I felt completely bewildered. No biological theory could account for the *discovery* of the lens. The medium might, by means of biological *rapport* with my mind, have gone so far as to read my questions, and reply to them coherently. But biology could not enable her to discover that magnetic currents would so alter the crystals of the diamond as to remedy its previous defects, and admit of its being polished into a perfect lens. Some such theory may have passed through my head, it is true; but if so, I had forgotten it. In my excited condition of mind there was no course left but to become a convert, and it was in a state of the most painful nervous exaltation that I left the medium's house that evening. She accompanied me to the door, hoping that I was satisfied.

The raps followed us as we went through the hall, sounding on the balusters, the flooring, and even the lintels of the door. I hastily expressed my satisfaction, and escaped hurriedly into the cool night air. I walked home with but one thought possessing me,—how to obtain a diamond of the immense size required. My entire means multiplied a hundred times over would have been inadequate to its purchase. Besides, such stones are rare, and become historical. I could find such only in the regalia of Eastern or European monarchs.

4

THE EYE OF MORNING

There was a light in Simon's room as I entered my house. A vague impulse urged me to visit him. As I opened the door of his sitting-room unannounced, he was bending, with his back toward me, over a carcel lamp, apparently engaged in minutely examining some object which he held in his hands. As I entered, he started suddenly, thrust his hand into his breast pocket, and turned to me with a face crimson with confusion.

"What!" I cried, "poring over the miniature of some fair lady?

Well, don't blush so much; I won't ask to see it."

Simon laughed awkwardly enough, but made none of the negative protestations usual on such occasions. He asked me to take a seat.

"Simon," said I, "I have just come from Madame Vulpes."

This time Simon turned as white as a sheet, and seemed stupefied, as if a sudden electric shock had smitten him. He babbled some incoherent words, and went hastily to a small closet where he usually kept his liquors. Although astonished at his emotion, I was too preoccupied with my own idea to pay much attention to anything else.

"You say truly when you call Madame Vulpes a devil of a woman," I continued. "Simon, she told me wonderful things tonight, or rather was the means of telling me wonderful things. Ah! if I could only get a diamond that weighed one hundred and forty carats!"

Scarcely had the sigh with which I uttered this desire died upon my lips, when Simon, with the aspect of a wild beast, glared at me savagely, and, rushing to the mantelpiece, where some foreign weapons hung on the wall, caught up a Malay *creese*, and brandished it furiously before him.

"No!" he cried in French, into which he always broke when excited. "No! you shall not have it! You are perfidious! You have consulted with that demon, and desire my treasure! But I will die first! Me! I am brave! You cannot make me fear!"

All this, uttered in a loud voice trembling with excitement, astounded me. I saw at a glance that I had accidentally trodden upon the edges of Simon's secret, whatever it was. It was necessary to reassure him.

"My dear Simon," I said, "I am entirely at a loss to know what you mean. I went to Madame Vulpes to consult with her on a scientific problem, to the solution of which I discovered that a diamond of the size I just mentioned was necessary. You were never alluded to during the evening, nor, so far as I was concerned, even thought of. What can be the meaning of this outburst? If you happen to have a set of valuable diamonds in your possession, you need fear nothing from me. The diamond which I require you could not possess; or, if you did possess it, you would not be living here."

Something in my tone must have completely reassured him; for his expression immediately changed to a sort of constrained merriment, combined, however, with a certain suspicious attention to my movements. He laughed, and said that I must bear with him; that he was at certain moments subject to a species of vertigo, which betrayed itself in incoherent speeches, and that the attacks passed off as rapidly as they came. He put his weapon aside while making this explanation, and endeavoured, with some success, to assume a more cheerful air.

All this did not impose on me in the least. I was too much accustomed to analytical labours to be baffled by so flimsy a veil. I determined to probe the mystery to the bottom.

"Simon," I said, gayly, "let us forget all this over a bottle of Burgundy. I have a case of Lausseure's *Clos Vougeot* downstairs, fragrant with the odours and ruddy with the sunlight of the Côte d'Or. Let us have up a couple of bottles. What say you?"

"With all my heart," answered Simon, smilingly.

I produced the wine and we seated ourselves to drink. It was of a famous vintage, that of 1848, a year when war and wine throve together,—and its pure but powerful juice seemed to impart renewed vitality to the system. By the time we had half finished the second bottle, Simon's head, which I knew was a weak one, had begun to yield, while I remained calm as ever, only that every draught seemed to send a flush of vigour through my limbs. Simon's utterance became more and more indistinct. He took to singing French *chansons* of a not very moral tendency. I rose suddenly from the table just at the conclusion of one of those incoherent verses, and, fixing my eyes on him with a quiet smile, said: "Simon, I have deceived you. I learned your secret this evening. You may as well be frank with me. Mrs. Vulpes, or rather one of her spirits, told me all."

He started with horror. His intoxication seemed for the moment to fade away, and he made a movement towards the weapon that he had a short time before laid down. I stopped him with my hand.

"Monster!" he cried, passionately, "I am ruined! What shall I do? You shall never have it! I swear by my mother!"

"I don't want it," I said; "rest secure, but be frank with me. Tell me all about it."

The drunkenness began to return. He protested with maudlin earnestness that I was entirely mistaken,—that I was intoxicated; then asked me to swear eternal secrecy, and promised to disclose the mystery to me. I pledged myself, of course, to all. With an uneasy look in his eyes, and hands unsteady with drink and nervousness, he drew a small case from his breast and opened it. Heavens! How the mild lamplight was shivered into a thousand prismatic arrows, as it fell upon a vast rose-diamond that glittered in the case! I was no judge of diamonds, but I saw at a glance that this was a gem of rare size and purity.

I looked at Simon with wonder, and—must I confess it?—with envy. How could he have obtained this treasure?

In reply to my questions, I could just gather from his drunken statements (of which, I fancy, half the incoherence was affected) that he had been superintending a gang of slaves engaged in diamond-washing in Brazil; that he had seen one of them secrete a diamond, but, instead of informing his employers, had quietly watched the negro until he saw him bury his treasure; that he had dug it up and fled with it, but that as yet he was afraid to attempt to dispose of it publicly,—so valuable a gem being almost certain to attract too much attention to its owner's antecedents,—and he had not been able to discover any of those obscure channels by which such matters are conveyed away safely. He added, that, in accordance with oriental practice, he had named his diamond with the fanciful title of "The Eye of Morning."

While Simon was relating this to me, I regarded the great diamond attentively. Never had I beheld anything so beautiful. All the glories of light, ever imagined or described, seemed to pulsate in its crystalline chambers. Its weight, as I learned from Simon, was exactly one hundred and forty carats. Here was an amazing coincidence. The hand of destiny seemed in it. On the very evening when the spirit of Leeuwenhoek communicates to me the great secret of the microscope, the priceless means which he directs me to employ start up within my easy reach! I determined, with the most perfect deliberation, to possess myself of Simon's diamond.

I sat opposite to him while he nodded over his glass, and calmly revolved the whole affair. I did not for an instant contemplate so foolish an act as a common theft, which would of course be discovered or at least necessitate flight and concealment, all of which must interfere with my scientific plans. There was but one step to be taken,—to kill Simon. After all, what was the life of a little peddling Jew, in comparison with the interests of science? Human beings are taken every day from the condemned prisons to be experimented on by surgeons. This man, Simon, was by his own confession a criminal, a robber, and I believed on my soul a murderer. He deserved death quite as much as any felon condemned by the laws: why should I not, like government, contrive that his punishment should contribute to the progress of human knowledge?

The means for accomplishing everything I desired lay within my reach. There stood upon the mantelpiece a bottle half full of French laudanum. Simon was so occupied with his diamond, which I had just restored to him, that it was an affair of no difficulty to drug his glass. In a quarter of an hour he was in a profound sleep.

I now opened his waistcoat, took the diamond from the inner pocket in which he had placed it, and removed him to the bed, on which I laid him so that his feet hung down over the edge. I had possessed myself of the Malay *creese*, which I held in my right hand, while with the other I discovered as accurately as I could by pulsation the exact locality of the heart. It was essential that all the aspects of his death should lead to the surmise of self-murder. I calculated the exact angle at which it was probable that the weapon, if levelled by Simon's own hand, would enter his breast; then with one powerful blow I thrust it up to the hilt in the very spot which I desired to penetrate. A convulsive thrill ran through Simon's limbs. I heard a smothered sound issue from his throat, precisely like the bursting of a large air-bubble, sent up by a diver, when it reaches the surface of the water; he turned half round on his side, and, as if to assist my plans more effectually, his right hand, moved by some mere spasmodic impulse, clasped the handle of the *creese*, which it remained holding with extraordinary muscular tenacity. Beyond this there was no apparent struggle. The laudanum, I presume, paralyzed the usual nervous action. He must have died instantly.

There was yet something to be done. To make it certain that all suspicion of the act should be diverted from any inhabitant of the house to Simon himself, it was necessary that the door should be in the morning *locked on the inside*. How to do this, and afterwards escape myself? Not by the window; that was a physical impossibility. Besides, I was determined that the windows *also* should be found bolted. The solution was simple enough. I descended softly to my own room for a peculiar instrument which I had used for holding small slippery substances, such as minute spheres of glass, etc. This instrument was nothing more than a long slender hand-vice, with a very powerful grip, and a considerable leverage, which last was accidentally owing to the shape of the handle. Nothing was simpler than, when the key was in the lock, to seize the end of its stem in this vice, through the keyhole, from the outside, and lock the door.

Previously, however, to doing this, I burned a number of papers on Simon's hearth. Suicides almost always burn papers before they destroy themselves. I also emptied some more *laudanum* into Simon's glass,—having first removed from it all traces of wine,—cleaned the other wine-glass, and brought the bottles away with me. If traces of two persons drinking had been found in the room, the question naturally would have arisen, Who was the second? Besides, the wine-bottles might have been identified as belonging to me. The laudanum I poured out to account for its presence in his stomach, in case of a *post-mortem* examination. The theory naturally would be, that he first intended to poison himself, but, after swallowing a little of the drug, was either disgusted with its taste, or changed his mind from other motives, and chose the dagger. These arrangements made, I walked out, leaving the gas burning, locked the door with my vice, and went to bed.

Simon's death was not discovered until nearly three in the afternoon. The servant, astonished at seeing the gas burning,—the light streaming on the dark landing from under the door,—peeped through the keyhole and saw Simon on the bed. She gave the alarm. The door was burst open, and the neighbourhood was in a fever of excitement.

Everyone in the house was arrested, myself included. There was an inquest; but no clew to his death beyond that of suicide could be obtained. Curiously enough, he had made several speeches to his friends the preceding week, that seemed to point to self-destruction. One gentleman swore that Simon had said in his presence that "he was tired of life." His landlord affirmed that Simon, when paying him his last month's rent, remarked that "he should not pay him rent much longer." All the other evidence corresponded,—the door locked inside, the position of the corpse, the burnt papers. As I anticipated, no one knew of the possession of the diamond by Simon, so that no motive was suggested for his murder. The jury, after a prolonged examination, brought in the usual verdict, and the neighbourhood once more settled down into its accustomed quiet.

5

ANIMULA

The three months succeeding Simon's catastrophe I devoted night and day to my diamond lens. I had constructed a vast galvanic battery, composed of nearly two thousand pairs of plates,—a higher power I dared not use, lest the diamond should be calcined. By means of this enormous engine I was enabled to send a powerful current of electricity continually through my great diamond, which it seemed to me gained in lustre every day. At the expiration of a month I commenced the grinding and polishing of the lens, a work of intense toil and exquisite delicacy. The great density of the stone, and the care required to be taken with the curvatures of the surfaces of the lens, rendered the labour the severest and most harassing that I had yet undergone.

At last the eventful moment came; the lens was completed. I stood trembling on the threshold of new worlds. I had the realization of Alexander's famous wish before me. The lens lay on the table, ready to be placed upon its platform. My hand fairly shook as I enveloped a drop of water with a thin coating of oil of turpentine, preparatory to its examination,—a process necessary in order to prevent the rapid evaporation of the water. I now placed the drop on a thin slip of glass under the lens, and throwing upon it, by the combined aid of a prism and a mirror, a powerful stream of light, I approached my eye to the minute hole drilled through the axis of the lens. For an instant I saw nothing save what seemed to be an illuminated chaos, a vast luminous abyss. A pure white light, cloudless and serene, and seemingly as limitless as space itself, was my first impression. Gently, and with the greatest care, I depressed the lens a few hair's-breadths. The wondrous illumination still continued, but as the lens approached the object a scene of indescribable beauty was unfolded to my view.

I seemed to gaze upon a vast space, the limits of which extended far beyond my vision. An atmosphere of magical luminousness permeated the entire field of view. I was amazed to see no trace of *animalculous* life. Not a living thing, apparently, inhabited that dazzling expanse. I comprehended instantly that, by the wondrous power of my lens, I had penetrated beyond the grosser particles of aqueous matter, beyond the realms of *infusoria* and *protozoa*, down to the original gaseous globule, into whose luminous interior I was gazing, as into an almost boundless dome filled with a supernatural radiance.

It was, however, no brilliant void into which I looked. On every side I beheld beautiful inorganic forms, of unknown texture, and coloured with the most enchanting hues. These forms presented the appearance of what might be called, for want of a more specific definition, foliated clouds of the highest rarity; that is, they undulated and broke into vegetable formations, and were tinged with splendours compared with which the gilding of our autumn woodlands is as dross compared with gold. Far away into the illimitable distance stretched long avenues of these gaseous forests, dimly transparent, and painted with prismatic hues of unimaginable brilliancy. The pendent branches waved along the fluid glades until every vista seemed to break through half-lucent ranks of many-coloured drooping silken pennons.

What seemed to be either fruits or flowers, pied with a thousand hues lustrous and ever varying, bubbled from the crowns of this fairy foliage. No hills, no lakes, no rivers, no forms animate or inanimate, were to be seen, save those vast *auroral* copses that floated serenely in the luminous stillness, with leaves and fruits and flowers gleaming with unknown fires, unrealizable by mere imagination.

How strange, I thought, that this sphere should be thus condemned to solitude! I had hoped, at least, to discover some new form of animal life—perhaps of a lower class than any with which we are at present acquainted, but still, some living organism. I found my newly discovered world, if I may so speak, a beautiful chromatic desert.

While I was speculating on the singular arrangements of the internal economy of Nature, with which she so frequently splinters into atoms our most compact theories, I thought I beheld a form moving slowly through the glades of one of the prismatic forests. I looked more attentively, and found that I was not mistaken. Words cannot depict the anxiety with which I awaited the nearer approach of this mysterious object. Was it merely some inanimate substance, held in suspense in the attenuated atmosphere of the globule, or was it an animal endowed with vitality and motion? It approached, flitting behind the gauzy, coloured veils of cloud-foliage, for seconds dimly revealed, then vanishing. At last the violet pennons that trailed nearest to me vibrated; they were gently pushed aside, and the form floated out into the broad light.

It was a female human shape. When I say human, I mean it possessed the outlines of humanity,—but there the analogy ends. Its adorable beauty lifted it illimitable heights beyond the loveliest daughter of Adam.

I cannot, I dare not, attempt to inventory the charms of this divine revelation of perfect beauty. Those eyes of mystic violet, dewy and serene, evade my words. Her long, lustrous hair following her glorious head in a golden wake, like the track sown in heaven by a falling star, seems to quench my most burning phrases with its splendours. If all the bees of Hybla nestled upon my lips, they would still sing but hoarsely the wondrous harmonies of outline that enclosed her form.

She swept out from between the rainbow-curtains of the cloud-trees into the broad sea of light that lay beyond. Her motions were those of some graceful naiad, cleaving, by a mere effort of her will, the clear, unruffled waters that fill the chambers of the sea. She floated forth with the serene grace of a frail bubble ascending through the still atmosphere of a June day. The perfect roundness of her limbs formed suave and enchanting curves. It was like listening to the most spiritual symphony of Beethoven the divine, to watch the harmonious flow of lines. This, indeed, was a pleasure cheaply purchased at any price. What cared I if I had waded to the portal of this wonder through another's blood? I would have given my own to enjoy one such moment of intoxication and delight.

Breathless with gazing on this lovely wonder, and forgetful for an instant of everything save her presence, I withdrew my eye from the microscope eagerly,—alas! As my gaze fell on the thin slide that lay beneath my instrument, the bright light from mirror and from prism sparkled on a colourless drop of water! There, in that tiny bead of dew, this beautiful being was forever imprisoned. The planet Neptune was not more distant from me than she. I hastened once more to apply my eye to the microscope.

Animula (let me now call her by that dear name which I subsequently bestowed on her) had changed her position. She had again approached the wondrous forest, and was gazing earnestly upwards. Presently one of the trees—as I must call them—unfolded a long ciliary process, with which it seized one of the gleaming fruits that glittered on its summit, and, sweeping slowly down, held it within reach of Animula. The sylph took it in her delicate hand and began to eat. My attention was so entirely absorbed by her, that I could not apply myself to the task of determining whether this singular plant was or was not instinct with volition.

I watched her, as she made her repast, with the most profound attention. The suppleness of her motions sent a thrill of delight through my frame; my heart beat madly as she turned her beautiful eyes in the direction of the spot in which I stood. What would I not have given to have had the power to precipitate myself into that luminous ocean, and float with her through those groves of purple and gold! While I was thus breathlessly following her every movement, she suddenly started, seemed to listen for a moment, and then cleaving the brilliant ether in which she was floating, like a flash of light, pierced through the *opaline* forest, and disappeared.

Instantly a series of the most singular sensations attacked me. It seemed as if I had suddenly gone blind. The luminous sphere was still before me, but my daylight had vanished. What caused this sudden disappearance? Had she a lover or a husband? Yes, that was the solution! Some signal from a happy fellow-being had vibrated through the avenues of the forest, and she had obeyed the summons.

The agony of my sensations, as I arrived at this conclusion, startled me. I tried to reject the conviction that my reason forced upon me. I battled against the fatal conclusion,—but in vain. It was so. I had no escape from it. I loved an animalcule!

It is true that, thanks to the marvellous power of my microscope, she appeared of human proportions. Instead of presenting the revolting aspect of the coarser creatures, that live and struggle and die, in the more easily resolvable portions of the water-drop, she was fair and delicate and of surpassing beauty. But of what account was all that? Every time that my eye was withdrawn from the instrument, it fell on a miserable drop of water, within which, I must be content to know, dwelt all that could make my life lovely.

Could she but see me once! Could I for one moment pierce the mystical walls that so inexorably rose to separate us, and whisper all that filled my soul, I might consent to be satisfied for the rest of my life with the knowledge of her remote sympathy. It would be something to have established even the faintest personal link to bind us together,—to know that at times, when roaming through those enchanted glades, she might think of the wonderful stranger, who had broken the monotony of her life with his presence, and left a gentle memory in her heart!

But it could not be. No invention of which human intellect was capable could break down the barriers that nature had erected. I might feast my soul upon the wondrous beauty, yet she must always remain ignorant of the adoring eyes that day and night gazed upon her, and, even when closed, beheld her in dreams. With a bitter cry of anguish I fled from the room, and, flinging myself on my bed, sobbed myself to sleep like a child.

6

THE SPILLING OF THE CUP

I arose the next morning almost at daybreak, and rushed to my microscope. I trembled as I sought the luminous world in miniature that contained my all. Animula was there. I had left the gas-lamp, surrounded by its moderators, burning when I went to bed the night before. I found the sylph bathing, as it were, with an expression of pleasure animating her features, in the brilliant light which surrounded her. She tossed her lustrous golden hair over her shoulders with innocent *coquetry*. She lay at full length in the transparent medium, in which she supported herself with ease, and gambolled with the enchanting grace that the nymph Salmacis might have exhibited when she sought to conquer the modest Hermaphroditus. I tried an experiment to satisfy myself if her powers of reflection were developed. I lessened the lamplight considerably. By the dim light that remained, I could see an expression of pain flit across her face. She looked upward suddenly, and her brows contracted. I flooded the stage of the microscope again with a full stream of light, and her whole expression changed. She sprang forward like some substance deprived of all weight. Her eyes sparkled and her lips moved. Ah! if science had only the means of conducting and reduplicating sounds, as it does the rays of light, what carols of happiness would then have entranced my ears! what jubilant hymns to Adonais would have thrilled the illumined air!

I now comprehended how it was that the Count de Gabalis peopled his mystic world with sylphs,—beautiful beings whose breath of life was lambent fire, and who sported forever in regions of purest ether and purest light. The Rosicrucian had anticipated the wonder that I had practically realized.

How long this worship of my strange divinity went on thus I scarcely know. I lost all note of time. All day from early dawn, and far into the night, I was to be found peering through that wonderful lens. I saw no one, went nowhere, and scarce allowed myself sufficient time for my meals. My whole life was absorbed in contemplation as rapt as that of any of the Romish saints. Every hour that I gazed upon the divine form strengthened my passion,—a passion that was always overshadowed by the maddening conviction that, although I could gaze on her at will, she never, never could behold me!

At length I grew so pale and emaciated from want of rest and continual brooding over my insane love and its cruel conditions that I determined to make some effort to wean myself from it. "Come," I said, "this is at best but a fantasy. Your imagination has bestowed on Animula charms which in reality she does not possess. Seclusion from female society has produced this morbid condition of mind. Compare her with the beautiful women of your own world, and this false enchantment will vanish."

I looked over the newspapers by chance. There I beheld the advertisement of a celebrated *danseuse* who appeared nightly at Niblo's. The Signorina Caradolce had the reputation of being the most beautiful as well as the most graceful woman in the world. I instantly dressed and went to the theatre.

The curtain drew up. The usual semicircle of fairies in white muslin were standing on the right toe around the enamelled flower-bank, of green canvas, on which the belated prince was sleeping. Suddenly a flute is heard. The fairies start. The trees open, the fairies all stand on the left toe, and the queen enters. It was the *signorina*. She bounded forward amid thunders of applause, and, lighting on one foot, remained poised in air. Heavens! was this the great enchantress that had drawn monarchs at her chariot-wheels? Those heavy muscular limbs, those thick ankles, those cavernous eyes, that stereotyped smile, those crudely painted cheeks! Where were the vermeil blooms, the liquid expressive eyes, the harmonious limbs of Animula?

The *signorina* danced. What gross, discordant movements! The play of her limbs was all false and artificial. Her bounds were painful athletic efforts; her poses were angular and distressed the eye. I could bear it no longer; with an exclamation of disgust that drew every eye upon me, I rose from my seat in the very middle of the Signorina's *pas-de-fascination*, and abruptly quitted the house.

I hastened home to feast my eyes once more on the lovely form of my sylph. I felt that henceforth to combat this passion would be impossible. I applied my eye to the lens. Animula was there,—but what could have happened? Some terrible change seemed to have taken place during my absence. Some secret grief seemed to cloud the lovely features of her I gazed upon. Her face had grown thin and haggard; her limbs trailed heavily; the wondrous lustre of her golden hair had faded. She was ill!—ill, and I could not assist her! I believe at that moment I would have gladly forfeited all claims to my human birthright, if I could only have been dwarfed to the size of an animalcule, and permitted to console her from whom fate had forever divided me.

I racked my brain for the solution of this mystery. What was it that afflicted the sylph? She seemed to suffer intense pain. Her features contracted, and she even writhed, as if with some internal agony. The wondrous forests appeared also to have lost half their beauty. Their hues were dim and in some places faded away altogether. I watched Animula for hours with a breaking heart, and she seemed absolutely to wither away under my very eye. Suddenly I remembered that I had not looked at the water-drop for several days. In fact, I hated to see it; for it reminded me of the natural barrier between Animula and myself. I hurriedly looked down on the stage of the microscope. The slide was still there,—but, great heavens! the water-drop had vanished! The awful truth burst upon me; it had evaporated; until it had become so minute as to be invisible to the naked eye; I had been gazing on its last atom, the one that contained Animula,—and she was dying!

I rushed again to the front of the lens, and looked through. Alas! the last agony had seized her. The rainbow-hued forests had all melted away, and Animula lay struggling feebly in what seemed to be a spot of dim light. Ah! the sight was horrible; the limbs once so round and lovely shrivelling up into nothings; the eyes,—those eyes that shone like heaven—being quenched into black dust; the lustrous golden hair now lank and discoloured. The last throe came. I beheld that final struggle of the blackening form—and I fainted.

When I awoke out of a trance of many hours, I found myself lying amid the wreck of my instrument, myself as shattered in mind and body as it. I crawled feebly to my bed, from which I did not rise for months.

They say now that I am mad; but they are mistaken. I am poor, for I have neither the heart nor the will to work; all my money is spent, and I live on charity. Young men's associations that love a joke invite me to lecture on Optics before them, for which they pay me and laugh at me while I lecture. "Linley, the mad microscopist," is the name I go by. I suppose that I talk incoherently while I lecture. Who could talk sense when his brain is haunted by such ghastly memories, while ever and *anon* among the shapes of death I behold the radiant form of my lost Animula!

The Eyes of the Panther
By Ambrose Bierce

1
ONE DOES NOT ALWAYS MARRY WHEN INSANE

A man and a woman—nature had done the grouping—sat on a rustic seat, in the late afternoon. The man was middle-aged, slender, swarthy, with the expression of a poet and the complexion of a pirate—a man at whom one would look again. The woman was young, blonde, graceful, with something in her figure and movements suggesting the word "lithe." She was habited in a gray gown with odd brown markings in the texture. She may have been beautiful; one could not readily say, for her eyes denied attention to all else. They were gray-green, long and narrow, with an expression defying analysis. One could only know that they were disquieting. Cleopatra may have had such eyes.

The man and the woman talked.

"Yes," said the woman, "I love you, God knows! But marry you, no. I cannot, will not."

"Irene, you have said that many times, yet always have denied me a reason. I've a right to know, to understand, to feel and prove my fortitude if I have it. Give me a reason."

"For loving you?"

The woman was smiling through her tears and her pallor. That did not stir any sense of humour in the man.

"No; there is no reason for that. A reason for not marrying me. I've a right to know. I must know. I will know!"

He had risen and was standing before her with clenched hands, on his face a frown—it might have been called a scowl. He looked as if he might attempt to learn by strangling her. She smiled no more—merely sat looking up into his face with a fixed, set regard that was

236

utterly without emotion or sentiment. Yet it had something in it that tamed his resentment and made him shiver.

"You are determined to have my reason?" she asked in a tone that was entirely mechanical—a tone that might have been her look made audible.

"If you please—if I'm not asking too much."

Apparently this lord of creation was yielding some part of his dominion over his co-creature.

"Very well, you shall know: I am insane."

The man started, then looked incredulous and was conscious that he ought to be amused. But, again, the sense of humour failed him in his need and despite his disbelief he was profoundly disturbed by that which he did not believe. Between our convictions and our feelings there is no good understanding.

"That is what the physicians would say," the woman continued, "if they knew. I might myself prefer to call it a case of 'possession.' Sit down and hear what I have to say."

The man silently resumed his seat beside her on the rustic bench by the wayside. Over against them on the eastern side of the valley the hills were already sunset-flushed and the stillness all about was of that peculiar quality that foretells the twilight. Something of its mysterious and significant solemnity had imparted itself to the man's mood. In the spiritual, as in the material world, are signs and presages of night. Rarely meeting her look, and whenever he did so conscious of the indefinable dread with which, despite their feline beauty, her eyes always affected him, Jenner Brading listened in silence to the story told by Irene Marlowe. In deference to the reader's possible prejudice against the artless method of an unpracticed historian the author ventures to substitute his own version for hers.

2

A ROOM MAY BE TOO NARROW FOR THREE, THOUGH
ONE IS OUTSIDE

In a little log house containing a single room sparely and rudely furnished, crouching on the floor against one of the walls, was a woman, clasping to her breast a child. Outside, a dense unbroken forest extended for many miles in every direction. This was at night and the room was black dark; no human eye could have discerned the woman and the child. Yet they were observed, narrowly, vigilantly, with never even a momentary slackening of attention; and that is the pivotal fact upon which this narrative turns.

Charles Marlowe was of the class, now extinct in this country, of woodmen pioneers—men who found their most acceptable surroundings in sylvan solitudes that stretched along the eastern slope of the Mississippi Valley, from the Great Lakes to the Gulf of Mexico. For more than a hundred years these men pushed ever westward, generation after generation, with rifle and axe, reclaiming from Nature and her savage children here and there an isolated acreage for the plough, no sooner reclaimed than surrendered to their less venturesome but more thrifty successors. At last they burst through the edge of the forest into the open country and vanished as if they had fallen over a cliff. The woodman pioneer is no more; the pioneer of the plains—he whose easy task it was to subdue for occupancy two-thirds of the country in a single generation—is another and inferior creation.

With Charles Marlowe in the wilderness, sharing the dangers, hardships and privations of that strange unprofitable life, were his wife and child, to whom, in the manner of his class in which the domestic virtues were a religion, he was passionately attached. The woman was still young enough to be comely, new enough to the awful isolation of her lot to be cheerful. By withholding the large capacity for happiness which the simple satisfactions of the forest life could not have filled, Heaven had dealt honourably with her. In her light household tasks, her child, her husband and her few foolish books, she found abundant provision for her needs.

One morning in midsummer Marlowe took down his rifle from the wooden hooks on the wall and signified his intention of getting game.

"We've meat enough," said the wife; "please don't go out today. I dreamed last night, O, such a dreadful thing! I cannot recollect it, but I'm almost sure that it will come to pass if you go out."

It is painful to confess that Marlowe received this solemn statement with less of gravity than was due to the mysterious nature of the calamity foreshadowed. In truth, he laughed.

"Try to remember," he said. "Maybe you dreamed that Baby had lost the power of speech."

The conjecture was obviously suggested by the fact that Baby, clinging to the fringe of his hunting-coat with all her ten pudgy thumbs, was at that moment uttering her sense of the situation in a series of exultant goo-goos inspired by sight of her father's raccoon-skin cap.

The woman yielded: lacking the gift of humour she could not

hold out against his kindly badinage. So, with a kiss for the mother and a kiss for the child, he left the house and closed the door upon his happiness forever.

At nightfall he had not returned. The woman prepared supper and waited. Then she put Baby to bed and sang softly to her until she slept. By this time the fire on the hearth, at which she had cooked supper, had burned out and the room was lighted by a single candle. This she afterward placed in the open window as a sign and welcome to the hunter if he should approach from that side. She had thoughtfully closed and barred the door against such wild animals as might prefer it to an open window—of the habits of beasts of prey in entering a house uninvited she was not advised, though with true female prevision she may have considered the possibility of their entrance by way of the chimney. As the night wore on she became not less anxious, but more drowsy, and at last rested her arms upon the bed by the child and her head upon the arms. The candle in the window burned down to the socket, sputtered and flared a moment and went out unobserved; for the woman slept and dreamed.

In her dreams she sat beside the cradle of a second child. The first one was dead. The father was dead. The home in the forest was lost and the dwelling in which she lived was unfamiliar. There were heavy oaken doors, always closed, and outside the windows, fastened into the thick stone walls, were iron bars, obviously (so she thought) a provision against Indians. All this she noted with an infinite self-pity, but without surprise—an emotion unknown in dreams. The child in the cradle was invisible under its coverlet which something impelled her to remove. She did so, disclosing the face of a wild animal! In the shock of this dreadful revelation the dreamer awoke, trembling in the darkness of her cabin in the wood.

As a sense of her actual surroundings came slowly back to her she felt for the child that was not a dream, and assured herself by its breathing that all was well with it; nor could she forbear to pass a hand lightly across its face. Then, moved by some impulse for which she probably could not have accounted, she rose and took the sleeping babe in her arms, holding it close against her breast. The head of the child's cot was against the wall to which the woman now turned her back as she stood. Lifting her eyes she saw two bright objects starring the darkness with a reddish-green glow. She took them to be two coals on the hearth, but with her returning sense of direction came the disquieting consciousness that they were not in that quarter of the room, moreover were too high, being nearly at the level of the eyes—of her own eyes. For these were the eyes of a panther.

The beast was at the open window directly opposite and not five paces away. Nothing but those terrible eyes was visible, but in the dreadful tumult of her feelings as the situation disclosed itself to her understanding she somehow knew that the animal was standing on its hinder feet, supporting itself with its paws on the window-ledge. That signified a malign interest—not the mere gratification of an indolent curiosity. The consciousness of the attitude was an added horror, accentuating the menace of those awful eyes, in whose steadfast fire her strength and courage were alike consumed. Under their silent questioning she shuddered and turned sick.

Her knees failed her, and by degrees, instinctively striving to avoid a sudden movement that might bring the beast upon her, she sank to the floor, crouched against the wall and tried to shield the babe with her trembling body without withdrawing her gaze from the luminous orbs that were killing her. No thought of her husband came to her in her agony—no hope nor suggestion of rescue or escape. Her capacity for thought and feeling had narrowed to the dimensions of a single emotion—fear of the animal's spring, of the impact of its body, the buffeting of its great arms, the feel of its teeth in her throat, the mangling of her babe. Motionless now and in absolute silence, she awaited her doom, the moments growing to hours, to years, to ages; and still those devilish eyes maintained their watch.

★★★★★★

Returning to his cabin late at night with a deer on his shoulders Charles Marlowe tried the door. It did not yield. He knocked; there was no answer. He laid down his deer and went around to the window. As he turned the angle of the building he fancied he heard a sound as of stealthy footfalls and a rustling in the undergrowth of the forest, but they were too slight for certainty, even to his practiced ear. Approaching the window, and to his surprise finding it open, he threw his leg over the sill and entered. All was darkness and silence. He groped his way to the fire-place, struck a match and lit a candle. Then he looked about. Cowering on the floor against a wall was his wife, clasping his child. As he sprang toward her she rose and broke into laughter, long, loud, and mechanical, devoid of gladness and devoid of sense—the laughter that is not out of keeping with the clanking of a chain. Hardly knowing what he did he extended his arms. She laid the babe in them. It was dead—pressed to death in its mother's embrace.

3
THE THEORY OF THE DEFENCE

That is what occurred during a night in a forest, but not all of it did Irene Marlowe relate to Jenner Brading; not all of it was known to her. When she had concluded the sun was below the horizon and the long summer twilight had begun to deepen in the hollows of the land. For some moments Brading was silent, expecting the narrative to be carried forward to some definite connection with the conversation introducing it; but the narrator was as silent as he, her face averted, her hands clasping and unclasping themselves as they lay in her lap, with a singular suggestion of an activity independent of her will.

"It is a sad, a terrible story," said Brading at last, "but I do not understand. You call Charles Marlowe father; that I know. That he is old before his time, broken by some great sorrow, I have seen, or thought I saw. But, pardon me, you said that you—that you—"

"That I am insane," said the girl, without a movement of head or body.

"But, Irene, you say—please, dear, do not look away from me—you say that the child was dead, not demented."

"Yes, that one—I am the second. I was born three months after that night, my mother being mercifully permitted to lay down her life in giving me mine."

Brading was again silent; he was a trifle dazed and could not at once think of the right thing to say. Her face was still turned away. In his embarrassment he reached impulsively toward the hands that lay closing and unclosing in her lap, but something—he could not have said what—restrained him. He then remembered, vaguely, that he had never altogether cared to take her hand.

"Is it likely," she resumed, "that a person born under such circumstances is like others—is what you call sane?"

Brading did not reply; he was preoccupied with a new thought that was taking shape in his mind—what a scientist would have called an hypothesis; a detective, a theory. It might throw an added light, albeit a lurid one, upon such doubt of her sanity as her own assertion had not dispelled.

The country was still new and, outside the villages, sparsely populated. The professional hunter was still a familiar figure, and among his trophies were heads and pelts of the larger kinds of game. Tales variously credible of nocturnal meetings with savage animals in lonely roads were sometimes current, passed through the customary stages of growth and decay, and were forgotten. A recent addition to these popular apocrypha, originating, apparently, by spontaneous generation in several households, was of a panther which had frightened some of their members by looking in at windows by night. The yarn had caused its little ripple of excitement—had even attained to the distinction of a place in the local newspaper; but Brading had given it no attention. Its likeness to the story to which he had just listened now impressed him as perhaps more than accidental. Was it not possible that the one story had suggested the other—that finding congenial conditions in a morbid mind and a fertile fancy, it had grown to the tragic tale that he had heard?

Brading recalled certain circumstances of the girl's history and disposition of which, with love's incuriosity, he had hitherto been heedless—such as her solitary life with her father, at whose house no one apparently was an acceptable visitor, and her strange fear of the night by which those who knew her best accounted for her never being seen after dark. Surely in such a mind imagination once kindled might burn with a lawless flame, penetrating and enveloping the entire structure. That she was mad, though the conviction gave him the acutest pain, he could no longer doubt; she had only mistaken an effect of her mental disorder for its cause, bringing into imaginary relation with her own personality the vagaries of the local myth-makers. With some vague intention of testing his new "theory," and no very definite notion of how to set about it he said gravely, but with hesitation:

"Irene, dear, tell me—I beg you will not take offense, but tell me—"

"I have told you," she interrupted, speaking with a passionate earnestness that he had not known her to show, "I have already told you that we cannot marry; is anything else worth saying?"

Before he could stop her she had sprung from her seat and without another word or look was gliding away among the trees toward her father's house. Brading had risen to detain her; he stood watching her in silence until she had vanished in the gloom.

Suddenly he started as if he had been shot, his face took on an expression of amazement and alarm: in one of the black shadows into which she had disappeared he had caught a quick, brief glimpse of shining eyes! For an instant he was dazed and irresolute; then he dashed into the wood after her, shouting, "Irene, Irene, look out! The panther! The panther!"

In a moment he had passed through the fringe of forest into open ground and saw the girl's gray skirt vanishing into her father's door. No panther was visible.

4

AN APPEAL TO THE CONSCIENCE OF GOD

Jenner Brading, attorney-at-law, lived in a cottage at the edge of the town. Directly behind the dwelling was the forest. Being a bachelor, and therefore by the Draconian moral code of the time and place denied the services of the only species of domestic servant known thereabout, the "hired girl," he boarded at the village hotel where also was his office. The woodside cottage was merely a lodging maintained—at no great cost, to be sure—as an evidence of prosperity and respectability. It would hardly do for one to whom the local newspaper had pointed with pride as "the foremost jurist of his time" to be "homeless," albeit he may sometimes have suspected that the words "home" and "house" were not strictly synonymous. Indeed, his consciousness of the disparity and his will to harmonize it were matters of logical inference, for it was generally reported that soon after the cottage was built its owner had made a futile venture in the direction of marriage—had, in truth, gone so far as to be rejected by the beautiful but eccentric daughter of Old Man Marlowe, the recluse. This was publicly believed because he had told it himself and she had not—a reversal of the usual order of things which could hardly fail to carry conviction.

Brading's bedroom was at the rear of the house, with a single window facing the forest. One night he was awakened by a noise at that window—he could hardly have said what it was like. With a little thrill of the nerves he sat up in bed and laid hold of the revolver which, with a forethought most commendable in one addicted to the habit of sleeping on the ground floor with an open window, he had put under his pillow. The room was in absolute darkness, but being unterrified he knew where to direct his eyes, and there he held them, awaiting in silence what further might occur. He could now dimly discern the aperture—a square of lighter black. Presently there appeared at its lower edge two gleaming eyes that burned with a malignant lustre inexpressibly terrible! Brading's heart gave a great jump, then seemed to stand still. A chill passed along his spine and through his hair; he felt the blood forsake his cheeks. He could not have cried out—not to save his life; but being a man of courage he would not, to save his life, have done so if he had been able. Some trepidation his coward body might feel, but his spirit was of sterner stuff. Slowly the shining eyes rose with a steady motion that seemed an approach, and slowly rose Brading's right hand, holding the pistol. He fired!

Blinded by the flash and stunned by the report, Brading nevertheless heard, or fancied that he heard, the wild high scream of the panther, so human in sound, so devilish in suggestion. Leaping from the bed he hastily clothed himself and pistol in hand, sprang from the door, meeting two or three men who came running up from the road. A brief explanation was followed by a cautious search of the house. The grass was wet with dew; beneath the window it had been trodden and partly levelled for a wide space, from which a devious trail, visible in the light of a lantern, led away into the bushes. One of the men stumbled and fell upon his hands, which as he rose and rubbed them together were slippery. On examination they were seen to be red with blood.

An encounter, unarmed, with a wounded panther was not agreeable to their taste; all but Brading turned back. He, with lantern and pistol, pushed courageously forward into the wood. Passing through a difficult undergrowth he came into a small opening, and there his courage had its reward, for there he found the body of his victim. But it was no panther. What it was is told, even to this day, upon a weather-worn headstone in the village churchyard, and for many years was attested daily at the graveside by the bent figure and sorrow-seamed face of Old Man Marlowe, to whose soul, and to the soul of his strange, unhappy child, peace—peace and reparation.

The Woman's Ghost Story
By Algernon Blackwood

"Yes," she said, from her seat in the dark corner, "I'll tell you an experience if you care to listen. And, what's more, I'll tell it briefly, without trimmings—I mean without unessentials. That's a thing story-tellers never do, you know," she laughed. "They drag in all the unessentials and leave their listeners to disentangle; but I'll give you just the essentials, and you can make of it what you please. But on one condition: that at the end you ask no questions, because I can't explain it and have no wish to."

We agreed. We were all serious. After listening to a dozen prolix stories from people who merely wished to "talk" but had nothing to tell, we wanted "essentials."

"In those days," she began, feeling from the quality of our silence that we were with her, "in those days I was interested in psychic things, and had arranged to sit up alone in a haunted house in the middle of London. It was a cheap and dingy lodging-house in a mean street, unfurnished. I had already made a preliminary examination in daylight that afternoon, and the keys from the caretaker, who lived next door, were in my pocket. The story was a good one—satisfied me, at any rate, that it was worth investigating; and I won't weary you with details as to the woman's murder and all the tiresome elaboration as to *why* the place was *alive*. Enough that it was.

"I was a good deal bored, therefore, to see a man, whom I took to be the talkative old caretaker, waiting for me on the steps when I went in at 11 p.m., for I had sufficiently explained that I wished to be there alone for the night.

"'I wished to show you *the* room,' he mumbled, and of course I couldn't exactly refuse, having tipped him for the temporary loan of a chair and table.

"'Come in, then, and let's be quick,' I said.

"We went in, he shuffling' after me through the unlighted hall up to the first floor where the murder had taken place, and I prepared myself to hear his inevitable account before turning him out with the half-crown his persistence had earned. After lighting the gas I sat down in the arm-chair he had provided—a faded, brown plush armchair—and turned for the first time to face him and get through with the performance as quickly as possible. And it was in that instant I got my first shock. The man was not the caretaker. It was not the old fool, Carey, I had interviewed earlier in the day and made my plans with. My heart gave a horrid jump.

"'Now who are *you*, pray?' I said. 'You're not Carey, the man I arranged with this afternoon. Who are you?'

"I felt uncomfortable, as you may imagine. I was a 'psychical researcher,' and a young woman of new tendencies, and proud of my liberty, but I did not care to find myself in an empty house with a stranger. Something of my confidence left me. Confidence with women, you know, is all humbug after a certain point. Or perhaps you don't know, for most of you are men. But anyhow my pluck ebbed in a quick rush, and I felt afraid.

"'Who are you?' I repeated quickly and nervously. The fellow was well dressed, youngish and good-looking, but with a face of great sadness. I myself was barely thirty. I am giving you essentials, or I would not mention it. Out of quite ordinary things comes this story. I think that's why it has value.

"'No,' he said; 'I'm the man who was frightened to death.'

"His voice and his words ran through me like a knife, and I felt ready to drop. In my pocket was the book I had bought to make notes in. I felt the pencil sticking in the socket. I felt, too, the extra warm things I had put on to sit up in, as no bed or sofa was available—a hundred things dashed through my mind, foolishly and without sequence or meaning, as the way is when one is really frightened. Unessentials leaped up and puzzled me, and I thought of what the papers might say if it came out, and what my 'smart' brother-in-law would think, and whether it would be told that I had cigarettes in my pocket, and was a freethinker.

"'The man who was frightened to death!' I repeated aghast.

"'That's me,' he said stupidly.

"I stared at him just as you would have done—any one of you men now listening to me—and felt my life ebbing and flowing like a sort of hot fluid. You needn't laugh! That's how I felt. Small things, you know, touch the mind with great earnestness when terror is there—*real terror*. But I might have been at a middle-class tea-party, for all the ideas I had: they were so ordinary!

"'But I thought you were the caretaker I tipped this afternoon to let me sleep here!' I gasped. 'Did—did Carey send you to meet me?'

"'No,' he replied in a voice that touched my boots somehow. 'I am the man who was frightened to death. And what is more, I am frightened *now!*'

"'So am I!' I managed to utter, speaking instinctively. 'I'm simply terrified.'

"'Yes,' he replied in that same odd voice that seemed to sound within me. 'But you are still in the flesh, and I—*am not!*'

"I felt the need for vigorous self-assertion. I stood up in that empty, unfurnished room, digging the nails into my palms and clenching my teeth. I was determined to assert my individuality and my courage as a new woman and a free soul.

"'You mean to say you are not in the flesh!' I gasped. 'What in the world are you talking about?'

"The silence of the night swallowed up my voice. For the first time I realized that darkness was over the city; that dust lay upon the stairs; that the floor above was untenanted and the floor below empty. I was alone in an unoccupied and haunted house, unprotected, and a woman. I chilled. I heard the wind round the house, and knew the stars were hidden. My thoughts rushed to policemen and omnibuses, and everything that was useful and comforting. I suddenly realized what a fool I was to come to such a house alone. I was icily afraid. I thought the end of my life had come. I was an utter fool to go in for psychical research when I had not the necessary nerve.

"'Good God!' I gasped. 'If you're not Carey, the man I arranged with, who are you?'

"I was really stiff with terror. The man moved slowly towards me across the empty room. I held out my arm to stop him, getting up out of my chair at the same moment, and he came to halt just opposite to me, a smile on his worn, sad face.

"'I told you who I am,' he repeated quietly with a sigh, looking at me with the saddest eyes I have ever seen, 'and I am frightened *still.*'

"By this time I was convinced that I was entertaining either a rogue or a madman, and I cursed my stupidity in bringing the man in without having seen his face. My mind was quickly made up, and I knew what to do. Ghosts and psychic phenomena flew to the winds. If I angered the creature my life might pay the price. I must humour him till I got to the door, and then race for the street. I stood bolt upright and faced him. We were about of a height, and I was a strong, athletic woman who played hockey in winter and climbed Alps in summer. My hand itched for a stick, but I had none.

"'Now, of course, I remember,' I said with a sort of stiff smile that was very hard to force. 'Now I remember your case and the wonderful way you behaved—'

"The man stared at me stupidly, turning his head to watch me as I backed more and more quickly to the door. But when his face broke into a smile I could control myself no longer. I reached the door in a run, and shot out on to the landing. Like a fool, I turned the wrong way, and stumbled over the stairs leading to the next story. But it was too late to change. The man was after me, I was sure, though no sound of footsteps came; and I dashed up the next flight, tearing my skirt and banging my ribs in the darkness, and rushed headlong into the first room I came to. Luckily the door stood ajar, and, still more fortunate, there was a key in the lock. In a second I had slammed the door, flung my whole weight against it, and turned the key.

"I was safe, but my heart was beating like a drum. A second later it seemed to stop altogether, for I saw that there was someone else in the room besides myself. A man's figure stood between me and the windows, where the street lamps gave just enough light to outline his shape against the glass. I'm a plucky woman, you know, for even then I didn't give up hope, but I may tell you that I have never felt so vilely frightened in all my born days. I had locked myself in with him!

"The man leaned against the window, watching me where I lay in a collapsed heap upon the floor. So there were two men in the house with me, I reflected. Perhaps other rooms were occupied too! What could it all mean? But, as I stared something changed in the room, or in me—hard to say which—and I realized my mistake, so that my fear, which had so far been physical, at once altered its character and became *psychical*, I became afraid in my soul instead of in my heart, and I knew immediately who this man was.

"'How in the world did you get up here?' I stammered to him across the empty room, amazement momentarily stemming my fear.

" 'Now, let me tell you,' he began, in that odd faraway voice of his that went down my spine like a knife. 'I'm in different space, for one thing, and you'd find me in any room you went into; for according to

248

your way of measuring, I'm *all over the house*. Space is a bodily condition, but I am out of the body, and am not affected by space. It's my condition that keeps me here. I want something to change my condition for me, for then I could get away. What I want is sympathy. Or, really, more than sympathy; I want affection—I want *love!*'

"While he was speaking I gathered myself slowly upon my feet. I wanted to scream and cry and laugh all at once, but I only succeeded in sighing, for my emotion was exhausted and a numbness was coming over me. I felt for the matches in my pocket and made a movement towards the gas jet.

"'I should be much happier if you didn't light the gas,' he said at once, 'or the vibrations of your light hurt me a good deal. You need not be afraid that I shall injure you. I can't touch your body to begin with, for there's a great gulf fixed, you know; and really this half-light suits me best. Now, let me continue what I was trying to say before. You know, so many people have come to this house to see me, and most of them have seen me, and one and all have been terrified. If only, oh, if only someone would be *not* terrified, but kind and loving to me! Then, you see, I might be able to change my condition and get away.'

"His voice was so sad that I felt tears start somewhere at the back of my eyes; but fear kept all else in check, and I stood shaking and cold as I listened to him.

"'Who are you then? Of course Carey didn't send you, I know now,' I managed to utter. My thoughts scattered dreadfully and I could think of nothing to say. I was afraid of a stroke.

"'I know nothing about Carey, or who he is,' continued the man quietly, 'and the name my body had I have forgotten, thank God; but I am the man who was frightened to death in this house ten years ago, and I have been frightened ever since, and am frightened still; for the succession of cruel and curious people who come to this house to see the ghost, and thus keep alive its atmosphere of terror, only helps to render my condition worse. If only someone would be kind to me— *laugh*, speak gently and rationally with me, cry if they like, pity, comfort, soothe me—anything but come here in curiosity and tremble as you are now doing in that corner. Now, madam, won't you take pity on me?' His voice rose to a dreadful cry. 'Won't you step out into the middle of the room and try to love me a little?'

"A horrible laughter came gurgling up in my throat as I heard him, but the sense of pity was stronger than the laughter, and I found myself actually leaving the support of the wall and approaching the centre of the floor.

"'By God!' he cried, at once straightening up against the window, 'you have done a kind act. That's the first attempt at sympathy that has been shown me since I died, and I feel better already. In life, you know, I was a misanthrope. Everything went wrong with me, and I came to hate my fellow men so much that I couldn't bear to see them even. Of course, like begets like, and this hate was returned. Finally I suffered from horrible delusions, and my room became haunted with demons that laughed and grimaced, and one night I ran into a whole cluster of them near the bed—and the fright stopped my heart and killed me. It's hate and remorse, as much as terror, that clogs me so thickly and keeps me here. If only someone could feel pity, and sympathy, and perhaps a little love for me, I could get away and be happy. When you came this afternoon to see over the house I watched you, and a little hope came to me for the first time. I saw you had courage, originality, resource—*love*. If only I could touch your heart, without frightening you, I knew I could perhaps tap that love you have stored up in your being there, and thus borrow the wings for my escape!'

"Now I must confess my heart began to ache a little, as fear left me and the man's words sank their sad meaning into me. Still, the whole affair was so incredible, and so touched with unholy quality, and the story of a woman's murder I had come to investigate had so obviously nothing to do with this thing, that I felt myself in a kind of wild dream that seemed likely to stop at any moment and leave me somewhere in bed after a nightmare,

"Moreover, his words possessed me to such an extent that I found it impossible to reflect upon anything else at all, or to consider adequately any ways or means of action or escape.

"I moved a little nearer to him in the gloom, horribly frightened, of course, but with the beginnings of a strange determination in my heart.

"'You women,' he continued, his voice plainly thrilling at my approach, 'you wonderful women, to whom life often brings no opportunity of spending your great love, oh, if you only could know how many of us simply yearn for it I It would save our souls, if but you knew. Few might find the chance that you now have, but if you only spent your love freely, without definite object, just letting it flow openly for all who need, you would reach hundreds and thou- sands of souls like me, and *release us!* Oh, madam, I ask you again to feel with me, to be kind and gentle—and if you can to love me a little!'

"My heart did leap within me and this time the tears did come, for I could not restrain them. I laughed too, for the way he called me 'madam' sounded so odd, here in this empty room at midnight in a London street, but my laughter stopped dead and merged in a flood of weeping when I saw how my change of feeling affected him. He had left his place by the window and was kneeling on the floor at my feet, his hands stretched out towards me, and the first signs of a kind of glory about his head.

"'Put your arms round me and kiss me, for the love of God!'' he cried. 'Kiss me, oh, kiss me, and I shall be freed! You have done so much already—now do this!'

"I stuck there, hesitating, shaking, my determination on the verge of action, yet not quite able to compass it. But the terror had almost gone.

"'Forget that I'm a man and you're a woman,' he continued in the most beseeching voice I ever heard. 'Forget that I'm a ghost, and come out boldly and press me to you with a great kiss, and let your love flow into me. Forget. yourself just for one minute and do a brave thing! Oh, love me, *love me*, love me! and I shall be free!'

"The words, or the deep force they somehow released in the centre of my being, stirred me profoundly, and an emotion infinitely greater than fear surged up over me and carried me with it across the edge of action. Without hesitation I took two steps forward towards him where he knelt, and held out my arms. Pity and love were in my heart at that moment, genuine pity, I swear, and genuine love. I forgot myself and my little tremblings in a great desire to help another soul.

"'I love you I poor, aching, unhappy thing! I love you,' I cried through hot tears; 'and I am not the least bit afraid in the world.'

"The man uttered a curious sound, like laughter, yet not laughter, and turned his face up to me. The light from the street below fell on it, but there was another light, too, shining all round it that seemed to come from the eyes and skin. He rose to his feet and met me, and in that second I folded him to my breast and kissed him full on the lips again and again."

All our pipes had gone out, and not even a skirt rustled in that dark studio as the story-teller paused a moment to steady her voice, and put a hand softly up to her eyes before going on again.

"Now, what can I say, and how can I describe to you, all you sceptical men sitting there with pipes in your mouths, the amazing sensation I experienced of holding an intangible, impalpable thing so closely to my heart that it touched my body with equal pressure all the way down, and then melted away somewhere into my very being? For it was like seizing a rush of cool wind and feeling a touch of burning fire the moment it had struck its swift blow and passed on. A series of shocks ran all over and all through me; a momentary ecstasy of flaming sweetness and wonder thrilled down into me; my heart gave another great leap—and then I was alone.

"The room was empty. I turned on the gas and struck a match to prove it. All fear had left me, and something was singing round me in the air and in my heart like the joy of a spring morning in youth. Not all the devils or shadows or hauntings in the world could then have caused me a single tremor.

"I unlocked the door and went all over the dark house, even into kitchen and cellar and up among the ghostly attics. But the house was empty. Something had left it I lingered a short hour, analyzing, thinking, wondering— you can guess what and how, perhaps, but I won't detail, for I promised only essentials, remember—and then went out to sleep the remainder of the night in my own flat, locking the door behind me upon a house no longer haunted.

"But my uncle. Sir Henry, the owner of the house, required an account of my adventure, and of course I was in duty bound to give him some kind of a true story. Before I could begin, however, he held up his hand to stop me.

"'First,' he said, 'I wish to tell you a little deception I ventured to practice on you. So many people have been to that house and seen the ghost that I came to think the story acted on their imaginations, and I wished to make a better test. So I invented for their benefit another story, with the idea that if you did see anything I could be sure it was not due merely to an excited imagination.'

"'Then what you told me about a woman having been murdered, and all that, was not the true story of the haunting?'

"'It was not. The true story is that a cousin of mine went mad in that house, and killed himself in a fit of morbid terror following upon years of miserable hypochondriasis. It is his figure that investigators see.'

"'That explains, then,' I gasped

"'Explains what?'

"I thought of that poor struggling soul, longing all these years for escape, and determined to keep my story for the present to myself.

"'Explains, I mean, why I did not see the ghost of the murdered woman,' I concluded.

"'Precisely,' said Sir Henry, 'and why, if you had seen anything, it would have had value, inasmuch as it could not have been caused by the imagination working upon a story you already knew.'"

The Great Valdez Sapphire
(Anonymous)

I know more about it than anyone else in the world, its present
owner not excepted. I can give its whole history, from the Cingalese
who found it, the Spanish adventurer who stole it, the cardinal who
bought it, the Pope who graciously accepted it, the favoured son of
the Church who received it, the gay and giddy duchess who pawned
it, down to the eminent prelate who now holds it in trust as a family
heirloom.

It will occupy a chapter to itself in my forthcoming work on *Historic Stones*, where full details of its weight, size, colour, and value may
be found. At present I am going to relate an incident in its history
which, for obvious reasons, will not be published—which, in fact, I
trust the reader will consider related in strict confidence.

I had never seen the stone itself when I began to write about
it, and it was not till one evening last spring, while staying with my
nephew, Sir Thomas Acton, that I came within measurable distance of
it. A dinner party was impending, and, at my instigation, the Bishop of
Northchurch and Miss Panton, his daughter and heiress, were among
the invited guests.

The dinner was a particularly good one, I remember that distinctly.
In fact, I felt myself partly responsible for it, having engaged the new
cook—a talented young Italian, pupil of the admirable old *chef* at my
club. We had gone over the *menu* carefully together, with a result re-
freshing in its novelty, but not so daring as to disturb the minds of the
innocent country guests who were bidden thereto.

The first spoonful of soup was reassuring, and I looked to the end
of the table to exchange a congratulatory glance with Leta. What was
amiss? No response. Her pretty face was flushed, her smile constrained,
she was talking with quite unnecessary *empressement* to her neighbour,

Sir Harry Landor, though Leta is one of those few women who understand the importance of letting a man settle down tranquilly and with an undisturbed mind to the business of dining, allowing no topic of serious interest to come on before the *relevés*, and reserving mere conversational brilliancy for the *entremets*.

Guests all right? No disappointments? I had gone through the list with her, selecting just the right people to be asked to meet the Landors, our new neighbours. Not a mere cumbrous county gathering, nor yet a showy imported party from town, but a skilful blending of both. Had anything happened already? I had been late for dinner and missed the arrivals in the drawing-room. It was Leta's fault. She has got into a way of coming into my room and putting the last touches to my toilet. I let her, for I am doubtful of myself nowadays after many years' dependence on the best of valets. Her taste is generally beyond dispute, but to-day she had indulged in a feminine vagary that provoked me and made me late for dinner.

"Are you going to wear your sapphire, Uncle Paul!" she cried in a tone of dismay. "Oh, why not the ruby?"

"You *would* have your way about the table decorations," I gently reminded her. "With that service of Crown Derby *repoussé* and orchids, the ruby would look absolutely barbaric. Now if you would have had the Limoges set, white candles, and a yellow silk centre—"

"Oh, but—I'm *so* disappointed—I wanted the bishop to see your ruby—or one of your engraved gems—"

"My dear, it is on the bishop's account I put this on. You know his daughter is heiress of the great Valdez sapphire—"

"Of course she is, and when he has the charge of a stone three times as big as yours, what's the use of wearing it? The ruby, dear Uncle Paul, *please!*"

She was desperately in earnest I could see, and considering the obligations which I am supposed to be under to her and Tom, it was but a little matter to yield, but it involved a good deal of extra trouble. Studs, sleeve-links, watch-guard, all carefully selected to go with the sapphire, had to be changed, the emerald which I chose as a compromise requiring more florid accompaniments of a deeper tone of gold; and the dinner hour struck as I replaced my jewel case, the one relic left me of a once handsome fortune, in my fireproof safe.

The emerald looked very well that evening, however. I kept my eyes upon it for comfort when Miss Panton proved trying.

She was a lean, yellow, dictatorial young person with no conversation. I spoke of her father's celebrated sapphires. "*My* sapphires," she amended sourly; "though I am legally debarred from making any profitable use of them." She furthermore informed me that she viewed them as useless gauds, which ought to be disposed of for the benefit of the heathen. I gave the subject up, and while she discoursed of the work of the Blue Ribbon Army among the Bosjesmans I tried to understand a certain dislocation in the arrangement of the table. Surely we were more or less in number than we should be? Opposite side all right. Who was extra on ours?

I leaned forward. Lady Landor on one side of Tom, on the other who? I caught glimpses of plumes pink and green nodding over a dinner plate, and beneath them a pink nose in a green visage with a nutcracker chin altogether unknown to me. A sharp gray eye shot a sideway glance down the table and caught me peeping, and I retreated, having only marked in addition two clawlike hands, with pointed ruffles and a mass of brilliant rings, making good play with a knife and fork. Who was she? At intervals a high acid voice could be heard addressing Tom, and a laugh that made me shudder; it had the quality of the scream of a bird of prey or the yell of a jackal. I had heard that sort of laugh before, and it always made me feel like a defenceless rabbit.

Every time it sounded I saw Leta's fan flutter more furiously and her manner grow more nervously animated. Poor dear girl! I never in all my recollection wished a dinner at an end so earnestly so as to assure her of my support and sympathy, though without the faintest conception why either should be required.

The ices at last. A *menu* card folded in two was laid beside me. I read it unobserved. "Keep the B. from joining us in the drawing-room." The B.—? The bishop, of course. With pleasure. But why? And how? *That's* the question, never mind "why." Could I lure him into the library—the billiard room—the conservatory? I doubted it, and I doubted still more what I should do with him when I got him there.

The bishop is a grand and stately ecclesiastic of the mediæval type, broad-chested, deep-voiced, martial of bearing. I could picture him charging mace in hand at the head of his vassals, or delivering over a dissenter of the period to the rack and thumb-screw, but not pottering among rare editions, tall copies and Grolier bindings, nor condescending to a quiet cigar among the tree ferns and orchids. Leta must and should be obeyed, I swore, nevertheless, even if I were driven to lock the door in the fearless old fashion of a bygone day, and declare I'd shoot any man who left while a drop remained in the bottles.

The ladies were rising. The lady at the head of the line smirked and nodded her pink plumes coquettishly at Tom, while her hawk's eyes roved keen and predatory over us all. She stopped suddenly, creating a block and confusion.

"Ah, the dear bishop! *You* there, and I never saw you! You must come and have a nice long chat presently. By-by—!" She shook her fan at him over my shoulder and tripped on. Leta, passing me last, gave me a look of profound despair.

"Lady Carwitchet!" somebody exclaimed. "I couldn't believe my eyes."

"Thought she was dead or in penal servitude. Never should have expected to see her *here*," said someone else behind me confidentially.

"What Carwitchet? Not the mother of the Carwitchet who—"

"Just so. The Carwitchet who—" Tom assented with a shrug. "We needn't go farther, as she's my guest. Just my luck. I met them at Buxton, thought them uncommonly good company—in fact, Carwitchet laid me under a great obligation about a horse I was nearly let in for buying—and gave them a general invitation here, as one does, you know. Never expected her to turn up with her luggage this afternoon just before dinner, to stay a week, or a fortnight if Carwitchet can join her." A groan of sympathy ran round the table. "It can't be helped. I've told you this just to show that I shouldn't have asked you here to meet this sort of people of my own free will; but, as it is, please say no more about them." The subject was not dropped by any means, and I took care that it should not be. At our end of the table one story after another went buzzing round—*sotto voce*, out of deference to Tom—but perfectly audible.

"Carwitchet? Ah, yes. Mixed up in that Rawlings divorce case, wasn't he? A bad lot. Turned out of the Dragoon Guards for cheating at cards, or picking pockets, or something—remember the row at the Cerulean Club? Scandalous exposure—and that forged letter business—oh, that was the mother—prosecution hushed up somehow. Ought to be serving her fourteen years—and that business of poor Farrars, the banker—got hold of some of his secrets and blackmailed him till he blew his brains out—"

It was so exciting that I clean forgot the bishop, till a low gasp at my elbow startled me. He was lying back in his chair, his mighty shaven jowl a ghastly white, his fierce imperious eyebrows drooping limp over his fishlike eyes, his splendid figure shrunk and contracted.

He was trying with a shaken hand to pour out wine. The decanter clattered against the glass and the wine spilled on the cloth.

"I'm afraid you find the room too warm. Shall we go into the library?"

He rose hastily and followed me like a lamb.

He recovered himself once we got into the hall, and affably rejected all my proffers of brandy and soda—medical advice—everything else my limited experience could suggest. He only demanded his carriage "directly" and that Miss Panton should be summoned forthwith.

I made the best use I could of the time left me.

"I'm uncommonly sorry you do not feel equal to staying a little longer, my lord. I counted on showing you my few trifles of precious stones, the salvage from the wreck of my possessions. Nothing in comparison with your own collection."

The bishop clasped his hand over his heart. His breath came short and quick.

"A return of that dizziness," he explained with a faint smile. "You are thinking of the Valdez sapphire, are you not? Someday," he went on with forced composure, "I may have the pleasure of showing it to you. It is at my banker's just now."

Miss Panton's steps were heard in the hall. "You are well known as a connoisseur, Mr. Acton," he went on hurriedly. "Is your collection valuable? If so, *keep it safe; don' trust a ring off your hand, or the key of your jewel-case out of your pocket till the house is clear again.*" The words rushed from his lips in an impetuous whisper, he gave me a meaning glance, and departed with his daughter. I went back to the drawing-room, my head swimming with bewilderment.

"What! The dear bishop gone!" screamed Lady Carwitchet from the central ottoman where she sat, surrounded by most of the gentlemen, all apparently well entertained by her conversation. "And I wanted to talk over old times with him so badly. His poor wife was my greatest friend. Mira Montanaro, daughter of the great banker, you know. It's not possible that that miserable little prig is my poor Mira's girl. The heiress of all the Montanaros in a black-lace gown worth twopence! When I think of her mother's beauty and her toilets! Does she ever wear the sapphires? Has anyone ever seen her in them? Eleven large stones in a lovely antique setting, and the great Valdez sapphire—worth thousands and thousands—for the pendant." No one replied. "I wanted to get a rise out of the bishop tonight. It used to make him so mad when I wore this."

She fumbled among the laces at her throat, and clawed out a pendant that hung to a velvet band around her neck. I fairly gasped when she removed her hand. A sapphire of irregular shape flashed out its blue lightning on us. Such a stone! A true, rich, cornflower blue even by that wretched artificial light, with soft velvety depths of colour and dazzling clearness of tint in its lights and shades—a stone to remember! I stretched out my hand involuntarily, but Lady Carwitchet drew back with a coquettish squeal. "No! no! You mustn't look any closer. Tell me what you think of it now. Isn't it pretty?"

"Superb!" was all I could ejaculate, staring at the azure splendour of that miraculous jewel in a sort of trance.

She gave a shrill cackling laugh of mockery.

"The great Mr. Acton taken in by a bit of Palais Royal gimcrackery! What an advertisement for Bogaerts et Cie! They are perfect artists in frauds. Don't you remember their stand at the first Paris Exhibition? They had imitations there of every celebrated stone; but I never expected anything made by man could delude Mr. Acton, never!" And she went off into another mocking cackle, and all the idiots round her haw-hawed knowingly, as if they had seen the joke all along. I was too bewildered to reply, which was on the whole lucky. "I suppose I musn't tell why I came to give quite a big sum in *francs* for this?" she went on, tapping her closed lips with her closed fan, and cocking her eye at us all like a parrot wanting to be coaxed to talk. "It's a queer story."

I didn't want to hear her anecdote, especially as I saw she wanted to tell it. What I *did* want was to see that pendant again. She had thrust it back among her laces, only the loop which held it to the velvet being visible. It was set with three small sapphires, and even from a distance I clearly made them out to be imitations, and poor ones. I felt a queer thrill of self-mistrust. Was the large stone no better? Could I, even for an instant, have been dazzled by a sham, and a sham of that quality? The events of the evening had flurried and confused me. I wished to think them over in quiet. I would go to bed.

My rooms at the Manor are the best in the house. Leta will have it so. I must explain their position for a reason to be understood later. My bedroom is in the southeast angle of the house; it opens on one side into a sitting-room in the east corridor, the rest of which is taken up by the suite of rooms occupied by Tom and Leta; and on the other side into my bathroom, the first room in the south corridor where the principal guest chambers are, to one of which it was originally the dressing-room. Passing this room I noticed a couple of housemaids preparing it for the night, and discovered with a shiver that Lady Carwitchet was to be my next-door neighbour. It gave me a turn.

The bishop's strange warning must have unnerved me. I was perfectly safe from her ladyship. The disused door into her room was locked, and the key safe on the housekeeper's bunch. It was also undiscoverable on her side, the recess in which it stood being completely filled by a large wardrobe. On my side hung a thick sound-proof *portière*. Nevertheless, I resolved not to use that room while she inhabited the next one. I removed my possessions, fastened the door of communication with my bedroom and dragged a heavy ottoman across it.

Then I stowed away my emerald in my strong-box. It is built into the wall of my sitting-room, and masked by the lower part of an old carved oak bureau. I put away even the rings I wore habitually, keeping out only an inferior cat's-eye for workaday wear. I had just made all safe when Leta tapped at the door and came in to wish me good night. She looked flushed and harassed and ready to cry. "Uncle Paul," she began, "I want you to go up to town at once, and stay away till I send for you."

"My dear—!" I was too amazed to expostulate.

"We've got a—a pestilence among us," she declared, her foot tapping the ground angrily, "and the least we can do is to go into quarantine. Oh, I'm so sorry and so ashamed! The poor bishop! I'll take good care that no one else shall meet that woman here. You did your best for me, Uncle Paul, and managed admirably, but it was all no use. I hoped against hope that what between the dusk of the drawing-room before dinner, and being put at opposite ends of the table, we might get through without a meeting—"

"But, my dear, explain. Why shouldn't the bishop and Lady Carwitchet meet? Why is it worse for him than anyone else?"

"Why? I thought everybody had heard of that dreadful wife of his who nearly broke his heart. If he married her for her money it served him right, but Lady Landor says she was very handsome and really in love with him at first. Then Lady Carwitchet got hold of her and led her into all sorts of mischief. She left her husband—he was only a rector with a country living in those days—and went to live in town, got into a horrid fast set, and made herself notorious. You *must* have heard of her."

"I heard of her sapphires, my dear. But I was in Brazil at the time."

"I wish you had been at home. You might have found her out. She was furious because her husband refused to let her wear the great Valdez sapphire. It had been in the Montanaro family for some generations, and her father settled it first on her and then on her little girl—the bishop being trustee. He felt obliged to take away the little girl, and send her off to be brought up by some old aunts in the country, and he locked up the sapphire. Lady Carwitchet tells as a splendid joke how they got the copy made in Paris, and it did just as well for the people to stare at. No wonder the bishop hates the very name of the stone."

"How long will she stay here?" I asked dismally.

"Till Lord Carwitchet can come and escort her to Paris to visit some American friends. Goodness knows when that will be! Do go up to town, Uncle Paul!"

I refused indignantly. The very least I could do was to stand by my poor young relatives in their troubles and help them through. I did so. I wore that inferior cat's eye for six weeks!

It is a time I cannot think of even now without a shudder. The more I saw of that terrible old woman the more I detested her, and we saw a very great deal of her. Leta kept her word, and neither accepted nor gave invitations all that time. We were cut off from all society but that of old General Fairford, who would go anywhere and meet anyone to get a rubber after dinner; the doctor, a sporting widower; and the Duberlys, a giddy, rather rackety young couple who had taken the Dower House for a year. Lady Carwitchet seemed perfectly content. She revelled in the soft living and good fare of the Manor House, the drives in Leta's big *barouche*, and Domenico's dinners, as one to whom short commons were not unknown. She had a hungry way of grabbing and grasping at everything she could—the shillings she won at whist, the best fruit at dessert, the postage stamps in the library inkstand—that was infinitely suggestive.

Sometimes I could have pitied her, she was so greedy, so spiteful, so friendless. She always made me think of some wicked old pirate putting into a peaceful port to provision and repair his battered old hulk, obliged to live on friendly terms with the natives, but his piratical old nostrils asniff for plunder and his piratical old soul longing to be off marauding once more. When would that be? Not till the arrival in Paris of her distinguished American friends, of whom we heard a great deal. "Charming people, the Bokums of Chicago, the American branch of the English Beauchamps, you know!" They seemed to be taking an unconscionable time to get there. She would have insisted on being driven over to Northchurch to call at the palace, but that the bishop was understood to be holding confirmations at the other end of the diocese.

I was alone in the house one afternoon sitting by my window, toying with the key of my safe, and wondering whether I dare treat myself to a peep at my treasures, when a suspicious movement in the park below caught my attention. A black figure certainly dodged from behind one tree to the next, and then into the shadow of the park paling instead of keeping to the footpath. It looked queer. I caught up my field glass and marked him at one point where he was bound to come into the open for a few steps. He crossed the strip of turf with giant strides and got into cover again, but not quick enough to prevent me recognizing him. It was—great heavens!—the bishop! In a soft hat pulled over his forehead, with a long cloak and a big stick he looked like a poacher.

Guided by some mysterious instinct I hurried to meet him. I opened the conservatory door, and in he rushed like a hunted rabbit. Without explanation I led him up the wide staircase to my room, where he dropped into a chair and wiped his face.

"You are astonished, Mr. Acton," he panted. "I will explain directly. Thanks." He tossed off the glass of brandy I had poured out without waiting for the qualifying soda, and looked better.

"I am in serious trouble. You can help me. I've had a shock to-day—a grievous shock." He stopped and tried to pull himself together. "I must trust you implicitly, Mr. Acton, I have no choice. Tell me what you think of this." He drew a case from his breast pocket and opened it. "I promised you should see the Valdez sapphire. Look there!"

The Valdez sapphire! A great big shining lump of blue crystal—flawless and of perfect colour—that was all. I took it up, breathed on it, drew out my magnifier, looked at it in one light and another. What was wrong with it? I could not say. Nine experts out of ten would undoubtedly have pronounced the stone genuine. I, by virtue of some mysterious instinct that has hitherto always guided me aright, was the unlucky tenth. I looked at the bishop. His eyes met mine. There was no need of spoken word between us.

"Has Lady Carwitchet shown you her sapphire?" was his most unexpected question. "She has? Now, Mr. Acton, on your honour as a connoisseur and a gentleman, which of the two is the Valdez?"

"Not this one." I could say naught else.

"You were my last hope." He broke off, and dropped his face on his folded arms with a groan that shook the table on which he rested, while I stood dismayed at myself for having let so hasty a judgment escape me. He lifted a ghastly countenance to me. "She vowed she would see me ruined and disgraced. I made her my enemy by crossing some of her schemes once, and she never forgives. She will keep her word. I shall appear before the world as a fraudulent trustee. I can neither produce the valuable confided to my charge nor make the loss good. I have only an incredible story to tell," he dropped his head and groaned again. "Who will believe me?"

"I will, for one."

"Ah, you? Yes, you know her. She took my wife from me, Mr. Acton. Heaven only knows what the hold was that she had over poor Mira. She encouraged her to set me at defiance and eventually to leave me. She was answerable for all the scandalous folly and extravagance of poor Mira's life in Paris—spare me the telling of the story. She left her at last to die alone and uncared for. I reached my wife to find her dying of a fever from which Lady Carwitchet and her crew had fled. She was raving in delirium, and died without recognizing me. Some trouble she had been in which I must never know oppressed her. At the very last she roused from a long stupor and spoke to the nurse. 'Tell him to get the sapphire back—she stole it. She has robbed my child.' Those were her last words. The nurse understood no English, and treated them as wandering; but I heard them, and knew she was sane when she spoke."

"What did you do?"

"What could I? I saw Lady Carwitchet, who laughed at me, and defied me to make her confess or disgorge. I took the pendant to more than one eminent jeweller on pretence of having the setting seen to, and all have examined and admired without giving a hint of there being anything wrong. I allowed a celebrated mineralogist to see it; he gave no sign—"

"Perhaps they are right and we are wrong."

"No, no. Listen. I heard of an old Dutchman celebrated for his imitations. I went to him, and he told me at once that he had been allowed by Montanaro to copy the Valdez—setting and all—for the Paris Exhibition. I showed him this, and he claimed it for his own work at once, and pointed out his private mark upon it. You must take your magnifier to find it; a Greek Beta. He also told me that he had sold it to Lady Carwitchet more than a year ago."

"It is a terrible position."

"It is. My co-trustee died lately. I have never dared to have another appointed. I am bound to hand over the sapphire to my daughter on her marriage, if her husband consents to take the name of Montanaro."

The bishop's face was ghastly pale, and the moisture started on his brow. I racked my brain for some word of comfort.

"Miss Panton may never marry."

"But she will!" he shouted. "That is the blow that has been dealt me today. My chaplain—actually, my chaplain—tells me that he is going out as a temperance missionary to equatorial Africa, and has the assurance to add that he believes my daughter is not indisposed to accompany him!" His consummating wrath acted as a momentary stimulant. He sat upright, his eyes flashing and his brow thunderous. I felt for that chaplain. Then he collapsed miserably. "The sapphires will have to be produced, identified, revalued. How shall I come out of it? Think of the disgrace, the ripping up of old scandals! Even if I were to compound with Lady Carwitchet, the sum she hinted at was too monstrous. She wants more than my money. Help me, Mr. Acton! For the sake of your own family interest, help me!"

"I beg your pardon—family interests? I don't understand."

"If my daughter is childless, her next of kin is poor Marmaduke Panton, who is dying at Cannes, not married, or likely to marry; and failing him, your nephew, Sir Thomas Acton, succeeds."

My nephew Tom! Leta, or Leta's baby, might come to be the possible inheritor of the great Valdez sapphire! The blood rushed to my head as I looked at the great shining swindle before me. "What diabolic jugglery was at work when the exchange was made?" I demanded fiercely.

"It must have been on the last occasion of her wearing the sapphires in London. I ought never to have let her out of my sight."

"You must put a stop to Miss Panton's marriage in the first place," I pronounced as autocratically as he could have done himself.

"Not to be thought of," he admitted helplessly. "Mira has my force of character. She knows her rights, and she will have her jewels. I want you to take charge of the—thing for me. If it's in the house she'll make me produce it. She'll inquire at the banker's. If *you* have it we can gain time, if but for a day or two." He broke off. Carriage wheels were crashing on the gravel outside. We looked at one another in consternation. Flight was imperative. I hurried him downstairs and out of the conservatory just as the door-bell rang. I think we both lost our heads in the confusion. He shoved the case into my hands, and I pocketed it, without a thought of the awful responsibility I was incurring, and saw him disappear into the shelter of the friendly night.

When I think of what my feelings were that evening—of my murderous hatred of that smirking jesting Jezebel who sat opposite me at dinner, my wrathful indignation at the thought of the poor little expected heir defrauded ere his birth; of the crushing contempt I felt for myself and the bishop as a pair of witless idiots unable to see our way out of the dilemma; all this boiling and surging through my soul, I can only wonder—Domenico having given himself a holiday, and the kitchen-maid doing her worst and wickedest—that gout or jaundice did not put an end to this story at once.

"Uncle Paul!" Leta was looking her sweetest when she tripped into my room next morning. "I've news for you. She," pointing a delicate forefinger in the direction of the corridor, "is going! Her Bokums have reached Paris at last, and sent for her to join them at the Grand Hotel."

I was thunderstruck. The longed-for deliverance had but come to remove hopelessly and forever out of my reach Lady Carwitchet and the great Valdez sapphire.

"Why, aren't you overjoyed? I am. We are going to celebrate the event by a dinner-party. Tom's hospitable soul is vexed by the lack of entertainment we had provided for her. We must ask the Brownleys someday or other, and they will be delighted to meet anything in the way of a ladyship, or such smart folks as the Duberly-Parkers. Then we may as well have the Blomfields, and air that awful modern Sèvres dessert-service she gave us when we were married." I had no objection to make, and she went on, rubbing her soft cheek against my shoulder like the purring little cat she was: "Now I want you to do something to please me—and Mrs. Blomfield. She has set her heart on seeing your rubies, and though I know you hate her about as much as you do that Sèvres china—"

"What! Wear my rubies with that! I won't. I'll tell you what I will do, though. I've got some carbuncles as big as prize gooseberries, a whole set. Then you have only to put those Bohemian glass vases and candelabra on the table, and let your gardener do his worst with his great forced, scentless, vulgar blooms, and we shall all be in keeping." Leta pouted. An idea struck me. "Or I'll do as you wish, on one condi-

265

tion. You get Lady Carwitchet to wear her big sapphire, and don't tell her I wish it."

I lived through the next few days as one in some evil dream. The sapphires, like twin spectres, haunted me day and night. Was ever man so tantalized? To hold the shadow and see the substance dangled temptingly within reach. The bishop made no sign of ridding me of my unwelcome charge, and the thought of what might happen in a case of burglary—fire—earthquake—made me start and tremble at all sorts of inopportune moments.

I kept faith with Leta, and reluctantly produced my beautiful rubies on the night of her dinner party. Emerging from my room I came full upon Lady Carwitchet in the corridor. She was dressed for dinner, and at her throat I caught the blue gleam of the great sapphire. Leta had kept faith with me. I don't know what I stammered in reply to her ladyship's remarks; my whole soul was absorbed in the contemplation of the intoxicating loveliness of the gem. *That* a Palais Royal deception! Incredible! My fingers twitched, my breath came short and fierce with the lust of possession. She must have seen the covetous glare in my eyes. A look of gratified spiteful complacency overspread her features, as she swept on ahead and descended the stairs before me. I followed her to the drawing-room door. She stopped suddenly, and murmuring something unintelligible hurried back again.

Everybody was assembled there that I expected to see, with an addition. Not a welcome one by the look on Tom's face. He stood on the hearth-rug conversing with a great hulking, high-shouldered fellow, sallow-faced, with a heavy moustache and drooping eyelids, from the corners of which flashed out a sudden suspicious look as I approached, which lighted up into a greedy one as it rested on my rubies, and seemed unaccountably familiar to me, till Lady Carwitchet tripping past me exclaimed:

"He has come at last! My naughty, naughty boy! Mr. Acton, this is my son, Lord Carwitchet!"

I broke off short in the midst of my polite acknowledgments to stare blankly at her. The sapphire was gone! A great gilt cross, with a Scotch pebble like an acid drop, was her sole decoration.

"I had to put my pendant away," she explained confidentially; "the clasp had got broken somehow." I didn't believe a word.

Lord Carwitchet contributed little to the general entertainment at dinner, but fell into confidential talk with Mrs. Duberly-Parker. I caught a few unintelligible remarks across the table. They referred,

I subsequently discovered, to the lady's little book on Northchurch races, and I recollected that the Spring Meeting was on, and tomorrow "Cup Day." After dinner there was great talk about getting up a party to go on General Fairford's drag. Lady Carwitchet was in ecstasies and tried to coax me into joining. Leta declined positively. Tom accepted sulkily.

The look in Lord Carwitchet's eye returned to my mind as I locked up my rubies that night. It made him look so like his mother! I went round my fastenings with unusual care. Safe and closets and desk and doors, I tried them all. Coming at last to the bathroom, it opened at once. It was the housemaid's doing. She had evidently taken advantage of my having abandoned the room to give it "a thorough spring cleaning," and I anathematized her. The furniture was all piled together and veiled with sheets, the carpet and felt curtain were gone, there were new brooms about. As I peered around, a voice close at my ear made me jump—Lady Carwitchet's!

"I tell you I have nothing, not a penny! I shall have to borrow my train fare before I can leave this. They'll be glad enough to lend it."

Not only had the *portière* been removed, but the door behind it had been unlocked and left open for convenience of dusting behind the wardrobe. I might as well have been in the bedroom.

"Don't tell me," I recognized Carwitchet's growl. "You've not been here all this time for nothing. You've been collecting for a Kilburn cot or getting subscriptions for the distressed Irish landlords. I know you. Now I'm not going to see myself ruined for the want of a paltry hundred or so. I tell you the colt is a dead certainty. If I could have got a thousand or two on him last week, we might have ended our dog days millionaires. Hand over what you can. You've money's worth, if not money. Where's that sapphire you stole?"

"I didn't. I can show you the receipted bill. All *I* possess is honestly come by. What could you do with it, even if I gave it you? You couldn't sell it as the Valdez, and you can't get it cut up as you might if it were real."

"If it's only bogus, why are you always in such a flutter about it? I'll do something with it, never fear. Hand over."

"I can't. I haven't got it. I had to raise something on it before I left town."

"Will you swear it's not in that wardrobe? I dare say you will. I mean to see. Give me those keys."

I heard a struggle and a jingle, then the wardrobe door must have been flung open, for a streak of light struck through a crack in the wood of the back. Creeping close and peeping through, I could see an awful sight. Lady Carwitchet in a flannel wrapper, minus hair, teeth, complexion, pointing a skinny forefinger that quivered with rage at her son, who was out of the range of my vision.

"Stop that, and throw those keys down here directly, or I'll rouse the house. Sir Thomas is a magistrate, and will lock you up as soon as look at you." She clutched at the bell rope as she spoke. "I'll swear I'm in danger of my life from you and give you in charge. Yes, and when you're in prison I'll keep you there till you die. I've often thought I'd do it. How about the hotel robberies last summer at Cowes, eh? Mightn't the police be grateful for a hint or two? And how about—"

The keys fell with a crash on the bed, accompanied by some bad language in an apologetic tone, and the door slammed to. I crept trembling to bed.

This new and horrible complication of the situation filled me with dismay. Lord Carwitchet's wolfish glance at my rubies took a new meaning. They were safe enough, I believed—but the sapphire! If he disbelieved his mother, how long would she be able to keep it from his clutches? That she had some plot of her own of which the bishop would eventually be the victim I did not doubt, or why had she not made her bargain with him long ago? But supposing she took fright, lost her head, allowed her son to wrest the jewel from her, or gave consent to its being mutilated, divided! I lay in a cold perspiration till morning.

My terrors haunted me all day. They were with me at breakfast time when Lady Carwitchet, tripping in smiling, made a last attempt to induce me to accompany her and keep her "bad, bad boy" from getting among "those horrid betting men."

They haunted me through the long peaceful day with Leta and the *tête-à-tête* dinner, but they swarmed around and beset me sorest when, sitting alone over my sitting-room fire, I listened for the return of the drag party. I read my newspaper and brewed myself some hot strong drink, but there comes a time of night when no fire can warm and no drink can cheer. The bishop's despairing face kept me company, and his troubles and the wrongs of the future heir took possession of me. Then the uncanny noises that make all old houses ghostly during the small hours began to make themselves heard. Muffled footsteps trod the corridor, stopping to listen at every door, door latches gently clicked, boards creaked unreasonably, sounds of stealthy movements came from the locked-up bathroom.

The welcome crash of wheels at last, and the sound of the front-door bell. I could hear Lady Carwitchet making her shrill *adieux* to her friends and her steps in the corridor. She was softly humming a little song as she approached. I heard her unlock her bedroom door before she entered—an odd thing to do. Tom came sleepily stumbling to his room later. I put my head out. "Where is Lord Carwitchet?"

"Haven't you seen him? He left us hours ago. Not come home, eh? Well, he's welcome to stay away. I don't want to see more of him." Tom's brow was dark and his voice surly. "I gave him to understand as much." Whatever had happened, Tom was evidently too disgusted to explain just then.

I went back to my fire unaccountably relieved, and brewed myself another and a stronger brew. It warmed me this time, but excited me foolishly. There must be some way out of the difficulty. I felt now as if I could almost see it if I gave my mind to it. Why—suppose—there might be no difficulty after all! The bishop was a nervous old gentleman. He might have been mistaken all through, Bogaerts might have been mistaken, I might—no. I could not have been mistaken—or I thought not. I fidgeted and fumed and argued with myself till I found I should have no peace of mind without a look at the stone in my possession, and I actually went to the safe and took the case out.

The sapphire certainly looked different by lamplight. I sat and stared, and all but overpersuaded my better judgment into giving it a verdict. Bogaerts's mark—I suddenly remembered it. I took my magnifier and held the pendant to the light. There, scratched upon the stone, was the Greek *Beta!* There came a tap on my door, and before I could answer, the handle turned softly and Lord Carwitchet stood before me. I whipped the case into my dressing-gown pocket and stared at him. He was not pleasant to look at, especially at that time of night. He had a dishevelled, desperate air, his voice was hoarse, his red-rimmed eyes wild.

"I beg your pardon," he began civilly enough. "I saw your light burning, and thought, as we go by the early train tomorrow, you might allow me to consult you now on a little business of my mother's." His eyes roved about the room. Was he trying to find the whereabouts of my safe? "You know a lot about precious stones, don't you?"

"So my friends are kind enough to say. Won't you sit down? I have unluckily little chance of indulging the taste on my own account," was my cautious reply.

"But you've written a book about them, and know them when you see them, don't you? Now my mother has given me something, and would like you to give a guess at its value. Perhaps you can put me in the way of disposing of it?"

"I certainly can do so if it is worth anything. Is that it?" I was in a fever of excitement, for I guessed what was clutched in his palm. He held out to me the Valdez sapphire.

How it shone and sparkled like a great blue star! I made myself a deprecating smile as I took it from him, but how dare I call it false to its face? As well accuse the sun in heaven of being a cheap imitation. I faltered and prevaricated feebly. Where was my moral courage, and where was the good, honest, thumping lie that should have aided me? "I have the best authority for recognizing this as a very good copy of a famous stone in the possession of the Bishop of Northchurch." His scowl grew so black that I saw he believed me, and I went on more cheerily: "This was manufactured by Johannes Bogaerts—I can give you his address, and you can make inquiries yourself—by special permission of the then owner, the late Leone Montanaro."

"Hand it back!" he interrupted (his other remarks were outrageous, but satisfactory to hear); but I waved him off. I couldn't give it up. It fascinated me. I toyed with it, I caressed it. I made it display its different tones of colour. I must see the two stones together. I must see it outshine its paltry rival. It was a whimsical frenzy that seized me—I can call it by no other name.

"Would you like to see the original? Curiously enough, I have it here. The bishop has left it in my charge."

The wolfish light flamed up in Carwitchet's eyes as I drew forth the case. He laid the Valdez down on a sheet of paper, and I placed the other, still in its case, beside it. In that moment they looked identical, except for the little loop of sham stones, replaced by a plain gold band in the bishop's jewel. Carwitchet leaned across the table eagerly, the table gave a lurch, the lamp tottered, crashed over, and we were left in semidarkness.

"Don't stir!" Carwitchet shouted. "The paraffin is all over the place!" He seized my sofa blanket, and flung it over the table while I stood helpless. "There, that's safe now. Have you candles on the chimney-piece? I've got matches."

He looked very white and excited as he lit up. "Might have been an awkward job with all that burning paraffin running about," he said quite pleasantly. "I hope no real harm is done." I was lifting the rug with shaking hands. The two stones lay as I had placed them. No! I nearly dropped it back again. It was the stone in the case that had the loop with the three sham sapphires!

Carwitchet picked the other up hastily. "So you say this is rubbish?" he asked, his eyes sparkling wickedly, and an attempt at mortification in his tone.

"Utter rubbish!" I pronounced, with truth and decision, snapping up the case and pocketing it. "Lady Carwitchet must have known it."

"Ah, well, it's disappointing, isn't it? Goodbye, we shall not meet again."

I shook hands with him most cordially. "Goodbye, Lord Carwitchet. *So* glad to have met you and your mother. It has been a source of the *greatest* pleasure, I assure you."

I have never seen the Carwitchets since. The bishop drove over next day in rather better spirits. Miss Panton had refused the chaplain.

"It doesn't matter, my lord," I said to him heartily. "We've all been under some strange misconception. The stone in your possession is the veritable one. I could swear to that anywhere. The sapphire Lady Carwitchet wears is only an excellent imitation, and—I have seen it with my own eyes—is the one bearing Bogaerts's mark, the Greek *Beta*."

The Inmost Light
By Arthur Machen

1

One evening in autumn, when the deformities of London were veiled in faint, blue mist and its vistas and far-reaching streets seemed splendid, Mr. Charles Salisbury was slowly pacing down Rupert Street, drawing nearer to his favourite restaurant by slow degrees. His eyes were downcast in study of the pavement, and thus it was that as he passed in at the narrow door a man who had come up from the lower end of the street jostled against him.

"I beg your pardon—wasn't looking where I was going. Why, it's Dyson!"

"Yes, quite so. How are you, Salisbury?"

"Quite well. But where have you been, Dyson? I don't think I can have seen you for the last five years."

"No; I dare say not. You remember I was getting rather hard up when you came to my place at Charlotte Street?"

"Perfectly. I think I remember your telling me that you owed five weeks' rent, and that you had parted with your watch for a comparatively small sum."

"My dear Salisbury, your memory is admirable. Yes, I was hard up. But the curious thing is that soon after you saw me I became harder up. My financial state was described by a friend as 'stone broke.' I don't approve of slang, mind you, but such was my condition. But suppose we go in; there might be other people who would like to dine—it's a human weakness, Salisbury."

"Certainly; come along. I was wondering as I walked down whether the corner table were taken. It has a velvet back, you know."

"I know the spot; it's vacant. Yes, as I was saying, I became even harder up."

"What did you do then?" asked Salisbury, disposing of his hat, and settling down in the corner of the seat, with a glance of fond anticipation at the *menu*.

"What did I do? Why, I sat down and reflected. I had a good classical education, and a positive distaste for business of any kind; that was the capital with which I faced the world. Do you know, I have heard people describe olives as nasty! What lamentable philistinism! I have often thought, Salisbury, that I could write genuine poetry under the influence of olives and red wine. Let us have Chianti; it may not be very good, but the flasks are simply charming."

"It is pretty good here. We may as well have a big flask."

"Very good. I reflected, then, on my want of prospects, and I determined to embark in literature."

"Really, that was strange. You seem in pretty comfortable circumstances, though."

"Though! What a satire upon a noble profession. I am afraid, Salisbury, you haven't a proper idea of the dignity of an artist. You see me sitting at my desk,—or at least you can see me if you care to call,—with pen and ink, and simple nothingness before me, and if you come again in a few hours you will (in all probability) find a creation!"

"Yes, quite so. I had an idea that literature was not remunerative."

"You are mistaken; its rewards are great. I may mention, by the way, that shortly after you saw me I succeeded to a small income. An uncle died, and proved unexpectedly generous."

"Ah, I see. That must have been convenient."

"It was pleasant,—undeniably pleasant. I have always considered it in the light of an endowment of my researches. I told you I was a man of letters; it would, perhaps, be more correct to describe myself as a man of science."

"Dear me, Dyson, you have really changed very much in the last few years. I had a notion, don't you know, that you were a sort of idler about town, the kind of man one might meet on the north side of Piccadilly every day from May to July."

"Exactly. I was even then forming myself, though all unconsciously. You know my poor father could not afford to send me to the university. I used to grumble in my ignorance at not having completed my education. That was the folly of youth, Salisbury; my university was Piccadilly. There I began to study the great science which still occupies me."

"What science do you mean?"

"The science of the great city; the physiology of London; literally and metaphysically the greatest subject that the mind of man can conceive. What an admirable *salmi* this is; undoubtedly the final end of the pheasant. Yes, I feel sometimes positively overwhelmed with the thought of the vastness and complexity of London. Paris a man may get to understand thoroughly with a reasonable amount of study; but London is always a mystery. In Paris you may say, 'Here live the actresses, here the Bohemians, and the *Ratés*;' but it is different in London. You may point out a street, correctly enough, as the abode of washerwomen; but, in that second floor, a man may be studying Chaldee roots, and in the garret over the way a forgotten artist is dying by inches."

"I see you are Dyson, unchanged and unchangeable," said Salisbury, slowly sipping his Chianti. "I think you are misled by a too fervid imagination; the mystery of London exists only in your fancy. It seems to me a dull place enough. We seldom hear of a really artistic crime in London, whereas I believe Paris abounds in that sort of thing."

"Give me some more wine. Thanks. You are mistaken, my dear fellow, you are really mistaken. London has nothing to be ashamed of in the way of crime. Where we fail is for want of Homers, not Agamemnons. *Carent quia vate sacro*, you know."

"I recall the quotation. But I don't think I quite follow you."

"Well, in plain language, we have no good writers in London who make a specialty of that kind of thing. Our common reporter is a dull dog; every story that he has to tell is spoilt in the telling. His idea of horror and of what excites horror is so lamentably deficient. Nothing will content the fellow but blood, vulgar red blood, and when he can get it he lays it on thick, and considers that he has produced a telling story. It's a poor notion. And, by some curious fatality, it is the most commonplace and brutal murders which always attract the most attention and get written up the most. For instance, I dare say that you never heard of the Harlesden case?"

"No, no; I don't remember anything about it."

"Of course not. And yet the story is a curious one. I will tell it you over our coffee. Harlesden, you know, or I expect you don't know, is quite on the out-quarters of London; something curiously different from your fine old crusted suburb like Norwood or Hampstead, different as each of these is from the other. Hampstead, I mean, is where you look for the head of your great China house with his three acres of land and pine houses, though of late there is the artistic substratum;

while Norwood is the home of the prosperous middle-class family who took the house 'because it was near the palace,' and sickened of the palace six months afterwards; but Harlesden is a place of no character. It's too new to have any character as yet. There are the rows of red houses and the rows of white houses and the bright green venetians, and the blistering doorways, and the little back-yards they call gardens, and a few feeble shops, and then, just as you think you're going to grasp the physiognomy of the settlement it all melts away."

"How the dickens is that? The houses don't tumble down before one's eyes I suppose."

"Well, no, not exactly that. But Harlesden as an entity disappears. Your street turns into a quiet lane, and your staring houses into elm trees, and the back gardens into green meadows. You pass instantly from town to country; there is no transition as in a small country town, no soft gradations of wider lawns and orchards, with houses gradually becoming less dense, but a dead stop. I believe the people who live there mostly go into the city. I have seen once or twice a laden 'bus bound thitherwards. But however that may be, I can't conceive a greater loneliness in a desert at midnight than there is there at midday. It is like a city of the dead; the streets are glaring and desolate, and as you pass it suddenly strikes you that this, too, is part of London. Well, a year or two ago there was a doctor living there; he had set up his brass plate and his red lamp at the very end of one of those shining streets, and from the back of the house the fields stretched away to the north. I don't know what his reason was in settling down in such an out-of-the-way place, perhaps Dr. Black, as we will call him, was a far-seeing man and looked ahead.

His relations, so it appeared afterwards, had lost sight of him for many years and didn't even know he was a doctor, much less where he lived. However, there he was, settled in Harlesden, with some fragments of a practice, and an uncommonly pretty wife. People used to see them walking out together in the summer evenings soon after they came to Harlesden, and, so far as could be observed, they seemed a very affectionate couple. These walks went on through the autumn, and then ceased; but, of course, as the days grew dark and the weather cold, the lanes near Harlesden might be expected to lose many of their attractions. All through the winter nobody saw anything of Mrs. Black; the doctor used to reply to his patients' inquiries that she was a 'little out of sorts, would be better, no doubt, in the spring.'

But the spring came, and the summer, and no Mrs. Black appeared, and at last people began to rumour and talk amongst themselves, and all sorts of queer things were said at 'high teas,' which you may possibly have heard are the only form of entertainment known in such suburbs. Dr. Black began to surprise some very odd looks cast in his direction, and the practice, such as it was, fell off before his eyes. In short, when the neighbours whispered about the matter, they whispered that Mrs. Black was dead, and that the doctor had made away with her.

But this wasn't the case; Mrs. Black was seen alive in June. It was a Sunday afternoon, one of those few exquisite days that an English climate offers, and half London had strayed out into the fields North, South, East, and West, to smell the scent of the white May, and to see if the wild roses were yet in blossom in the hedges. I had gone out myself early in the morning, and had had a long ramble, and somehow or other, as I was steering homeward, I found myself in this very Harlesden we have been talking about. To be exact, I had a glass of beer in the 'General Gordon,' the most flourishing house in the neighbourhood, and as I was wandering rather aimlessly about I saw an uncommonly tempting gap in a hedgerow, and resolved to explore the meadow beyond. Soft grass is very grateful to the feet after the infernal grit strewn on suburban sidewalks, and after walking about for some time, I thought I should like to sit down on a bank and have a smoke.

While I was getting out my pouch, I looked up in the direction of the houses, and as I looked I felt my breath caught back, and my teeth began to chatter, and the stick I had in one hand snapped in two with the grip I gave it. It was as if I had had an electric current down my spine, and yet for some moment of time which seemed long, but which must have been very short, I caught myself wondering what on earth was the matter. Then I knew what had made my very heart shudder and my bones grind together in an agony. As I glanced up I had looked straight towards the last house in the row before me, and in an upper window of that house I had seen for some short fraction of a second a face. It was the face of a woman, and yet it was not human. You and I, Salisbury, have heard in our time, as we sat in our seats in church in sober English fashion, of a lust that cannot be satiated, and of a fire that is unquenchable, but few of us have any notion what these words mean. I hope you never may, for as I saw that face at the window, with the blue sky above me and the warm air playing in gusts about me, I knew I had looked into another world—looked through the window of a commonplace, brand-new house, and seen hell open before me.

When the first shock was over, I thought once or twice that I should have fainted; my face streamed with a cold sweat, and my breath came and went in sobs, as if I had been half drowned. I managed to get up at last, and walked round to the street, and there I saw the name Dr. Black on the post by the front gate. As fate or my luck would have it, the door opened and a man came down the steps as I passed by. I had no doubt it was the doctor himself. He was of a type rather common in London,—long and thin with a pasty face and a dull black moustache. He gave me a look as we passed each other on the pavement, and though it was merely the casual glance which one foot-passenger bestows on another, I felt convinced in my mind that here was an ugly customer to deal with. As you may imagine I went my way a good deal puzzled and horrified, too, by what I had seen; for I had paid another visit to the 'General Gordon,' and had got together a good deal of the common gossip of the place about the Blacks.

I didn't mention the fact that I had seen a woman's face in the window; but I heard that Mrs. Black had been much admired for her beautiful golden hair, and round what had struck me with such a nameless terror there was a mist of flowing yellow hair, as it were an aureole of glory round the visage of a satyr. The whole thing bothered me in an indescribable manner; and when I got home I tried my best to think of the impression I had received as an illusion, but it was no use. I knew very well I had seen what I have tried to describe to you, and I was morally certain that I had seen Mrs. Black. And then there was the gossip of the place, the suspicion of foul play, which I knew to be false, and my own conviction that there was some deadly mischief or other going on in that bright red house at the corner of the Devon Road,—how to construct a theory of a reasonable kind out of these two elements.

In short, I found myself in a world of mystery; I puzzled my head over it and filled up my leisure moments by gathering together odd threads of speculation, but I never moved a step toward any real solution, and as the summer days went on the matter seemed to grown misty and indistinct, shadowing some vague terror, like a nightmare of last month. I suppose it would before long have faded into the background of my brain—I should not have forgotten it, for such a thing could never be forgotten—but one morning as I was looking over the paper my eye was caught by a heading over some two dozen lines of small type. The words I had seen were simply, 'The Harlesden Case,' and I knew what I was going to read. Mrs. Black was dead. Black had called in another medical man to certify as to cause of death, and something or other had aroused the strange doctor's suspicions, and there had been an inquest and *post-mortem*.

And the result? That, I will confess, did astonish me considerably; it was the triumph of the unexpected. The two doctors who made the autopsy were obliged to confess that they could not discover the faintest trace of any kind of foul play; their most exquisite tests and reagents failed to detect the presence of poison in the most infinitesimal quantity. Death, they found, had been caused by a somewhat obscure and scientifically interesting form of brain disease. The tissue of the brain and the molecules of the gray matter had undergone a most extraordinary series of changes; and the younger of the two doctors, who has some reputation, I believe, as a specialist in brain trouble, made some remarks in giving his evidence, which struck me deeply at the time, though I did not then grasp their full significance.

He said: 'At the commencement of the examination I was astonished to find appearances of a character entirely new to me, notwithstanding my somewhat large experience. I need not specify these appearances at present; it will be sufficient for me to state that as I proceeded in my task I could scarcely believe that the brain before me was that of a human being at all.' There was some surprise at this statement, as you may imagine, and the coroner asked the doctor if he meant to say that the brain resembled that of an animal.

'No,' he replied, 'I should not put it in that way. Some of the appearances I noticed seemed to point in that direction, but others, and these were the more surprising, indicated a nervous organization of a wholly different character to that either of man or of the lower animals.' It was a curious thing to say, but of course the jury brought in a verdict of death from natural causes, and, so far as the public was concerned, the case came to an end. But after I had read what the doctor said, I made up my mind that I should like to know a good deal more, and I set to work on what seemed likely to prove an interesting investigation. I had really a good deal of trouble, but I was successful in a measure. Though—why, my dear fellow, I had no notion of the time. Are you aware that we have been here nearly four hours? The waiters are staring at us. Let's have the bill and be gone."

The two men went out in silence, and stood a moment in the cool air, watching the hurrying traffic of Coventry Street pass before them to the accompaniment of ringing bells of hansoms and the cries of the newsboys, the deep far murmur of London surging up ever and again from beneath these louder noises.

"It is a strange case, isn't it?" said Dyson, at length. "What do you think of it?"

"My dear fellow, I haven't heard the end, so I will reserve my opinion. When will you give me the sequel?"

"Come to my rooms some evening; say next Thursday. Here's the address. Goodnight; I want to get down to the Strand."

Dyson hailed a passing hansom, and Salisbury turned northward to walk home to his lodgings.

2

Mr. Salisbury, as may have been gathered from the few remarks which he had found it possible to introduce in the course of the evening, was a young gentleman of a peculiarly solid form of intellect, coy and retiring before the mysterious and the uncommon, with a constitutional dislike of paradox. During the restaurant dinner he had been forced to listen in almost absolute silence to a strange tissue of improbabilities strung together with the ingenuity of a born meddler in plots and mysteries, and it was with a feeling of weariness that he crossed Shaftesbury Avenue, and dived into the recesses of Soho, for his lodgings were in a modest neighbourhood to the north of Oxford Street. As he walked he speculated on the probable fate of Dyson, relying on literature unbefriended by a thoughtful relative; and could not help concluding that so much subtlety united to a too vivid imagination would in all likelihood have been rewarded with a pair of sandwich-boards or a super's banner.

Absorbed in this train of thought, and admiring the perverse dexterity which could transmute the face of a sickly woman and a case of brain disease into the crude elements of romance, Salisbury strayed on through the dimly lighted streets, not noticing the gusty wind which drove sharply round corners and whirled the stray rubbish of the pavement into the air in eddies, while black clouds gathered over the sickly yellow moon. Even a stray drop or two of rain blown into his face did not rouse him from his meditations, and it was only when with a sudden rush the storm tore down upon the street that he began to consider the expediency of finding some shelter. The rain, driven by the wind, pelted down with the violence of a thunderstorm, dashing up from the stones and hissing through the air, and soon a perfect

279

torrent of water coursed along the kennels and accumulated in pools over the choked-up drains.

The few stray passengers who had been loafing rather than walking about the street, had scuttered away like frightened rabbits to some invisible places of refuge, and though Salisbury whistled loud and long for a hansom, no hansom appeared. He looked about him, as if to discover how far he might be from the haven of Oxford Street; but strolling carelessly along he had turned out of his way, and found himself in an unknown region, and one to all appearance devoid even of a public-house where shelter could be bought for the modest sum of twopence. The street lamps were few and at long intervals, and burned behind grimy glasses with the sickly light of oil lamps, and by this wavering light Salisbury could make out the shadowy and vast old houses of which the street was composed.

As he passed along, hurrying, and shrinking from the full sweep of the rain, he noticed the innumerable bell-handles, with names that seemed about to vanish of old age graven on brass plates beneath them, and here and there a richly carved pent-house overhung the door, blackening with the grime of fifty years. The storm seemed to grow more and more furious; he was wet through, and a new hat had become a ruin, and still Oxford Street seemed as far off as ever. It was with deep relief that the dripping man caught sight of a dark archway which seemed to promise shelter from the rain if not from the wind. Salisbury took up his position in the driest corner and looked about him; he was standing in a kind of passage contrived under part of a house, and behind him stretched a narrow footway leading between blank walls to regions unknown.

He had stood there for some time, vainly endeavouring to rid himself of some of his superfluous moisture, and listening for the passing wheel of a hansom, when his attention was aroused by a loud noise coming from the direction of the passage behind, and growing louder as it drew nearer. In a couple of minutes he could make out the shrill, raucous voice of a woman, threatening and denouncing and making the very stones echo with her accents, while now and then a man grumbled and expostulated. Though to all appearance devoid of romance, Salisbury had some relish for street rows, and was, indeed, somewhat of an amateur in the more amusing phases of drunkenness; he therefore composed himself to listen and observe with something of the air of a subscriber to grand opera. To his annoyance, however, the tempest seemed suddenly to be composed, and he could hear nothing but the impatient steps of the woman and the slow lurch of the man as they came toward him.

Keeping back in the shadow of the wall, he could see the two drawing nearer; the man was evidently drunk, and had much ado to avoid frequent collision with the wall as he tacked across from one side to the other, like some bark beating up against a wind. The woman was looking straight in front of her, with tears streaming from her eyes, but suddenly as they went by, the flame blazed up again, and she burst forth into a torrent of abuse, facing round upon her companion.

"You low rascal! You mean, contemptible cur!" she went on, after an incoherent storm of curses: "You think I'm to work and slave for you always, I suppose, while you're after that Green Street girl and drinking every penny you've got. But you're mistaken, Sam,—indeed, I'll bear it no longer. Damn you, you dirty thief, I've done with you and your master too, so you can go your own errands, and I only hope they'll get you into trouble."

The woman tore at the bosom of her dress, and taking something out that looked like paper, crumpled it up and flung it away. It fell at Salisbury's feet. She ran out and disappeared in the darkness, while the man lurched slowly into the street, grumbling indistinctly to himself in a perplexed tone of voice. Salisbury looked out after him, and saw him maundering along the pavement, halting now and then and swaying indecisively, and then starting off at some fresh tangent. The sky had cleared, and white fleecy clouds were fleeting across the moon, high in the heaven. The light came and went by turns as the clouds passed by, and, turning round as the clear white rays shone into the passage, Salisbury saw the little ball of crumpled paper which the woman had cast down. Oddly curious to know what it might contain, he picked it up and put it in his pocket, and set out afresh on his journey.

3

Salisbury was a man of habit. When he got home, drenched to the skin, his clothes hanging lank about him, and a ghastly dew besmearing his hat, his only thought was of his health, of which he took studious care. So, after changing his clothes and encasing himself in a warm dressing-gown he proceeded to prepare a sudorific in the shape of hot gin and water, warming the latter over one of those spirit lamps which mitigate the austerities of the modern hermit's life. By the time this preparation had been imbibed, and Salisbury's disturbed feelings had been soothed by a pipe of tobacco, he was able to get into bed in a happy state of vacuity, without a thought of his adventure in the dark archway, or of the weird fancies with which Dyson had seasoned his dinner.

It was the same at breakfast the next morning, for Salisbury made a point of not thinking of anything until that meal was over; but when the cup and saucer were cleared away, and the morning pipe was lit, he remembered the little ball of paper, and began fumbling in the pockets of his wet coat. He did not remember into which pocket he had put it, and as he dived now into one, and now into another, he experienced a strange feeling of apprehension lest it should not be there at all, though he could not for the life of him have explained the importance he attached to what was in all probability mere rubbish. But he sighed with relief when his fingers touched the crumpled surface in an inside pocket, and he drew it out gently and laid it on the little desk by his easy chair with as much care as if it had been some rare jewel. Salisbury sat smoking and staring at his find for a few minutes, an odd temptation to throw the thing in the fire and have done with it struggling with as odd a speculation as to its possible contents and as to the reason why the infuriated woman should have flung a bit of paper from her with such vehemence.

As might be expected, it was the latter feeling that conquered in the end, and yet it was with something like repugnance that he at last took the paper and unrolled it, and laid it out before him. It was a piece of common dirty paper, to all appearance torn out of a cheap exercise book, and in the middle were a few lines written in a queer cramped hand. Salisbury bent his head and stared eagerly at it for a moment, drawing a long breath, and then fell back in his chair gazing blankly before him, till at last with a sudden revulsion he burst into a peal of laughter, so long and loud and uproarious that the landlady's baby in the floor below awoke from sleep and echoed his mirth with hideous yells. But he laughed again and again, and took up the paper to read a second time what seemed such meaningless nonsense. It began:

Q. has had to go and see his friends in Paris. Traverse Handel S.
'Once around the grass, and twice around the lass, and thrice around the maple tree.'

Salisbury took up the paper and crumpled it as the angry woman had done, and aimed it at the fire. He did not throw it there, however, but tossed it carelessly into the well of the desk, and laughed again.

The sheer folly of the thing offended him, and he was ashamed of his own eager speculation, as one who pores over the high-sounding announcements in the agony column of the daily paper, and finds nothing but advertisement and triviality. He walked to the window, and stared out at the languid morning life of his quarter; the maids in slatternly print-dresses washing doorsteps, the fishmonger and the butcher on their rounds, and the tradesmen standing at the doors of their small shops, drooping for lack of trade and excitement. In the distance a blue haze gave some grandeur to the prospect, but the view as a whole was depressing, and would have only interested a student of the life of London, who finds something rare and choice in its every aspect.

Salisbury turned away in disgust, and settled himself in the easy chair, upholstered in a bright shade of green, and decked with yellow gimp, which was the pride and attraction of the apartments. Here he composed himself to his morning's occupation, the perusal of a novel that dealt with sport and love in a manner that suggested the collaboration of a stud-groom and a ladies' college. In an ordinary way, however, Salisbury would have been carried on by the interest of the story up to lunch time, but this morning he fidgeted in and out of his chair, took the book up and laid it down again, and swore at last to himself and at himself in mere irritation. In point of fact the jingle of the paper found in the archway had "got into his head," and do what he would he could not help muttering over and over, "*Once around the grass, and twice around the lass, and thrice around the maple tree.*"

It became a positive pain, like the foolish burden of a music-hall song, everlastingly quoted, and sung at all hours of the day and night, and treasured by the street boys as an unfailing resource for six months together. He went out into the streets, and tried to forget his enemy in the jostling of the crowds, and the roar and clatter of the traffic; but presently he would find himself stealing quietly aside and pacing some deserted byway, vainly puzzling his brains, and trying to fix some meaning to phrases that were meaningless. It was a positive relief when Thursday came, and he remembered that he had made an appointment to go and see Dyson; the flimsy reveries of the self-styled man of letters appeared entertaining when compared with this ceaseless iteration, this maze of thought from which there seemed no possibility of escape.

Dyson's abode was in one of the quietest of the quiet streets that lead down from the Strand to the river, and when Salisbury passed from the narrow stairway into his friend's room, he saw that the uncle had been beneficent indeed. The floor glowed and flamed with all the colours of the east; it was, as Dyson pompously remarked, "a sunset in a dream," and the lamplight, the twilight of London streets, was shut out with strangely worked curtains, glittering here and there with threads of gold. In the shelves of an oak *armoire* stood jars and plates of old French china, and the black and white of etchings not to be found in the Haymarket or in Bond Street, stood out against the splendour of a Japanese paper. Salisbury sat down on the settle by the hearth, and sniffed the mingled fumes of incense and tobacco, wondering and dumb before all this splendour after the green rep and the oleographs, the gilt-framed mirror and the lustres of his own apartment.

"I am glad you have come," said Dyson. "Comfortable little room, isn't it? But you don't look very well, Salisbury. Nothing disagreed with you, has it?"

"No; but I have been a good deal bothered for the last few days. The fact is I had an odd kind of—of—adventure, I suppose I may call it, that night I saw you, and it has worried me a good deal. And the provoking part of it is that it's the merest nonsense—but, however, I will tell you all about it, by and by. You were going to let me have the rest of that odd story you began at the restaurant."

"Yes. But I am afraid, Salisbury, you are incorrigible. You are a slave to what you call matter of fact. You know perfectly well that in your heart you think the oddness in that case is of my making, and that it is all really as plain as the police reports. However, as I have begun, I will go on. But first we will have something to drink, and you may as well light your pipe."

Dyson went up to the oak cupboard, and drew from its depths a rotund bottle and two little glasses quaintly gilded.

"It's Benedictin," he said. "You'll have some, won't you?"

Salisbury assented, and the two men sat sipping and smoking reflectively for some minutes before Dyson began.

"Let me see," he said at last; "we were at the inquest, weren't we? No, we had done with that. Ah, I remember. I was telling you that on the whole I had been successful in my inquiries, investigation, or whatever you like to call it, into the matter. Wasn't that where I left off?"

"Yes, that was it. To be precise, I think 'though' was the last word you said on the matter."

"Exactly. I have been thinking it all over since the other night, and

I have come to the conclusion that that 'though' is a very big 'though' indeed. Not to put too fine a point on it, I have had to confess that what I found out, or thought I found out, amounts in reality to nothing. I am as far away from the heart of the case as ever. However, I may as well tell you what I do know. You may remember my saying that I was impressed a good deal by some remarks of one of the doctors who gave evidence at the inquest.

"Well, I determined that my first step must be to try if I could get something more definite and intelligible out of that doctor. Somehow or other I managed to get an introduction to the man, and he gave me an appointment to come and see him. He turned out to be a pleasant, genial fellow; rather young and not in the least like the typical medical man, and he began the conference by offering me whiskey and cigars. I didn't think it worthwhile to beat about the bush, so I began by saying that part of his evidence at the Harlesden Inquest struck me as very peculiar, and I gave him the printed report, with the sentences in question underlined. He just glanced at the slip, and gave me a queer look. 'It struck you as peculiar, did it?' said he. 'Well, you must remember the Harlesden case was very peculiar. In fact, I think I may safely say that in some features it was unique—quite unique.' 'Quite so,' I replied, 'and that's exactly why it interests me, and why I want to know more about it. And I thought that if anybody could give me any information it would be you. What is your opinion of the matter?'

"It was a pretty downright sort of question, and my doctor looked rather taken aback.

"'Well,' he said, 'as I fancy your motive in inquiring into the question must be mere curiosity, I think I may tell you my opinion with tolerable freedom. So, Mr.—Mr. Dyson, if you want to know my theory, it is this: I believe that Dr. Black killed his wife.'

"'But the verdict,' I answered, 'the verdict was given from your own evidence.'

"'Quite so, the verdict was given in accordance with the evidence of my colleague and myself, and, under the circumstances, I think the jury acted very sensibly. In fact I don't see what else they could have done. But I stick to my opinion, mind you, and I say this also: I don't wonder at Black's doing what I firmly believe he did. I think he was justified.'

"'Justified! How could that be?' I asked. I was astonished, as you may imagine, at the answer I had got. The doctor wheeled round his chair, and looked steadily at me for a moment before he answered.

"'I suppose you are not a man of science yourself? No; then it would be of no use my going into detail. I have always been firmly opposed myself to any partnership between physiology and psychology. I believe that both are bound to suffer. No one recognizes more decidedly than I do the impassable gulf, the fathomless abyss that separates the world of consciousness from the sphere of matter. We know that every change of consciousness is accompanied by a rearrangement of the molecules in the gray matter; and that is all. What the link between them is, or why they occur together, we do not know, and most authorities believe that we never can know. Yet, I will tell you that as I did my work, the knife in my hand, I felt convinced, in spite of all theories, that what lay before me was not the brain of a dead woman; not the brain of a human being at all. Of course I saw the face; but it was quite placid, devoid of all expression. It must have been a beautiful face, no doubt; but I can honestly say that I would not have looked in that face when there was life behind it for a thousand guineas, no, nor for twice that sum.'

"'My dear sir,' I said, 'you surprise me extremely. You say that it was not the brain of a human being. What was it then?'

"'The brain of a devil.' He spoke quite coolly, and never moved a muscle. 'The brain of a devil,' he repeated, 'and I have no doubt that Black put a pillow over her mouth and kept it there for a few minutes. I don't blame him if he did. Whatever Mrs. Black was, she was not fit to stay in this world. Will you have anything more? No? Goodnight, goodnight.'

"It was a queer sort of opinion to get from a man of science, wasn't it? When he was saying that he would not have looked on that face when alive for a thousand guineas or two thousand guineas, I was thinking of the face I had seen, but I said nothing. I went again to Harlesden, and passed from one shop to another, making small purchases, and trying to find out whether there was anything about the Blacks which was not already common property; but there was very little to hear. One of the tradesmen to whom I spoke said he had known the dead woman well—she used to buy of him such quantities of grocery as were required for their small household, for they never kept a servant, but had a charwoman in occasionally, and she had not seen Mrs. Black for months before she died. According to this man, Mrs. Black was 'a nice lady,' always kind and considerate, so fond of her husband, and he of her, as everyone thought.

"And yet, to put the doctor's opinion on one side, I knew what

I had seen. And then, after thinking it all over and putting one thing with another, it seemed to me that the only person likely to give me much assistance would be Black himself, and I made up my mind to find him. Of course he wasn't to be found in Harlesden; he had left, I was told, directly after the funeral. Everything in the house had been sold, and one fine day Black got into the train with a small portmanteau, and went nobody knew where. It was a chance if he were ever heard of again, and it was by a mere chance that I came across him at last. I was walking one day along Gray's Inn Road, not bound for anywhere in particular, but looking about me, as usual, and holding on to my hat, for it was a gusty day in early March, and the wind was making the tree-tops in the Inn rock and quiver. I had come up from the Holborn end, and I had almost got to Theobald's Road, when I noticed a man walking in front of me, leaning on a stick and to all appearance very feeble.

"There was something about his look that made me curious, I don't know why; and I began to walk briskly, with the idea of overtaking him, when of a sudden his hat blew off, and came bounding along the pavement to my feet. Of course I rescued the hat, and gave it a glance as I went towards its owner. It was a biography in itself; a Piccadilly maker's name in the inside, but I don't think a beggar would have picked it out of the gutter. Then I looked up, and saw Dr. Black of Harlesden waiting for me. A queer thing, wasn't it? But, Salisbury, what a change! When I saw Dr. Black come down the steps of his house at Harlesden, he was an upright man, walking firmly with well-built limbs; a man, I should say, in the prime of his life. And now before me there crouched this wretched creature, bent and feeble, with shrunken cheeks, and hair that was whitening fast, and limbs that trembled and shook together, and misery in his eyes.

"He thanked me for bringing him his hat, saying, 'I don't think I should ever have got it, I can't run much now. A gusty day, sir, isn't it?' and with this he was turning away; but by little and little I contrived to draw him into the current of conversation, and we walked together eastward. I think the man would have been glad to get rid of me, but I didn't intend to let him go, and he stopped at last in front of a miserable house in a miserable street. It was, I verily believe, one of the most wretched quarters I have ever seen,—houses that must have been sordid and hideous enough when new, that had gathered foulness with every year, and now seemed to lean and totter to their fall. 'I live up there,' said Black, pointing to the tiles, 'not in the front,—in the back. I am very quiet there. I won't ask you to come in now, but perhaps some other day———'

"I caught him up at that, and told him I should be only too glad to come and see him. He gave me an odd sort of glance, as if he was wondering what on earth I or anybody else could care about him, and I left him fumbling with his latch-key. I think you will say I did pretty well, when I tell you that within a few weeks I had made myself an intimate friend of Black's. I shall never forget the first time I went to this room; I hope I shall never see such abject, squalid misery again. The foul paper, from which all pattern or trace of a pattern had long vanished, subdued and penetrated with the grime of the evil street, was hanging in mouldering pennons from the wall. Only at the end of the room was it possible to stand upright; and the sight of the wretched bed and the odour of corruption that pervaded the place made me turn faint and sick.

"Here I found him munching a piece of bread; he seemed surprised to find that I had kept my promise, but he gave me his chair, and sat on the bed while we talked. I used to go and see him often, and we had long conversations together, but he never mentioned Harlesden or his wife. I fancy that he supposed me ignorant of the matter, or thought that if I had heard of it, I should never connect the respectable Dr. Black of Harlesden with a poor garreteer in the backwoods of London. He was a strange man, and as we sat together smoking, I often wondered whether he were mad or sane, for I think the wildest dreams of Paracelsus and the Rosicrucians would appear plain and sober fact, compared with the theories I have heard him earnestly advance in that grimy den of his. I once ventured to hint something of the sort to him; I suggested that something he had said was in flat contradiction to all science and all experience.

"'No, Dyson,' he answered, 'not all experience, for mine counts for something. I am no dealer in unproved theories; what I say I have proved for myself, and at a terrible cost. There is a region of knowledge of which you will never know, which wise men, seeing from afar off, shun like the plague, as well they may; but into that region I have gone. If you knew, if you could even dream of what may be done, of what one or two men have done, in this quiet world of ours, your very soul would shudder and faint within you. What you have heard from me has been but the merest husk and outer covering of true science,—that science which means death and that which is more awful than death to those who gain it. No, Dyson, when men say that there are strange things in the world, they little know the awe and the terror that dwell always within them and about them.'"

There was a sort of fascination about the man that drew me to him, and I was quite sorry to have to leave London for a month or two; I missed his odd talk. A few days after I came back to town I thought I would go and look him up; but when I gave the two rings at the bell that used to summon him, there was no answer. I rang and rang again, and was just turning to go away, when the door opened and a dirty woman asked me what I wanted.

"From her look I fancy she took me for a plain-clothes officer after one of her lodgers; but when I inquired if Mr. Black was in, she gave me a stare of another kind. 'There's no Mr. Black lives here,' she said. 'He's gone. He's dead this six weeks. I always thought he was a bit queer in his head, or else had been and got into some trouble or other. He used to go out every morning from ten till one, and one Monday morning we heard him come in and go into his room and shut the door, and a few minutes after, just as we was a-sitting down to our dinner, there was such a scream that I thought I should have gone right off. And then we heard a stamping, and down he came raging and cursing most dreadful, swearing he had been robbed of something that was worth millions. And then he just dropped down in the passage, and we thought he was dead.

"'We got him up to his room, and put him on his bed, and I just sat there and waited, while my 'usband he went for the doctor. And there was the winder wide open, and a little tin box he had lying on the floor open and empty; but of course nobody could possible have got in at the winder, and as for him having anything that was worth anything, it's nonsense, for he was often weeks and weeks behind with his rent, and my 'usband he threatened often and often to turn him into the street, for, as he said, we've got a living to myke like other people, and of course that's true; but somehow I didn't like to do it, though he was an odd kind of a man, and I fancy had been better off. And then the doctor came and looked at him, and said as he couldn't do nothing, and that night he died as I was a-sitting by his bed; and I can tell you that, with one thing and another, we lost money by him, for the few bits of clothes as he had were worth next to nothing when they came to be sold.'

"I gave the woman half a sovereign for her trouble, and went home thinking of Dr. Black and the epitaph she had made him, and wondering at his strange fancy that he had been robbed. I take it that he had very little to fear on that score, poor fellow; but I suppose that he was really mad, and died in a sudden access of his mania. His landlady said that once or twice when she had had occasion to go into his room (to dun the poor wretch for his rent, most likely), he would keep her at the door for about a minute, and that when she came in she would find him putting away his tin box in the corner by the window. I suppose he had become possessed with the idea of some great treasure, and fancied himself a wealthy man in the midst of all his misery.

"*Explicit*, my tale is ended; and you see that though I knew Black I know nothing of his wife or of the history of her death. That's the Harlesden case, Salisbury, and I think it interests me all the more deeply because there does not seem the shadow of a possibility that I or anyone else will ever know more about it. What do you think of it?"

"Well, Dyson, I must say that I think you have contrived to surround the whole thing with a mystery of your own making. I go for the doctor's solution,—Black murdered his wife, being himself, in all probability, an undeveloped lunatic."

"What? Do you believe, then, that this woman was something too awful, too terrible, to be allowed to remain on the earth? You will remember that the doctor said it was the brain of a devil?"

"Yes, yes; but he was speaking, of course, metaphorically. It's really quite a simple matter, Dyson, if you only look at it like that."

"Ah, well, you may be right; but yet I am sure you are not. Well, well, it's no good discussing it anymore. A little more Benedictine? That's right; try some of this tobacco. Didn't you say that you had been bothered by something,—something which happened that night we dined together?"

"Yes, I have been worried, Dyson,—worried a great deal. I—But it's such a trivial matter, indeed, such an absurdity, that I feel ashamed to trouble you with it."

"Never mind; let's have it, absurd or not."

With many hesitations, and with much inward resentment of the folly of the thing, Salisbury told his tale, and repeated reluctantly the absurd intelligence and the absurder doggerel of the scrap of paper, expecting to hear Dyson burst out into a roar of laughter.

"Isn't it too bad that I should let myself be bothered by such stuff as that?" he asked, when he had stuttered out the jingle of once and twice and thrice.

Dyson had listened to it all gravely, even to the end, and meditated for a few minutes in silence.

"Yes," he said at length, "it was a curious chance, your taking shelter in that archway just as those two went by. But I don't know that I should call what was written on the paper nonsense; it is bizarre certainly, but I expect it has a meaning for somebody. Just repeat it again, will you? and I will write it down. Perhaps we might find a cipher of some sort, though I hardly think we shall."

Again had the reluctant lips of Salisbury to slowly stammer out the rubbish he abhorred, while Dyson jotted it down on a slip of paper.

"Look over it, will you?" he said, when it was done; "it may be important that I should have every word in its place. Is that all right?"

"Yes, that is an accurate copy. But I don't think you will get much out of it. Depend upon it, it is mere nonsense, a wanton scribble. I must be going now, Dyson. No, no more; that stuff of yours is pretty strong. Goodnight."

"I suppose you would like to hear from me, if I did find out anything?"

"No, not I; I don't want to hear about the thing again. You may regard the discovery, if it is one as your own."

"Very well. Goodnight."

4

A good many hours after Salisbury had returned to the company of the green rep chairs, Dyson still sat at his desk, itself a Japanese romance, smoking many pipes, and meditating over his friend's story. The bizarre quality of the inscription which had annoyed Salisbury was to him an attraction; and now and again he took it up and scanned thoughtfully what he had written, especially the quaint jingle at the end. It was a token, a symbol, he decided, and not a cipher; and the woman who had flung it away was, in all probability, entirely ignorant of its meaning. She was but the agent of the "Sam" she had abused and discarded, and he, too, was again the agent of someone unknown,— possibly of the individual styled Q., who had been forced to visit his French friends. But what to make of "Traverse Handel S.?" Here was the root and source of the enigma, and not all the tobacco of Virginia seemed likely to suggest any clew here.

It seemed almost hopeless; but Dyson regarded himself as the Wellington of mysteries, and went to bed feeling assured that sooner or later he would hit upon the right track. For the next few days he was deeply engaged in his literary labours,—labours which were a profound mystery even to the most intimate of his friends, who searched the railway bookstalls in vain for the result of so many hours spent at the Japanese bureau in company with strong tobacco and black tea. On this occasion Dyson confined himself to his room for four days, and it was with genuine relief that he laid down his pen and went out into the streets in quest of relaxation and fresh air. The gas lamps were being lighted, and the fifth edition of the evening papers was being howled through the streets; and Dyson, feeling that he wanted quiet, turned away from the clamorous Strand, and began to trend away to the northwest. Soon he found himself in streets that echoed to his footsteps; and crossing a broad new thoroughfare, and verging still to the west, Dyson discovered that he had penetrated to the depths of Soho.

Here again was life; rare vintages of France and Italy, at prices which seemed contemptibly small, allured the passer-by; here were cheeses, vast and rich; here olive oil, and here a grove of Rabelaisian sausages; while in a neighbouring shop the whole press of Paris appeared to be on sale. In the middle of the roadway a strange miscellany of nations sauntered to and fro; for there cab and hansom rarely ventured, and from window over window the inhabitants looked forth in pleased contemplation of the scene. Dyson made his way slowly along, mingling with the crowd on the cobblestones, listening to the queer babel of French and German and Italian and English, glancing now and again at the shop windows with their levelled batteries of bottles, and had almost gained the end of the street, when his attention was arrested by a small shop at the corner, a vivid contrast to its neighbours.

It was the typical shop of the poor quarter, a shop entirely English. Here were vended tobacco and sweets, cheap pipes of clay and cherry wood; penny exercise-books and penholders jostled for precedence with comic songs, and story papers with appalling cuts showed that romance claimed its place beside the actualities of the evening paper, the bills of which fluttered at the doorway. Dyson glanced up at the name above the door, and stood by the kennel trembling; for a sharp pang, the pang of one who has made a discovery, had for a moment left him incapable of motion. The name over the little shop was Travers. Dyson looked up again, this time at the corner of the wall above the lamp-post, and read, in white letters on a blue ground, the words "Handel Street, W.C.," and the legend was repeated in fainter letters just below. He gave a little sigh of satisfaction, and without more ado walked boldly into the shop, and stared the fat man who was sitting behind the counter full in the face. The fellow rose to his feet and returned the stare a little curiously, and then began in stereotyped phrase,—

"What can I do for you, sir?"

Dyson enjoyed the situation, and a dawning perplexity on the man's face. He propped his stick carefully against the counter, and leaning over it, said slowly and impressively:

"Once around the grass, and twice around the lass, and thrice around the maple-tree."

Dyson had calculated on his words producing an effect, and he was not disappointed. The vendor of miscellanies gasped, open-mouthed, like a fish, and steadied himself against the counter. When he spoke, after a short interval, it was in a hoarse mutter, tremulous and unsteady.

"Would you mind saying that again, sir? I didn't quite catch it."

"My good man, I shall most certainly do nothing of the kind. You heard what I said perfectly well. You have got a clock in your shop, I see; an admirable timekeeper I have no doubt. Well, I give you a minute by your own clock."

The man looked about him in perplexed indecision, and Dyson felt that it was time to be bold.

"Look here, Travers, the time is nearly up. You have heard of Q., I think. Remember, I hold your life in my hands. Now!"

Dyson was shocked at the result of his own audacity. The man shrunk and shrivelled in terror, the sweat poured down a face of ashy white, and he held up his hands before him.

"Mr. Davies, Mr. Davies, don't say that, don't for Heaven's sake. I didn't know you at first, I didn't indeed. Good God! Mr. Davies, you wouldn't ruin me? I'll get it in a moment."

"You had better not lose any more time."

The man slunk piteously out of his shop, and went into a back parlour. Dyson heard his trembling fingers fumbling with a bunch of keys, and the creak of an opening box. He came back presently with a small package neatly tied up in brown paper in his hands, and, still full of terror, handed it to Dyson.

"I'm glad to be rid of it," he said. "I'll take no more jobs of this sort."

Dyson took the parcel and his stick, and walked out of the shop with a nod, turning round as he passed the door. Travers had sunk into his seat, his face still white with terror, with one hand over his eyes, and Dyson speculated a good deal as he walked rapidly away as to what queer chords those could be on which he had played so roughly. He hailed the first hansom he could see, and drove home, and when he had lit his hanging lamp, and laid his parcel on the table, he paused for a moment, wondering on what strange thing the lamplight would soon shine. He locked his door, and cut the strings, and unfolded the paper layer after layer, and came at last to a small wooden box, simply but solidly made. There was no lock, and Dyson had simply to raise the lid, and as he did so he drew a long breath and started back. The lamp seemed to glimmer feebly like a single candle, but the whole room blazed with light—and not with light alone but with a thousand colours, with all the glories of some painted window; and upon the walls of his room and on the familiar furniture, the glow flamed back and seemed to flow again to its source, the little wooden box.

For there upon a bed of soft wool lay the most splendid jewel,—a jewel such as Dyson had never dreamed of, and within it shone the blue of far skies, and the green of the sea by the shore, and the red of the ruby, and deep violet rays, and in the middle of all it seemed aflame as if a fountain of fire rose up, and fell, and rose again with sparks like stars for drops. Dyson gave a long deep sigh, and dropped into his chair, and put his hands over his eyes to think. The jewel was like an opal, but from a long experience of the shop windows he knew there was no such thing as an opal one quarter or one eighth of its size. He looked at the stone again, with a feeling that was almost awe, and placed it gently on the table under the lamp, and watched the wonderful flame that shone and sparkled in its centre, and then turned to the box, curious to know whether it might contain other marvels. He lifted the bed of wool on which the opal had reclined, and saw beneath, no more jewels, but a little old pocket-book, worn and shabby with use. Dyson opened it at the first leaf, and dropped the book again appalled. He had read the name of the owner, neatly written in blue ink:—

Steven Black, M.D.,
Oranmore,
Devon Road,
Harlesden.

It was several minutes before Dyson could bring himself to open the book a second time; he remembered the wretched exile in his garret and his strange talk, and the memory too of the face he had seen at the window, and of what the specialist had said surged up in his mind, and as he held his finger on the cover he shivered, dreading what might be written within. When at last he held it in his hand, and turned the pages, he found that the first two leaves were blank, but the third was covered with clear minute writing, and Dyson began to read with the light of the opal flaming in his eyes.

5

The record began:

> Ever since I was a young man I devoted all my leisure and a good deal of time that ought to have been given to other studies to the investigation of curious and obscure branches of knowledge. What are commonly called the pleasures of life had never any attractions for me, and I lived alone in London, avoiding my fellow-students, and in my turn avoided by them as a man self-absorbed and unsympathetic. So long as I could gratify my desire of knowledge of a peculiar kind, knowledge of which the very existence is a profound secret to most men, I was intensely happy, and I have often spent whole nights sitting in the darkness of my room, and thinking of the strange world on the brink of which I trod.
>
> My professional studies, however, and the necessity of obtaining a degree, for some time forced my more obscure employment into the background, and soon after I had qualified I met Agnes, who became my wife. We took a new house in this remote suburb, and I began the regular routine of a sober practice, and for some months lived happily enough, sharing in the life about me, and only thinking at odd intervals of that occult science which had once fascinated my whole being. I had learnt enough of the paths I had begun to tread to know that they were beyond all expression difficult and dangerous, that to persevere meant in all probability the wreck of a life, and that they lead to regions so terrible that the mind of man shrinks appalled at the very thought.
>
> Moreover, the quiet and the peace I had enjoyed since my marriage had wiled me away to a great extent from places where I knew no peace could dwell. But suddenly,—I think, indeed, it was the work of a single night, as I lay awake on my bed gazing into the darkness,—suddenly, I say, the old desire, the former longing returned, and returned with a force that had been intensified ten times by its absence; and when the day dawned

and I looked out of the window and saw with haggard eyes the sun rise in the East, I knew that my doom had been pronounced; that as I had gone far, so now I must go farther with steps that know no faltering.

I turned to the bed where my wife was sleeping peacefully, and lay down again weeping bitter tears, for the sun had set on our happy life and had risen with a dawn of terror to us both. I will not set down here in minute detail what followed; outwardly I went about the day's labour as before, saying nothing to my wife. But she soon saw that I had changed. I spent my spare time in a room which I had fitted up as a laboratory, and often I crept upstairs in the gray dawn of the morning, when the light of many lamps still glowed over London; and each night I had stolen a step nearer to that great abyss which I was to bridge over, the gulf between the world of consciousness and the world of matter.

My experiments were many and complicated in their nature, and it was some months before I realized whither they all pointed, and when this was borne in upon me in a moment's time, I felt my face whiten and my heart still within me. But the power to draw back, the power to stand before the doors that now opened wide before me and not to enter in, had long ago been absent; the way was closed, and I could only pass onward. My position was as utterly hopeless as that of the prisoner in an utter dungeon, whose only light is that of the dungeon above him; the doors were shut and escape was impossible. Experiment after experiment gave the same result, and I knew, and shrank even as the thought passed through my mind, that in the work I had to do there must be elements which no laboratory could furnish, which no scales could ever measure.

In that work, from which even I doubted to escape with life, life itself must enter; from some human being there must be drawn that essence which men call the soul, and in its place (for in the scheme of the world there is no vacant chamber), in its place would enter in what the lips can hardly utter, what the mind cannot conceive without a horror more awful than the horror of death itself. And when I knew this, I knew also on whom this fate would fall; I looked into my wife's eyes. Even at that hour, if I had gone out and taken a rope and hanged myself I might have escaped, and she also, but in no other way.

At last I told her all. She shuddered, and wept, and called on her dead mother for help, and asked me if I had no mercy, and I could only sigh. I concealed nothing from her; I told her what she would become, and what would enter in where her life had been; I told her of all the shame and of all the horror. You who will read this when I am dead,—if indeed I allow this record to survive—you who have opened the box and have seen what lies there, if you could understand what lies hidden in that opal! For one night my wife consented to what I asked of her, consented with the tears running down her beautiful face, and hot shame flushing red over her neck and breast, consented to undergo this for me. I threw open the window, and we looked together at the sky and the dark earth for the last time; it was a fine starlight night, and there was a pleasant breeze blowing, and I kissed her on her lips, and her tears ran down upon my face. That night she came down to my laboratory, and there, with shutters bolted and barred down, with curtains drawn thick and close so that the very stars might be shut out from the sight of that room, while the crucible hissed and boiled over the lamp, I did what had to be done, and led out what was no longer a woman. But on the table the opal flamed and sparkled with such light as no eyes of man have ever gazed on, and the rays of the flame that was within it flashed and glittered, and shone even to my heart. My wife had only asked one thing of me; that when there came at last what I had told her, I would kill her. I have kept that promise.

★★★★★★

There was nothing more. Dyson let the little pocket-book fall, and turned and looked again at the opal with its flaming inmost light, and then, with unutterable irresistible horror surging up in his heart, grasped the jewel, and flung it on the ground, and trampled it beneath his heel. His face was white with terror as he turned away, and for a moment stood sick and trembling, and then with a start he leapt across the room and steadied himself against the door. There was an angry hiss, as of steam escaping under great pressure, and as he gazed, motionless, a volume of heavy yellow smoke was slowly issuing from the very centre of the jewel, and wreathing itself in snake-like coils above it. And then a thin white flame burst forth from the smoke, and shot up into the air and vanished; and on the ground there lay a thing like a cinder, black, and crumbling to the touch.

The Lost Room
By Fitz-James O'Brien

It was oppressively warm. The sun had long disappeared, but seemed to have left its vital spirit of heat behind it. The air rested; the leaves of the acacia-trees that shrouded my windows hung plumb-like on their delicate stalks. The smoke of my cigar scarce rose above my head, but hung about me in a pale blue cloud, which I had to dissipate with languid waves of my hand. My shirt was open at the throat, and my chest heaved laboriously in the effort to catch some breaths of fresher air. The noises of the city seemed to be wrapped in slumber, and the shrilling of the mosquitoes was the only sound that broke the stillness.

As I lay with my feet elevated on the back of a chair, wrapped in that peculiar frame of mind in which thought assumes a species of lifeless motion, the strange fancy seized me of making a languid inventory of the principal articles of furniture in my room. It was a task well suited to the mood in which I found myself. Their forms were duskily defined in the dim twilight that floated shadowily through the chamber; it was no labour to note and particularize each, and from the place where I sat I could command a view of all my possessions without even turning my head.

There was, *imprimis*, that ghostly lithograph by Calame. It was a mere black spot on the white wall, but my inner vision scrutinized every detail of the picture. A wild, desolate, midnight heath, with a spectral oak-tree in the centre of the foreground. The wind blows fiercely, and the jagged branches, clothed scantily with ill-grown leaves, are swept to the left continually by its giant force.

A formless wrack of clouds streams across the awful sky, and the rain sweeps almost parallel with the horizon. Beyond, the heath stretches off into endless blackness, in the extreme of which either fancy or art has conjured up some undefinable shapes that seem riding into space. At the base of the huge oak stands a shrouded figure. His mantle is wound by the blast in tight folds around his form, and the long cock's feather in his hat is blown upright, till it seems as if it stood on end with fear. His features are not visible, for he has grasped his cloak with both hands, and drawn it from either side across his face. The picture is seemingly objectless. It tells no tale, but there is a weird power about it that haunts one, and it was for that I bought it.

Next to the picture comes the round blot that hangs below it, which I know to be a smoking-cap. It has my coat of arms embroidered on the front, and for that reason I never wear it; though, when properly arranged on my head, with its long blue silken tassel hanging down by my cheek, I believe it becomes me well. I remember the time when it was in the course of manufacture. I remember the tiny little hands that pushed the coloured silks so nimbly through the cloth that was stretched on the embroidery-frame,—the vast trouble I was put to to get a coloured copy of my armorial bearings for the heraldic work which was to decorate the front of the band,—the pursings up of the little mouth, and the contractions of the young forehead, as their possessor plunged into a profound sea of cogitation touching the way in which the cloud should be represented from which the armed hand, that is my crest, issues,—the heavenly moment when the tiny hands placed it on my head, in a position that I could not bear for more than a few seconds, and I, kinglike, immediately assumed my royal prerogative after the coronation, and instantly levied a tax on my only subjects which was, however, not paid unwillingly. Ah! the cap is there, but the embroiderer has fled; for Atropos was severing the web of life above her head while she was weaving that silken shelter for mine!

How uncouthly the huge piano that occupies the corner at the left of the door looms out in the uncertain twilight! I neither play nor sing, yet I own a piano. It is a comfort to me to look at it, and to feel that the music is there, although I am not able to break the spell that binds it. It is pleasant to know that Bellini and Mozart, Cimarosa, Porpora, Glück and all such,—or at least their souls,—sleep in that unwieldy case. There lie embalmed, as it were, all operas, *sonatas, oratorios, nocturnos*, marches, songs and dances, that ever climbed into existence through the four bars that wall in melody. Once I was entirely repaid for the investment of my funds in that instrument which I never use. Blokeeta, the composer, came to see me. Of course his instincts urged him as irresistibly to my piano as if some magnetic power lay within it compelling him to approach. He tuned it, he played on it. All night long, until the gray and spectral dawn rose out of the depths of the midnight, he sat and played, and I lay smoking by the window listening.

Wild, unearthly, and sometimes insufferably painful, were the improvisations of Blokeeta. The chords of the instrument seemed breaking with anguish. Lost souls shrieked in his dismal preludes; the half-heard utterances of spirits in pain, that groped at inconceivable distances from anything lovely or harmonious, seemed to rise dimly up out of the waves of sound that gathered under his hands. Melancholy human love wandered out on distant heaths, or beneath dank and gloomy cypresses, murmuring its unanswered sorrow, or hateful gnomes sported and sang in the stagnant swamps triumphing in unearthly tones over the knight whom they had lured to his death. Such was Blokeeta's night's entertainment; and when he at length closed the piano, and hurried away through the cold morning, he left a memory about the instrument from which I could never escape.

Those snow-shoes that hang in the space between the mirror and the door recall Canadian wanderings,—a long race through the dense forests, over the frozen snow through whose brittle crust the slender hoofs of the caribou that we were pursuing sank at every step, until the poor creature despairingly turned at bay in a small juniper coppice, and we heartlessly shot him down. And I remember how Gabriel, the *habitant*, and François, the half-breed, cut his throat, and how the hot blood rushed out in a torrent over the snowy soil; and I recall the snow *cabane* that Gabriel built, where we all three slept so warmly; and the great fire that glowed at our feet, painting all kinds of demoniac shapes on the black screen of forest that lay without; and the deer-steaks that we roasted for our breakfast; and the savage drunkenness of Gabriel in the morning, he having been privately drinking out of my brandy-flask all the night long.

That long haftless dagger that dangles over the mantelpiece makes my heart swell. I found it, when a boy, in a hoary old castle in which one of my maternal ancestors once lived. That same ancestor—who, by the way, yet lives in history—was a strange old sea-king, who dwelt on the extremest point of the southwestern coast of Ireland. He owned the whole of that fertile island called Inniskeiran, which directly faces Cape Clear, where between them the Atlantic rolls furiously, forming what the fishermen of the place call "the Sound." An awful place in winter is that same Sound. On certain days no boat can live there for a moment, and Cape Clear is frequently cut off for days from any communication with the mainland.

This old sea-king—Sir Florence O'Driscoll by name—passed a stormy life. From the summit of his castle he watched the ocean, and when any richly laden vessels bound from the South to the industrious Galway merchants, hove in sight, Sir Florence hoisted the sails of his galley, and it went hard with him if he did not tow into harbour ship and crew. In this way he lived; not a very honest mode of livelihood, certainly, according to our modern ideas, but quite reconcilable with the morals of the time. As may be supposed, Sir Florence got into trouble. Complaints were laid against him at the English court by the plundered merchants, and the Irish viking set out for London, to plead his own cause before good Queen Bess, as she was called. He had one powerful recommendation: he was a marvellously handsome man. Not Celtic by descent, but half Spanish, half Danish in blood, he had the great northern stature with the regular features, flashing eyes, and dark hair of the Iberian race. This may account for the fact that his stay at the English court was much longer than was necessary, as also for the tradition, which a local historian mentions, that the English queen evinced a preference for the Irish chieftain, of other nature than that usually shown by monarch to subject.

Previous to his departure, Sir Florence had intrusted the care of his property to an Englishman named Hull. During the long absence of the knight, this person managed to ingratiate himself with the local authorities, and gain their favour so far that they were willing to support him in almost any scheme. After a protracted stay, Sir Florence, pardoned of all his misdeeds, returned to his home. Home no longer. Hull was in possession, and refused to yield an acre of the lands he had so nefariously acquired. It was no use appealing to the law, for its officers were in the opposite interest. It was no use appealing to the queen, for she had another lover, and had forgotten the poor Irish knight by this time; and so the Viking passed the best portion of his life in unsuccessful attempts to reclaim his vast estates, and was eventually, in his old age, obliged to content himself with his castle by the sea and the island of Inniskeiran, the only spot of which the usurper was unable to deprive him. So this old story of my kinsman's fate looms up out of the darkness that enshrouds that haftless dagger hanging on the wall.

It was somewhat after the foregoing fashion that I dreamily made the inventory of my personal property. As I turned my eyes on each object, one after the other,—or the places where they lay, for the room was now so dark that it was almost impossible to see with any distinctness,—a crowd of memories connected with each rose up before me, and, perforce, I had to indulge them. So I proceeded but slowly, and at last my cigar shortened to a hot and bitter morsel that I could barely hold between my lips, while it seemed to me that the night grew each moment more insufferably oppressive.

While I was revolving some impossible means of cooling my wretched body, the cigar stump began to burn my lips. I flung it angrily through the open window, and stooped out to watch it falling. It first lighted on the leaves of the acacia, sending out a spray of red sparkles, then, rolling off, it fell plump on the dark walk in the garden, faintly illuminating for a moment the dusky trees and breathless flowers. Whether it was the contrast between the red flash of the cigarstump and the silent darkness of the garden, or whether it was that I detected by the sudden light a faint waving of the leaves, I know not; but something suggested to me that the garden was cool. I will take a turn there, thought I, just as I am; it cannot be warmer than this room, and however still the atmosphere, there is always a feeling of liberty and spaciousness in the open air, that partially supplies one's wants. With this idea running through my head, I arose, lit another cigar, and passed out into the long, intricate corridors that led to the main staircase. As I crossed the threshold of my room, with what a different feeling I should have passed it had I known that I was never to set foot in it again!

I lived in a very large house, in which I occupied two rooms on the second floor. The house was old-fashioned, and all the floors communicated by a huge circular staircase that wound up through the centre of the building, while at every landing long, rambling corridors stretched off into mysterious nooks and corners. This palace of mine was very high, and its resources, in the way of crannies and windings, seemed to be interminable. Nothing seemed to stop anywhere. *Cul-de-sacs* were unknown on the premises. The corridors and passages, like mathematical lines, seemed capable of indefinite extension, and the object of the architect must have been to erect an edifice in which people might go ahead forever. The whole place was gloomy, not so much because it was large, but because an unearthly nakedness seemed to pervade the structure. The staircases, corridors, halls, and vestibules all partook of a desert-like desolation. There was nothing on the walls to break the sombre monotony of those long *vistas* of shade. No carvings on the wainscoting, no moulded masks peering down from the simply severe cornices, no marble vases on the landings. There was an eminent dreariness and want of life—so rare in an American establishment—all over the abode. It was Hood's haunted house put in order and newly painted.

The servants, too, were shadowy, and chary of their visits. Bells rang three times before the gloomy chambermaid could be induced to present herself; and the negro waiter, a ghoul-like looking creature from Congo, obeyed the summons only when one's patience was exhausted or one's want satisfied in some other way. When he did come, one felt sorry that he had not stayed away altogether, so sullen and savage did he appear. He moved along the echoless floors with a slow, noiseless shamble, until his dusky figure, advancing from the gloom, seemed like some reluctant *afreet*, compelled by the superior power of his master to disclose himself. When the doors of all the chambers were closed, and no light illuminated the long corridor save the red, unwholesome glare of a small oil lamp on a table at the end, where late lodgers lit their candles, one could not by any possibility conjure up a sadder or more desolate prospect.

Yet the house suited me. Of meditative and sedentary habits, I enjoyed the extreme quiet. There were but few lodgers, from which I infer that the landlord did not drive a very thriving trade; and these, probably oppressed by the sombre spirit of the place, were quiet and ghost-like in their movements. The proprietor I scarcely ever saw. My bills were deposited by unseen hands every month on my table, while I was out walking or riding, and my pecuniary response was intrusted to the attendant *afreet*. On the whole, when the bustling, wide-awake spirit of New York is taken into consideration, the sombre, half-vivified character of the house in which I lived was an anomaly that no one appreciated better than I who lived there.

I felt my way down the wide, dark staircase in my pursuit of zephyrs. The garden, as I entered it, did feel somewhat cooler than my own room, and I puffed my cigar along the dim, cypress-shrouded walks with a sensation of comparative relief. It was very dark. The tall-growing flowers that bordered the path were so wrapped in gloom as to present the aspect of solid pyramidal masses, all the details of leaves and blossoms being buried in an embracing darkness, while the trees had lost all form, and seemed like masses of overhanging cloud. It was a place and time to excite the imagination; for in the impenetrable cavities of endless gloom there was room for the most riotous fancies to play at will. I walked and walked, and the echoes of my footsteps on the ungravelled and mossy path suggested a double feeling. I felt alone and yet in company at the same time. The solitariness of the place made itself distinct enough in the stillness, broken alone by the hollow reverberations of my step, while those very reverberations seemed to imbue me with an undefined feeling that I was not alone. I was not, therefore, much startled when I was suddenly accosted from beneath the solid darkness of an immense cypress by a voice saying, "Will you give me a light, sir?"

"Certainly," I replied, trying in vain to distinguish the speaker amidst the impenetrable dark.

Somebody advanced, and I held out my cigar. All I could gather definitively about the individual who thus accosted me was that he must have been of extremely small stature; for I, who am by no means an overgrown man, had to stoop considerably in handing him my cigar. The vigorous puff that he gave his own lighted up my Havana for a moment, and I fancied that I caught a glimpse of long, wild hair. The flash was, however, so momentary that I could not even say certainly whether this was an actual impression or the mere effort of imagination to embody that which the senses had failed to distinguish.

"Sir, you are out late," said this unknown to me, as he, with half-uttered thanks, handed me back my cigar, for which I had to grope in the gloom.

"Not later than usual," I replied, dryly.

"Hum! you are fond of late wanderings, then?"

"That is just as the fancy seizes me."

"Do you live here?"

"Yes."

"Queer house, isn't it?"

"I have only found it quiet."

"Hum! But you *will* find it queer, take my word for it." This was earnestly uttered; and I felt at the same time a bony finger laid on my arm, that cut it sharply like a blunted knife.

"I cannot take your word for any such assertion," I replied rudely, shaking off the bony finger with an irrepressible motion of disgust.

"No offence, no offence," muttered my unseen companion rapidly, in a strange, subdued voice, that would have been shrill had it been louder; "your being angry does not alter the matter. You will find it a queer house. Everybody finds it a queer house. Do you know who lives there?"

304

"I never busy myself, sir, about other people's affairs," I answered sharply, for the individual's manner, combined with my utter uncertainty as to his appearance, oppressed me with an irksome longing to be rid of him.

"O, you don't? Well, I do. I know what they are—well, well, well!" and as he pronounced the three last words his voice rose with each, until, with the last, it reached a shrill shriek that echoed horribly among the lonely walks. "Do you know what they eat?" he continued.

"No, sir,—nor care."

"O, but you will care. You must care. You shall care. I'll tell you what they are. They are enchanters. They are ghouls. They are cannibals. Did you never remark their eyes, and how they gloated on you when you passed? Did you never remark the food that they served up at your table? Did you never in the dead of night hear muffled and unearthly footsteps gliding along the corridors, and stealthy hands turning the handle of your door? Does not some magnetic influence fold itself continually around you when they pass, and send a thrill through spirit and body, and a cold shiver that no sunshine will chase away? O, you have! You have felt all these things! I know it!"

The earnest rapidity, the subdued tones, the eagerness of accent, with which all this was uttered, impressed me most uncomfortably. It really seemed as if I could recall all those weird occurrences and influences of which he spoke; and I shuddered in spite of myself in the midst of the impenetrable darkness that surrounded me.

"Hum!" said I, assuming, without knowing it, a confidential tone, "may I ask you how you know these things?"

"How I know them? Because I am their enemy; because they tremble at my whisper; because I hang upon their track with the perseverance of a bloodhound and the stealthiness of a tiger; because—because—I was *of* them once!"

"Wretch!" I cried excitedly, for involuntarily his eager tones had wrought me up to a high pitch of spasmodic nervousness, "then you mean to say that you——"

As I uttered this word, obeying an uncontrollable impulse, I stretched forth my hand in the direction of the speaker and made a blind clutch. The tips of my fingers seemed to touch a surface as smooth as glass, that glided suddenly from under them. A sharp, angry hiss sounded through the gloom, followed by a whirring noise, as if some projectile passed rapidly by, and the next moment I felt instinctively that I was alone.

A most disagreeable feeling instantly assailed me;—a prophetic instinct that some terrible misfortune menaced me; an eager and overpowering anxiety to get back to my own room without loss of time. I turned and ran blindly along the dark cypress alley, every dusky clump of flowers that rose blackly in the borders making my heart each moment cease to beat. The echoes of my own footsteps seemed to redouble and assume the sounds of unknown pursuers following fast upon my track. The boughs of lilac-bushes and syringas, that here and there stretched partly across the walk, seemed to have been furnished suddenly with hooked hands that sought to grasp me as I flew by, and each moment I expected to behold some awful and impassable barrier fall across my track and wall me up forever.

At length I reached the wide entrance. With a single leap I sprang up the four or five steps that formed the stoop, and dashed along the hall, up the wide, echoing stairs, and again along the dim, funereal corridors until I paused, breathless and panting, at the door of my room. Once so far, I stopped for an instant and leaned heavily against one of the panels, panting lustily after my late run. I had, however, scarcely rested my whole weight against the door, when it suddenly gave way, and I staggered in head-foremost. To my utter astonishment the room I had left in profound darkness was now a blaze of light. So intense was the illumination that, for a few seconds while the pupils of my eyes were contracting under the sudden change, I saw absolutely nothing save the dazzling glare. This fact in itself, coming on me with such utter suddenness, was sufficient to prolong my confusion, and it was not until after several minutes had elapsed that I perceived the room was not only illuminated, but occupied. And such occupants! Amazement at the scene took such possession of me that I was incapable of either moving or uttering a word. All that I could do was to lean against the wall, and stare blankly at the strange picture.

It might have been a scene out of *Faublas*, or *Gramont's Memoirs*, or happened in some palace of Minister Foucque.

Round a large table in the centre of the room, where I had left a student-like litter of books and papers, were seated half a dozen persons. Three were men and three were women. The table was heaped with a prodigality of luxuries. Luscious eastern fruits were piled up in silver filigree vases, through whose meshes their glowing rinds shone in the contrasts of a thousand hues. Small silver dishes that Benvenuto might have designed, filled with succulent and aromatic meats, were distributed upon a cloth of snowy damask. Bottles of every shape, slender ones from the Rhine, stout fellows from Holland, sturdy ones from Spain, and quaint basket-woven flasks from Italy, absolutely littered the board. Drinking-glasses of every size and hue filled up the interstices, and the thirsty German flagon stood side by side with the *aërial* bubbles of Venetian glass that rest so lightly on their threadlike stems. An odour of luxury and sensuality floated through the apartment. The lamps that burned in every direction seemed to diffuse a subtle incense on the air, and in a large vase that stood on the floor I saw a mass of magnolias, tuberoses, and jasmines grouped together, stifling each other with their honeyed and heavy fragrance.

The inhabitants of my room seemed beings well suited to so sensual an atmosphere. The women were strangely beautiful, and all were attired in dresses of the most fantastic devices and brilliant hues. Their figures were round, supple, and elastic; their eyes dark and languishing; their lips full, ripe, and of the richest bloom. The three men wore half-masks, so that all I could distinguish were heavy jaws, pointed beards, and brawny throats that rose like massive pillars out of their doublets. All six lay reclining on Roman couches about the table, drinking down the purple wines in large draughts, and tossing back their heads and laughing wildly.

I stood, I suppose, for some three minutes, with my back against the wall staring vacantly at the bacchanal vision, before any of the revellers appeared to notice my presence. At length, without any expression to indicate whether I had been observed from the beginning or not, two of the women arose from their couches, and, approaching, took each a hand and led me to the table. I obeyed their motions mechanically. I sat on a couch, between them as they indicated. I unresistingly permitted them to wind their arms about my neck.

"You must drink," said one, pouring out a large glass of red wine, "here is Clos Vougeout of a rare vintage; and here," pushing a flask of amber-hued wine before me, "is Lachryma Christi."

"You must eat," said the other, drawing the silver dishes toward her. "Here are cutlets stewed with olives, and here are slices of a *filet* stuffed with bruised sweet chestnuts"—and as she spoke, she, without waiting for a reply, proceeded to help me.

The sight of the food recalled to me the warnings I had received in the garden. This sudden effort of memory restored to me my other faculties at the same instant. I sprang to my feet, thrusting the women from me with each hand.

"Demons!" I almost shouted. "I will have none of your accursed food. I know you. You are cannibals, you are ghouls, you are enchanters. Begone, I tell you! Leave my room in peace!"

A shout of laughter from all six was the only effect that my passionate speech produced. The men rolled on their couches, and their half-masks quivered with the convulsions of their mirth. The women shrieked, and tossed the slender wine-glasses wildly aloft, and turned to me and flung themselves on my bosom fairly sobbing with laughter.

"Yes," I continued, as soon as the noisy mirth had subsided, "yes, I say, leave my room instantly! I will have none of your unnatural orgies here!"

"His room!" shrieked the woman on my right.

"His room!" echoed she on my left.

"His room! He calls it his room!" shouted the whole party, as they rolled once more into jocular convulsions.

"How know you that it is your room?" said one of the men who sat opposite to me, at length, after the laughter had once more somewhat subsided.

"How do I know?" I replied indignantly. "How do I know my own room? How could I mistake it, pray? There's my furniture—my piano——"

"He calls that a piano," shouted my neighbours, again in convulsions as I pointed to the corner where my huge piano, sacred to the memory of Blokeeta, used to stand. "O, yes! It is his room. There—there is his piano!"

The peculiar emphasis they laid on the word "piano" caused me to scrutinize the article I was indicating more thoroughly. Up to this time, though utterly amazed at the entrance of these people into my chamber, and connecting them somewhat with the wild stories I had heard in the garden, I still had a sort of indefinite idea that the whole thing was a masquerading freak got up in my absence, and that the Bacchanalian orgy I was witnessing was nothing more than a portion of some elaborate hoax of which I was to be the victim. But when my eyes turned to the corner where I had left a huge and cumbrous piano, and beheld a vast and sombre organ lifting its fluted front to the very ceiling, and convinced myself, by a hurried process of memory, that it occupied the very spot in which I had left my own instrument, the little self-possession that I had left forsook me. I gazed around me bewildered.

In like manner everything was changed. In the place of that old haftless dagger, connected with so many historic associations personal to myself, I beheld a Turkish *yataghan* dangling by its belt of crimson silk, while the jewels in the hilt blazed as the lamplight played upon them. In the spot where hung my cherished smoking cap, memorial of a buried love, a knightly *casque* was suspended on the crest of which a golden dragon stood in the act of springing. That strange lithograph of Calame was no longer a lithograph, but it seemed to me that the portion of the wall which it covered, of the exact shape and size, had been cut out, and, in place of the picture, a *real* scene on the same scale, and with real actors, was distinctly visible.

The old oak was there, and the stormy sky was there; but I saw the branches of the oak sway with the tempest, and the clouds drive before the wind. The wanderer in his cloak was gone; but in his place I beheld a circle of wild figures, men and women, dancing with linked hands around the hole of the great tree, chanting some wild fragment of a song, to which the winds roared an unearthly chorus. The snow-shoes, too, on whose sinewy woof I had sped for many days amidst Canadian wastes, had vanished, and in their place lay a pair of strange up-curled Turkish slippers, that had, perhaps, been many a time shuffled off at the doors of mosques, beneath the steady blaze of an orient sun.

All was changed. Wherever my eyes turned they missed familiar objects, yet encountered strange representatives. Still, in all the substitutes there seemed to me a reminiscence of what they replaced. They seemed only for a time transmuted into other shapes, and there lingered around them the atmosphere of what they once had been. Thus I could have sworn the room to have been mine, yet there was nothing in it that I could rightly claim. Everything reminded me of some former possession that it was not. I looked for the acacia at the window, and lo! long silken palm-leaves swayed in through the open lattice; yet they had the same motion and the same air of my favourite tree, and seemed to murmur to me, "Though we seem to be palm-leaves, yet are we acacia-leaves; yea, those very ones on which you used to watch the butterflies alight and the rain patter while you smoked and dreamed!" So in all things; the room was, yet was not, mine; and a sickening consciousness of my utter inability to reconcile its identity with its appearance overwhelmed me, and choked my reason.

"Well, have you determined whether or not this is your room?" asked the girl on my left, proffering me a huge tumbler creaming over with champagne, and laughing wickedly as she spoke.

"It is mine," I answered, doggedly, striking the glass rudely with my hand, and dashing the aromatic wine over the white cloth. "I know that it is mine; and ye are jugglers and enchanters who want to drive me mad."

"Hush! hush!" she said, gently, not in the least angered by my rough treatment. "You are excited. Alf shall play something to soothe you."

At her signal, one of the men sat down at the organ. After a short, wild, spasmodic prelude, he began what seemed to me to be a symphony of recollections. Dark and sombre, and all through full of quivering and intense agony, it appeared to recall a dark and dismal night, on a cold reef, around which an unseen but terribly audible ocean broke with eternal fury. It seemed as if a lonely pair were on the reef, one living, the other dead; one clasping his arms around the tender neck and naked bosom of the other, striving to warm her into life, when his own vitality was being each moment sucked from him by the icy breath of the storm.

Here and there a terrible wailing minor key would tremble through the chords like the shriek of sea-birds, or the warning of advancing death. While the man played I could scarce restrain myself. It seemed to be Blokeeta whom I listened to, and on whom I gazed. That wondrous night of pleasure and pain that I had once passed listening to him seemed to have been taken up again at the spot where it had broken off, and the same hand was continuing it. I stared at the man called Alf. There he sat with his cloak and doublet, and long rapier and mask of black velvet. But there was something in the air of the peaked beard, a familiar mystery in the wild mass of raven hair that fell as if wind-blown over his shoulders, which riveted my memory.

"Blokeeta! Blokeeta!" I shouted, starting up furiously from the couch on which I was lying, and bursting the fair arms that were linked around my neck as if they had been hateful chains,—"Blokeeta! my friend! speak to me, I entreat you! Tell these horrid enchanters to leave me. Say that I hate them. Say that I command them to leave my room."

The man at the organ stirred not in answer to my appeal. He ceased playing, and the dying sound of the last note he had touched faded off into a melancholy moan. The other men and the women burst once more into peals of mocking laughter.

"Why will you persist in calling this your room?" said the woman next me, with a smile meant to be kind, but to me inexpressibly loathsome. "Have we not shown you by the furniture, by the general appearance of the place, that you are mistaken, and that this cannot be your apartment? Rest content, then, with us. You are welcome here, and need no longer trouble yourself about your room."

"Rest content!" I answered madly; "live with ghosts, eat of awful meats, and see awful sights! Never! never! You have cast some enchantment over the place that has disguised it; but for all that I know it to be my room. You shall leave it!"

"Softly, softly!" said another of the sirens. "Let us settle this amicably. This poor gentleman seems obstinate and inclined to make an uproar. Now we do not want an uproar. We love the night and its quiet; and there is no night that we love so well as that on which the moon is coffined in clouds. Is it not so, my brothers?"

An awful and sinister smile gleamed on the countenances of her unearthly audience, and seemed to glide visibly from underneath their masks.

"Now," she continued, "I have a proposition to make. It would be ridiculous for us to surrender this room simply because this gentleman states that it is his; and yet I feel anxious to gratify, as far as may be fair, his wild assertion of ownership. A room, after all, is not much to us; we can get one easily enough, but still we should be loath to give this apartment up to so imperious a demand. We are willing, however, to *risk* its loss. That is to say,"—turning to me,—"I propose that we play for the room. If you win, we will immediately surrender it to you just as it stands; if, on the contrary, you lose, you shall bind yourself to depart and never molest us again."

Agonized at the ever-darkening mysteries that seemed to thicken around me, and despairing of being able to dissipate them by the mere exercise of my own will, I caught almost gladly at the chance thus presented to me. The idea of my loss or my gain scarce entered into my calculations. All I felt was an indefinite knowledge that I might, in the way proposed, regain in an instant, that quiet chamber and that peace of mind of which I had so strangely been deprived.

"I agree!" I cried eagerly; "I agree. Anything to rid myself of such unearthly company!"

The woman touched a small golden bell that stood near her on the table, and it had scarce ceased to tinkle when a negro dwarf entered with a silver tray on which were dice-boxes and dice. A shudder passed over me as I thought in this stunted African I could trace a resemblance to the ghoul-like black servant to whose attendance I had been accustomed.

"Now," said my neighbour, seizing one of the dice-boxes and giving me the other, "the highest wins. Shall I throw first?"

I nodded assent. She rattled the dice, and I felt an inexpressible load lifted from my heart as she threw fifteen.

"It is your turn," she said, with a mocking smile; "but before you throw, I repeat the offer I made you before. Live with us. Be one of us. We will initiate you into our mysteries and enjoyments,—enjoyments of which you can form no idea unless you experience them. Come; it is not too late yet to change your mind. Be with us!"

My reply was a fierce oath, as I rattled the dice with spasmodic nervousness and flung them on the board. They rolled over and over again, and during that brief instant I felt a suspense, the intensity of which I have never known before or since. At last they lay before me. A shout of the same horrible, maddening laughter rang in my ears. I peered in vain at the dice, but my sight was so confused that I could not distinguish the amount of the cast. This lasted for a few moments. Then my sight grew clear, and I sank back almost lifeless with despair as I saw that I had thrown but *twelve*!

"Lost! lost!" screamed my neighbour, with a wild laugh. "Lost! lost!" shouted the deep voices of the masked men. "Leave us, coward!" they all cried; "you are not fit to be one of us. Remember your promise; leave us!"

Then it seemed as if some unseen power caught me by the shoulders and thrust me toward the door. In vain I resisted. In vain I screamed and shouted for help. In vain I implored them for pity. All the reply I had was those mocking peals of merriment, while, under the invisible influence, I staggered like a drunken man toward the door. As I reached the threshold the organ pealed out a wild triumphal strain. The power that impelled me concentrated itself into one vigorous impulse that sent me blindly staggering out into the echoing corridor, and as the door closed swiftly behind me, I caught one glimpse of the apartment I had left forever. A change passed like a shadow over it. The lamps died out, the siren women and masked men vanished, the flowers, the fruits, the bright silver and bizarre furniture faded swiftly, and I saw again, for the tenth of a second, my own old chamber restored. There was the acacia waving darkly; there was the table littered with books; there was the ghostly lithograph, the dearly beloved smoking-cap, the Canadian snow-shoes, the ancestral dagger. And there, at the piano, organ no longer, sat Blokeeta playing.

The next instant the door closed violently, and I was left standing in the corridor stunned and despairing.

As soon as I had partially recovered my comprehension I rushed madly to the door, with the dim idea of beating it in. My fingers touched a cold and solid wall. There was no door! I felt all along the corridor for many yards on both sides. There was not even a crevice to give me hope. I rushed downstairs shouting madly. No one answered. In the vestibule I met the negro; I seized him by the collar and demanded my room. The demon showed his white and awful teeth, which were filed into a saw-like shape, and extricating himself from my grasp with a sudden jerk, fled down the passage with a gibbering laugh. Nothing but echo answered to my despairing shrieks. The lonely garden resounded with my cries as I strode madly through the dark walls, and the tall funereal cypresses seemed to bury me beneath their heavy shadows. I met no one,—could find no one. I had to bear my sorrow and despair alone.

Since that awful hour I have never found my room. Everywhere I look for it, yet never see it. Shall I ever find it?

The Mummy's Foot

By Théophile Gautier

I had entered, in an idle mood, the shop of one of those curiosity venders who are called *marchands de bric-à-brac* in that Parisian *argot*
which is so perfectly unintelligible elsewhere in France.

You have doubtless glanced occasionally through the windows of
some of these shops, which have become so numerous now that it is
fashionable to buy antiquated furniture, and that every petty stock
broker thinks he must have his *chambre au moyen âge*.

There is one thing there which clings alike to the shop of the
dealer in old iron, the ware-room of the tapestry maker, the laboratory
of the chemist, and the studio of the painter: in all those gloomy dens
where a furtive daylight filters in through the window-shutters the
most manifestly ancient thing is dust. The cobwebs are more authentic
than the guimp laces, and the old pear-tree furniture on exhibition
is actually younger than the mahogany which arrived but yesterday
from America.

The warehouse of my *bric-à-brac* dealer was a veritable Caphar-
naum. All ages and all nations seemed to have made their rendezvous
there. An Etruscan lamp of red clay stood upon a Boule cabinet, with
ebony panels, brightly striped by lines of inlaid brass; a duchess of the
court of Louis XV. nonchalantly extended her fawn-like feet under a
massive table of the time of Louis XIII., with heavy spiral supports of
oak, and carven designs of chimeras and foliage intermingled.

Upon the denticulated shelves of several sideboards glittered immense Japanese dishes with red and blue designs relieved by gilded
hatching, side by side with enamelled works by Bernard Palissy, representing serpents, frogs, and lizards in relief.

From disembowelled cabinets escaped cascades of silver-lustrous
Chinese silks and waves of tinsels which an oblique sunbeam shot

through with luminous beads; while portraits of every era, in frames more or less tarnished, smiled through their yellow varnish.

The striped breastplate of a damascened suit of Milanese armour glittered in one corner; loves and nymphs of porcelain, Chinese grotesques, vases of *celadon* and crackle-ware, Saxon and old Sèvres cups encumbered the shelves and nooks of the apartment.

The dealer followed me closely through the tortuous way contrived between the piles of furniture, warding off with his hand the hazardous sweep of my coat-skirts, watching my elbows with the uneasy attention of an antiquarian and a usurer.

It was a singular face, that of the merchant; an immense skull, polished like a knee, and surrounded by a thin aureole of white hair, which brought out the clear salmon tint of his complexion all the more strikingly, lent him a false aspect of patriarchal *bonhomie*, counteracted, however, by the scintillation of two little yellow eyes which trembled in their orbits like two *louis d'or* upon quicksilver. The curve of his nose presented an aquiline silhouette, which suggested the Oriental or Jewish type. His hands—thin, slender, full of nerves which projected like strings upon the finger-board of a violin, and armed with claws like those on the terminations of bats' wings—shook with senile trembling; but those convulsively agitated hands became firmer than steel pincers or lobsters' claws when they lifted any precious article—an onyx cup, a Venetian glass, or a dish of Bohemian crystal. This strange old man had an aspect so thoroughly rabbinical and cabalistic that he would have been burnt on the mere testimony of his face three centuries ago.

"Will you not buy something from me today, sir? Here is a Malay *kreese* with a blade undulating like flame. Look at those grooves contrived for the blood to run along, those teeth set backward so as to tear out the entrails in withdrawing the weapon. It is a fine character of ferocious arm, and will look well in your collection. This two-handed sword is very beautiful. It is the work of Josepe de la Hera; and this *colichemarde*, with its fenestrated guard—what a superb specimen of handicraft!"

"No; I have quite enough weapons and instruments of carnage. I want a small figure, something which will suit me as a paper-weight, for I cannot endure those trumpery bronzes which the stationers sell, and which may be found on everybody's desk."

The old gnome foraged among his ancient wares, and finally arranged before me some antique bronzes, so-called at least; fragments of malachite, little Hindoo or Chinese idols, a kind of *poussah*-toys in jade-stone, representing the incarnations of Brahma or Vishnoo, and wonderfully appropriate to the very undivine office of holding papers and letters in place.

I was hesitating between a porcelain dragon, all constellated with warts, its mouth formidable with bristling tusks and ranges of teeth, and an abominable little Mexican fetish, representing the god Vitzili-putzili *au naturel*, when I caught sight of a charming foot, which I at first took for a fragment of some antique Venus.

It had those beautiful ruddy and tawny tints that lend to Florentine bronze that warm living look so much preferable to the gray-green aspect of common bronzes, which might easily be mistaken for statues in a state of putrefaction. Satiny gleams played over its rounded forms, doubtless polished by the amorous kisses of twenty centuries, for it seemed a Corinthian bronze, a work of the best era of art, perhaps moulded by Lysippus himself.

"That foot will be my choice," I said to the merchant, who regarded me with an ironical and saturnine air, and held out the object desired that I might examine it more fully.

I was surprised at its lightness. It was not a foot of metal, but in sooth a foot of flesh, an embalmed foot, a mummy's foot. On examining it still more closely the very grain of the skin, and the almost imperceptible lines impressed upon it by the texture of the bandages, became perceptible. The toes were slender and delicate, and terminated by perfectly formed nails, pure and transparent as agates. The great toe, slightly separated from the rest, afforded a happy contrast, in the antique style, to the position of the other toes, and lent it an *aërial* lightness—the grace of a bird's foot. The sole, scarcely streaked by a few almost imperceptible cross lines, afforded evidence that it had never touched the bare ground, and had only come in contact with the finest matting of Nile rushes and the softest carpets of panther skin.

"Ha, ha, you want the foot of the Princess Hermonthis!" exclaimed the merchant, with a strange giggle, fixing his owlish eyes upon me. "Ha, ha, ha! For a paper-weight! An original idea!—an artistic idea! Old Pharaoh would certainly have been surprised had someone told him that the foot of his adored daughter would be used for a paper-weight after he had had a mountain of granite hollowed out as a receptacle for the triple coffin, painted and gilded, covered with hieroglyphics and beautiful paintings of the Judgment of Souls," continued the queer little merchant, half audibly, as though talking to himself.

"How much will you charge me for this mummy fragment?"

"Ah, the highest price I can get, for it is a superb piece. If I had the match of it you could not have it for less than five hundred *francs*. The daughter of a Pharaoh! Nothing is more rare."

"Assuredly that is not a common article, but still, how much do you want? In the first place let me warn you that all my wealth consists of just five *louis*. I can buy anything that costs five *louis*, but nothing dearer. You might search my vest pockets and most secret drawers without even finding one poor five-*franc* piece more."

"Five *louis* for the foot of the Princess Hermonthis! That is very little, very little indeed. 'Tis an authentic foot," muttered the merchant, shaking his head, and imparting a peculiar rotary motion to his eyes. "Well, take it, and I will give you the bandages into the bargain," he added, wrapping the foot in an ancient damask rag. "Very fine! Real damask—Indian damask which has never been redyed. It is strong, and yet it is soft," he mumbled, stroking the frayed tissue with his fingers, through the trade-acquired habit which moved him to praise even an object of such little value that he himself deemed it only worth the giving away.

He poured the gold coins into a sort of medieval alms-purse hanging at his belt, repeating:

"The foot of the Princess Hermonthis to be used for a paper-weight!"

Then turning his phosphorescent eyes upon me, he exclaimed in a voice strident as the crying of a cat which has swallowed a fish-bone:

"Old Pharaoh will not be well pleased. He loved his daughter, the dear man!"

"You speak as if you were a contemporary of his. You are old enough, goodness knows! but you do not date back to the Pyramids of Egypt," I answered, laughingly, from the threshold.

I went home, delighted with my acquisition.

With the idea of putting it to profitable use as soon as possible, I placed the foot of the divine Princess Hermonthis upon a heap of papers scribbled over with verses, in themselves an undecipherable mosaic work of erasures; articles freshly begun; letters forgotten, and posted in the table drawer instead of the letter-box, an error to which absent-minded people are peculiarly liable. The effect was charming, *bizarre*, and romantic.

Well satisfied with this embellishment, I went out with the gravity and pride becoming one who feels that he has the ineffable advantage over all the passers-by whom he elbows, of possessing a piece of the Princess Hermonthis, daughter of Pharaoh.

I looked upon all who did not possess, like myself, a paper-weight so authentically Egyptian as very ridiculous people, and it seemed to me that the proper occupation of every sensible man should consist in the mere fact of having a mummy's foot upon his desk.

Happily I met some friends, whose presence distracted me in my infatuation with this new acquisition. I went to dinner with them, for I could not very well have dined with myself.

When I came back that evening, with my brain slightly confused by a few glasses of wine, a vague whiff of Oriental perfume delicately titillated my olfactory nerves. The heat of the room had warmed the natron, bitumen, and myrrh in which the *paraschistes*, who cut open the bodies of the dead, had bathed the corpse of the princess. It was a perfume at once sweet and penetrating, a perfume that four thousand years had not been able to dissipate.

The Dream of Egypt was Eternity. Her odours have the solidity of granite and endure as long.

I soon drank deeply from the black cup of sleep. For a few hours all remained opaque to me. Oblivion and nothingness inundated me with their sombre waves.

Yet light gradually dawned upon the darkness of my mind. Dreams commenced to touch me softly in their silent flight.

The eyes of my soul were opened, and I beheld my chamber as it actually was. I might have believed myself awake but for a vague consciousness which assured me that I slept, and that something fantastic was about to take place.

The odour of the myrrh had augmented in intensity, and I felt a slight headache, which I very naturally attributed to several glasses of champagne that we had drunk to the unknown gods and our future fortunes.

I peered through my room with a feeling of expectation which I saw nothing to justify. Every article of furniture was in its proper place. The lamp, softly shaded by its globe of ground crystal, burned upon its bracket; the water-colour sketches shone under their Bohemian glass; the curtains hung down languidly; everything wore an aspect of tranquil slumber.

After a few moments, however, all this calm interior appeared to become disturbed. The woodwork cracked stealthily, the ash-covered log suddenly emitted a jet of blue flame, and the disks of the *pateras* seemed like great metallic eyes, watching, like myself, for the things which were about to happen.

My eyes accidentally fell upon the desk where I had placed the foot of the Princess Hermonthis.

Instead of remaining quiet, as behooved a foot which had been embalmed for four thousand years, it commenced to act in a nervous manner, contracted itself, and leaped over the papers like a startled frog. One would have imagined that it had suddenly been brought into contact with a galvanic battery. I could distinctly hear the dry sound made by its little heel, hard as the hoof of a gazelle.

I became rather discontented with my acquisition, inasmuch as I wished my paper-weights to be of a sedentary disposition, and thought it very unnatural that feet should walk about without legs, then I commenced to experience a feeling closely akin to fear.

Suddenly I saw the folds of my bed-curtain stir, and heard a bumping sound, like that caused by some person hopping on one foot across the floor. I must confess I became alternately hot and cold, that I felt a strange wind chill my back, and that my suddenly rising hair caused my night-cap to execute a leap of several yards.

The bed-curtains opened and I beheld the strangest figure imaginable before me.

It was a young girl of a very deep coffee-brown complexion, like the *bayadere* Amani, and possessing the purest Egyptian type of perfect beauty. Her eyes were almond-shaped and oblique, with eyebrows so black that they seemed blue; her nose was exquisitely chiselled, almost Greek in its delicacy of outline; and she might indeed have been taken for a Corinthian statue of bronze but for the prominence of her cheek-bones and the slightly African fullness of her lips, which compelled one to recognize her as belonging beyond all doubt to the hieroglyphic race which dwelt upon the banks of the Nile.

Her arms, slender and spindle-shaped like those of very young girls, were encircled by a peculiar kind of metal bands and bracelets of glass beads; her hair was all twisted into little cords, and she wore upon her bosom a little idol-figure of green paste, bearing a whip with seven lashes, which proved it to be an image of Isis; her brow was adorned with a shining plate of gold, and a few traces of paint relieved the coppery tint of her cheeks.

As for her costume, it was very odd indeed.

Fancy a *pagne*, or skirt, all formed of little strips of material bedizened with red and black hieroglyphics, stiffened with bitumen, and apparently belonging to a freshly unbandaged mummy.

In one of those sudden flights of thought so common in dreams I heard the hoarse *falsetto* of the *bric-à-brac* dealer, repeating like a monotonous refrain the phrase he had uttered in his shop with so enigmatical an intonation:

"Old Pharaoh will not be well pleased. He loved his daughter, the dear man!"

One strange circumstance, which was not at all calculated to restore my equanimity, was that the apparition had but one foot; the other was broken off at the ankle!

She approached the table where the foot was starting and fidgeting about more than ever, and there supported herself upon the edge of the desk. I saw her eyes fill with pearly gleaming tears.

Although she had not as yet spoken, I fully comprehended the thoughts which agitated her. She looked at her foot—for it was indeed her own—with an exquisitely graceful expression of *coquettish* sadness, but the foot leaped and ran hither and thither, as though impelled on steel springs.

Twice or thrice she extended her hand to seize it, but could not succeed.

Then commenced between the Princess Hermonthis and her foot—which appeared to be endowed with a special life of its own—a very fantastic dialogue in a most ancient Coptic tongue, such as might have been spoken thirty centuries ago in the *syrinxes* of the land of Ser. Luckily I understood Coptic perfectly well that night.

The Princess Hermonthis cried, in a voice sweet and vibrant as the tones of a crystal bell:

"Well, my dear little foot, you always flee from me, yet I always took good care of you. I bathed you with perfumed water in a bowl of alabaster; I smoothed your heel with pumice-stone mixed with palm oil; your nails were cut with golden scissors and polished with a hippopotamus tooth; I was careful to select *tatbebs* for you, painted and embroidered and turned up at the toes, which were the envy of all the young girls in Egypt. You wore on your great toe rings bearing the device of the sacred Scarabæus, and you supported one of the lightest bodies that a lazy foot could sustain."

The foot replied in a pouting and chagrined tone:

"You know well that I do not belong to myself any longer. I have been bought and paid for. The old merchant knew what he was about.

He bore you a grudge for having refused to espouse him. This is an ill turn which he has done you. The Arab who violated your royal coffin in the subterranean pits of the necropolis of Thebes was sent thither by him. He desired to prevent you from being present at the reunion of the shadowy nations in the cities below. Have you five pieces of gold for my ransom?"

"Alas, no! My jewels, my rings, my purses of gold and silver were all stolen from me," answered the Princess Hermonthis, with a sob.

"Princess," I then exclaimed, "I never retained anybody's foot unjustly. Even though you have not got the five *louis* which it cost me, I present it to you gladly. I should feel unutterably wretched to think that I were the cause of so amiable a person as the Princess Hermonthis being lame."

I delivered this discourse in a royally gallant, troubadour tone which must have astonished the beautiful Egyptian girl.

She turned a look of deepest gratitude upon me, and her eyes shone with bluish gleams of light.

She took her foot, which surrendered itself willingly this time, like a woman about to put on her little shoe, and adjusted it to her leg with much skill.

This operation over, she took a few steps about the room, as though to assure herself that she was really no longer lame.

"Ah, how pleased my father will be! He who was so unhappy because of my mutilation, and who from the moment of my birth set a whole nation at work to hollow me out a tomb so deep that he might preserve me intact until that last day, when souls must be weighed in the balance of Amenthi! Come with me to my father. He will receive you kindly, for you have given me back my foot."

I thought this proposition natural enough. I arrayed myself in a dressing-gown of large-flowered pattern, which lent me a very Pharaonic aspect, hurriedly put on a pair of Turkish slippers, and informed the Princess Hermonthis that I was ready to follow her.

Before starting, Hermonthis took from her neck the little idol of green paste, and laid it on the scattered sheets of paper which covered the table.

"It is only fair," she observed, smilingly, "that I should replace your paper-weight."

She gave me her hand, which felt soft and cold, like the skin of a serpent, and we departed.

We passed for some time with the velocity of an arrow through a fluid and grayish expanse, in which half-formed silhouettes flitted swiftly by us, to right and left.

For an instant we saw only sky and sea.

A few moments later obelisks commenced to tower in the distance; pylons and vast flights of steps guarded by sphinxes became clearly outlined against the horizon.

We had reached our destination.

The princess conducted me to a mountain of rose-coloured granite, in the face of which appeared an opening so narrow and low that it would have been difficult to distinguish it from the fissures in the rock, had not its location been marked by two *stelæ* wrought with sculptures.

Hermonthis kindled a torch and led the way before me.

We traversed corridors hewn through the living rock. These walls covered with hieroglyphics and paintings of allegorical processions, might well have occupied thousands of arms for thousands of years in their formation. These corridors of interminable length opened into square chambers, in the midst of which pits had been contrived, through which we descended by cramp-irons or spiral stairways. These pits again conducted us into other chambers, opening into other corridors, likewise decorated with painted sparrow-hawks, serpents coiled in circles, the symbols of the *tau* and *pedum*—prodigious works of art which no living eye can ever examine—interminable legends of granite which only the dead have time to read through all eternity.

At last we found ourselves in a hall so vast, so enormous, so immeasurable, that the eye could not reach its limits. Files of monstrous columns stretched far out of sight on every side, between which twinkled livid stars of yellowish flame; points of light which revealed further depths incalculable in the darkness beyond.

The Princess Hermonthis still held my hand, and graciously saluted the mummies of her acquaintance.

My eyes became accustomed to the dim twilight, and objects became discernible.

I beheld the kings of the subterranean races seated upon thrones—grand old men, though dry, withered, wrinkled like parchment, and blackened with naphtha and bitumen—all wearing *pshents* of gold, and breast-plates and gorgets glittering with precious stones, their eyes immovably fixed like the eyes of sphinxes, and their long beards whitened by the snow of centuries. Behind them stood their peoples, in the stiff and constrained posture enjoined by Egyptian art, all eternally preserving the attitude prescribed by the hieratic code. Behind these nations, the cats, ibixes, and crocodiles contemporary with them—rendered monstrous of aspect by their swathing bands—mewed, flapped their wings, or extended their jaws in a saurian giggle.

All the Pharaohs were there—Cheops, Chephrenes, Psammetichus, Sesostris, Amenotaph—all the dark rulers of the pyramids and *syrinxes*. On yet higher thrones sat Chronos and Xixouthros, who was contemporary with the deluge, and Tubal Cain, who reigned before it.

The beard of King Xixouthros had grown seven times around the granite table, upon which he leaned, lost in deep reverie, and buried in dreams.

Farther back, through a dusty cloud, I beheld dimly the seventy-two preadamite kings, with their seventy-two peoples, forever passed away.

After permitting me to gaze upon this bewildering spectacle a few moments, the Princess Hermonthis presented me to her father Pharaoh, who favoured me with a most gracious nod.

"I have found my foot again! I have found my foot!" cried the princess, clapping her little hands together with every sign of frantic joy. "It was this gentleman who restored it to me."

The races of Kemi, the races of Nahasi—all the black, bronzed, and copper-coloured nations repeated in chorus:

"The Princess Hermonthis has found her foot again!"

Even Xixouthros himself was visibly affected.

He raised his heavy eyelids, stroked his moustache with his fingers, and turned upon me a glance weighty with centuries.

"By Oms, the dog of Hell, and Tmei, daughter of the Sun and of Truth, this is a brave and worthy lad!" exclaimed Pharaoh, pointing to me with his sceptre, which was terminated with a lotus-flower.

"What recompense do you desire?"

Filled with that daring inspired by dreams in which nothing seems impossible, I asked him for the hand of the Princess Hermonthis. The hand seemed to me a very proper antithetic recompense for the foot.

Pharaoh opened wide his great eyes of glass in astonishment at my witty request.

"What country do you come from, what is your age?"

"I am a Frenchman, and I am twenty-seven years old, venerable Pharaoh."

"Twenty-seven years old, and he wishes to espouse the Princess Hermonthis who is thirty centuries old!" cried out at once all the

Thrones and all the Circles of Nations.

Only Hermonthis herself did not seem to think my request unreasonable.

"If you were even only two thousand years old," replied the ancient king, "I would willingly give you the princess, but the disproportion is too great; and, besides, we must give our daughters husbands who will last well. You do not know how to preserve yourselves any longer. Even those who died only fifteen centuries ago are already no more than a handful of dust. Behold, my flesh is solid as basalt, my bones are bones of steel!

"I will be present on the last day of the world with the same body and the same features which I had during my lifetime. My daughter Hermonthis will last longer than a statue of bronze.

"Then the last particles of your dust will have been scattered abroad by the winds, and even Isis herself, who was able to find the atoms of Osiris, would scarce be able to recompense your being.

"See how vigorous I yet remain, and how mighty is my grasp," he added, shaking my hand in the English fashion with a strength that buried my rings in the flesh of my fingers.

He squeezed me so hard that I awoke, and found my friend Alfred shaking me by the arm to make me get up.

"Oh, you everlasting sleeper! Must I have you carried out into the middle of the street, and fireworks exploded in your ears? It is afternoon. Don't you recollect your promise to take me with you to see M. Aguado's Spanish pictures?"

"God! I forgot all, all about it," I answered, dressing myself hurriedly. "We will go there at once. I have the permit lying there on my desk."

I started to find it, but fancy my astonishment when I beheld, instead of the mummy's foot I had purchased the evening before, the little green paste idol left in its place by the Princess Hermonthis!

The Mysterious Card

By Cleveland Moffett

1

Richard Burwell, of New York, will never cease to regret that the French language was not made a part of his education.

This is why:

On the second evening after Burwell arrived in Paris, feeling lonely without his wife and daughter, who were still visiting a friend in London, his mind naturally turned to the theatre. So, after consulting the daily amusement calendar, he decided to visit the *Folies Bergère*, which he had heard of as one of the notable sights. During an intermission he went into the beautiful garden, where gay crowds were strolling among the flowers, and lights, and fountains. He had just seated himself at a little three-legged table, with a view to enjoying the novel scene, when his attention was attracted by a lovely woman, gowned strikingly, though in perfect taste, who passed near him, leaning on the arm of a gentleman. The only thing that he noticed about this gentleman was that he wore eye-glasses.

Now Burwell had never posed as a captivator of the fair sex, and could scarcely credit his eyes when the lady left the side of her escort and, turning back as if she had forgotten something, passed close by him, and deftly placed a card on his table. The card bore some French words written in purple ink, but, not knowing that language, he was unable to make out their meaning. The lady paid no further heed to him, but, rejoining the gentleman with the eye-glasses, swept out of the place with the grace and dignity of a princess. Burwell remained staring at the card.

Needless to say, he thought no more of the performance or of the other attractions about him. Everything seemed flat and tawdry compared with the radiant vision that had appeared and disappeared so mysteriously. His one desire now was to discover the meaning of the words written on the card.

Calling a *fiacre*, he drove to the Hôtel Continental, where he was staying. Proceeding directly to the office and taking the manager aside, Burwell asked if he would be kind enough to translate a few words of French into English. There were no more than twenty words in all.

"Why, certainly," said the manager, with French politeness, and cast his eyes over the card. As he read, his face grew rigid with astonishment, and, looking at his questioner sharply, he exclaimed: "Where did you get this, *monsieur?*"

Burwell started to explain, but was interrupted by: "That will do, that will do. You must leave the hotel."

"What do you mean?" asked the man from New York, in amazement.

"You must leave the hotel now—tonight—without fail," commanded the manager excitedly.

Now it was Burwell's turn to grow angry, and he declared heatedly that if he wasn't wanted in this hotel there were plenty of others in Paris where he would be welcome. And, with an assumption of dignity, but piqued at heart, he settled his bill, sent for his belongings, and drove up the Rue de la Paix to the Hôtel Bellevue, where he spent the night.

The next morning he met the proprietor, who seemed to be a good fellow, and, being inclined now to view the incident of the previous evening from its ridiculous side, Burwell explained what had befallen him, and was pleased to find a sympathetic listener.

"Why, the man was a fool," declared the proprietor. "Let me see the card; I will tell you what it means." But as he read, his face and manner changed instantly.

"This is a serious matter," he said sternly. "Now I understand why my *confrère* refused to entertain you. I regret, *monsieur*, but I shall be obliged to do as he did."

"What do you mean?"

"Simply that you cannot remain here."

With that he turned on his heel, and the indignant guest could not prevail upon him to give any explanation.

"We'll see about this," said Burwell, thoroughly angered.

It was now nearly noon, and the New Yorker remembered an engagement to lunch with a friend from Boston, who, with his family, was stopping at the Hôtel de l'Alma. With his luggage on the carriage, he ordered the *cocher* to drive directly there, determined to take counsel with his countryman before selecting new quarters. His friend was highly indignant when he heard the story—a fact that gave Burwell no little comfort, knowing, as he did, that the man was accustomed to foreign ways from long residence abroad.

"It is some silly mistake, my dear fellow; I wouldn't pay any attention to it. Just have your luggage taken down and stay here. It is a nice, homelike place, and it will be very jolly, all being together. But, first, let me prepare a little 'nerve settler' for you."

After the two had lingered a moment over their Manhattan cocktails, Burwell's friend excused himself to call the ladies. He had proceeded only two or three steps when he turned, and said: "Let's see that mysterious card that has raised all this row."

He had scarcely withdrawn it from Burwell's hand when he started back, and exclaimed:—

"Great God, man! Do you mean to say—this is simply—"

Then, with a sudden movement of his hand to his head, he left the room.

He was gone perhaps five minutes, and when he returned his face was white.

"I am awfully sorry," he said nervously; "but the ladies tell me they—that is, my wife—she has a frightful headache. You will have to excuse us from the lunch."

Instantly realizing that this was only a flimsy pretence, and deeply hurt by his friend's behaviour, the mystified man arose at once and left without another word. He was now determined to solve this mystery at any cost. What could be the meaning of the words on that infernal piece of pasteboard?

Profiting by his humiliating experiences, he took good care not to show the card to any one at the hotel where he now established himself,—a comfortable little place near the Grand Opera House.

All through the afternoon he thought of nothing but the card, and turned over in his mind various ways of learning its meaning without getting himself into further trouble. That evening he went again to the *Folies Bergère* in the hope of finding the mysterious woman, for he was now more than ever anxious to discover who she was. It even occurred to him that she might be one of those beautiful Nihilist conspirators, or, perhaps, a Russian spy, such as he had read of in novels. But he failed to find her, either then or on the three subsequent evenings which he passed in the same place. Meanwhile the card was burning in his pocket like a hot coal. He dreaded the thought of meeting anyone that he knew, while this horrible cloud hung over him. He bought a French-English dictionary and tried to pick out the meaning word by word, but failed. It was all Greek to him. For the first time in his life, Burwell regretted that he had not studied French at college.

After various vain attempts to either solve or forget the torturing riddle, he saw no other course than to lay the problem before a detective agency. He accordingly put his case in the hands of an *agent de la sûreté* who was recommended as a competent and trustworthy man. They had a talk together in a private room, and, of course, Burwell showed the card. To his relief, his adviser at least showed no sign of taking offence. Only he did not and would not explain what the words meant.

"It is better," he said, "that *monsieur* should not know the nature of this document for the present. I will do myself the honour to call upon *monsieur* tomorrow at his hotel, and then *monsieur* shall know everything."

"Then it is really serious?" asked the unfortunate man.

"Very serious," was the answer.

The next twenty-four hours Burwell passed in a fever of anxiety. As his mind conjured up one fearful possibility after another he deeply regretted that he had not torn up the miserable card at the start. He even seized it,—prepared to strip it into fragments, and so end the whole affair. And then his Yankee stubbornness again asserted itself, and he determined to see the thing out, come what might.

"After all," he reasoned, "it is no crime for a man to pick up a card that a lady drops on his table."

Crime or no crime, however, it looked very much as if he had committed some grave offence when, the next day, his detective drove up in a carriage, accompanied by a uniformed official, and requested the astounded American to accompany them to the police headquarters.

"What for?" he asked.

"It is only a formality," said the detective; and when Burwell still protested the man in uniform remarked: "You'd better come quietly, *monsieur*; you will have to come, anyway."

An hour later, after severe cross-examination by another official, who demanded many facts about the New Yorker's age, place of birth, residence, occupation, etc., the bewildered man found himself in the

Conciergerie prison. Why he was there or what was about to befall him Burwell had no means of knowing; but before the day was over he succeeded in having a message sent to the American Legation, where he demanded immediate protection as a citizen of the United States. It was not until evening, however, that the Secretary of Legation, a consequential person, called at the prison. There followed a stormy interview, in which the prisoner used some strong language, the French officers gesticulated violently and talked very fast, and the secretary calmly listened to both sides, said little, and smoked a good cigar.

"I will lay your case before the American minister," he said as he rose to go, "and let you know the result tomorrow."

"But this is an outrage. Do you mean to say—" Before he could finish, however, the secretary, with a strangely suspicious glance, turned and left the room.

That night Burwell slept in a cell.

The next morning he received another visit from the non-committal secretary, who informed him that matters had been arranged, and that he would be set at liberty forthwith.

"I must tell you, though," he said, "that I have had great difficulty in accomplishing this, and your liberty is granted only on condition that you leave the country within twenty-four hours, and never under any conditions return."

Burwell stormed, raged, and pleaded; but it availed nothing. The secretary was inexorable, and yet he positively refused to throw any light upon the causes of this monstrous injustice.

"Here is your card," he said, handing him a large envelope closed with the seal of Legation. "I advise you to burn it and never refer to the matter again."

That night the ill-fated man took the train for London, his heart consumed by hatred for the whole French nation, together with a burning desire for vengeance. He wired his wife to meet him at the station, and for a long time debated with himself whether he should at once tell her the sickening truth. In the end he decided that it was better to keep silent. No sooner, however, had she seen him than her woman's instinct told her that he was labouring under some mental strain. And he saw in a moment that to withhold from her his burning secret was impossible, especially when she began to talk of the trip they had planned through France. Of course no trivial reason would satisfy her for his refusal to make this trip, since they had been looking forward to it for years; and yet it was impossible now for him to set foot on French soil.

So he finally told her the whole story, she laughing and weeping in turn. To her, as to him, it seemed incredible that such overwhelming disasters could have grown out of so small a cause, and, being a fluent French scholar, she demanded a sight of the fatal piece of pasteboard. In vain her husband tried to divert her by proposing a trip through Italy. She would consent to nothing until she had seen the mysterious card which Burwell was now convinced he ought long ago to have destroyed. After refusing for awhile to let her see it, he finally yielded. But, although he had learned to dread the consequences of showing that cursed card, he was little prepared for what followed. She read it turned pale, gasped for breath, and nearly fell to the floor.

"I told you not to read it," he said; and then, growing tender at the sight of her distress, he took her hand in his and begged her to be calm. "At least tell me what the thing means," he said. "We can bear it together; you surely can trust me."

But she, as if stung by rage, pushed him from her and declared, in a tone such as he had never heard from her before, that never, never again would she live with him. "You are a monster!" she exclaimed. And those were the last words he heard from her lips.

Failing utterly in all efforts at reconciliation, the half-crazed man took the first steamer for New York, having suffered in scarcely a fortnight more than in all his previous life. His whole pleasure trip had been ruined, he had failed to consummate important business arrangements, and now he saw his home broken up and his happiness ruined. During the voyage he scarcely left his stateroom, but lay there prostrated with agony. In this black despondency the one thing that sustained him was the thought of meeting his partner, Jack Evelyth, the friend of his boyhood, the sharer of his success, the bravest, most loyal fellow in the world. In the face of even the most damning circumstances, he felt that Evelyth's rugged common sense would evolve some way of escape from this hideous nightmare. Upon landing at New York he hardly waited for the gang-plank to be lowered before he rushed on shore and grasped the hand of his partner, who was waiting on the wharf.

"Jack," was his first word, "I am in dreadful trouble, and you are the only man in the world who can help me."

An hour later Burwell sat at his friend's dinner table, talking over the situation.

Evelyth was all kindness, and several times as he listened to Burwell's story his eyes filled with tears.

"It does not seem possible, Richard," he said, "that such things can be; but I will stand by you; we will fight it out together. But we cannot strike in the dark. Let me see this card."

"There is the damned thing," Burwell said, throwing it on the table.

Evelyth opened the envelope, took out the card, and fixed his eyes on the sprawling purple characters.

"Can you read it?" Burwell asked excitedly.

"Perfectly," his partner said. The next moment he turned pale, and his voice broke. Then he clasped the tortured man's hand in his with a strong grip. "Richard," he said slowly, "if my only child had been brought here dead it would not have caused me more sorrow than this does. You have brought me the worst news one man could bring another."

His agitation and genuine suffering affected Burwell like a death sentence.

"Speak, man," he cried; "do not spare me. I can bear anything rather than this awful uncertainty. Tell me what the card means."

Evelyth took a swallow of brandy and sat with head bent on his clasped hands.

"No, I can't do it; there are some things a man must not do."

Then he was silent again, his brows knitted. Finally he said solemnly:—

"No, I can't see any other way out of it. We have been true to each other all our lives; we have worked together and looked forward to never separating. I would rather fail and die than see this happen. But we have got to separate, old friend; we have got to separate."

They sat there talking until late into the night. But nothing that Burwell could do or say availed against his friend's decision. There was nothing for it but that Evelyth should buy his partner's share of the business or that Burwell buy out the other. The man was more than fair in the financial proposition he made; he was generous, as he always had been, but his determination was inflexible; the two must separate. And they did.

With his old partner's desertion, it seemed to Burwell that the world was leagued against him. It was only three weeks from the day on which he had received the mysterious card; yet in that time he had lost all that he valued in the world,—wife, friends, and business. What next to do with the fatal card was the sickening problem that now possessed him.

He dared not show it; yet he dared not destroy it. He loathed it; yet he could not let it go from his possession. Upon returning to his house he locked the accursed thing away in his safe as if it had been a package of dynamite or a bottle of deadly poison. Yet not a day passed that he did not open the drawer where the thing was kept and scan with loathing the mysterious purple scrawl.

In desperation he finally made up his mind to take up the study of the language in which the hateful thing was written. And still he dreaded the approach of the day when he should decipher its awful meaning.

One afternoon, less than a week after his arrival in New York, as he was crossing Twenty-third Street on the way to his French teacher, he saw a carriage rolling up Broadway. In the carriage was a face that caught his attention like a flash. As he looked again he recognized the woman who had been the cause of his undoing. Instantly he sprang into another cab and ordered the driver to follow after. He found the house where she was living. He called there several times; but always received the same reply, that she was too much engaged to see anyone. Next he was told that she was ill, and on the following day the servant said she was much worse. Three physicians had been summoned in consultation. He sought out one of these and told him it was a matter of life or death that he see this woman. The doctor was a kindly man and promised to assist him. Through his influence, it came about that on that very night Burwell stood by the bedside of this mysterious woman. She was beautiful still, though her face was worn with illness.

"Do you recognize me?" he asked tremblingly, as he leaned over the bed, clutching in one hand an envelope containing the mysterious card. "Do you remember seeing me at the *Folies Bergère* a month ago?"

"Yes," she murmured, after a moment's study of his face; and he noted with relief that she spoke English.

"Then, for God's sake, tell me, what does it all mean?" he gasped, quivering with excitement.

"I gave you the card because I wanted you to—to—"

Here a terrible spasm of coughing shook her whole body, and she fell back exhausted.

An agonizing despair tugged at Burwell's heart. Frantically snatching the card from its envelope, he held it close to the woman's face.

"Tell me! Tell me!"

With a supreme effort, the pale figure slowly raised itself on the pillow, its fingers clutching at the counterpane.

Then the sunken eyes fluttered—forced themselves open—and stared in stony amazement upon the fatal card, while the trembling lips moved noiselessly, as if in an attempt to speak. As Burwell, choking with eagerness, bent his head slowly to hers, a suggestion of a smile flickered across the woman's face. Again the mouth quivered, the man's head bent nearer and nearer to hers, his eyes riveted upon the lips. Then, as if to aid her in deciphering the mystery, he turned his eyes to the card.

With a cry of horror he sprang to his feet, his eyeballs starting from their sockets. Almost at the same moment the woman fell heavily upon the pillow.

Every vestige of the writing had faded! The card was blank!

The woman lay there dead.

2

The Card Unveiled

No physician was ever more scrupulous than I have been, during my thirty years of practice, in observing the code of professional secrecy; and it is only for grave reasons, partly in the interests of medical science, largely as a warning to intelligent people, that I place upon record the following statements.

One morning a gentleman called at my offices to consult me about some nervous trouble. From the moment I saw him, the man made a deep impression on me, not so much by the pallor and worn look of his face as by a certain intense sadness in his eyes, as if all hope had gone out of his life. I wrote a prescription for him, and advised him to try the benefits of an ocean voyage. He seemed to shiver at the idea, and said that he had been abroad too much, already.

As he handed me my fee, my eye fell upon the palm of his hand, and I saw there, plainly marked on the Mount of Saturn, a cross surrounded by two circles. I should explain that for the greater part of my life I have been a constant and enthusiastic student of palmistry. During my travels in the Orient, after taking my degree, I spent months studying this fascinating art at the best sources of information in the world. I have read everything published on palmistry in every known language, and my library on the subject is perhaps the most complete in existence. In my time I have examined at least fourteen thousand palms, and taken casts of many of the more interesting of them. But I had never seen such a palm as this; at least, never but once, and the horror of the case was so great that I shudder even now when I call it to mind.

"Pardon me," I said, keeping the patient's hand in mine, "would you let me look at your palm?"

I tried to speak indifferently, as if the matter were of small consequence, and for some moments I bent over the hand in silence. Then, taking a magnifying glass from my desk, I looked at it still more closely. I was not mistaken; here was indeed the sinister double circle on Saturn's mount, with the cross inside,—a marking so rare as to portend some stupendous destiny of good or evil, more probably the latter.

I saw that the man was uneasy under my scrutiny, and, presently, with some hesitation, as if mustering courage, he asked: "Is there anything remarkable about my hand?"

"Yes," I said, "there is. Tell me, did not something very unusual, something very horrible, happen to you about ten or eleven years ago?"

I saw by the way the man started that I had struck near the mark, and, studying the stream of fine lines that crossed his lifeline from the Mount of Venus, I added: "Were you not in some foreign country at that time?"

The man's face blanched, but he only looked at me steadily out of those mournful eyes. Now I took his other hand, and compared the two, line by line, mount by mount, noting the short square fingers, the heavy thumb, with amazing willpower in its upper joint, and gazing again and again at that ominous sign on Saturn.

"Your life has been strangely unhappy, your years have been clouded by some evil influence."

"My God," he said weakly, sinking into a chair, "how can you know these things?"

"It is easy to know what one sees," I said, and tried to draw him out about his past, but the words seemed to stick in his throat.

"I will come back and talk to you again," he said, and he went away without giving me his name or any revelation of his life.

Several times he called during subsequent weeks, and gradually seemed to take on a measure of confidence in my presence. He would talk freely of his physical condition, which seemed to cause him much anxiety. He even insisted upon my making the most careful examination of all his organs, especially of his eyes, which, he said, had troubled him at various times. Upon making the usual tests, I found that he was suffering from a most uncommon form of colour blindness, that seemed to vary in its manifestations, and to be connected with certain hallucinations or abnormal mental states which recurred periodically, and about which I had great difficulty in persuading him to speak. At each visit I took occasion to study his hand anew, and each reading of the palm gave me stronger conviction that here was a life mystery that would abundantly repay any pains taken in unravelling it.

While I was in this state of mind, consumed with a desire to know more of my unhappy acquaintance and yet not daring to press him with questions, there came a tragic happening that revealed to me with startling suddenness the secret I was bent on knowing. One night, very late,—in fact it was about four o'clock in the morning,—I received an urgent summons to the bedside of a man who had been shot. As I bent over him I saw that it was my friend, and for the first time I realized that he was a man of wealth and position, for he lived in a beautifully furnished house filled with art treasures and looked after by a retinue of servants. From one of these I learned that he was Richard Burwell, one of New York's most respected citizens—in fact, one of her best-known philanthropists, a man who for years had devoted his life and fortune to good works among the poor.

But what most excited my surprise was the presence in the house of two officers, who informed me that Mr. Burwell was under arrest, charged with murder. The officers assured me that it was only out of deference to his well-known standing in the community that the prisoner had been allowed the privilege of receiving medical treatment in his own home; their orders were peremptory to keep him under close surveillance.

Giving no time to further questionings, I at once proceeded to examine the injured man, and found that he was suffering from a bullet wound in the back at about the height of the fifth rib. On probing for the bullet, I found that it had lodged near the heart, and decided that it would be exceedingly dangerous to try to remove it immediately. So I contented myself with administering a sleeping potion.

As soon as I was free to leave Burwell's bedside I returned to the officers and obtained from them details of what had happened. A woman's body had been found a few hours before, shockingly mutilated, on Water Street, one of the dark ways in the swarming region along the river front. It had been found at about two o'clock in the morning by some printers from the office of the *Courier des Etats Unis*, who, in coming from their work, had heard cries of distress and hurried to the rescue. As they drew near they saw a man spring away from something huddled on the sidewalk, and plunge into the shadows of the night, running from them at full speed.

Suspecting at once that here was the mysterious assassin so long vainly sought for many similar crimes, they dashed after the fleeing man, who darted right and left through the maze of dark streets, giving out little cries like a squirrel as he ran. Seeing that they were losing ground, one of the printers fired at the fleeing shadow, his shot being followed by a scream of pain, and hurrying up they found a man writhing on the ground. The man was Richard Burwell.

The news that my sad-faced friend had been implicated in such a revolting occurrence shocked me inexpressibly, and I was greatly relieved the next day to learn from the papers that a most unfortunate mistake had been made. The evidence given before the coroner's jury was such as to abundantly exonerate Burwell from all shadow of guilt. The man's own testimony, taken at his bedside, was in itself almost conclusive in his favour. When asked to explain his presence so late at night in such a part of the city, Burwell stated that he had spent the evening at the Florence Mission, where he had made an address to some unfortunates gathered there, and that later he had gone with a young missionary worker to visit a woman living on Frankfort Street, who was dying of consumption. This statement was borne out by the missionary worker himself, who testified that Burwell had been most tender in his ministrations to the poor woman and had not left her until death had relieved her sufferings.

Another point which made it plain that the printers had mistaken their man in the darkness, was the statement made by all of them that, as they came running up, they had overheard some words spoken by the murderer, and that these words were in their own language, French. Now it was shown conclusively that Burwell did not know the French language, that indeed he had not even an elementary knowledge of it.

Another point in his favour was a discovery made at the spot where the body was found. Some profane and ribald words, also in French, had been scrawled in chalk on the door and doorsill, being in the nature of a coarse defiance to the police to find the assassin, and experts in handwriting who were called testified unanimously that Burwell, who wrote a refined, scholarly hand, could never have formed those misshapen words.

Furthermore, at the time of his arrest no evidence was found on the clothes or person of Burwell, nothing in the nature of bruises or bloodstains that would tend to implicate him in the crime. The outcome of the matter was that he was honourably discharged by the coroner's jury, who were unanimous in declaring him innocent, and who brought in a verdict that the unfortunate woman had come to her death at the hand of some person or persons unknown.

On visiting my patient late on the afternoon of the second day I saw that his case was very grave, and I at once instructed the nurses and attendants to prepare for an operation. The man's life depended upon my being able to extract the bullet, and the chance of doing this was very small. Mr. Burwell realized that his condition was critical, and, beckoning me to him, told me that he wished to make a statement he felt might be his last. He spoke with agitation which was increased by an unforeseen happening. For just then a servant entered the room and whispered to me that there was a gentleman downstairs who insisted upon seeing me, and who urged business of great importance. This message the sick man overheard, and lifting himself with an effort, he said excitedly: "Tell me, is he a tall man with glasses?"

The servant hesitated.

"I knew it; you cannot deceive me; that man will haunt me to my grave. Send him away, doctor; I beg of you not to see him."

Humouring my patient, I sent word to the stranger that I could not see him, but, in an undertone, instructed the servant to say that the man might call at my office the next morning. Then, turning to Burwell, I begged him to compose himself and save his strength for the ordeal awaiting him.

"No, no," he said, "I need my strength now to tell you what you must know to find the truth. You are the only man who has understood that there has been some terrible influence at work in my life. You are the only man competent to study out what that influence is, and I have made provision in my will that you shall do so after I am gone. I know that you will heed my wishes?"

The intense sadness of his eyes made my heart sink; I could only grip his hand and remain silent.

"Thank you; I was sure I might count on your devotion. Now, tell me, doctor, you have examined me carefully, have you not?"

I nodded.

"In every way known to medical science?"

I nodded again.

"And have you found anything wrong with me,—I mean, besides this bullet, anything abnormal?"

"As I have told you, your eyesight is defective; I should like to examine your eyes more thoroughly when you are better."

"I shall never be better; besides it isn't my eyes; I mean myself, my soul,—you haven't found anything wrong there?"

"Certainly not; the whole city knows the beauty of your character and your life."

"Tut, tut; the city knows nothing. For ten years I have lived so much with the poor that people have almost forgotten my previous active life when I was busy with money-making and happy in my home. But there is a man out West, whose head is white and whose heart is heavy, who has not forgotten, and there is a woman in London, a silent, lonely woman, who has not forgotten. The man was my partner, poor Jack Evelyth; the woman was my wife. How can a man be so cursed, doctor, that his love and friendship bring only misery to those who share it? How can it be that one who has in his heart only good thoughts can be constantly under the shadow of evil? This charge of murder is only one of several cases in my life where, through no fault of mine, the shadow of guilt has been cast upon me.

"Years ago, when my wife and I were perfectly happy, a child was born to us, and a few months later, when it was only a tender, helpless little thing that its mother loved with all her heart, it was strangled in its cradle, and we never knew who strangled it, for the deed was done one night when there was absolutely no one in the house but my wife and myself. There was no doubt about the crime, for there on the tiny neck were the finger marks where some cruel hand had closed until life went.

"Then a few years later, when my partner and I were on the eve of fortune, our advance was set back by the robbery of our safe. Someone opened it in the night, someone who knew the combination, for it was the work of no burglar, and yet there were only two persons in the world who knew that combination, my partner and myself. I tried to be brave when these things happened, but as my life went on it seemed more and more as if some curse were on me.

"Eleven years ago I went abroad with my wife and daughter. Business took me to Paris, and I left the ladies in London, expecting to have them join me in a few days. But they never did join me, for the curse was on me still, and before I had been forty-eight hours in the

338

French capital something happened that completed the wreck of my life. It doesn't seem possible, does it, that a simple white card with some words scrawled on it in purple ink could effect a man's undoing? And yet that was my fate. The card was given me by a beautiful woman with eyes like stars. She is dead long ago, and why she wished to harm me I never knew. You must find that out.

"You see I did not know the language of the country, and, wishing to have the words translated,—surely that was natural enough,—I showed the card to others. But no one would tell me what it meant. And, worse than that, wherever I showed it, and to whatever person, there evil came upon me quickly. I was driven from one hotel after another; an old acquaintance turned his back on me; I was arrested and thrown into prison; I was ordered to leave the country."

The sick man paused for a moment in his weakness, but with an effort forced himself to continue:—

"When I went back to London, sure of comfort in the love of my wife, she too, on seeing the card, drove me from her with cruel words. And when finally, in deepest despair, I returned to New York, dear old Jack, the friend of a life-time, broke with me when I showed him what was written. What the words were I do not know, and suppose no one will ever know, for the ink has faded these many years. You will find the card in my safe with other papers. But I want you, when I am gone, to find out the mystery of my life; and—and—about my fortune, that must be held until you have decided. There is no one who needs my money as much as the poor in this city, and I have bequeathed it to them unless—"

In an agony of mind, Mr. Burwell struggled to go on, I soothing and encouraging him.

"Unless you find what I am afraid to think, but—but—yes, I must say it,—that I have not been a good man, as the world thinks, but have—O doctor, if you find that I have unknowingly harmed any human being, I want that person, or these persons, to have my fortune. Promise that."

Seeing the wild light in Burwell's eyes, and the fever that was burning him, I gave the promise asked of me, and the sick man sank back calmer.

A little later, the nurse and attendants came for the operation. As they were about to administer the ether, Burwell pushed them from him, and insisted on having brought to his bedside an iron box from the safe.

"The card is here," he said, laying his trembling hand upon the box, "you will remember your promise!"

Those were his last words, for he did not survive the operation.

Early the next morning I received this message: "The stranger of yesterday begs to see you"; and presently a gentleman of fine presence and strength of face, a tall, dark-complexioned man wearing glasses, was shown into the room.

"Mr. Burwell is dead, is he not?" were his first words.

"Who told you?"

"No one told me, but I know it, and I thank God for it."

There was something in the stranger's intense earnestness that convinced me of his right to speak thus, and I listened attentively.

"That you may have confidence in the statement I am about to make, I will first tell you who I am"; and he handed me a card that caused me to lift my eyes in wonder, for it bore a very great name, that of one of Europe's most famous *savants*.

"You have done me much honour, sir," I said with respectful inclination.

"On the contrary you will oblige me by considering me in your debt, and by never revealing my connection with this wretched man. I am moved to speak partly from considerations of human justice, largely in the interest of medical science. It is right for me to tell you, doctor, that your patient was beyond question the Water Street assassin."

"Impossible!" I cried.

"You will not say so when I have finished my story, which takes me back to Paris, to the time, eleven years ago, when this man was making his first visit to the French capital."

"The mysterious card!" I exclaimed.

"Ah, he has told you of his experience, but not of what befell the night before, when he first met my sister."

"Your sister?"

"Yes, it was she who gave him the card, and, in trying to befriend him, made him suffer. She was in ill health at the time, so much so that we had left our native India for extended journeyings. Alas! we delayed too long, for my sister died in New York, only a few weeks later, and I honestly believe her taking off was hastened by anxiety inspired by this man."

"Strange," I murmured, "how the life of a simple New York merchant could become entangled with that of a great lady of the East."

"Yet so it was. You must know that my sister's condition was due mainly to an over fondness for certain occult investigations, from which I had vainly tried to dissuade her. She had once befriended some adepts, who, in return, had taught her things about the soul she had better have left unlearned. At various times while with her I had seen strange things happen, but I never realized what unearthly powers were in her until that night in Paris. We were returning from a drive in the Bois; it was about ten o'clock, and the city lay beautiful around us as Paris looks on a perfect summer's night. Suddenly my sister gave a cry of pain and put her hand to her heart. Then, changing from French to the language of our country, she explained to me quickly that something frightful was taking place there, where she pointed her finger across the river, that we must go to the place at once—the driver must lash his horses—every second was precious.

"So affected was I by her intense conviction, and such confidence had I in my sister's wisdom, that I did not oppose her, but told the man to drive as she directed. The carriage fairly flew across the bridge, down the Boulevard St. Germain, then to the left, threading its way through the narrow streets that lie along the Seine. This way and that, straight ahead here, a turn there, she directing our course, never hesitating, as if drawn by some unseen power, and always urging the driver on to greater speed. Finally, we came to a black-mouthed, evil-looking alley, so narrow and roughly paved that the carriage could scarcely advance.

"'Come on!' my sister cried, springing to the ground; 'we will go on foot, we are nearly there. Thank God, we may yet be in time.'

"No one was in sight as we hurried along the dark alley, and scarcely a light was visible, but presently a smothered scream broke the silence, and, touching my arm, my sister exclaimed:—

"'There, draw your weapon, quick, and take the man at any cost!'

"So swiftly did everything happen after that that I hardly know my actions, but a few minutes later I held pinioned in my arms a man whose blows and writhings had been all in vain; for you must know that much exercise in the jungle had made me strong of limb. As soon as I had made the fellow fast I looked down and found moaning on the ground a poor woman, who explained with tears and broken words that the man had been in the very act of strangling her. Searching him I found a long-bladed knife of curious shape, and keen as a razor, which had been brought for what horrible purpose you may perhaps divine.

"Imagine my surprise, on dragging the man back to the carriage, to find, instead of the ruffianly assassin I expected, a gentleman as far as could be judged from face and manner. Fine eyes, white hands, careful speech, all the signs of refinement and the dress of a man of means.

"'How can this be?' I said to my sister in our own tongue as we drove away, I holding my prisoner on the opposite seat where he sat silent.

"'It is a *kulos*-man,' she said, shivering, 'it is a fiend-soul. There are a few such in the whole world, perhaps two or three in all.'

"'But he has a good face.'

"'You have not seen his real face yet; I will show it to you, presently.'

"In the strangeness of these happenings and the still greater strangeness of my sister's words, I had all but lost the power of wonder. So we sat without further word until the carriage stopped at the little *château* we had taken near the Parc Monteau.

"I could never properly describe what happened that night; my knowledge of these things is too limited. I simply obeyed my sister in all that she directed, and kept my eyes on this man as no hawk ever watched its prey. She began by questioning him, speaking in a kindly tone which I could ill understand. He seemed embarrassed, dazed, and professed to have no knowledge of what had occurred, or how he had come where we found him. To all my inquiries as to the woman or the crime he shook his head blankly, and thus aroused my wrath.

"'Be not angry with him, brother; he is not lying, it is the other soul.'

"She asked him about his name and country, and he replied without hesitation that he was Richard Burwell, a merchant from New York, just arrived in Paris, travelling for pleasure in Europe with his wife and daughter. This seemed reasonable, for the man spoke English, and, strangely enough, seemed to have no knowledge of French, although we both remember hearing him speak French to the woman.

"'There is no doubt,' my sister said, 'It is indeed a *kulos*-man; It knows that I am here, that I am Its master. Look, look!' she cried sharply, at the same time putting her eyes so close to the man's face that their fierce light seemed to burn into him. What power she exercised I do not know, nor whether some words she spoke, unintelligible to me, had to do with what followed, but instantly there came over this man, this pleasant-looking, respectable American citizen, such a change as is not made by death worms gnawing in a grave. Now there was a fiend grovelling at her feet, a foul, sin-stained fiend.

"'Now you see the demon-soul,' said my sister. 'Watch It writhe and struggle; it has served me well, brother, sayest thou not so, the lore I gained from our wise men?'

"The horror of what followed chilled my blood; nor would I trust my memory were it not that there remained and still remains plain proof of all that I affirm. This hideous creature, dwarfed, crouching, devoid of all resemblance to the man we had but now beheld, chattering to us in curious old-time French, poured out such horrid blasphemy as would have blanched the cheek of Satan, and made recital of such evil deeds as never mortal ear gave heed to. And as she willed my sister checked It or allowed It to go on. What it all meant was more than I could tell. To me it seemed as if these tales of wickedness had no connection with our modern life, or with the world around us, and so I judged presently from what my sister said.

"'Speak of the later time, since thou wast in this clay.'

"Then I perceived that the creature came to things of which I knew: It spoke of New York, of a wife, a child, a friend. It told of strangling the child, of robbing the friend; and was going on to tell God knows what other horrid deeds when my sister stopped It.

"'Stand as thou didst in killing the little babe, stand, stand!' and once more she spoke some words unknown to me. Instantly the demon sprang forward, and, bending Its clawlike hands, clutched them around some little throat that was not there,—but I could see it in my mind. And the look on its face was a blackest glimpse of hell.

"'And now stand as thou didst in robbing the friend, stand, stand'; and again came the unknown words, and again the fiend obeyed.

"'These we will take for future use,' said my sister. And bidding me watch the creature carefully until she should return, she left the room, and, after none too short an absence, returned bearing a black box that was an apparatus for photography, and something more besides,— some newer, stranger kind of photography that she had learned. Then, on a strangely fashioned card, a transparent white card, composed of many layers of finest Oriental paper, she took the pictures of the creature in those two creeping poses. And when it all was done, the card seemed as white as before, and empty of all meaning until one held it up and examined it intently. Then the pictures showed.

And between the two there was a third picture, which somehow seemed to show, at the same time, two faces in one, two souls, my sister said, the kindly visaged man we first had seen, and then the fiend.

"Now my sister asked for pen and ink and I gave her my pocket pen which was filled with purple ink. Handing this to the *kulos*-man she bade him write under the first picture: 'Thus I killed my babe.' And under the second picture: 'Thus I robbed my friend.' And under the third, the one that was between the other two: 'This is the soul of Richard Burwell.' An odd thing about this writing was that it was in the same old French the creature had used in speech, and yet Burwell knew no French.

"My sister was about to finish with the creature when a new idea took her, and she said, looking at It as before:—'Of all thy crimes which one is the worst? Speak, I command thee!'

"Then the fiend told how once It had killed every soul in a house of holy women and buried the bodies in a cellar under a heavy door.

"'Where was the house?'

"'At No. 19 Rue Picpus, next to the old graveyard.'

"'And when was this?'

"Here the fiend seemed to break into fierce rebellion, writhing on the floor with hideous contortions, and pouring forth words that meant nothing to me, but seemed to reach my sister's understanding, for she interrupted from time to time, with quick, stern words that finally brought It to subjection.

"'Enough,' she said, 'I know all,' and then she spoke some words again, her eyes fixed as before, and the reverse change came. Before us stood once more the honest-looking, fine-appearing gentleman, Richard Burwell, of New York.

"'Excuse me, *madame*,' he said, awkwardly, but with deference; 'I must have dosed a little. I am not myself tonight.'

"'No,' said my sister, 'you have not been yourself tonight.'

"A little later I accompanied the man to the Continental Hotel, where he was stopping, and, returning to my sister, I talked with her until late into the night. I was alarmed to see that she was wrought to a nervous tension that augured ill for her health. I urged her to sleep, but she would not.

"'No,' she said, 'think of the awful responsibility that rests upon me.' And then she went on with her strange theories and explanations, of which I understood only that here was a power for evil more terrible than a pestilence, menacing all humanity.

"'Once in many cycles it happens,' she said, 'that a *kulos*-soul pushes itself within the body of a new-born child, when the pure soul waiting to enter is delayed. Then the two live together through that life,

344

and this hideous principle of evil has a chance upon the earth. It is my will, as I feel it my duty, to see this poor man again. The chances are that he will never know us, for the shock of this night to his normal soul is so great as to wipe out memory.'

"The next evening, about the same hour, my sister insisted that I should go with her to the *Folies Bergère*, a concert garden, none too well frequented, and when I remonstrated, she said: 'I must go,—It is there,' and the words sent a shiver through me.

"We drove to this place, and passing into the garden, presently discovered Richard Burwell seated at a little table, enjoying the scene of pleasure, which was plainly new to him. My sister hesitated a moment what to do, and then, leaving my arm, she advanced to the table and dropped before Burwell's eyes the card she had prepared. A moment later, with a look of pity on her beautiful face, she rejoined me and we went away. It was plain he did not know us."

To so much of the *savant's* strange recital I had listened with absorbed interest, though without a word, but now I burst in with questions.

"What was your sister's idea in giving Burwell the card?" I asked.

"It was in the hope that she might make the man understand his terrible condition, that is, teach the pure soul to know its loathsome companion."

"And did her effort succeed?"

"Alas! it did not; my sister's purpose was defeated by the man's inability to see the pictures that were plain to every other eye. It is impossible for the *kulos*-man to know his own degradation."

"And yet this man has for years been leading a most exemplary life?"

My visitor shook his head. "I grant you there has been improvement, due largely to experiments I have conducted upon him according to my sister's wishes. But the fiend soul was never driven out. It grieves me to tell you, doctor, that not only was this man the Water Street assassin, but he was the mysterious murderer, the long-sought-for mutilator of women, whose red crimes have baffled the police of Europe and America for the past ten years."

"You know this," said I, starting up, "and yet did not denounce him?"

"It would have been impossible to prove such a charge, and besides, I had made oath to my sister that I would use the man only for these soul-experiments. What are his crimes compared with the great secret of knowledge I am now able to give the world?"

"A secret of knowledge?"

"Yes," said the *savant*, with intense earnestness, "I may tell you now, doctor, what the whole world will know, ere long, that it is possible to compel every living person to reveal the innermost secrets of his or her life, so long as memory remains, for memory is only the power of producing in the brain material pictures that may be projected externally by the thought rays and made to impress themselves upon the photographic plate, precisely as ordinary pictures do."

"You mean," I exclaimed, "that you can photograph the two principles of good and evil that exist in us?"

"Exactly that. The great truth of a dual soul existence, that was dimly apprehended by one of your Western novelists, has been demonstrated by me in the laboratory with my camera. It is my purpose, at the proper time, to entrust this precious knowledge to a chosen few who will perpetuate it and use it worthily."

"Wonderful, wonderful!" I cried, "and now tell me, if you will, about the house on the Rue Picpus. Did you ever visit the place?"

"We did, and found that no buildings had stood there for fifty years, so we did not pursue the search."[1]

"And the writing on the card, have you any memory of it, for Burwell told me that the words have faded?"

"I have something better than that; I have a photograph of both card and writing, which my sister was careful to take. I had a notion that the ink in my pocket pen would fade, for it was a poor affair. This photograph I will bring you tomorrow."

"Bring it to Burwell's house," I said.

★★★★★★

The next morning the stranger called as agreed upon.

"Here is the photograph of the card," he said.

"And here is the original card," I answered, breaking the seal of

---

1. Years later, some workmen in Paris, making excavations in the Rue Picpus, came upon a heavy door buried under a mass of debris, under an old cemetery. On lifting the door they found a vault-like chamber in which were a number of female skeletons, and graven on the walls were blasphemous words written in French, which experts declared dated from fully two hundred years before. They also declared this handwriting identical with that found on the door at the Water Street murder in New York. Thus we may deduce a theory of fiend reincarnation; for it would seem clear, almost to the point of demonstration, that this murder of the seventeenth century was the work of the same evil soul that killed the poor woman on Water Street towards the end of the nineteenth century.

the envelope I had taken from Burwell's iron box. "I have waited for your arrival to look at it. Yes, the writing has indeed vanished; the card seems quite blank."

"Not when you hold it this way," said the stranger, and as he tipped the card I saw such a horrid revelation as I can never forget. In an instant I realized how the shock of seeing that card had been too great for the soul of wife or friend to bear. In these pictures was the secret of a cursed life. The resemblance to Burwell was unmistakable, the proof against him was overwhelming. In looking upon that piece of pasteboard the wife had seen a crime which the mother could never forgive, the partner had seen a crime which the friend could never forgive. Think of a loved face suddenly melting before your eyes into a grinning skull, then into a mass of putrefaction, then into the ugliest fiend of hell, leering at you, distorted with all the marks of vice and shame. That is what I saw, that is what they had seen!

"Let us lay these two cards in the coffin," said my companion impressively, "we have done what we could."

Eager to be rid of the hateful piece of pasteboard (for who could say that the curse was not still clinging about it?), I took the strange man's arm, and together we advanced into the adjoining room where the body lay. I had seen Burwell as he breathed his last, and knew that there had been a peaceful look on his face as he died. But now, as we laid the two white cards on the still, breast, the *savant* suddenly touched my arm, and pointing to the dead man's face, now frightfully distorted, whispered:—"See, even in death It followed him. Let us close the coffin quickly."

The Oblong Box
By Edgar Allan Poe

Some years ago I engaged passage from Charleston, S. C., to the city of New York, in the fine packet-ship *Independence*, Captain Hardy. We were to sail on the fifteenth of the month (June), weather permitting; and on the fourteenth I went on board to arrange some matters in my stateroom.

I found that we were to have a great many passengers, including a more than usual number of ladies. On the list were several of my acquaintances; and among other names I was rejoiced to see that of Mr. Cornelius Wyatt, a young artist, for whom I entertained feelings of warm friendship. He had been, with me, a fellow-student at C—— University, where we were very much together. He had the ordinary temperament of genius, and was a compound of misanthropy, sensibility, and enthusiasm. To these qualities he united the warmest and truest heart which ever beat in a human bosom.

I observed that his name was carded upon three staterooms: and upon again referring to the list of passengers I found that he had engaged passage for himself, wife, and two sisters—his own. The staterooms were sufficiently roomy, and each had two berths, one above the other. These berths, to be sure, were so exceedingly narrow as to be insufficient for more than one person; still, I could not comprehend why there were three staterooms for these four persons. I was, just at that epoch, in one of those moody frames of mind which make a man abnormally inquisitive about trifles: and I confess with shame that I busied myself in a variety of ill-bred and preposterous conjectures about this matter of the supernumerary stateroom. It was no business of mine, to be sure; but with none the less pertinacity did I occupy myself in attempts to resolve the enigma. At last I reached a conclusion which wrought in me great wonder why I had not arrived at it before.

"It is a servant, of course," I said; "what a fool I am not sooner to have thought of so obvious a solution!" And then I again repaired to the list, but here I saw distinctly that no servant was to come with the party: although, in fact, it had been the original design to bring one, for the words "and servant" had been first written and then over-scored. "Oh, extra baggage, to be sure," I now said to myself; "something he wishes not to be put in the hold, something to be kept under his own eye,—ah, I have it! a painting or so, and this is what he has been bargaining about with Nicolino, the Italian Jew." This idea satisfied me and I dismissed my curiosity for the nonce.

Wyatt's two sisters I knew very well, and most amiable and clever girls they were. His wife he had newly married, and I had never yet seen her. He had often talked about her in my presence, however, and in his usual style of enthusiasm. He described her as of surpassing beauty, wit, and accomplishment. I was, therefore, quite anxious to make her acquaintance.

On the day in which I visited the ship (the fourteenth), Wyatt and party were also to visit it, so the captain informed me, and I waited on board an hour longer than I had designed in hope of being presented to the bride; but then an apology came. "Mrs. W. was a little indisposed, and would decline coming on board until tomorrow at the hour of sailing."

The morrow having arrived, I was going from my hotel to the wharf, when Captain Hardy met me and said that, "owing to circumstances" (a stupid but convenient phrase), "he rather thought the *Independence* would not sail for a day or two, and that when all was ready he would send up and let me know." This I thought strange, for there was a stiff southerly breeze; but as "the circumstances" were not forthcoming, although I pumped for them with much perseverance, I had nothing to do but to return home and digest my impatience at leisure.

I did not receive the expected message from the captain for nearly a week. It came at length, however, and I immediately went on board. The ship was crowded with passengers, and everything was in the bustle attendant upon making sail. Wyatt's party arrived in about ten minutes after myself. There were the two sisters, the bride, and the artist—the latter in one of his customary fits of moody misanthropy. I was too well used to these, however, to pay them any special attention. He did not even introduce me to his wife; this courtesy devolving, perforce, upon his sister Marian, a very sweet and intelligent girl, who in a few hurried words made us acquainted.

Mrs. Wyatt had been closely veiled; and when she raised her veil in acknowledging my bow, I confess that I was very profoundly astonished. I should have been much more so, however, had not long experience advised me not to trust, with too implicit a reliance, the enthusiastic descriptions of my friend the artist, when indulging in comments upon the loveliness of woman. When beauty was the theme, I well knew with what facility he soared into the regions of the purely ideal.

The truth is, I could not help regarding Mrs. Wyatt as a decidedly plain-looking woman. If not positively ugly, she was not, I think, very far from it. She was dressed, however, in exquisite taste, and then I had no doubt that she had captivated my friend's heart by the more enduring graces of the intellect and soul. She said very few words, and passed at once into her stateroom with Mr. W.

My old inquisitiveness now returned. There was no servant, that was a settled point. I looked, therefore, for the extra baggage. After some delay a cart arrived at the wharf with an oblong pine box, which was everything that seemed to be expected. Immediately upon its arrival we made sail, and in a short time were safely over the bar and standing out to sea.

The box in question was, as I say, oblong. It was about six feet in length by two and a half in breadth: I observed it attentively and like to be precise. Now, this shape was peculiar; and no sooner had I seen it than I took credit to myself for the accuracy of my guessing. I had reached the conclusion, it will be remembered, that the extra baggage of my friend the artist would prove to be pictures, or at least a picture, for I knew he had been for several weeks in conference with Nicolino; and now here was a box, which, from its shape, could possibly contain nothing in the world but a copy of Leonardo's *Last Supper*; and a copy of this very *Last Supper*, done by Rubini the younger at Florence, I had known for some time to be in the possession of Nicolino. This point, therefore, I considered as sufficiently settled. I chuckled excessively when I thought of my acumen. It was the first time I had ever known Wyatt to keep from me any of his artistical secrets; but here he evidently intended to steal a march upon me and smuggle a fine picture to New York, under my very nose; expecting me to know nothing of the matter. I resolved to quiz him well, now and hereafter.

One thing, however, annoyed me not a little. The box did not go into the extra stateroom. It was deposited in Wyatt's own; and there, too, it remained, occupying very nearly the whole of the floor, no doubt to the exceeding discomfort of the artist and his wife; this the more especially as the tar or paint with which it was lettered in sprawling capitals emitted a strong, disagreeable, and, to my fancy, a peculiarly disgusting odour. On the lid were painted the words:

Mrs. Adelaide Curtis, Albany, New York. Charge of Cornelius Wyatt, Esq. This side up. To be handled with care.

Now, I was aware that Mrs. Adelaide Curtis of Albany was the artist's wife's mother; but then I looked upon the whole address as a mystification, intended especially for myself. I made up my mind, of course, that the box and contents would never get farther north than the studio of my misanthropic friend in Chambers Street, New York.

For the first three or four days we had fine weather, although the wind was dead ahead, having chopped round to the northward immediately upon our losing sight of the coast. The passengers were, consequently, in high spirits and disposed to be social. I must except, however, Wyatt and his sisters, who behaved stiffly, and, I could not help thinking, uncourteously, to the rest of the party. Wyatt's conduct I did not so much regard. He was gloomy, even beyond his usual habit,—in fact, he was morose; but in him I was prepared for eccentricity. For the sisters, however, I could make no excuse. They secluded themselves in their staterooms during the greater part of the passage, and absolutely refused, although I repeatedly urged them, to hold communication with any person on board.

Mrs. Wyatt herself was far more agreeable. That is to say, she was chatty; and to be chatty is no slight recommendation at sea. She became excessively intimate with most of the ladies; and, to my profound astonishment, evinced no equivocal disposition to coquet with the men. She amused us all very much. I say "amused," and scarcely know how to explain myself. The truth is, I soon found that Mrs. W. was far oftener laughed at than with. The gentlemen said little about her; but the ladies in a little while pronounced her "a good-hearted thing, rather indifferent-looking, totally uneducated, and decidedly vulgar." The great wonder was, how Wyatt had been entrapped into such a match. Wealth was the general solution, but this I knew to be no solution at all; for Wyatt had told me that she neither brought him a dollar nor had any expectations from any source whatever. "He had married," he said, "for love, and for love only; and his bride was far more than worthy of his love."

When I thought of these expressions on the part of my friend, I confess that I felt indescribably puzzled. Could it be possible that he was taking leave of his senses? What else could I think? He, so refined, so intellectual, so fastidious, with so exquisite a perception of the faulty, and so keen an appreciation of the beautiful! To be sure, the lady seemed especially fond of him, particularly so in his absence, when she made herself ridiculous by frequent quotations of what had been said by her "beloved husband, Mr. Wyatt." The word "husband" seemed forever, to use one of her own delicate expressions,—forever "on the tip of her tongue." In the meantime it was observed by all on board that he avoided her in the most pointed manner, and, for the most part, shut himself up alone in his stateroom, where, in fact, he might have been said to live altogether, leaving his wife at full liberty to amuse herself as she thought best in the public society of the main cabin.

My conclusion, from what I saw and heard, was that the artist, by some unaccountable freak of fate, or perhaps in some fit of enthusiastic and fanciful passion, had been induced to unite himself with a person altogether beneath him, and that the natural result, entire and speedy disgust, had ensued. I pitied him from the bottom of my heart, but could not, for that reason, quite forgive his incommunicativeness in the matter of the *Last Supper*. For this I resolved to have my revenge.

One day he came up on deck, and, taking his arm as had been my wont, I sauntered with him backward and forward. His gloom, however (which I considered quite natural under the circumstances), seemed entirely unabated. He said little, and that moodily, and with evident effort. I ventured a jest or two, and he made a sickening attempt at a smile. Poor fellow! as I thought of his wife I wondered that he could have heart to put on even the semblance of mirth. At last I ventured a home thrust. I determined to commence a series of covert insinuations, or innuendos, about the oblong box, just to let him perceive, gradually, that I was not altogether the butt, or victim, of his little bit of pleasant mystification. My first observation was by way of opening a masked battery. I said something about the "peculiar shape of that box"; and, as I spoke the words I smiled knowingly, winked, and touched him gently with my forefinger in the ribs.

The manner in which Wyatt received this harmless pleasantry convinced me at once that he was mad. At first he stared at me as if he found it impossible to comprehend the witticism of my remark; but as its point seemed slowly to make its way into his brain, his eyes, in the same proportion, seemed protruding from their sockets. Then he grew very red, then hideously pale, then, as if highly amused with what I had insinuated, he began a loud and boisterous laugh, which, to my astonishment, he kept up, with gradually increasing vigour, for ten minutes or more. In conclusion, he fell flat and heavily upon the deck. When I ran to uplift him, to all appearance he was dead.

I called assistance, and, with much difficulty, we brought him to himself. Upon reviving he spoke incoherently for some time. At length we bled him and put him to bed. The next morning he was quite recovered, so far as regarded his mere bodily health. Of his mind I say nothing, of course. I avoided him during the rest of the passage, by advice of the captain, who seemed to coincide with me altogether in my views of his insanity, but cautioned me to say nothing on this head to any person on board.

Several circumstances occurred immediately after this fit of Wyatt's which contributed to heighten the curiosity with which I was already possessed. Among other things, this: I had been nervous; drank too much strong green tea, and slept ill at night,—in fact, for two nights I could not be properly said to sleep at all. Now, my stateroom opened into the main cabin or dining-room, as did those of all the single men on board. Wyatt's three rooms were in the after-cabin, which was separated from the main one by a slight sliding door, never locked even at night. As we were almost constantly on a wind, and the breeze was not a little stiff, the ship heeled to leeward very considerably; and whenever her starboard side was to leeward the sliding door between the cabins slid open and so remained, nobody taking the trouble to get up and shut it.

But my berth was in such a position that when my own stateroom door was open, as well as the sliding door in question (and my own door was always open on account of the heat), I could see into the after-cabin quite distinctly, and just at that portion of it, too, where were situated the staterooms of Mr. Wyatt. Well, during two nights (not consecutive), while I lay awake, I clearly saw Mrs. W., about eleven o'clock upon each night, steal cautiously from the stateroom of Mr. W. and enter the extra room, where she remained until daybreak, when she was called by her husband and went back. That they were virtually separated was clear. They had separate apartments, no doubt in contemplation of a more permanent divorce; and here, after all, I thought, was the mystery of the extra stateroom.

There was another circumstance, too, which interested me much. During the two wakeful nights in question, and immediately after the disappearance of Mrs. Wyatt into the extra stateroom, I was attracted by certain singular, cautious, subdued noises in that of her husband. After listening to them for some time with thoughtful attention, I at length succeeded perfectly in translating their import. They were sounds occasioned by the artist in prying open the oblong box by means of a chisel and mallet, the latter being apparently muffled or deadened by some soft woollen or cotton substance in which its head was enveloped.

In this manner I fancied I could distinguish the precise moment when he fairly disengaged the lid, also that I could determine when he removed it altogether, and when he deposited it upon the lower berth in his room; this latter point I knew, for example, by certain slight taps which the lid made in striking against the wooden edges of the berth as he endeavoured to lay it down very gently, there being no room for it on the floor. After this there was a dead stillness, and I heard nothing more, upon either occasion, until nearly daybreak; unless, perhaps, I may mention a low sobbing or murmuring sound, so very much suppressed as to be nearly inaudible, if, indeed, the whole of this latter noise were not rather produced by my own imagination.

I say it seemed to resemble sobbing or sighing, but, of course, it could not have been either. I rather think it was a ringing in my own ears. Mr. Wyatt, no doubt, according to custom, was merely giving the rein to one of his hobbies, indulging in one of his fits of artistic enthusiasm. He had opened his oblong box in order to feast his eyes on the pictorial treasure within. There was nothing in this, however, to make him sob. I repeat, therefore, that it must have been simply a freak of my own fancy, distempered by good Captain Hardy's green tea. Just before dawn, on each of the two nights of which I speak, I distinctly heard Mr. Wyatt replace the lid upon the oblong box, and force the nails into their old places by means of the muffled mallet. Having done this, he issued from his stateroom, fully dressed, and proceeded to call Mrs. W. from hers.

We had been at sea seven days, and were now off Cape Hatteras, when there came a tremendously heavy blow from the southwest. We were, in a measure, prepared for it, however, as the weather had been holding out threats for some time. Everything was made snug, alow and aloft; and, as the wind steadily freshened, we lay to, at length, under spanker and foretopsail, both double-reefed.

In this trim we rode safely enough for forty-eight hours, the ship proving herself an excellent sea-boat in many respects, and shipping no water of any consequence. At the end of this period, however, the gale had freshened into a hurricane, and our after-sail split into ribbons, bringing us so much in the trough of the water that we shipped several prodigious seas, one immediately after the other. By this accident we lost three men overboard with the caboose, and nearly the whole of the larboard bulwarks. Scarcely had we recovered our senses before the foretopsail went into shreds, when we got up a storm staysail, and with this did pretty well for some hours, the ship heading the sea much more steadily than before.

The gale still held on, however, and we saw no signs of its abating. The rigging was found to be ill-fitted and greatly strained; and on the third day of the blow, about five in the afternoon, our mizzen-mast, in a heavy lurch to windward, went by the board. For an hour or more we tried in vain to get rid of it, on account of the prodigious rolling of the ship; and, before we had succeeded, the carpenter came aft and announced four feet water in the hold. To add to our dilemma, we found the pumps choked and nearly useless.

All was now confusion and despair, but an effort was made to lighten the ship by throwing overboard as much of her cargo as could be reached, and by cutting away the two masts that remained. This we at last accomplished, but we were still unable to do anything at the pumps; and, in the meantime, the leak gained on us very fast.

At sundown the gale had sensibly diminished in violence, and, as the sea went down with it, we still entertained faint hopes of saving ourselves in the boats. At eight p.m., the clouds broke away to windward, and we had the advantage of a full moon, a piece of good fortune which served wonderfully to cheer our drooping spirits.

After incredible labour we succeeded, at length, in getting the long-boat over the side without material accident, and into this we crowded the whole of the crew and most of the passengers. This party made off immediately, and, after undergoing much suffering, finally arrived in safety at Ocracoke Inlet, on the third day after the wreck.

Fourteen passengers, with the captain, remained on board, resolving to trust their fortunes to the jolly-boat at the stern. We lowered it without difficulty, although it was only by a miracle that we prevented it from swamping as it touched the water. It contained, when afloat, the captain and his wife, Mr. Wyatt and party, a Mexican officer, wife, four children, and myself, with a negro valet.

We had no room, of course, for anything except a few positively necessary instruments, some provisions, and the clothes upon our backs. No one had thought of even attempting to save anything more. What must have been the astonishment of all, then, when, having proceeded a few fathoms from the ship, Mr. Wyatt stood up in the stern-sheets and coolly demanded of Captain Hardy that the boat should be put back for the purpose of taking in his oblong box!

"Sit down, Mr. Wyatt," replied the captain, somewhat sternly; "you will capsize us if you do not sit quite still. Our gunwale is almost in the water now."

"The box!" vociferated Mr. Wyatt, still standing, "the box, I say! Captain Hardy, you cannot, you will not refuse me. Its weight will be but a trifle, it is nothing, mere nothing. By the mother who bore you—for the love of Heaven—by your hope of salvation, I implore you to put back for the box!"

The captain for a moment seemed touched by the earnest appeal of the artist, but he regained his stern composure, and merely said:

"Mr. Wyatt, you are mad. I cannot listen to you. Sit down, I say, or you will swamp the boat. Stay! hold him, seize him! he is about to spring overboard! There—I knew it—he is over!"

As the captain said this, Mr. Wyatt, in fact, sprang from the boat, and, as we were yet in the lee of the wreck, succeeded, by almost superhuman exertion, in getting hold of a rope which hung from the forechains. In another moment he was on board, and rushing frantically down into the cabin.

In the meantime we had been swept astern of the ship, and being quite out of her lee, were at the mercy of the tremendous sea which was still running. We made a determined effort to put back, but our little boat was like a feather in the breath of the tempest. We saw at a glance that the doom of the unfortunate artist was sealed.

As our distance from the wreck rapidly increased, the madman (for as such only could we regard him) was seen to emerge from the companionway, up which, by dint of strength that appeared gigantic, he dragged, bodily, the oblong box. While we gazed in the extremity of astonishment, he passed rapidly several turns of a three-inch rope, first around the box and then around his body. In another instant both body and box were in the sea, disappearing suddenly, at once and forever.

We lingered awhile sadly upon our oars, with our eyes riveted upon the spot. At length we pulled away. The silence remained unbroken for an hour. Finally I hazarded a remark.

"Did you observe, captain, how suddenly they sank? Was not that an exceedingly singular thing? I confess that I entertained some feeble hope of his final deliverance when I saw him lash himself to the box and commit himself to the sea."

"They sank as a matter of course," replied the captain, "and that like a shot. They will soon rise again, however, but not till the salt melts."

"The salt!" I ejaculated.

"Hush!" said the captain, pointing to the wife and sisters of the deceased. "We must talk of these things at some more appropriate time."

★★★★★★

We suffered much and made a narrow escape; but fortune befriended us, as well as our mates in the long-boat. We landed, in fine, more dead than alive, after four days of intense distress, upon the beach opposite Roanoke Island. We remained here a week, were not ill-treated by the wreckers, and at length obtained a passage to New York.

About a month after the loss of the *Independence*, I happened to meet Captain Hardy in Broadway. Our conversation turned, naturally, upon the disaster, and especially upon the sad fate of poor Wyatt. I thus learned the following particulars:

The artist had engaged passage for himself, wife, two sisters, and a servant. His wife was indeed, as she had been represented, a most lovely and most accomplished woman. On the morning of the fourteenth of June (the day in which I first visited the ship), the lady suddenly sickened and died. The young husband was frantic with grief, but circumstances imperatively forbade the deferring his voyage to New York. It was necessary to take to her mother the corpse of his adored wife, and, on the other hand, the universal prejudice which would prevent his doing so openly was well known. Nine tenths of the passengers would have abandoned the ship rather than take passage with a dead body.

In this dilemma Captain Hardy arranged that the corpse, being first partially embalmed and packed, with a large quantity of salt in a box of suitable dimensions, should be conveyed on board as merchandise. Nothing was to be said of the lady's decease; and, as it was well understood that Mr. Wyatt had engaged passage for his wife, it became necessary that some person should personate her during the voyage.

357

This the deceased lady's maid was easily prevailed on to do. The extra stateroom, originally engaged for this girl during her mistress's life, was now merely retained. In this stateroom the pseudo-wife slept, of course, every night. In the daytime she performed, to the best of her ability, the part of her mistress, whose person, it had been carefully ascertained, was unknown to any of the passengers on board.

My own mistake arose, naturally enough, through too careless, too inquisitive, and too impulsive a temperament. But of late it is a rare thing that I sleep soundly at night. There is a countenance which haunts me, turn as I will. There is an hysterical laugh which will forever ring within my ears.

The Return

By Algernon Blackwood

It was curious—that sense of dull uneasiness that came over him so suddenly, so stealthily at first he scarcely noticed it, but with such marked increase after a time that he presently got up and left the theatre. His seat was on the gangway of the dress circle, and he slipped out awkwardly in the middle of what seemed to be the best and jolliest song of the piece. The full house was shaking with laughter; so infectious was the gaiety that even strangers turned to one another as much as to say, "Now, isn't that funny?"

It was curious, too, the way the feeling first got into him at all, and in the full swing of laughter, music, light-heartedness; for it came as a vague suggestion, "I've forgotten something—something I meant to do—something of importance. What in the world was it, now?" And he thought hard, searching vainly through his mind; then dismissed it as the dancing caught his attention. It came back a little later again, during a passage of long-winded talk that bored him and set his attention free once more, but came more strongly this time, insisting on an answer. What could it have been that he had overlooked, left undone, omitted to see to? It went on nibbling at the subconscious part of him. Several times this happened, this dismissal and return, till at last the thing declared itself more plainly—and he felt bothered, troubled, distinctly uneasy.

He was wanted somewhere. There was somewhere else he ought to be. That describes it best, perhaps. Some engagement of moment had entirely slipped his memory—an engagement that involved another person, too. But where, what, with whom? And, at length, this vague uneasiness amounted to positive discomfort, so that he felt unable to enjoy the piece, and left abruptly. Like a man to whom comes suddenly the horrible idea that the match he lit his cigarette with and flung into the waste-paper basket on leaving was not really out—a sort of panic distress—he jumped into a taxicab and hurried to his flat to find everything in order, of course; no smoke, no fire, no smell of burning.

But his evening was spoiled. He sat smoking in his armchair at home, this business man of forty, practical in mind, of character some called stolid, cursing himself for an imaginative fool. It was now too late to go back to the theatre; the club bored him; he spent an hour with the evening papers, dipping into books, sipping a long cool drink, doing odds and ends about the flat. "I'll go to bed early for a change," he laughed, but really all the time fighting—yes, deliberately fighting—this strange attack of uneasiness that so insidiously grew upwards, outwards from the buried depths of him that sought so strenuously to deny it. It never occurred to him that he was ill. He was not ill. His health was thunderingly good. He was as robust as a coal-heaver.

The flat was roomy, high up on the top floor, yet in a busy part of town, so that the roar of traffic mounted round it like a sea. Through the open windows came the fresh night air of June. He had never noticed before how sweet the London night air could be, and that not all the smoke and dust could smother a certain touch of wild fragrance that tinctured it with perfume—yes, almost perfume—as of the country. He swallowed a draught of it as he stood there, staring out across the tangled world of roofs and chimney-pots. He saw the procession of the clouds; he saw the stars; he saw the moonlight falling in a shower of silver spears upon the slates and wires and steeples. And something in him quickened—something that had never stirred before.

He turned with a horrid start, for the uneasiness had of a sudden leaped within him like an animal. There was someone in the flat.

Instantly, with action—even this slight action—the fancy vanished; but, all the same, he switched on the electric lights and made a search. For it seemed to him that someone had crept up close behind him while he stood there watching the night—someone, whose silent presence fingered with unerring touch both this new thing that had quickened in his heart and that sense of original deep uneasiness. He was amazed at himself—angry—indignant that he could be thus foolishly upset over nothing, yet at the same time profoundly distressed at this vehement growth of a new thing in his well-ordered personality. Growth? He dismissed the word the moment it occurred to him—but it had occurred to him. It stayed. While he searched the empty flat, the long passages, the gloomy bedroom at the end, the little hall where he kept his overcoats and golf sticks, it stayed. Growth! It was oddly disquieting. Growth to him involved, though he neither acknowledged nor recognized the truth perhaps, some kind of undesirable changeableness, instability, unbalance.

Yet singular as it all was, he realized that the uneasiness and the sudden appreciation of beauty that was so new to him had both entered by the same door into his being. When he came back to the front room he noticed that he was perspiring. There were little drops of moisture on his forehead. And down his spine ran chills, little, faint quivers of cold. He was shivering.

He lit his big *meerschaum* pipe, and left the lights all burning. The feeling that there was something he had overlooked, forgotten, left undone, had vanished. Whatever the original cause of this absurd uneasiness might be—he called it absurd on purpose because he now realized in the depths of him that it was really more vital than he cared about—it was much nearer to discovery than before. It dodged about just below the threshold of discovery. It was as close as that. Any moment he would know what it was; he would remember. Yes, he would *remember*. Meanwhile, he was in the right place. No desire to go elsewhere afflicted him, as in the theatre. Here was the place, here in the flat.

And then it was with a kind of sudden burst and rush—it seemed to him the only way to phrase it—memory gave up her dead.

At first he only caught her peeping round the corner at him, drawing aside a corner of an enormous curtain, as it were; striving for more complete entrance as though the mass of it were difficult to move. But he understood, he knew, he recognized. It was enough for that. As an entrance into his being—heart, mind, soul—was being attempted and the entrance because of his stolid temperament was difficult of accomplishment, there was effort, strain. Something in him had first to be opened up, widened, made soft and ready as by an operation, before full entrance could be effected. This much he grasped though for the life of him he could not have put it into words. Also he knew who it was that sought an entrance. Deliberately from himself he withheld the name. But he knew as surely as though Straughan stood in the room and faced him with a knife saying, "Let me in, let me in. I wish you to know I'm here. I'm clearing a way! You recall our promise?"

He rose from his chair and went to the open window again, the strange fear slowly passing. The cool air fanned his cheeks. Beauty till now had scarcely ever brushed the surface of his soul. He had never troubled his head about it. It passed him by indifferent; and he had ever loathed the mouthy prating of it on others' lips. He was practical; beauty was for dreamers, for women, for men who had means and leisure. He had not exactly scorned it; rather it had never touched his life, to sweeten, to cheer, to uplift. Artists for him were like monks— another sex almost—useless beings who never helped the world go round. He was for action always, work, activity, achievement as he saw them. He remembered Straughan vaguely—Straughan, the ever impecunious friend of his youth, always talking of colour and sound—mysterious, ineffectual things. He even forgot what they had quarrelled about, if they had quarrelled at all even; or why they had gone apart all these years ago. And certainly he had forgotten any promise. Memory as yet only peeped at him round the corner of that huge curtain tentatively, suggestively, yet—he was obliged to admit it—somewhat winningly. He was conscious of this gentle, sweet seductiveness that now replaced his fear.

And as he stood now at the open window peering over huge London, beauty came close and smote him between the eyes. She came blindingly, with her train of stars and clouds and perfumes. Night, mysterious, myriad-eyed, and flaming across her sea of haunted shadows invaded his heart and shook him with her immemorial wonder and delight. He found no words of course to clothe the new unwonted sensations. He only knew that all his former dread, uneasiness, distress, and with them this idea of growth that had seemed so repugnant to him were merged, swept up, and gathered magnificently home into a wave of beauty that enveloped him. "See it, and understand," ran a secret inner whisper across his mind. He saw. He understood. . . .

He went back and turned the lights out. Then he took his place again at that open window, drinking in the night. He saw a new world; a species of intoxication held him. He sighed, as his thoughts blundered for expression among words and sentences that knew him not. But the delight was there, the wonder, the mystery. He watched with heart alternately tightening and expanding the transfiguring play of moon and shadow over the sea of buildings. He saw the dance of the hurrying clouds, the open patches into outer space, the veiling and unveiling of that ancient silvery face; and he caught strange whispers of the hierophantic, sacerdotal power that has echoed down the world since Time began and dropped strange magic phrases into every poet's heart, since first "*God dawned on Chaos*"—the Beauty of the Night.

A long time passed—it may have been one hour, it may have been three—when at length he turned away and went slowly to his bedroom. A deep peace lay over him. Something quite new and blessed had crept into his life and thought. He could not quite understand it all. He only knew that it uplifted. There was no longer the least sign of affliction or distress. Even the inevitable reaction that set in could not destroy that.

And then as he lay in bed nearing the borderland of sleep, suddenly and without any obvious suggestion to bring it, he remembered another thing. He remembered the promise. Memory got past the big curtain for an instant and showed her face. She looked into his eyes. It must have been a dozen years ago when Straughan and he had made that foolish solemn promise, that whoever died first should show himself if possible to the other.

He had utterly forgotten it—till now. But Straughan had not forgotten it. The letter came three weeks later from India. That very evening Straughan had died—at nine o'clock. And he had come back— in the Beauty that he loved.

The Second Generation

By Algernon Blackwood

Sometimes, in a moment of sharp experience, comes that vivid flash of insight that makes a platitude suddenly seem a revelation— its full content is abruptly realized. "Ten years *is* a long time, yes," he thought, as he walked up the drive to the great Kensington house where she still lived.

Ten years—long enough, at any rate, for her to have married and for her husband to have died. More than that he had not heard, in the outlandish places where life had cast him in the interval. He wondered whether there had been any children. All manner of thoughts and questions, confused a little, passed across his mind. He was well-to-do now, though probably his entire capital did not amount to her income for a single year. He glanced at the huge, forbidding mansion. Yet that pride was false which had made of poverty an insuperable obstacle. He saw it now. He had learned values in his long exile.

But he was still ridiculously timid. This confusion of thought, of mental images rather, was due to a kind of fear, since worship ever is akin to awe. He was as nervous as a boy going up for a *viva voce*; and with the excitement was also that unconquerable sinking—that horrid shrinking sensation that excessive shyness brings. Why in the world had he come? Why had he telegraphed the very day after his arrival in England? Why had he not sent a tentative, tactful letter, feeling his way a little?

Very slowly he walked up the drive, feeling that if a reasonable chance of escape presented itself he would almost take it. But all the windows stared so hard at him that retreat was really impossible now and though no faces were visible behind the curtains, all had seen him, possibly she herself—his heart beat absurdly at the extravagant suggestion. Yet it was odd—he felt so certain of being seen, and that someone watched him. He reached the wide stone steps that were clean as marble, and shrank from the mark his boots must make upon their spotlessness. In desperation, then, before he could change his mind, he touched the bell. But he did not hear it ring—mercifully; that irrevocable sound must have paralyzed him altogether.

If no one came to answer, he might still leave a card in the letter-box and slip away. Oh, how utterly he despised himself for such a thought! A man of thirty with such a chicken heart was not fit to protect a child, much less a woman. And he recalled with a little stab of pain that the man she married had been noted for his courage, his determined action, his inflexible firmness in various public situations, head and shoulders above lesser men. What presumption on his own part ever to dream! ... He remembered, too, with no apparent reason in particular, that this man had a grown-up son already, by a former marriage.

And still no one came to open that huge, contemptuous door with its so menacing, so hostile air. His back was to it, as he carelessly twirled his umbrella, but he felt its sneering expression behind him while it looked him up and down. It seemed to push him away. The entire mansion focused its message through that stern portal: Little timid men are not welcomed here.

How well he remembered the house! How often in years gone by had he not stood and waited just like this, trembling with delight and anticipation, yet terrified lest the bell should be answered and the great door actually swung wide! Then, as now, he would have run, had he dared. He was still afraid—his worship was so deep. But in all these years of exile in wild places, farming, mining, working for the position he had at last attained, her face and the memory of her gracious presence had been his comfort and support, his only consolation, though never his actual joy. There was so little foundation for it all, yet her smile and the words she had spoken to him from time to time in friendly conversation had clung, inspired, kept him going—for he knew them all by heart. And more than once in foolish optimistic moods, he had imagined, greatly daring, that she possibly had meant more....

He touched the bell a second time—with the point of his umbrella. He meant to go in, carelessly as it were, saying as lightly as might be, "Oh, I'm back in England again—if you haven't *quite* forgotten my existence—I could not forego the pleasure of saying 'How-do-you-do?' and hearing that you are well ... ," and the rest; then presently bow himself easily out—into the old loneliness again. But he would at least have seen her; he would have heard her voice, and looked into her gentle, amber eyes; he would have touched her hand. She might even ask him to come in another day and see her! He had rehearsed it all a hundred times, as certain feeble temperaments do rehearse such scenes. And he came rather well out of that rehearsal, though always with an aching heart, the old great yearnings unfulfilled. All the way across the Atlantic he had thought about it, though with lessening confidence as the time drew near. The very night of his arrival in London he wrote, then, tearing up the letter (after sleeping over it), he had telegraphed next morning, asking if she would be in. He signed his surname—such a very common name, alas! but surely she would know—and her reply, "Please call 4:30," struck him as rather oddly worded. Yet here he was.

There was a rattle of the big door knob, that aggressive, hostile knob that thrust out at him insolently like a fist of bronze. He started, angry with himself for doing so. But the door did not open. He became suddenly conscious of the wilds he had lived in for so long; his clothes were hardly fashionable; his voice probably had a twang in it, and he used tricks of speech that must betray the rough life so recently left. What would she think of him, now? He looked much older, too. And how brusque it was to have telegraphed like that! He felt awkward, gauche, tongue-tied, hot and cold by turns. The sentences, so carefully rehearsed, fled beyond recovery.

Good heavens—the door was open! It had been open for some minutes. It moved noiselessly on big hinges. He acted automatically; he heard himself asking if her ladyship was at home, though his voice was nearly inaudible. The next moment he was standing in the great, dim hall, so poignantly familiar, and the remembered perfume almost made him sway. He did not hear the door close, but he knew. He was caught. The butler betrayed an instant's surprise—or was it overwrought imagination again?—when he gave his name. It seemed to him—though only later did he grasp the significance of that curious intuition—that the man had expected another caller instead. The man took his card respectfully and disappeared. These flunkeys were so marvellously trained. He was too long accustomed to straight question and straight answer, but here, in the Old Country, privacy was jealously guarded with such careful ritual.

And almost immediately the butler returned, still expressionless, and showed him into the large drawing-room on the ground floor that he knew so well. Tea was on the table—tea for one. He felt puzzled. "If you will have tea first, sir, her ladyship will see you afterwards," was what he heard. And though his breath came thickly, he asked the question that forced itself out. Before he knew what he was saying he asked it, "Is she ill?"

"Oh, no, her ladyship is quite well, thank you, sir. If you will have tea first, sir, her ladyship will see you afterwards."

The horrid formula was repeated, word for word. He sank into an armchair and mechanically poured out his own tea. What he felt he did not exactly know. It seemed so unusual, so utterly unexpected, so unnecessary, too. Was it a special attention, or was it merely casual? That it could mean anything else did not occur to him. How was she busy, occupied—not here to give him tea? He could not understand it. It seemed such a farce having tea alone like this—it was like waiting for an audience, it was like a doctor's or a dentist's room. He felt bewildered, ill at ease, cheap. . . . But after ten years in primitive lands perhaps London usages had changed in some extraordinary manner. He recalled his first amazement at the motor-omnibuses, taxicabs, and electric tubes. All were new. London was otherwise than when he left it. Piccadilly and the Marble Arch themselves had altered. And, with his reflection, a shade more confidence stole in.

She knew that he was there and presently she would come in and speak with him, explaining everything by the mere fact of her delicious presence. He was ready for the ordeal, he would see her—and drop out again. It was worth all manner of pain, even of mortification. He was in her house, drinking her tea, sitting in a chair she used herself perhaps. Only he would never dare to say a word or make a sign that might betray his changeless secret. He still felt the boyish worshipper, worshipping in dumbness from a distance, one of a group of many others like himself. Their dreams had faded, his had continued, that was the difference. Memories tore and raced and poured upon him. How sweet and gentle she had always been to him! He used to wonder sometimes. . . . Once, he remembered, he had rehearsed a declaration, but while rehearsing the big man had come in and captured her, though he had only read the definite news long after by chance in an Arizona paper.

He gulped his tea down. His heart alternately leaped and stood still. A sort of numbness held him most of that dreadful interval, and no clear thought came at all. Every ten seconds his head turned towards the door that rattled, seemed to move, yet never opened. But any moment now it *must* open, and he would be in her very presence, breathing the same air with her. He would see her, charge himself with her beauty once more to the brim, and then go out again into the wilderness—the wilderness of life—without her, and not for a mere ten years but for always. She was so utterly beyond his reach. He felt like a backwoodsman, he was a backwoodsman.

For one thing only was he duly prepared, though he thought about it little enough—she would, of course, have changed. The photograph he owned, cut from an illustrated paper, was not true now. It might even be a little shock perhaps. He must remember that. Ten years cannot pass over a woman without—

Before he knew it the door was open, and she was advancing quietly towards him across the thick carpet that deadened sound. With both hands outstretched she came, and with the sweetest welcoming smile upon her parted lips he had seen in any human face. Her eyes were soft with joy. His whole heart leaped within him; for the instant he saw her it all flashed clear as sunlight—that she knew and understood. She had always known, had always understood. Speech came easily to him in a flood, had he needed it, but he did not need it. It was all so adorably easy, simple, natural, and true. He just took her hands—those welcoming, outstretched hands—in both of his own, and led her to the nearest sofa. He was not even surprised at himself. Inevitably, out of depths of truth, this meeting came about. And he uttered a little foolish commonplace, because he feared the huge revulsion that his sudden glory brought, and loved to taste it slowly:

"So you live here still?"

"Here, and here," she answered softly, touching his heart, and then her own. "I am attached to this house, too, because *you* used to come and see me here, and because it was here I waited so long for you, and still wait. I shall never leave it—unless you change. You see, we live together here."

He said nothing. He leaned forward to take and hold her. The abrupt knowledge of it all somehow did not seem abrupt—it was as though he had known it always; and the complete disclosure did not seem disclosure either—rather as though she told him something he had inexplicably left unrealized, yet not forgotten. He felt absolutely master of himself, yet, in a curious sense, outside of himself at the same time. His arms were already open—when she gently held her hands up to prevent. He heard a faint sound outside the door.

"But you are free," he cried, his great passion breaking out and flooding him, yet most oddly well controlled, "and I—"

She interrupted him in the softest, quietest whisper he had ever heard:

"You are not free, as I am free—not yet."

The sound outside came suddenly closer. It was a step. There was a faint click on the handle of the door. In a flash, then, came the dreadful shock that overwhelmed him—the abrupt realization of the truth that was somehow horrible—that Time, all these years, had left no mark upon her and that *she had not changed*. Her face was as young as when he saw her last.

With it there came cold and darkness into the great room. He shivered with cold, but an alien, unaccountable cold. Some great shadow dropped upon the entire earth, and though but a second could have passed before the handle actually turned, and the other person entered, it seemed to him like several minutes. He heard her saying this amazing thing that was question, answer, and forgiveness all in one— this, at least, he divined before the ghastly interruption came—"But, George—if you had only spoken—!"

With ice in his blood he heard the butler saying that her ladyship would be "pleased" to see him if he had finished his tea and would be "so good as to bring the papers and documents upstairs with him." He had just sufficient control of certain muscles to stand upright and murmur that he would come. He rose from a sofa that held no one but himself. All at once he staggered. He really did not know exactly what happened, or how he managed to stammer out the medley of excuses and semi-explanations that battered their way through his brain and issued somehow in definite words from his lips. Somehow or other he accomplished it. The sudden attack, the faintness, the collapse!... He vaguely remembered afterwards—with amazement too— the suavity of the butler as he suggested telephoning for a doctor, and that he just managed to forbid it, refusing the offered glass of brandy as well, remembered contriving to stumble into the taxicab and give his hotel address with a final explanation that he would call another day and "bring the papers." It was quite clear that his telegram had been attributed to someone else, someone "with papers"—perhaps a solicitor or architect. His name was such an ordinary one, there were so many Smiths. It was also clear that she whom he had come to see and *had* seen, no longer lived here in the flesh. . . .

And just as he left the hall he had the vision—mere fleeting glimpse it was—of a tall, slim, girlish figure on the stairs asking if anything was wrong, and realized vaguely through his atrocious pain that she was, of course, the wife of the son who had inherited. . . .

The Secret of Goresthorpe Grange

By A. Conan Doyle

I am sure that Nature never intended me to be a self-made man. There are times when I can hardly bring myself to realize that twenty years of my life were spent behind the counter of a grocer's shop in the East End of London, and that it was through such an avenue that I reached a wealthy independence and the possession of Goresthorpe Grange. My habits are Conservative, and my tastes refined and aristocratic. I have a soul which spurns the vulgar herd. Our family, the D'Odds, date back to a prehistoric era, as is to be inferred from the fact that their advent into British history is not commented on by any trustworthy historian. Some instinct tells me that the blood of a Crusader runs in my veins. Even now, after the lapse of so many years, such exclamations as "By'r Lady!" rise naturally to my lips, and I feel that, should circumstances require it, I am capable of rising in my stirrups and dealing an *infidel* a blow—say with a mace—which would considerably astonish him.

Goresthorpe Grange is a feudal mansion—or so it was termed in the advertisement which originally brought it under my notice. Its right to this adjective had a most remarkable effect upon its price, and the advantages gained may possibly be more sentimental than real. Still, it is soothing to me to know that I have slits in my staircase through which I can discharge arrows: and there is a sense of power in the fact of possessing a complicated apparatus by means of which I am enabled to pour molten lead upon the head of the casual visitor. These things chime in with my peculiar humour, and I do not grudge to pay for them. I am proud of my battlements and of the circular uncovered sewer which girds me round. I am proud of my portcullis and donjon and keep. There is but one thing wanting to round off the mediæval-ism of my abode, and to render it symmetrically and completely antique. Goresthorpe Grange is not provided with a ghost.

Any man with old-fashioned tastes and ideas as to how such establishments should be conducted would have been disappointed at the omission. In my case it was particularly unfortunate. From my childhood I had been an earnest student of the supernatural, and a firm believer in it. I have revelled in ghostly literature until there is hardly a tale bearing upon the subject which I have not perused. I learned the German language for the sole purpose of mastering a book upon demonology. When an infant I have secreted myself in dark rooms in the hope of seeing some of those bogies with which my nurse used to threaten me; and the same feeling is as strong in me now as then. It was a proud moment when I felt that a ghost was one of the luxuries which my money might command.

It is true that there was no mention of an apparition in the advertisement. On reviewing the mildewed walls, however, and the shadowy corridors, I had taken it for granted that there was such a thing on the premises. As the presence of a kennel presupposes that of a dog, so I imagined that it was impossible that such desirable quarters should be untenanted by one or more restless shades. Good heavens, what can the noble family from whom I purchased it have been doing during these hundreds of years! Was there no member of it spirited enough to make away with his sweetheart, or take some other steps calculated to establish a hereditary spectre? Even now I can hardly write with patience upon the subject.

For a long time I hoped against hope. Never did a rat squeak behind the wainscot, or rain drip upon the attic-floor, without a wild thrill shooting through me as I thought that at last I had come upon traces of some unquiet soul. I felt no touch of fear upon these occasions. If it occurred in the night-time, I would send Mrs. D'Odd— who is a strong-minded woman—to investigate the matter while I covered up my head with the bedclothes and indulged in an ecstasy of expectation. Alas, the result was always the same! The suspicious sound would be traced to some cause so absurdly natural and commonplace that the most fervid imagination could not clothe it with any of the glamour of romance.

I might have reconciled myself to this state of things had it not been for Jorrocks of Havistock Farm. Jorrocks is a coarse, burly, matter-of-fact fellow whom I only happen to know through the accidental circumstance of his fields adjoining my demesne. Yet this man, though utterly devoid of all appreciation of archæological unities, is in possession of a well authenticated and undeniable spectre. Its existence only dates back, I believe, to the reign of the Second George, when a young lady cut her throat upon hearing of the death of her lover at the battle of Dettingen. Still, even that gives the house an air of respectability, especially when coupled with bloodstains upon the floor. Jorrocks is densely unconscious of his good fortune; and his language when he reverts to the apparition is painful to listen to. He little dreams how I covet every one of those moans and nocturnal wails which he describes with unnecessary objurgation. Things are indeed coming to a pretty pass when democratic spectres are allowed to desert the landed proprietors and annul every social distinction by taking refuge in the houses of the great unrecognized.

I have a large amount of perseverance. Nothing else could have raised me into my rightful sphere, considering the uncongenial atmosphere in which I spent the earlier part of my life. I felt now that a ghost must be secured, but how to set about securing one was more than either Mrs. D'Odd or myself was able to determine. My reading taught me that such phenomena are usually the outcome of crime. What crime was to be done, then, and who was to do it? A wild idea entered my mind that Watkins, the house-steward, might be prevailed upon—for a consideration—to immolate himself or someone else in the interests of the establishment. I put the matter to him in a half jesting manner; but it did not seem to strike him in a favourable light. The other servants sympathized with him in his opinion—at least, I cannot account in any other way for their having left the house in a body the same afternoon.

"My dear," Mrs. D'Odd remarked to me one day after dinner as I sat moodily sipping a cup of sack—I love the good old names—"my dear, that odious ghost of Jorrocks' has been gibbering again."

"Let it gibber!" I answered recklessly.

Mrs. D'Odd struck a few chords on her virginal and looked thoughtfully into the fire.

"I'll tell you what it is, Argentine," she said at last, using the pet name which we usually substituted for Silas, "we must have a ghost sent down from London."

"How can you be so idiotic, Matilda?" I remarked severely. "Who could get us such a thing?"

"My cousin, Jack Brocket, could," she answered confidently.

Now, this cousin of Matilda's was rather a sore subject between us. He was a rakish clever young fellow, who had tried his hand at many things, but wanted perseverance to succeed at any. He was, at that time, in chambers in London, professing to be a general agent, and really living, to a great extent, upon his wits. Matilda managed so that most of our business should pass through his hands, which certainly saved me a great deal of trouble, but I found that Jack's commission was generally considerably larger than all the other items of the bill put together. It was this fact which made me feel inclined to rebel against any further negotiations with the young gentleman.

"O yes, he could," insisted Mrs. D., seeing the look of disapprobation upon my face. "You remember how well he managed that business about the crest?"

"It was only a resuscitation of the old family coat-of-arms, my dear," I protested.

Matilda smiled in an irritating manner. "There was a resuscitation of the family portraits, too, dear," she remarked. "You must allow that Jack selected them very judiciously."

I thought of the long line of faces which adorned the walls of my banqueting-hall, from the burly Norman robber, through every gradation of casque, plume, and ruff, to the sombre Chesterfieldian individual who appears to have staggered against a pillar in his agony at the return of a maiden MS. which he grips convulsively in his right hand. I was fain to confess that in that instance he had done his work well, and that it was only fair to give him an order—with the usual commission—for a family spectre, should such a thing be attainable.

It is one of my maxims to act promptly when once my mind is made up. Noon of the next day found me ascending the spiral stone staircase which leads to Mr. Brocket's chambers, and admiring the succession of arrows and fingers upon the whitewashed wall, all indicating the direction of that gentleman's sanctum. As it happened, artificial aids of the sort were entirely unnecessary, as an animated flap-dance overhead could proceed from no other quarter, though it was replaced by a deathly silence as I groped my way up the stair. The door was opened by a youth evidently astounded at the appearance of a client, and I was ushered into the presence of my young friend, who was writing furiously in a large ledger—upside down, as I afterwards discovered.

After the first greetings, I plunged into business at once.

"Look here, Jack," I said, "I want you to get me a spirit, if you can."

"Spirits you mean!" shouted my wife's cousin, plunging his hand into the waste-paper basket and producing a bottle with the celerity of a conjuring trick. "Let's have a drink!"

I held up my hand as a mute appeal against such a proceeding so early in the day; but on lowering it again I found that I had almost involuntarily closed my fingers round the tumbler which my adviser had pressed upon me. I drank the contents hastily off, lest anyone should come in upon us and set me down as a toper. After all there was something very amusing about the young fellow's eccentricities.

"Not spirits," I explained smilingly; "an apparition—a ghost. If such a thing is to be had, I should be very willing to negotiate."

"A ghost for Goresthorpe Grange?" inquired Mr. Brocket, with as much coolness as if I had asked for a drawing-room suite.

"Quite so," I answered.

"Easiest thing in the world," said my companion, filling up my glass again in spite of my remonstrance. "Let us see!" Here he took down a large red notebook, with all the letters of the alphabet in a fringe down the edge. "A ghost you said, didn't you? That's G. G— gems—gimlets—gaspipes—gauntlets—guns—galleys. Ah, here we are. Ghosts. Volume nine, section six, page forty-one. Excuse me!" And Jack ran up a ladder and began rummaging among a pile of ledgers on a high shelf. I felt half inclined to empty my glass into the spittoon when his back was turned; but on second thoughts I disposed of it in a legitimate way.

"Here it is!" cried my London agent, jumping off the ladder with a crash, and depositing an enormous volume of manuscript upon the table. "I have all these things tabulated, so that I may lay my hands upon them in a moment. It's all right—it's quite weak" (here he filled our glasses again). "What were we looking up, again?"

"Ghosts," I suggested.

"Of course; page 41. Here we are. 'J. H. Fowler & Son, Dunkel Street, suppliers of mediums to the nobility and gentry; charms sold— love-philtres—mummies—horoscopes cast.' Nothing in your line there, I suppose?"

I shook my head despondingly.

"Frederick Tabb," continued my wife's cousin, "solo channel of communication between the living and dead. Proprietor of the spirits of Byron, Kirke White, Grimaldi, Tom Cribb, and Inigo Jones. That's about the figure!"

"Nothing romantic enough there," I objected. "Good heavens! Fancy a ghost with a black eye and a handkerchief tied round its

waist, or turning summersaults, and saying, 'How are you tomorrow?'"
The very idea made me so warm that I emptied my glass and filled
it again.

"Here is another," said my companion, "Christopher McCarthy;
bi-weekly *séances*—attended by all the eminent spirits of ancient and
modern times. Nativities—charms—*abracadabras*, messages from the
dead. He might be able to help us. However, I shall have a hunt round
myself tomorrow, and see some of these fellows. I know their haunts,
and it's odd if I can't pick up something cheap. So there's an end of
business," he concluded, hurling the ledger into the corner, "and now
we'll have something to drink."

We had several things to drink—so many that my inventive faculties were dulled next morning, and I had some little difficulty in
explaining to Mrs. D'Odd why it was that I hung my boots and spectacles upon a peg along with my other garments before retiring to
rest. The new hopes excited by the confident manner in which my
agent had undertaken the commission caused me to rise superior to
alcoholic reaction, and I paced about the rambling corridors and old-
fashioned rooms, picturing to myself the appearance of my expected
acquisition, and deciding what part of the building would harmonize
best with its presence. After much consideration, I pitched upon the
banqueting-hall as being, on the whole, most suitable for its reception.
It was a long low room, hung round with valuable tapestry and interesting relics of the old family to whom it had belonged. Coats of mail
and implements of war glimmered fitfully as the light of the fire played
over them, and the wind crept under the door, moving the hangings
to and fro with a ghastly rustling.

At one end there was the raised dais, on which in ancient times
the host and his guests used to spread their table, while a descent of a
couple of steps led to the lower part of the hall, where the vassals and
retainers held wassail. The floor was uncovered by any sort of carpet,
but a layer of rushes had been scattered over it by my direction. In
the whole room there was nothing to remind one of the nineteenth
century; except, indeed, my own solid silver plate, stamped with the
resuscitated family arms, which was laid out upon an oak table in the
centre. This, I determined, should be the haunted room, supposing my
wife's cousin to succeed in his negotiation with the spirit mongers.
There was nothing for it now but to wait patiently until I heard some
news of the result of his inquiries.

A letter came in the course of a few days, which, if it was short, was at least encouraging. It was scribbled in pencil on the back of a play-bill, and sealed apparently with a tobacco-stopper. "Am on the track," it said. "Nothing of the sort to be had from any professional spiritual-ist, but picked up a fellow in a pub yesterday who says he can manage it for you. Will send him down unless you wire to the contrary. Abra-hams is his name, and he has done one or two of these jobs before." The letter wound up with some incoherent allusions to a cheque, and was signed by my affectionate cousin, John Brocket.

I need hardly say that I did not wire, but awaited the arrival of Mr. Abrahams with all impatience. In spite of my belief in the supernatu-ral, I could scarcely credit the fact that any mortal could have such a command over the spirit-world as to deal in them and barter them against mere earthly gold. Still, I had Jack's word for it that such a trade existed; and here was a gentleman with a Judaical name ready to demonstrate it by proof positive. How vulgar and commonplace Jorrock's eighteenth-century ghost would appear should I succeed in securing a real mediæval apparition! I almost thought that one had been sent down in advance, for, as I walked down the moat that night before retiring to rest, I came upon a dark figure engaged in surveying the machinery of my portcullis and drawbridge. His start of surprise, however, and the manner in which he hurried off into the darkness, speedily convinced me of his earthly origin, and I put him down as some admirer of one of my female retainers mourning over the muddy Hellespont which divided him from his love. Whoever he may have been, he disappeared and did not return, though I loitered about for some time in the hope of catching a glimpse of him and exercising my feudal rights upon his person.

Jack Brocket was as good as his word. The shades of another evening were beginning to darken round Goresthorpe Grange, when a peal at the outer bell, and the sound of a fly pulling up, announced the ar-rival of Mr. Abrahams. I hurried down to meet him, half expecting to see a choice assortment of ghosts crowding in at his rear. Instead, however, of being the sallow-faced, melancholy-eyed man that I had pictured to myself, the ghost-dealer was a sturdy little podgy fellow, with a pair of wonderfully keen sparkling eyes and a mouth which was constantly stretched in a good-humoured, if somewhat artificial, grin. His sole stock-in-trade seemed to consist of a small leather bag jealously locked and strapped, which emitted a metallic chink upon being placed on the stone flags of the hall.

"And 'ow are you, sir?" he asked, wringing my hand with the utmost effusion. "And the missis, 'ow is she? And all the others—'ow's all their 'ealth?"

I intimated that we were all as well as could reasonably be expected; but Mr. Abrahams happened to catch a glimpse of Mrs. D'Odd in the distance, and at once plunged at her with another string of inquiries as to her health, delivered so volubly and with such an intense earnestness that I half expected to see him terminate his cross-examination by feeling her pulse and demanding a sight of her tongue. All this time his little eyes rolled round and round, shifting perpetually from the floor to the ceiling, and from the ceiling to the walls, taking in apparently every article of furniture in a single comprehensive glance.

Having satisfied himself that neither of us was in a pathological condition, Mr. Abrahams suffered me to lead him upstairs, where a repast had been laid out for him to which he did ample justice. The mysterious little bag he carried along with him, and deposited it under his chair during the meal. It was not until the table had been cleared and we were left together that he broached the matter on which he had come down.

"I hunderstand," he remarked, puffing at a trichinopoly, "that you want my 'elp in fitting up this 'ere 'ouse with a happarition."

I acknowledged the correctness of his surmise, while mentally wondering at those restless eyes of his, which still danced about the room as if he were making an inventory of the contents.

"And you won't find a better man for the job, though I says it as shouldn't," continued my companion. "Wot did I say to the young gent wot spoke to me in the bar of the Lame Dog? 'Can you do it?' says he. 'Try me,' says I, 'me and my bag. Just try me.' I couldn't say fairer than that."

My respect for Jack Brocket's business capacities began to go up very considerably. He certainly seemed to have managed the matter wonderfully well. "You don't mean to say that you carry ghosts about in bags?" I remarked, with diffidence.

Mr. Abrahams smiled a smile of superior knowledge. "You wait," he said; "give me the right place and the right hour, with a little of the essence of Lucoptolycus"—here he produced a small bottle from his waistcoat-pocket—"and you won't find no ghost that I ain't up to. You'll see them yourself, and pick your own, and I can't say fairer than that."

As all Mr. Abraham's protestations of fairness were accompanied by a cunning leer and a wink from one or other of his wicked little eyes, the impression of candour was somewhat weakened.

"When are you going to do it?" I asked reverentially.

"Ten minutes to one in the morning," said Mr. Abrahams, with decision. "Some says midnight, but I says ten to one, when there ain't such a crowd, and you can pick your own ghost. And now," he continued, rising to his feet, "suppose you trot me round the premises, and let me see where you wants it; for there's some places as attracts 'em, and some as they won't hear of—not if there was no other place in the world."

Mr. Abrahams inspected our corridors and chambers with a most critical and observant eye, fingering the old tapestry with the air of a connoisseur, and remarking in an undertone that it would "match uncommon nice." It was not until he reached the banqueting-hall, however, which I had myself picked out, that his admiration reached the pitch of enthusiasm. "'Ere's the place!" he shouted, dancing, bag in hand, round the table on which my plate was lying, and looking not unlike some quaint little goblin himself. "'Ere's the place; we won't get nothin' to beat this! A fine room—noble, solid, none of your electro-plate trash! That's the way as things ought to be done, sir. Plenty of room for 'em to glide here. Send up some brandy and the box of weeds; I'll sit here by the fire and do the preliminaries, which is more trouble than you think; for them ghosts carries on hawful at times, before they finds out who they've got to deal with. If you was in the room they'd tear you to pieces as like as not. You leave me alone to tackle them, and at half-past twelve come in, and I'll lay they'll be quiet enough by then."

Mr. Abraham's request struck me as a reasonable one, so I left him with his feet upon the mantelpiece, and his chair in front of the fire, fortifying himself with stimulants against his refractory visitors. From the room beneath, in which I sat with Mrs. D'Odd, I could hear that after sitting for some time he rose up, and paced about the hall with quick impatient steps. We then heard him try the lock of the door, and afterwards drag some heavy article of furniture in the direction of the window, on which, apparently, he mounted, for I heard the creaking of the rusty hinges as the diamond-paned casement folded backwards, and I knew it to be situated several feet above the little man's reach. Mrs. D'Odd says that she could distinguish his voice speaking in low and rapid whispers after this, but that may have been her imagination. I confess that I began to feel more impressed than I had deemed it possible to be. There was something awesome in the thought of the solitary mortal standing by the open window and summoning in from the gloom outside the spirits of the nether world. It was with a trepidation which I could hardly disguise from Matilda that I observed that the clock was pointing to half-past twelve, and that the time had come for me to share the vigil of my visitor.

He was sitting in his old position when I entered, and there were no signs of the mysterious movements which I had overheard, though his chubby face was flushed as with recent exertion.

"Are you succeeding all right?" I asked as I came in, putting on as careless an air as possible, but glancing involuntarily round the room to see if we were alone.

"Only your help is needed to complete the matter," said Mr. Abrahams, in a solemn voice. "You shall sit by me and partake of the essence of Lucoptolycus, which removes the scales from our earthly eyes. Whatever you may chance to see, speak not and make no movement, lest you break the spell." His manner was subdued, and his usual cockney vulgarity had entirely disappeared. I took the chair which he indicated, and awaited the result.

My companion cleared the rushes from the floor in our neighbourhood, and going down upon his hands and knees, described a half circle with chalk, which enclosed the fireplace and ourselves. Round the edge of this half circle he drew several hieroglyphics, not unlike the signs of the zodiac. He then stood up and uttered a long invocation, delivered so rapidly that it sounded like a single gigantic word in some uncouth guttural language. Having finished this prayer, if prayer it was, he pulled out the small bottle which he had produced before, and poured a couple of teaspoonfuls of clear transparent fluid into a phial, which he handed to me with an intimation that I should drink it.

The liquid had a faintly sweet odour, not unlike the aroma of certain sorts of apples. I hesitated a moment before applying it to my lips, but an impatient gesture from my companion overcame my scruples, and I tossed it off. The taste was not unpleasant; and, as it gave rise to no immediate effects, I leaned back in my chair and composed myself for what was to come. Mr. Abrahams seated himself beside me, and I felt that he was watching my face from time to time while repeating some more of the invocations in which he had indulged before.

A sense of delicious warmth and languor began gradually to steal over me, partly, perhaps, from the heat of the fire, and partly from some unexplained cause. An uncontrollable impulse to sleep weighed down my eyelids, while, at the same time, my brain worked actively, and a hundred beautiful and pleasing ideas flitted through it. So utterly lethargic did I feel that, though I was aware that my companion put his hand over the region of my heart, as if to feel how it were beating, I did not attempt to prevent him, nor did I even ask him for the reason of his action. Everything in the room appeared to be reeling slowly round in a drowsy dance, of which I was the centre. The great elk's head at the far end wagged solemnly backward and forward, while the massive salvers on the tables performed *cotillons* with the claret cooler and the epergne. My head fell upon my breast from sheer heaviness, and I should have become unconscious had I not been recalled to myself by the opening of the door at the other end of the hall.

This door led on to the raised dais, which, as I have mentioned, the heads of the house used to reserve for their own use. As it swung slowly back upon its hinges, I sat up in my chair, clutching at the arms, and staring with a horrified glare at the dark passage outside. Something was coming down it—something unformed and intangible, but still a *something*. Dim and shadowy, I saw it flit across the threshold, while a blast of ice-cold air swept down the room, which seemed to blow through me, chilling my very heart. I was aware of the mysterious presence, and then I heard it speak in a voice like the sighing of an east wind among pine-trees on the banks of a desolate sea.

It said: "I am the invisible nonentity. I have affinities and am subtle. I am electric, magnetic, and spiritualistic. I am the great ethereal sigh-heaver. I kill dogs. Mortal, wilt thou choose me?"

I was about to speak, but the words seemed to be choked in my throat; and, before I could get them out, the shadow flitted across the hall and vanished in the darkness at the other side, while a long-drawn melancholy sigh quivered through the apartment.

I turned my eyes toward the door once more, and beheld, to my astonishment, a very small old woman, who hobbled along the corridor and into the hall. She passed backward and forward several times, and then, crouching down at the very edge of the circle upon the floor, she disclosed a face the horrible malignity of which shall never be banished from my recollection. Every foul passion appeared to have left its mark upon that hideous countenance.

"Ha! ha!" she screamed, holding out her wizened hands like the talons of an unclean bird. "You see what I am. I am the fiendish old woman. I wear snuff-coloured silks. My curse descends on people. Sir Walter was partial to me. Shall I be thine, mortal?"

I endeavoured to shake my head in horror; on which she aimed a blow at me with her crutch, and vanished with an eldritch scream.

By this time my eyes turned naturally toward the open door, and I was hardly surprised to see a man walk in of tall and noble stature. His face was deadly pale, but was surmounted by a fringe of dark hair which fell in ringlets down his back. A short pointed beard covered his chin. He was dressed in loose-fitting clothes, made apparently of yellow satin, and a large white ruff surrounded his neck. He paced across the room with slow and majestic strides. Then turning, he addressed me in a sweet, exquisitely-modulated voice.

"I am the cavalier," he remarked. "I pierce and am pierced. Here is my rapier. I clink steel. This is a bloodstain over my heart. I can emit hollow groans. I am patronized by many old Conservative families. I am the original manor-house apparition. I work alone, or in company with shrieking damsels."

He bent his head courteously, as though awaiting my reply, but the same choking sensation prevented me from speaking; and, with a deep bow, he disappeared.

He had hardly gone before a feeling of intense horror stole over me, and I was aware of the presence of a ghastly creature in the room of dim outlines and uncertain proportions. One moment it seemed to pervade the entire apartment, while at another it would become invisible, but always leaving behind it a distinct consciousness of its presence. Its voice, when it spoke, was quavering and gusty. It said, "I am the leaver of footsteps and the spiller of gouts of blood. I tramp upon corridors. Charles Dickens has alluded to me. I make strange and disagreeable noises. I snatch letters and place invisible hands on people's wrists. I am cheerful. I burst into peals of hideous laughter. Shall I do one now?" I raised my hand in a deprecating way, but too late to prevent one discordant outbreak which echoed through the room. Before I could lower it the apparition was gone.

I turned my head toward the door in time to see a man come hastily and stealthily into the chamber. He was a sunburned powerfully-built fellow, with earrings in his ears and a Barcelona handkerchief tied loosely round his neck. His head was bent upon his chest, and his whole aspect was that of one afflicted by intolerable remorse. He paced rapidly backward and forward like a caged tiger, and I observed that a drawn knife glittered in one of his hands, while he grasped what appeared to be a piece of parchment in the other. His voice, when he spoke, was deep and sonorous. He said, "I am a murderer. I am a ruffian. I crouch when I walk. I step noiselessly. I know something of the Spanish Main. I can do the lost treasure business. I have charts. Am able-bodied and a good walker. Capable of haunting a large park." He looked toward me beseechingly, but before I could make a sign I was paralyzed by the horrible sight which appeared at the door.

It was a very tall man, if, indeed, it might be called a man, for the gaunt bones were protruding through the corroding flesh, and the features of a leaden hue. A winding sheet was wrapped round the figure, and formed a hood over the head, from under the shadow of which two fiendish eyes, deep-set in their grisly sockets, blazed and sparkled like red-hot coals. The lower jaw had fallen upon the breast, disclosing a withered, shrivelled tongue and two lines of black and jagged fangs. I shuddered and drew back as this fearful apparition advanced to the edge of the circle.

"I am the American blood-curdler," it said, in a voice which seemed to come in a hollow murmur from the earth beneath it. "None other is genuine. I am the embodiment of Edgar Allan Poe. I am circumstantial and horrible. I am a low-caste spirit-subduing spectre. Observe my blood and my bones. I am grisly and nauseous. No depending on artificial aid. Work with grave-clothes, a coffin-lid, and a galvanic battery. Turn hair white in a night." The creature stretched out its fleshless arms to me as if in entreaty, but I shook my head; and it vanished, leaving a low sickening repulsive odour behind it. I sank back in my chair, so overcome by terror and disgust that I would have very willingly resigned myself to dispensing with a ghost altogether, could I have been sure that this was the last of the hideous procession.

A faint sound of trailing garments warned me that it was not so. I looked up, and beheld a white figure emerging from the corridor into the right. As it stepped across the threshold I saw that it was that of a young and beautiful woman dressed in the fashion of a bygone day. Her hands were clasped in front of her, and her pale proud face bore traces of passion and of suffering. She crossed the hall with a gentle sound, like the rustling of autumn leaves, and then, turning her lovely and unutterably sad eyes upon me, she said,

"I am the plaintive and sentimental, the beautiful and ill-used. I have been forsaken and betrayed. I shriek in the night-time and glide down passages. My antecedents are highly respectable and generally aristocratic. My tastes are æsthetic. Old oak furniture like this would do, with a few more coats of mail and plenty of tapestry. Will you not take me?"

Her voice died away in a beautiful cadence as she concluded, and she held out her hands as in supplication. I am always sensitive to female influences. Besides, what would Jorrocks' ghost be to this? Could anything be in better taste? Would I not be exposing myself to the chance of injuring my nervous system by interviews with such creatures as my last visitor, unless I decided at once? She gave me a seraphic smile, as if she knew what was passing in my mind. That smile settled the matter. "She will do!" I cried; "I choose this one;" and as, in my enthusiasm, I took a step toward her, I passed over the magic circle which had girdled me round.

"Argentine, we have been robbed!"

I had an indistinct consciousness of these words being spoken, or rather screamed, in my ear a great number of times without my being able to grasp their meaning. A violent throbbing in my head seemed to adapt itself to their rhythm, and I closed my eyes to the lullaby of "Robbed, robbed, robbed." A vigorous shake caused me to open them again, however, and the sight of Mrs. D'Odd in the scantiest of costumes and most furious of tempers was sufficiently impressive to recall all my scattered thoughts, and make me realize that I was lying on my back on the floor, with my head among the ashes which had fallen from last night's fire, and a small glass phial in my hand.

I staggered to my feet, but felt so weak and giddy that I was compelled to fall back into a chair. As my brain became clearer, stimulated by the exclamations of Matilda, I began gradually to recollect the events of the night. There was the door through which my supernatural visitors had filed. There was the circle of chalk with the hieroglyphics round the edge. There was the cigar-box and brandy bottle which had been honoured by the attentions of Mr. Abrahams. But the seer himself—where was he? and what was this open window with a rope running out of it? And where, O where, was the pride of Goresthorpe Grange, the glorious plate which was to have been the delectation of generations of D'Odds? And why was Mrs. D. standing in the gray light of dawn, wringing her hands and repeating her monotonous refrain? It was only very gradually that my misty brain took these things in, and grasped the connection between them.

Reader, I have never seen Mr. Abrahams since; I have never seen the plate stamped with the resuscitated family crest; hardest of all, I have never caught a glimpse of the melancholy spectre with the trailing garments, nor do I expect that I ever shall. In fact my night's experiences have cured me of my mania for the supernatural, and quite reconciled me to inhabiting the humdrum nineteenth century edifice on the outskirts of London which Mrs. D. has long had in her mind's eye.

As to the explanation of all that occurred—that is a matter which is open to several surmises. That Mr. Abrahams, the ghost-hunter, was identical with Jemmy Wilson, *alias* the Nottingham crackster, is considered more than probable at Scotland Yard, and certainly the description of that remarkable burglar tallied very well with the appearance of my visitor. The small bag which I have described was picked up in a neighbouring field next day, and found to contain a choice assortment of jimmies and centrebits. Footmarks deeply imprinted in the mud on either side of the moat showed that an accomplice from below had received the sack of precious metals which had been let down through the open window. No doubt the pair of scoundrels, while looking round for a job, had overheard Jack Brocket's indiscreet inquiries, and had promptly availed themselves of the tempting opening.

And now as to my less substantial visitors, and the curious grotesque vision which I had enjoyed—am I to lay it down to any real power over occult matters possessed by my Nottingham friend? For a long time I was doubtful upon the point, and eventually endeavoured to solve it by consulting a well-known analyst and medical man, sending him the few drops of the so-called essence of Lucoptolycus which remained in my phial. I append the letter which I received from him, only too happy to have the opportunity of winding up my little narrative by the weighty words of a man of learning.

Arundel Street.

Dear Sir,—Your very singular case has interested me extremely. The bottle which you sent contained a strong solution of chloral, and the quantity which you describe yourself as having swallowed must have amounted to at least eighty grains of the pure hydrate. This would of course have reduced you to a partial state of insensibility, gradually going on to complete coma. In this semi-unconscious state of chloralism it is not unusual for circumstantial and *bizarre* visions to present themselves— more especially to individuals unaccustomed to the use of the drug. You tell me in your note that your mind was saturated with ghostly literature, and that you had long taken a morbid interest in classifying and recalling the various forms in which apparitions have been said to appear. You must also remember

385

that you were expecting to see something of that very nature, and that your nervous system was worked up to an unnatural state of tension. Under the circumstances, I think that, far from the sequel being an astonishing one, it would have been very surprising indeed to anyone versed in narcotics had you not experienced some such effects.—I remain, dear sir, sincerely yours,

T. E. Stube, M.D.

Argentine D'Odd, Esq.,
The Elms, Brixton."

The Sin-Eater

By Fiona Macleod

Sin.
Taste this bread, this substance: tell me
Is it bread or flesh?
[The Senses approach.]
The Smell.
Its smell
Is the smell of bread.
Sin.
Touch, come. Why tremble?
Say what's this thou touchest?
The Touch.
Bread.
Sin.
Sight, declare what thou discernest
In this object.
The Sight.
Bread alone.
   —Calderon,
Los Encantos de la Culpa

A wet wind out of the south mazed and mooned through the sea-mist that hung over the Ross. In all the bays and creeks was a continuous weary lapping of water. There was no other sound anywhere.

Thus was it at daybreak; it was thus at noon; thus was it now in the darkening of the day. A confused thrusting and falling of sounds through the silence betokened the hour of the setting. Curlews wailed in the mist; on the seething limpet-covered rocks the *skuas* and terns screamed, or uttered hoarse, rasping cries. Ever and again the prolonged note of the oyster-catcher shrilled against the air, as an echo

387

flying blindly along a blank wall of cliff. Out of weedy places, wherein the tide sobbed with long, gurgling moans, came at intervals the barking of a seal.

Inland, by the hamlet of Contullich, there is a reedy tarn called the Loch-a-chaoruinn.[1] By the shores of this mournful water a man moved. It was a slow, weary walk that of the man Neil Ross. He had come from Duninch, thirty miles to the eastward, and had not rested foot, nor eaten, nor had word of man or woman, since his going west an hour after dawn.

At the bend of the loch nearest the clachan he came upon an old woman carrying peat. To his reiterated question as to where he was, and if the tarn were Feur-Lochan above Fionnaphort that is on the strait of Iona on the west side of the Ross of Mull, she did not at first make any answer. The rain trickled down her withered brown face, over which the thin gray locks hung limply. It was only in the deep-set eyes that the flame of life still glimmered, though that dimly.

The man had used the English when first he spoke, but as though mechanically. Supposing that he had not been understood, he repeated his question in the Gaelic.

After a minute's silence the old woman answered him in the native tongue, but only to put a question in return.

"I am thinking it is a long time since you have been in Iona?"

The man stirred uneasily.

"And why is that, mother?" he asked, in a weak voice hoarse with damp and fatigue; "how is it you will be knowing that I have been in Iona at all?"

"Because I knew your kith and kin there, Neil Ross."

"I have not been hearing that name, mother, for many a long year. And as for the old face o' you, it is unbeknown to me."

"I was at the naming of you, for all that. Well do I remember the day that Silis Macallum gave you birth; and I was at the house on the croft of Ballyrona when Murtagh Ross—that was your father— laughed. It was an ill laughing that."

"I am knowing it. The curse of God on him!"

"'Tis not the first, nor the last, though the grass is on his head three years agone now."

"You that know who I am will be knowing that I have no kith or kin now on Iona?"

---

1. Contullich: *i.e.* Ceann-nan-tulaich, "the end of the hillocks." Loch a chaoruinn means the loch of the rowan-trees.

"Ay; they are all under gray stone or running wave. Donald your brother, and Murtagh your next brother, and little Silis, and your mother Silis herself, and your two brothers of your father, Angus and Ian Macallum, and your father Murtagh Ross, and his lawful childless wife, Dionaid, and his sister Anna—one and all, they lie beneath the green wave or in the brown mould. It is said there is a curse upon all who live at Ballyrona. The owl builds now in the rafters, and it is the big sea-rat that runs across the fireless hearth."

"It is there I am going."

"The foolishness is on you, Neil Ross."

"Now it is that I am knowing who you are. It is old Sheen Macarthur I am speaking to."

"Tha mise . . . it is I."

"And you will be alone now, too, I am thinking, Sheen?"

"I am alone. God took my three boys at the one fishing ten years ago; and before there was moonrise in the blackness of my heart my man went. It was after the drowning of Anndra that my croft was taken from me. Then I crossed the Sound, and shared with my widow sister Elsie McVurie till *she* went; and then the two cows had to go; and I had no rent, and was old."

In the silence that followed, the rain dribbled from the sodden bracken and dripping loneroid. Big tears rolled slowly down the deep lines on the face of Sheen. Once there was a sob in her throat, but she put her shaking hand to it, and it was still.

Neil Ross shifted from foot to foot. The ooze in that marshy place squelched with each restless movement he made. Beyond them a plover wheeled, a blurred splatch in the mist, crying its mournful cry over and over and over.

It was a pitiful thing to hear—ah, bitter loneliness, bitter patience of poor old women. That he knew well. But he was too weary, and his heart was nigh full of its own burthen. The words could not come to his lips. But at last he spoke.

"*Tha mo chridhe goirt*," he said, with tears in his voice, as he put his hand on her bent shoulder; "my heart is sore."

She put up her old face against his.

"'*S tha e ruidhinn mo chridhe*," she whispered; "it is touching my heart you are."

After that they walked on slowly through the dripping mist, each dumb and brooding deep.

"Where will you be staying this night?" asked Sheen suddenly, when they had traversed a wide boggy stretch of land; adding, as by an afterthought—"Ah, it is asking you were if the tarn there were Feur-Lochan. No; it is Loch-a-chaoruinn, and the clachan that is near is Contullich."

"Which way?"

"Yonder, to the right."

"And you are not going there?"

"No. I am going to the steading of Andrew Blair. Maybe you are for knowing it? It is called the Baile-na-Chlais-nambuidheag."[2]

"I do not remember. But it is remembering a Blair I am. He was Adam, the son of Adam, the son of Robert. He and my father did many an ill deed together."

"Ay, to the stones be it said. Sure, now, there was, even till this weary day, no man or woman who had a good word for Adam Blair."

"And why that ... why till this day?"

"It is not yet the third hour since he went into the silence."

Neil Ross uttered a sound like a stifled curse. For a time he trudged wearily on.

"Then I am too late," he said at last, but as though speaking to himself. "I had hoped to see him face to face again, and curse him between the eyes. It was he who made Murtagh Ross break his troth to my mother, and marry that other woman, barren at that, God be praised! And they say ill of him, do they?"

"Ay, it is evil that is upon him. This crime and that, God knows; and the shadow of murder on his brow and in his eyes. Well, well, 'tis ill to be speaking of a man in corpse, and that nearby. 'Tis Himself only that knows, Neil Ross."

"Maybe ay and maybe no. But where is it that I can be sleeping this night, Sheen Macarthur?"

"They will not be taking a stranger at the farm this night of the nights, I am thinking. There is no place else for seven miles yet, when there is the clachan, before you will be coming to Fionnaphort. There is the warm byre, Neil, my man; or, if you can bide by my peats, you may rest, and welcome, though there is no bed for you, and no food either save some of the porridge that is over."

"And that will do well enough for me, Sheen; and Himself bless you for it."

And so it was.

★★★★★★

---

2. "The farm in the hollow of the yellow flowers."

After old Sheen Macarthur had given the wayfarer food—poor food at that, but welcome to one nigh starved, and for the heartsome way it was given, and because of the thanks to God that was upon it before even spoon was lifted—she told him a lie. It was the good lie of tender love.

"Sure now, after all, Neil, my man," she said, "it is sleeping at the farm I ought to be, for Maisie Macdonald, the wise woman, will be sitting by the corpse, and there will be none to keep her company. It is there I must be going; and if I am weary, there is a good bed for me just beyond the dead-board, which I am not minding at all. So, if it is tired you are sitting by the peats, lie down on my bed there, and have the sleep; and God be with you."

With that she went, and soundlessly, for Neil Ross was already asleep, where he sat on an upturned claar, with his elbows on his knees, and his flame-lit face in his hands.

The rain had ceased; but the mist still hung over the land, though in thin veils now, and these slowly drifting seaward. Sheen stepped wearily along the stony path that led from her bothy to the farm-house. She stood still once, the fear upon her, for she saw three or four blurred yellow gleams moving beyond her, eastward, along the dyke. She knew what they were—the corpse-lights that on the night of death go between the bier and the place of burial. More than once she had seen them before the last hour, and by that token had known the end to be near.

Good Catholic that she was, she crossed herself, and took heart. Then muttering:

Crois nan naoi aingeal leam
'O mhullach mo chin
Gu craican mo bhonn."
(The cross of the nine angels be about me,
From the top of my head
To the soles of my feet),

. . . . she went on her way fearlessly.

When she came to the White House, she entered by the milk-shed that was between the byre and the kitchen. At the end of it was a paved place, with washing-tubs. At one of these stood a girl that served in the house—an ignorant lass called Jessie McFall, out of Oban. She was ignorant, indeed, not to know that to wash clothes with a newly dead body nearby was an ill thing to do. Was it not a matter for the

391

knowing that the corpse could hear, and might rise up in the night and clothe itself in a clean white shroud?

She was still speaking to the lassie when Maisie Macdonald, the deid-watcher, opened the door of the room behind the kitchen to see who it was that was come. The two old women nodded silently. It was not till Sheen was in the closed room, midway in which something covered with a sheet lay on a board, that any word was spoken.

"*Duit sìth mòr*, Beann Macdonald."

"And deep peace to you, too, Sheen; and to him that is there."

"*Och, ochone, mise 'n diugh*; 'tis a dark hour this."

"Ay; it is bad. Will you have been hearing or seeing anything?"

"Well, as for that, I am thinking I saw lights moving betwixt here and the green place over there."

"The corpse-lights?"

"Well, it is calling them that they are."

"I *thought* they would be out. And I have been hearing the noise of the planks—the cracking of the boards, you know, that will be used for the coffin tomorrow."

A long silence followed. The old women had seated themselves by the corpse, their cloaks over their heads. The room was fireless, and was lit only by a tall wax death-candle, kept against the hour of the going.

At last Sheen began swaying slowly to and fro, crooning low the while. "I would not be for doing that, Sheen Macarthur," said the deid-watcher in a low voice, but meaningly; adding, after a moment's pause, "*The mice have all left the house.*"

Sheen sat upright, a look half of terror, half of awe in her eyes.

"God save the sinful soul that is hiding," she whispered.

Well she knew what Maisie meant. If the soul of the dead be a lost soul it knows its doom. The house of death is the house of sanctuary; but before the dawn that follows the death-night the soul must go forth, whosoever or whatsoever wait for it in the homeless, shelterless plains of air around and beyond. If it be well with the soul, it need have no fear; if it be not ill with the soul, it may fare forth with surety; but if it be ill with the soul, ill will the going be. Thus is it that the spirit of an evil man cannot stay, and yet dare not go; and so it strives to hide itself in secret places anywhere, in dark channels and blind walls; and the wise creatures that live near man smell the terror, and flee. Maisie repeated the saying of Sheen, then, after a silence, added:

"Adam Blair will not lie in his grave for a year and a day because of the sins that are upon him; and it is knowing that, they are here. He will be the Watcher of the Dead for a year and a day."

"Ay, sure, there will be dark prints in the dawn-dew over yonder."

Once more the old women relapsed into silence. Through the night there was a sighing sound. It was not the sea, which was too far off to be heard save in a day of storm. The wind it was, that was dragging itself across the sodden moors like a wounded thing, moaning and sighing.

Out of sheer weariness, Sheen twice rocked forward from her stool, heavy with sleep. At last Maisie led her over to the niche-bed opposite, and laid her down there, and waited till the deep furrows in the face relaxed somewhat, and the thin breath laboured slow across the fallen jaw.

"Poor old woman," she muttered, heedless of her own gray hairs and grayer years; "a bitter, bad thing it is to be old, old and weary. 'Tis the sorrow, that. God keep the pain of it!"

As for herself, she did not sleep at all that night, but sat between the living and the dead, with her plaid shrouding her. Once, when Sheen gave a low, terrified scream in her sleep, she rose, and in a loud voice cried, "*Sheeach-ad! Away with you!*" And with that she lifted the shroud from the dead man, and took the pennies off the eyelids, and lifted each lid; then, staring into these filmed wells, muttered an ancient incantation that would compel the soul of Adam Blair to leave the spirit of Sheen alone, and return to the cold corpse that was its coffin till the wood was ready.

The dawn came at last. Sheen slept, and Adam Blair slept a deeper sleep, and Maisie stared out of her wan, weary eyes against the red and stormy flares of light that came into the sky.

When, an hour after sunrise, Sheen Macarthur reached her bothy, she found Neil Ross, heavy with slumber, upon her bed. The fire was not out, though no flame or spark was visible; but she stooped and blew at the heart of the peats till the redness came, and once it came it grew. Having done this, she kneeled and said a rune of the morning, and after that a prayer, and then a prayer for the poor man Neil. She could pray no more because of the tears. She rose and put the meal and water into the pot for the porridge to be ready against his awaking. One of the hens that was there came and pecked at her ragged skirt. "Poor beastie," she said. "Sure, that will just be the way I am pulling at the white robe of the Mother o' God. 'Tis a bit meal for you, cluckie, and for me a healing hand upon my tears. O, *och, ochone,* the tears, the tears!"

It was not till the third hour after sunrise of that bleak day in that winter of the winters, that Neil Ross stirred and arose. He ate in silence. Once he said that he smelt the snow coming out of the north. Sheen said no word at all.

After the porridge, he took his pipe, but there was no tobacco. All that Sheen had was the pipeful she kept against the gloom of the Sabbath. It was her one solace in the long weary week. She gave him this, and held a burning peat to his mouth, and hungered over the thin, rank smoke that curled upward.

It was within half-an-hour of noon that, after an absence, she returned.

"Not between you and me, Neil Ross," she began abruptly, "but just for the asking, and what is beyond. Is it any money you are having upon you?"

"No."

"Nothing?"

"Nothing."

"Then how will you be getting across to Iona? It is seven long miles to Fionnaphort, and bitter cold at that, and you will be needing food, and then the ferry, the ferry across the Sound, you know."

"Ay, I know."

"What would you do for a silver piece, Neil, my man?"

"You have none to give me, Sheen Macarthur; and, if you had, it would not be taking it I would."

"Would you kiss a dead man for a crown-piece—a crown-piece of five good shillings?"

Neil Ross stared. Then he sprang to his feet.

"It is Adam Blair you are meaning, woman! God curse him in death now that he is no longer in life!"

Then, shaking and trembling, he sat down again, and brooded against the dull red glow of the peats.

But, when he rose, in the last quarter before noon, his face was white.

"The dead are dead, Sheen Macarthur. They can know or do nothing. I will do it. It is willed. Yes, I am going up to the house there. And now I am going from here. God Himself has my thanks to you, and my blessing too. They will come back to you. It is not forgetting you I will be. Goodbye."

"Goodbye, Neil, son of the woman that was my friend. A south wind to you! Go up by the farm. In the front of the house you will see what you will be seeing. Maisie Macdonald will be there. She will tell you what's for the telling. There is no harm in it, sure; sure, the dead are dead. It is praying for you I will be, Neil Ross. Peace to you!"

"And to you, Sheen."

And with that the man went.

★★★★★★

When Neil Ross reached the byres of the farm in the wide hollow, he saw two figures standing as though awaiting him, but separate, and unseen of the other. In front of the house was a man he knew to be Andrew Blair; behind the milk-shed was a woman he guessed to be Maisie Macdonald.

It was the woman he came upon first.

"Are you the friend of Sheen Macarthur?" she asked in a whisper, as she beckoned him to the doorway.

"I am."

"I am knowing no names or anything. And no one here will know you, I am thinking. So do the thing and begone."

"There is no harm to it?"

"None."

"It will be a thing often done, is it not?"

"Ay, sure."

"And the evil does not abide?"

"No. The . . . the . . . person . . . the person takes them away, . . . and. . . ."

"*Them?*"

"For sure, man! Them . . . the sins of the corpse. He takes them away; and are you for thinking God would let the innocent suffer for the guilty? No . . . the person . . . the Sin-Eater, you know . . . takes them away on himself, and one by one the air of heaven washes them away till he, the Sin-Eater, is clean and whole as before."

"But if it is a man you hate . . . if it is a corpse that is the corpse of one who has been a curse and a foe . . . if. . . ."

"*Sst!* Be still now with your foolishness. It is only an idle saying, I am thinking. Do it, and take the money and go. It will be hell enough for Adam Blair, miser as he was, if he is for knowing that five good shillings of his money are to go to a passing tramp because of an old, ancient silly tale."

Neil Ross laughed low at that. It was for pleasure to him.

"Hush wi' ye! Andrew Blair is waiting round there. Say that I have sent you round, as I have neither bite nor bit to give."

Turning on his heel, Neil walked slowly round to the front of the house. A tall man was there, gaunt and brown, with hairless face and lank brown hair, but with eyes cold and gray as the sea.

"Good day to you, an' good faring. Will you be passing this way to anywhere?"

"Health to you. I am a stranger here. It is on my way to Iona I am. But I have the hunger upon me. There is not a brown bit in my pocket. I asked at the door there, near the byres. The woman told me she could give me nothing—not a penny even, worse luck—nor, for that, a drink of warm milk. 'Tis a sore land this."

"You have the Gaelic of the Isles. Is it from Iona you are?"

"It is from the Isles of the West I come."

"From Tiree ... from Coll?"

"No."

"From the Long Island ... or from Uist ... or maybe from Benbecula?"

"No."

"Oh well, sure it is no matter to me. But may I be asking your name?"

"Macallum."

"Do you know there is a death here, Macallum?"

"If I didn't I would know it now, because of what lies yonder."

Mechanically Andrew Blair looked round. As he knew, a rough bier was there, that was made of a dead-board laid upon three milking-stools. Beside it was a *claar*, a small tub to hold potatoes. On the bier was a corpse, covered with a canvas sheeting that looked like a sail.

"He was a worthy man, my father," began the son of the dead man, slowly; "but he had his faults, like all of us. I might even be saying that he had his sins, to the Stones be it said. You will be knowing, Macallum, what is thought among the folk ... that a stranger, passing by, may take away the sins of the dead, and that, too, without any hurt whatever ... any hurt whatever."

"Ay, sure."

"And you will be knowing what is done?"

"Ay."

"With the bread ... and the water. ...?"

"Ay."

"It is a small thing to do. It is a Christian thing. I would be doing it myself, and that gladly, but the ... the ... passer-by who. ..."

"It is talking of the Sin-Eater you are?"

"Yes, yes, for sure. The Sin-Eater as he is called—and a good Christian act it is, for all that the ministers and the priests make a frowning at it—the Sin-Eater must be a stranger. He must be a stranger, and should know nothing of the dead man—above all, bear him no grudge."

At that Neil Ross's eyes lightened for a moment.

"And why that?"

"Who knows? I have heard this, and I have heard that. If the Sin-Eater was hating the dead man he could take the sins and fling them into the sea, and they would be changed into demons of the air that would harry the flying soul till Judgment-Day."

"And how would that thing be done?"

The man spoke with flashing eyes and parted lips, the breath coming swift. Andrew Blair looked at him suspiciously; and hesitated, before, in a cold voice, he spoke again.

"That is all folly, I am thinking, Macallum. Maybe it is all folly, the whole of it. But, see here, I have no time to be talking with you. If you will take the bread and the water you shall have a good meal if you want it, and . . . and . . . yes, look you, my man, I will be giving you a shilling too, for luck."

"I will have no meal in this house, Anndramhic-Adam; nor will I do this thing unless you will be giving me two silver half-crowns. That is the sum I must have, or no other."

"Two half-crowns! Why, man, for one half-crown . . ."

"Then be eating the sins o' your father yourself, Andrew Blair! It is going I am."

"Stop, man! Stop, Macallum. See here—I will be giving you what you ask."

"So be it. Is the . . . Are you ready?"

"Ay, come this way."

With that the two men turned and moved slowly towards the bier.

In the doorway of the house stood a man and two women; farther in, a woman; and at the window to the left, the serving-wench, Jessie McFall, and two men of the farm. Of those in the doorway, the man was Peter, the half-witted youngest brother of Andrew Blair; the taller and older woman was Catreen, the widow of Adam, the second brother; and the thin, slight woman, with staring eyes and drooping mouth, was Muireall, the wife of Andrew. The old woman behind these was Maisie Macdonald.

Andrew Blair stooped and took a saucer out of the *claar*. This he put upon the covered breast of the corpse. He stooped again, and brought forth a thick square piece of new-made bread. That also he placed upon the breast of the corpse. Then he stooped again, and with that he emptied a spoonful of salt alongside the bread.

"I must see the corpse," said Neil Ross simply.

"It is not needful, Macallum."

"I must be seeing the corpse, I tell you—and for that, too, the bread and the water should be on the naked breast."

"No, no, man; it . . ."

But here a voice, that of Maisie the wise woman, came upon them, saying that the man was right, and that the eating of the sins should be done in that way and no other.

With an ill grace the son of the dead man drew back the sheeting. Beneath it, the corpse was in a clean white shirt, a death-gown long ago prepared, that covered him from his neck to his feet, and left only the dusky yellowish face exposed.

While Andrew Blair unfastened the shirt and placed the saucer and the bread and the salt on the breast, the man beside him stood staring fixedly on the frozen features of the corpse. The new laird had to speak to him twice before he heard.

"I am ready. And you, now? What is it you are muttering over against the lips of the dead?"

"It is giving him a message I am. There is no harm in that, sure?"

"Keep to your own folk, Macallum. You are from the West you say, and we are from the North. There can be no messages between you and a Blair of Strathmore, no messages for *you* to be giving."

"He that lies here knows well the man to whom I am sending a message"—and at this response Andrew Blair scowled darkly. He would fain have sent the man about his business, but he feared he might get no other.

"It is thinking I am that you are not a Macallum at all. I know all of that name in Mull, Iona, Skye, and the near isles. What will the name of your naming be, and of your father, and of his place?"

Whether he really wanted an answer, or whether he sought only to divert the man from his procrastination, his question had a satisfactory result.

"Well, now, it's ready I am, Anndra-mhic-Adam."

With that, Andrew Blair stooped once more and from the *claar* brought a small jug of water. From this he filled the saucer.

"You know what to say and what to do, Macallum."

There was not one there who did not have a shortened breath because of the mystery that was now before them, and the fearfulness of it. Neil Ross drew himself up, erect, stiff, with white, drawn face. All who waited, save Andrew Blair, thought that the moving of his lips was because of the prayer that was slipping upon them, like the last lapsing of the ebb-tide. But Blair was watching him closely, and knew that it was no prayer which stole out against the blank air that was around the dead.

Slowly Neil Ross extended his right arm. He took a pinch of the salt and put it in the saucer, then took another pinch and sprinkled it upon the bread. His hand shook for a moment as he touched the saucer. But there was no shaking as he raised it towards his lips, or when he held it before him when he spoke.

"With this water that has salt in it, and has lain on thy corpse, O Adam mhic Anndra mhic Adam Mòr, I drink away all the evil that is upon thee . . ."

There was throbbing silence while he paused.

". . . And may it be upon me and not upon thee, if with this water it cannot flow away."

Thereupon, he raised the saucer and passed it thrice round the head of the corpse sunways; and, having done this, lifted it to his lips and drank as much as his mouth would hold. Thereafter he poured the remnant over his left hand, and let it trickle to the ground. Then he took the piece of bread. Thrice, too, he passed it round the head of the corpse sunways.

He turned and looked at the man by his side, then at the others, who watched him with beating hearts.

With a loud clear voice he took the sins.

"*Thoir dhomh do ciontachd, O Adam mhic Anndra mhic Adam Mòr!* Give me thy sins to take away from thee! Lo, now, as I stand here, I break this bread that has lain on thee in corpse, and I am eating it, I am, and in that eating I take upon me the sins of thee, O man that was alive and is now white with the stillness!"

Thereupon Neil Ross broke the bread and ate of it, and took upon himself the sins of Adam Blair that was dead. It was a bitter swallowing, that. The remainder of the bread he crumbled in his hand, and threw it on the ground, and trod upon it. Andrew Blair gave a sigh of relief. His cold eyes lightened with malice.

"Be off with you, now, Macallum. We are wanting no tramps at the farm here, and perhaps you had better not be trying to get work this side Iona; for it is known as the Sin-Eater you will be, and that won't be for the helping, I am thinking! There—there are the two half-crowns for you .. and may they bring you no harm, you that are *Scapegoat* now!"

The Sin-Eater turned at that, and stared like a hill-bull. *Scapegoat!* Ay, that's what he was. Sin-Eater, Scapegoat! Was he not, too, another Judas, to have sold for silver that which was not for the selling? No, no, for sure Maisie Macdonald could tell him the rune that would serve for the easing of this burden. He would soon be quit of it.

Slowly he took the money, turned it over, and put it in his pocket.

"I am going, Andrew Blair," he said quietly, "I am going now. I will not say to him that is there in the silence, *A chuid do Pharas da!*— nor will I say to you, *Gu'n gleidheadh Dia thu,*—nor will I say to this dwelling that is the home of thee and thine, *Gu'n beannaic-headh Dia an tigh!*"[3]

Here there was a pause. All listened. Andrew Blair shifted uneasily, the furtive eyes of him going this way and that, like a ferret in the grass.

"But, Andrew Blair, I will say this: when you fare abroad, *Droch caoidh ort!* and when you go upon the water, *Gaoth gun direadh ort!* Ay, ay, Anndra-mhic-Adam, *Dia ad aghaidh 's ad aodann . . . agus bas dunach ort! Dhonas 's dholas ort, agus leat-sa!*"[4]

The bitterness of these words was like snow in June upon all there. They stood amazed. None spoke. No one moved.

Neil Ross turned upon his heel, and, with a bright light in his eyes, walked away from the dead and the living. He went by the byres, whence he had come. Andrew Blair remained where he was, now glooming at the corpse, now biting his nails and staring at the damp sods at his feet.

When Neil reached the end of the milk-shed he saw Maisie Macdonald there, waiting.

"These were ill sayings of yours, Neil Ross," she said in a low voice,

3. *A chuid do Pharas da!* "His share of heaven be his." *Gu'n gleidheadh Dia thu,* "May God preserve you." *Gu'n beannaic-headh Dia an tigh!* "God's blessing on this house."
4. *Droch caoidh ort!* "May a fatal accident happen to you" (*lit.* "bad moan on you"). *Gaoth gun direadh ort!* "May you drift to your drowning" (*lit.* "wind without direction on you"). *Dia ad aghaidh, etc.,* "God against thee and in thy face . . . and may a death of woe be yours. . . . Evil and sorrow to thee and thine!"

so that she might not be overheard from the house.

"So, it is knowing me you are."

"Sheen Macarthur told me."

"I have good cause."

"That is a true word. I know it."

"Tell me this thing. What is the rune that is said for the throwing into the sea of the sins of the dead? See here, Maisie Macdonald. There is no money of that man that I would carry a mile with me. Here it is. It is yours, if you will tell me that rune."

Maisie took the money hesitatingly. Then, stooping, she said slowly the few lines of the old, old rune.

"Will you be remembering that?"

"It is not forgetting it I will be, Maisie."

"Wait a moment. There is some warm milk here."

With that she went, and then, from within, beckoned to him to enter.

"There is no one here, Neil Ross. Drink the milk."

He drank; and while he did so she drew a leather pouch from some hidden place in her dress.

"And now I have this to give you."

She counted out ten pennies and two farthings.

"It is all the coppers I have. You are welcome to them. Take them, friend of my friend. They will give you the food you need, and the ferry across the Sound."

"I will do that, Maisie Macdonald, and thanks to you. It is not forgetting it I will be, nor you, good woman. And now, tell me, is it safe that I am? He called me a 'scapegoat', he, Andrew Blair! Can evil touch me between this and the sea?"

"You must go to the place where the evil was done to you and yours—and that, I know, is on the west side of Iona. Go, and God preserve you. But here, too, is a *sian* that will be for the safety."

Thereupon, with swift mutterings she said this charm: an old, familiar Sian against Sudden Harm:

Sian a chuir Moire air Mac ort,
Sian ro' marbhadh, sian ro' lot ort,
Sian eadar a' chlioch 's a' ghlun,
Sian nan Tri ann an aon ort,
O mhullach do chinn gu bonn do chois ort:
Sian seachd eadar a h-aon ort,

Sian seachd eadar a dha ort,
Sian seachd eadar a tri ort,
Sian seachd eadar a ceithir ort,
Sian seachd eadar a coig ort,
Sian seachd eadar a sia ort,
Sian seachd paidir nan seach paidir dol deiseil ri diugh narach ort,
ga do ghleidheadh bho bheud 's bho mhi-thapadh!

Scarcely had she finished before she heard heavy steps approaching.

"Away with you," she whispered, repeating in a loud, angry tone, "Away with you! *Seachad! Seachad!*"

And with that Neil Ross slipped from the milk-shed and crossed the yard, and was behind the byres before Andrew Blair, with sullen mien and swift, wild eyes, strode from the house.

It was with a grim smile on his face that Neil tramped down the wet heather till he reached the high road, and fared thence as through a marsh because of the rains there had been.

For the first mile he thought of the angry mind of the dead man, bitter at paying of the silver. For the second mile he thought of the evil that had been wrought for him and his. For the third mile he pondered over all that he had heard and done and taken upon him that day.

Then he sat down upon a broken granite heap by the way, and brooded deep till one hour went, and then another, and the third was upon him.

A man driving two calves came towards him out of the west. He did not hear or see. The man stopped; spoke again. Neil gave no answer. The drover shrugged his shoulders, hesitated, and walked slowly on, often looking back.

An hour later a shepherd came by the way he himself had tramped. He was a tall, gaunt man with a squint. The small, pale-blue eyes glittered out of a mass of red hair that almost covered his face. He stood still, opposite Neil, and leaned on his *cromak*.

"*Latha math leat,*" he said at last; "I wish you good day."

Neil glanced at him, but did not speak.

"What is your name, for I seem to know you?"

But Neil had already forgotten him. The shepherd took out his snuff-mull, helped himself, and handed the mull to the lonely wayfarer. Neil mechanically helped himself.

"*Am bheil thu 'dol do Fhionphort?*" tried the shepherd again: "Are you going to Fionnaphort?"

"*Tha mise 'dol a dh' I-challum-chille*," Neil answered, in a low, weary voice, and as a man adream: "I am on my way to Iona."

"I am thinking I know now who you are. You are the man Macallum."

Neil looked, but did not speak. His eyes dreamed against what the other could not see or know. The shepherd called angrily to his dogs to keep the sheep from straying; then, with a resentful air, turned to his victim.

"You are a silent man for sure, you are. I'm hoping it is not the curse upon you already."

"What curse?"

"Ah, *that* has brought the wind against the mist! I was thinking so!"

"What curse?"

"You are the man that was the Sin-Eater over there?"

"Ay."

"The man Macallum?"

"Ay."

"Strange it is, but three days ago I saw you in Tobermory, and heard you give your name as Neil Ross to an Iona man that was there."

"Well?"

"Oh, sure, it is nothing to me. But they say the Sin-Eater should not be a man with a hidden lump in his pack."[5]

"Why?"

"For the dead know, and are content. There is no shaking off any sins, then—for that man."

"It is a lie."

"Maybe ay and maybe no."

"Well, have you more to be saying to me? I am obliged to you for your company, but it is not needing it I am, though no offense."

"Och, man, there's no offense between you and me. Sure, there's Iona in me, too; for the father of my father married a woman that was the granddaughter of Tomais Macdonald, who was a fisherman there. No, no; it is rather warning you I would be."

"And for what?"

"Well, well, just because of that laugh I heard about."

"What laugh?"

---

5. *i.e.* With a criminal secret, or an undiscovered crime.

"The laugh of Adam Blair that is dead."

Neil Ross stared, his eyes large and wild. He leaned a little forward. No word came from him. The look that was on his face was the question.

"Yes, it was this way. Sure, the telling of it is just as I heard it. After you ate the sins of Adam Blair, the people there brought out the coffin. When they were putting him into it, he was as stiff as a sheep dead in the snow—and just like that, too, with his eyes wide open. Well, someone saw you trampling the heather down the slope that is in front of the house, and said, 'It is the Sin-Eater!' With that, Andrew Blair sneered, and said—'Ay, 'tis the scapegoat he is!' Then, after a while, he went on, 'The Sin-Eater they call him; ay, just so; and a bitter good bargain it is, too, if all's true that's thought true!' And with that he laughed, and then his wife that was behind him laughed, and then. . . ."

"Well, what then?"

"Well, 'tis Himself that hears and knows if it is true! But this is the thing I was told: After that laughing there was a stillness and a dread. For all there saw that the corpse had turned its head and was looking after you as you went down the heather. Then, Neil Ross, if that be your true name, Adam Blair that was dead put up his white face against the sky, and laughed."

At this, Ross sprang to his feet with a gasping sob.

"It is a lie, that thing!" he cried, shaking his fist at the shepherd. "It is a lie."

"It is no lie. And by the same token, Andrew Blair shrank back white and shaking, and his woman had the swoon upon her, and who knows but the corpse might have come to life again had it not been for Maisie Macdonald, the deid-watcher, who clapped a handful of salt on his eyes, and tilted the coffin so that the bottom of it slid forward, and so let the whole fall flat on the ground, with Adam Blair in it sideways, and as likely as not cursing and groaning, as his wont was, for the hurt both to his old bones and his old ancient dignity."

Ross glared at the man as though the madness was upon him. Fear and horror and fierce rage swung him now this way and now that.

"What will the name of you be, shepherd?" he stuttered huskily.

"It is Eachainn Gilleasbuig I am to ourselves; and the English of that for those who have no Gaelic is Hector Gillespie; and I am Eachainn mac Ian mac Alasdair of Strathsheean that is where Sutherland lies against Ross."

"Then take this thing—and that is, the curse of the Sin-Eater! And a bitter bad thing may it be upon you and yours."

And with that Neil the Sin-Eater flung his hand up into the air, and then leaped past the shepherd, and a minute later was running through the frightened sheep, with his head low, and a white foam on his lips, and his eyes red with blood as a seal's that has the death-wound on it.

★★★★★★

On the third day of the seventh month from that day, Aulay Mac-neill, coming into Balliemore of Iona from the west side of the island, said to old Ronald MacCormick, that was the father of his wife, that he had seen Neil Ross again, and that he was "absent"—for though he had spoken to him, Neil would not answer, but only gloomed at him from the wet weedy rock where he sat.

The going back of the man had loosed every tongue that was in Iona. When, too, it was known that he was wrought in some terrible way, if not actually mad, the islanders whispered that it was because of the sins of Adam Blair. Seldom or never now did they speak of him by his name, but simply as "The Sin-Eater." The thing was not so rare as to cause this strangeness, nor did many (and perhaps none did) think that the sins of the dead ever might or could abide with the living who had merely done a good Christian charitable thing. But there was a reason.

Not long after Neil Ross had come again to Iona, and had settled down in the ruined roofless house on the croft of Ballyrona, just like a fox or a wild-cat, as the saying was, he was given fishing-work to do by Aulay Macneill, who lived at Ard-an-teine, at the rocky north end of the *machar* or plain that is on the west Atlantic coast of the island.

One moonlit night, either the seventh or the ninth after the earth-ing of Adam Blair at his own place in the Ross, Aulay Macneill saw Neil Ross steal out of the shadow of Ballyrona and make for the sea. Macneill was there by the rocks, mending a lobster-creel. He had gone there because of the sadness. Well, when he saw the Sin-Eater, he watched.

Neil crept from rock to rock till he reached the last fang that churns the sea into yeast when the tide sucks the land just opposite.

Then he called out something that Aulay Macneill could not catch. With that he springs up, and throws his arms above him.

"Then," says Aulay when he tells the tale, "it was like a ghost he was. The moonshine was on his face like the curl o' a wave. White!

405

there is no whiteness like that of the human face. It was whiter than the foam about the skerry it was; whiter than the moon shining; whiter than ... well, as white as the painted letters on the black boards of the fishing-cobles. There he stood, for all that the sea was about him, the slip-slop waves leapin' wild, and the tide making, too, at that. He was shaking like a sail two points off the wind. It was then that, all of a sudden, he called in a womany, screamin' voice—

"'I am throwing the sins of Adam Blair into the midst of ye, white dogs o' the sea! Drown them, tear them, drag them away out into the black deeps! Ay, ay, ay, ye dancin' wild waves, this is the third time I am doing it, and now there is none left; no, not a sin, not a sin!

> "'O-hi O-ri, dark tide o' the sea,
> I am giving the sins of a dead man to thee!
> By the Stones, by the Wind, by the Fire, by the Tree,
> From the dead man's sins set me free, set me free!
> Adam mhic Anndra mhic Adam and me,
> Set us free! Set us free!'

"Ay, sure, the Sin-Eater sang that over and over; and after the third singing he swung his arms and screamed:

> "'And listen to me, black waters an' running tide,
> That rune is the good rune told me by Maisie the wise,
> And I am Neil the son of Silis Macallum
> By the black-hearted evil man Murtagh Ross,
> That was the friend of Adam mac Anndra, God against him!'

"And with that he scrambled and fell into the sea. But, as I am Aulay mac Luais and no other, he was up in a moment, an' swimmin' like a seal, and then over the rocks again, an' away back to that lonely roofless place once more, laughing wild at times, an' muttering an' whispering."

It was this tale of Aulay Macneill's that stood between Neil Ross and the isle-folk. There was something behind all that, they whispered one to another.

So it was always the Sin-Eater he was called at last. None sought him. The few children who came upon him now and again fled at his approach, or at the very sight of him. Only Aulay Macneill saw him at times, and had word of him.

After a month had gone by, all knew that the Sin-Eater was wrought to madness because of this awful thing: the burden of Adam Blair's sins would not go from him! Night and day he could hear them laughing low, it was said.

But it was the quiet madness. He went to and fro like a shadow in the grass, and almost as soundless as that, and as voiceless. More and more the name of him grew as a terror. There were few folk on that wild west coast of Iona, and these few avoided him when the word ran that he had knowledge of strange things, and converse, too, with the secrets of the sea.

One day Aulay Macneill, in his boat, but dumb with amaze and terror for him, saw him at high tide swimming on a long rolling wave right into the hollow of the Spouting Cave. In the memory of man, no one had done this and escaped one of three things: a snatching away into oblivion, a strangled death, or madness. The islanders know that there swims into the cave, at full tide, a Mar-Tarbh, a dreadful creature of the sea that some call a *kelpie*; only it is not a *kelpie*, which is like a woman, but rather is a sea-bull, offspring of the cattle that are never seen. Ill indeed for any sheep or goat, ay, or even dog or child, if any happens to be leaning over the edge of the Spouting Cave when the Mar-tarv roars; for, of a surety, it will fall in and straightway be devoured.

With awe and trembling Aulay listened for the screaming of the doomed man. It was full tide, and the sea-beast would be there.

The minutes passed, and no sign. Only the hollow booming of the sea, as it moved like a baffled blind giant round the cavern-bases; only the rush and spray of the water flung up the narrow shaft high into the windy air above the cliff it penetrates.

At last he saw what looked like a mass of seaweed swirled out on the surge. It was the Sin-Eater. With a leap, Aulay was at his oars. The boat swung through the sea. Just before Neil Ross was about to sink for the second time, he caught him and dragged him into the boat.

But then, as ever after, nothing was to be got out of the Sin-Eater save a single saying: *Tha e lamhan fuar! Tha e lamhan fuar!*—"It has a cold, cold hand!"

The telling of this and other tales left none free upon the island to look upon the "scapegoat" save as one accursed.

It was in the third month that a new phase of his madness came upon Neil Ross.

The horror of the sea and the passion for the sea came over him at the same happening. Oftentimes he would race along the shore, screaming wild names to it, now hot with hate and loathing, now as the pleading of a man with the woman of his love. And strange chants to it, too, were upon his lips. Old, old lines of forgotten runes were overheard by Aulay Macneill, and not Aulay only; lines wherein the ancient sea-name of the island, *Ioua*, that was given to it long before it was called Iona, or any other of the nine names that are said to belong to it, occurred again and again.

The flowing tide it was that wrought him thus. At the ebb he would wander across the weedy slabs or among the rocks, silent, and more like a lost duinshee than a man.

Then again after three months a change in his madness came. None knew what it was, though Aulay said that the man moaned and moaned because of the awful burden he bore. No drowning seas for the sins that could not be washed away, no grave for the live sins that would be quick till the day of the Judgment!

For weeks thereafter he disappeared. As to where he was, it is not for the knowing.

Then at last came that third day of the seventh month when, as I have said, Aulay Macneill told old Ronald MacCormick that he had seen the Sin-Eater again.

It was only a half-truth that he told, though. For, after he had seen Neil Ross upon the rock, he had followed him when he rose, and wandered back to the roofless place which he haunted now as of yore. Less wretched a shelter now it was, because of the summer that was come, though a cold, wet summer at that.

"Is that you, Neil Ross?" he had asked, as he peered into the shadows among the ruins of the house.

"That's not my name," said the Sin-Eater; and he seemed as strange then and there, as though he were a castaway from a foreign ship.

"And what will it be, then, you that are my friend, and sure knowing me as Aulay mac Luais—Aulay Macneill that never grudges you bit or sup?"

"*I am Judas.*"

★★★★★★

"And at that word," says Aulay Macneill, when he tells the tale, "at that word the pulse in my heart was like a bat in a shut room. But after a bit I took up the talk.

"'Indeed,' I said; 'and I was not for knowing that. May I be so bold as to ask whose son, and of what place?'

"But all he said to me was, '*I am Judas.*'

"Well, I said, to comfort him, 'Sure, it's not such a bad name in itself, though I am knowing some which have a more home-like sound.'

408

But no, it was no good.

"'I am Judas. And because I sold the Son of God for five pieces of silver. . . .'

"But here I interrupted him and said, 'Sure, now, Neil—I mean, Judas—it was eight times five.' Yet the simpleness of his sorrow prevailed, and I listened with the wet in my eyes.

"'I am Judas. And because I sold the Son of God for five silver shillings, He laid upon me all the nameless black sins of the world. And that is why I am bearing them till the Day of Days.'"

★★★★★★

And this was the end of the Sin-Eater; for I will not tell the long story of Aulay Macneill, that gets longer and longer every winter; but only the unchanging close of it.

I will tell it in the words of Aulay.

★★★★★★

"A bitter, wild day it was, that day I saw him to see him no more. It was late. The sea was red with the flamin' light that burned up the air betwixt Iona and all that is west of West. I was on the shore, looking at the sea. The big green waves came in like the chariots in the Holy Book. Well, it was on the black shoulder of one of them, just short of the ton o' foam that swept above it, that I saw a spar surgin' by.

"'What is that?' I said to myself. And the reason of my wondering was this: I saw that a smaller spar was swung across it. And while I was watching that thing another great billow came in with a roar, and hurled the double spar back, and not so far from me but I might have gripped it. But who would have gripped that thing if he were for seeing what I saw?

"It is Himself knows that what I say is a true thing.

"On that spar was Neil Ross, the Sin-Eater. Naked he was as the day he was born. And he was lashed, too—ay, sure, he was lashed to it by ropes round and round his legs and his waist and his left arm. It was the Cross he was on. I saw that thing with the fear upon me. Ah, poor drifting wreck that he was! *Judas on the Cross!* It was his *eric!*

"But even as I watched, shaking in my limbs, I saw that there was life in him still. The lips were moving, and his right arm was ever for swinging this way and that. 'Twas like an oar, working him off a lee shore; ay, that was what I thought.

"Then, all at once, he caught sight of me. Well he knew me, poor man, that has his share of heaven now, I am thinking!

"He waved, and called, but the hearing could not be, because of a big surge o' water that came tumbling down upon him. In the stroke of an oar he was swept close by the rocks where I was standing. In that flounderin', seethin' whirlpool I saw the white face of him for a moment, an' as he went out on the re-surge like a hauled net, I heard these words fallin' against my ears:

"'*An eirig m'anama*. . . . In ransom for my soul!'

"And with that I saw the double-spar turn over and slide down the back-sweep of a drowning big wave. Ay, sure, it went out to the deep sea swift enough then. It was in the big eddy that rushes between Skerry-Mòr and Skerry-Beag. I did not see it again—no, not for the quarter of an hour, I am thinking. Then I saw just the whirling top of it rising out of the flying yeast of a great, black-blustering wave, that was rushing northward before the current that is called the Black-Eddy.

"With that you have the end of Neil Ross; ay, sure, him that was called the Sin-Eater. And that is a true thing; and may God save us the sorrow of sorrows.

"And that is all."

The Sylph and the Father
By Elsa Barker

Passing yesterday along the line where the great French army stands before its powerful opponent, and marking the spirit of courage and aspiration which makes it seem like a long line of living light, I saw a familiar face in the regions outside the physical.

I paused, highly pleased at the encounter, and the sylph—for it was a sylph whom I met—paused also with a little smile of recognition.

Do you recall in my former book the story of a sylph, Meriline, who was the companion and familiar of a student of magic who lived in the Rue de Vaugirard in Paris?

It was Meriline that I met above the line of light which shows to wanderers in the astral regions where the soldiers of *la belle France* fight and die for the same ideal which inspired Jeanne d'Arc—to drive the foreigner out of France.

"Where is your friend and master?" I asked the sylph, and she pointed below to a trench which spoke loud its determination to conquer.

"I am here, to be still with him," she said.

"And can you speak to him here?" I asked.

"I can always speak with him," she answered. "I have been very useful to him—and to France."

"To France?" I enquired, with growing interest.

"Oh, yes! When his commanding officer wants to know what is being plotted over there, he often asks my friend, and my friend asks me."

"Truly," I thought, "the French are an inspired people, when the officers of armies ask guidance from the realm of the invisible! But had not Jeanne her visions?"

"And how do you gain the information desired?" I asked, drawing nearer to Meriline, who seemed more serious than when we met some years before in Paris.

"Why," she answered, "I go over there and look around me. I have learned what to look for, he has taught me, and when I bring him news he rewards me with more love."

"And do you love him still, as of old?"

"As of old?"

"Yes, as you did back there in Paris."

"Time must have passed slowly with you," said the sylph, "if you call a few years ago 'as of old'."

"Are a few years, then, as nothing?"

"A few years are as nothing to me," she replied. "I have lived a long time."

"And do you know the future of your friend?" I asked.

A puzzled look came over the face of Meriline, and she said, slowly:

"I used to know everything that would happen to him, because I could read his will, and whatever he willed came to pass; but since we have been out here he seems to have lost his will."

"Lost his will!" I exclaimed, in surprise.

"Yes, lost his will; for he prays continually to a great Being whom he loves far more than me, and he always prays one prayer, '*Thy will be done!*' It used to be his will which was always done; but now, as I say, he seems to have lost his will."

"Perhaps," I said, "it is true of the will as was once said of the life, and he that loses his will shall find it."

"I hope he will find it soon," she answered, "for in the old days he was always giving me interesting things to do, to help him achieve the purposes of his will, and now he only sends me over there. I don't like *over there!*"

"Why not?"

"Because my friend is menaced by something over there."

"And what has his will to do with that?"

"Why, even about that, he says all day to the great Being that he loves so much more than me, 'Thy will be done.'"

"Do you think you could learn to say it, too?" I asked.

"I say it after him sometimes; but I don't know what it means."

"Have you never heard of God?"

"I have heard of many gods, of Isis and Osiris and Set, and of Horus, the son of Osiris."

"And is it to one of these that he says, '*Thy will be done*'?"

"Oh, no! It is not to any of the gods that he used to call upon in his magical working. This is some new god that he has found."

"Or the oldest of all gods that he has returned to," I suggested. "What does he call Him?"

"Our Father who art in heaven."

"If you also should learn to say '*Thy will be done*' to our Father who is in heaven," I said, "it might help you toward the attainment of that soul you were wanting and waiting for, when last we met in Paris."

"How could our Father help me?"

"It was He who gave souls to men," I said.

The eyes of the sylph were brilliant with something almost human.

"And could He give a soul to me?"

"It is said that He *can* do anything."

"Then I will ask Him for a soul."

"But to ask Him for a soul," I said, "is not to pray the prayer your friend prays."

"He only says——"

"Yes, I know. Suppose you say it after him."

"I will, if you will tell me what it means. I like to do what my friend does."

"'*Thy will be done*,'" I said, "when addressed to the Father in heaven, means that we give up all our desires, whether for pleasure or love or happiness, or anything else, and lay all those desires at His feet, sacrificing all we have or hope for to Him, because we love Him more than ourselves."

"That is a strange way to get what one desires," she said.

"It is not done to get what one desires," I answered.

"But what is it done for?"

"For love of the Father in heaven."

"But I do not know the Father in heaven. What is He?"

"He is the Source and the Goal of the being of your friend. He is the One that your friend will re-become some day, if he can forever say to Him, Thy will be done."

"The One he will re-become?"

"Yes, for when he blends his will with that of the Father in heaven, the Father in heaven dwells in his heart and the two become one."

"Then is the Father in heaven really the Self of my friend?"

"The greatest philosopher could not have expressed it more truly,"

413

I said.

"Then indeed do I love the Father in heaven," breathed the sylph, "and I will say now every day and all day, 'Thy will be done' to Him."

"Even if it separates you from your friend?"

"How can it separate me from my friend, if the Father is the Self of him?"

"I would that all angels were your equal in learning," I said.

But Meriline had turned from me in utter forgetfulness, and was saying over and over, with joy in her uplifted face, "Thy will be done! Thy will be done!"

"Truly," I said to myself, as I passed along the line, "he who worships the Father as the Self of the beloved has already acquired a soul."

The Torture by Hope

By Villiers de l'Isle Adam

Many years ago, as evening was closing in, the venerable Pedro Arbuez d'Espila, sixth prior of the Dominicans of Segovia, and third Grand Inquisitor of Spain, followed by a *fra redemptor*, and preceded by two familiars of the Holy Office, the latter carrying lanterns, made their way to a subterranean dungeon. The bolt of a massive door creaked, and they entered a mephitic *in-pace*, where the dim light revealed between rings fastened to the wall a blood-stained rack, a brazier, and a jug. On a pile of straw, loaded with fetters and his neck encircled by an iron *carcan*, sat a haggard man, of uncertain age, clothed in rags.

This prisoner was no other than Rabbi Aser Abarbanel, a Jew of Arragon, who—accused of usury and pitiless scorn for the poor—had been daily subjected to torture for more than a year. Yet "his blindness was as dense as his hide," and he had refused to abjure his faith.

Proud of a filiation dating back thousands of years, proud of his ancestors—for all Jews worthy of the name are vain of their blood—he descended Talmudically from Othoniel and consequently from Ipsiboa, the wife of the last judge of Israel, a circumstance which had sustained his courage amid incessant torture. With tears in his eyes at the thought of this resolute soul rejecting salvation, the venerable Pedro Arbuez d'Espila, approaching the shuddering rabbi, addressed him as follows:

"My son, rejoice: your trials here below are about to end. If in the presence of such obstinacy I was forced to permit, with deep regret, the use of great severity, my task of fraternal correction has its limits. You are the fig tree which, having failed so many times to bear fruit, at last withered, but God alone can judge your soul. Perhaps Infinite Mercy will shine upon you at the last moment! We must hope so.

415

There are examples. So sleep in peace tonight. Tomorrow you will be included in the *auto da fé*: that is, you will be exposed to the *quémadero*, the symbolical flames of the Everlasting Fire: It burns, as you know, only at a distance, my son; and Death is at least two hours (often three) in coming, on account of the wet, iced bandages, with which we protect the heads and hearts of the condemned. There will be forty-three of you. Placed in the last row, you will have time to invoke God and offer to Him this baptism of fire, which is of the Holy Spirit. Hope in the Light, and rest."

With these words, having signed to his companions to unchain the prisoner, the prior tenderly embraced him. Then came the turn of the *fra redemptor*, who, in a low tone, entreated the Jew's forgiveness for what he had made him suffer for the purpose of redeeming him; then the two familiars silently kissed him. This ceremony over, the captive was left, solitary and bewildered, in the darkness.

★★★★★★

Rabbi Aser Abarbanel, with parched lips and visage worn by suffering, at first gazed at the closed door with vacant eyes. Closed? The word unconsciously roused a vague fancy in his mind, the fancy that he had seen for an instant the light of the lanterns through a chink between the door and the wall. A morbid idea of hope, due to the weakness of his brain, stirred his whole being. He dragged himself toward the strange *appearance*. Then, very gently and cautiously, slipping one finger into the crevice, he drew the door toward him. Marvellous! By an extraordinary accident the familiar who closed it had turned the huge key an instant before it struck the stone casing, so that the rusty bolt not having entered the hole, the door again rolled on its hinges.

The *rabbi* ventured to glance outside. By the aid of a sort of luminous dusk he distinguished at first a semicircle of walls indented by winding stairs; and opposite to him, at the top of five or six stone steps, a sort of black portal, opening into an immense corridor, whose first arches only were visible from below.

Stretching himself flat he crept to the threshold. Yes, it was really a corridor, but endless in length. A wan light illumined it: lamps suspended from the vaulted ceiling lightened at intervals the dull hue of the atmosphere—the distance was veiled in shadow. Not a single door appeared in the whole extent! Only on one side, the left, heavily grated loopholes sunk in the walls, admitted a light which must be that of evening, for crimson bars at intervals rested on the flags of the pavement. What a terrible silence! Yet, yonder, at the far end of that passage there might be a doorway of escape! The Jew's vacillating hope was tenacious, for it was *the last.*

Without hesitating, he ventured on the flags, keeping close under the loopholes, trying to make himself part of the blackness of the long walls. He advanced slowly, dragging himself along on his breast, forcing back the cry of pain when some raw wound sent a keen pang through his whole body.

Suddenly the sound of a sandaled foot approaching reached his ears. He trembled violently, fear stifled him, his sight grew dim. Well, it was over, no doubt. He pressed himself into a niche and half lifeless with terror, waited.

It was a familiar hurrying along. He passed swiftly by, holding in his clenched hand an instrument of torture—a frightful figure—and vanished. The suspense which the *rabbi* had endured seemed to have suspended the functions of life, and he lay nearly an hour unable to move. Fearing an increase of tortures if he were captured, he thought of returning to his dungeon. But the old hope whispered in his soul that divine *perhaps*, which comforts us in our sorest trials. A miracle had happened. He could doubt no longer. He began to crawl toward the chance of escape. Exhausted by suffering and hunger, trembling with pain, he pressed onward. The sepulchral corridor seemed to lengthen mysteriously, while he, still advancing, gazed into the gloom where there *must* be some avenue of escape.

Oh! oh! He again heard footsteps, but this time they were slower, more heavy. The white and black forms of two inquisitors appeared, emerging from the obscurity beyond. They were conversing in low tones, and seemed to be discussing some important subject, for they were gesticulating vehemently.

At this spectacle Rabbi Aser Abarbanel closed his eyes: his heart beat so violently that it almost suffocated him; his rags were damp with the cold sweat of agony; he lay motionless by the wall, his mouth wide open, under the rays of a lamp, praying to the God of David.

Just opposite to him the two inquisitors paused under the light of the lamp—doubtless owing to some accident due to the course of their argument. One, while listening to his companion, gazed at the *rabbi!* And, beneath the look—whose absence of expression the hapless man did not at first notice—he fancied he again felt the burning pincers scorch his flesh, he was to be once more a living wound. Fainting, breathless, with fluttering eyelids, he shivered at the touch of the monk's floating robe. But—strange yet natural fact—the inquisitor's gaze was evidently that of a man deeply absorbed in his intended reply, engrossed by what he was hearing; his eyes were fixed—and seemed to look at the Jew *without seeing him.*

In fact, after the lapse of a few minutes, the two gloomy figures slowly pursued their way, still conversing in low tones, toward the place whence the prisoner had come; *he had not been seen!* Amid the horrible confusion of the *rabbi's* thoughts, the idea darted through his brain: "Can I be already dead that they did not see me?" A hideous impression roused him from his lethargy: in looking at the wall against which his face was pressed, he imagined he beheld two fierce eyes watching him! He flung his head back in a sudden frenzy of fright, his hair fairly bristling! Yet, no! No. His hand groped over the stones: it was the *reflection* of the inquisitor's eyes, still retained in his own, which had been refracted from two spots on the wall.

Forward! He must hasten toward that goal which he fancied (absurdly, no doubt) to be deliverance, toward the darkness from which he was now barely thirty paces distant. He pressed forward faster on his knees, his hands, at full length, dragging himself painfully along, and soon entered the dark portion of this terrible corridor.

Suddenly the poor wretch felt a gust of cold air on the hands resting upon the flags; it came from under the little door to which the two walls led.

Oh, Heaven, if that door should open outward. Every nerve in the miserable fugitive's body thrilled with hope. He examined it from top to bottom, though scarcely able to distinguish its outlines in the surrounding darkness. He passed his hand over it: no bolt, no lock! A latch! He started up, the latch yielded to the pressure of his thumb: the door silently swung open before him.

★★★★★★

"Halleluia!" murmured the *rabbi* in a transport of gratitude as, standing on the threshold, he beheld the scene before him.

The door had opened into the gardens, above which arched a star-lit sky, into spring, liberty, life! It revealed the neighbouring fields, stretching toward the sierras, whose sinuous blue lines were relieved against the horizon. Yonder lay freedom! O, to escape! He would journey all night through the lemon groves, whose fragrance reached him. Once in the mountains and he was safe! He inhaled the delicious air; the breeze revived him, his lungs expanded! He felt in his swelling heart the *Veni foràs* of Lazarus! And to thank once more the God who had bestowed this mercy upon him, he extended his arms, raising his

418

eyes toward Heaven. It was an ecstasy of joy!

Then he fancied he saw the shadow of his arms approach him—fancied that he felt these shadowy arms inclose, embrace him—and that he was pressed tenderly to some one's breast. A tall figure actually did stand directly before him. He lowered his eyes—and remained motionless, gasping for breath, dazed, with fixed eyes, fairly drivelling with terror.

Horror! He was in the clasp of the Grand Inquisitor himself, the venerable Pedro Arbuez d'Espila who gazed at him with tearful eyes, like a good shepherd who had found his stray lamb.

The dark-robed priest pressed the hapless Jew to his heart with so fervent an outburst of love, that the edges of the monochal haircloth rubbed the Dominican's breast. And while Aser Abarbanel with protruding eyes gasped in agony in the ascetic's embrace, vaguely comprehending that all the phases of this fatal evening were only a prearranged torture, that of Hope, the Grand Inquisitor, with an accent of touching reproach and a look of consternation, murmured in his ear, his breath parched and burning from long fasting:

"What, my son! On the eve, perchance, of salvation—you wished to leave us?"

When the World Was Young

By Jack London

1

He was a very quiet, self-possessed sort of man, sitting a moment on top of the wall to sound the damp darkness for warnings of the dangers it might conceal. But the plummet of his hearing brought nothing to him save the moaning of wind through invisible trees and the rustling of leaves on swaying branches. A heavy fog drifted and drove before the wind, and though he could not see this fog, the wet of it blew upon his face, and the wall on which he sat was wet.

Without noise he had climbed to the top of the wall from the out-side, and without noise he dropped to the ground on the inside. From his pocket he drew an electric night-stick, but he did not use it. Dark as the way was, he was not anxious for light. Carrying the night-stick in his hand, his finger on the button, he advanced through the dark-ness. The ground was velvety and springy to his feet, being carpeted with dead pine-needles and leaves and mould which evidently had been undisturbed for years. Leaves and branches brushed against his body, but so dark was it that he could not avoid them. Soon he walked with his hand stretched out gropingly before him, and more than once the hand fetched up against the solid trunks of massive trees. All about him he knew were these trees; he sensed the loom of them every-where; and he experienced a strange feeling of microscopic smallness in the midst of great bulks leaning toward him to crush him. Beyond, he knew, was the house, and he expected to find some trail or winding path that would lead easily to it.

Once, he found himself trapped. On every side he groped against trees and branches, or blundered into thickets of underbrush, until there seemed no way out. Then he turned on his light, circumspectly, directing its rays to the ground at his feet. Slowly and carefully he moved it about him, the white brightness showing in sharp detail all the obstacles to his progress. He saw an opening between huge-trunked trees, and advanced through it, putting out the light and treading on dry footing as yet protected from the drip of the fog by the dense foliage overhead. His sense of direction was good, and he knew he was going toward the house.

And then the thing happened—the thing unthinkable and unexpected. His descending foot came down upon something that was soft and alive, and that arose with a snort under the weight of his body. He sprang clear, and crouched for another spring, anywhere, tense and expectant, keyed for the onslaught of the unknown. He waited a moment, wondering what manner of animal it was that had arisen from under his foot and that now made no sound nor movement and that must be crouching and waiting just as tensely and expectantly as he. The strain became unbearable. Holding the night-stick before him, he pressed the button, saw, and screamed aloud in terror. He was prepared for anything, from a frightened calf or fawn to a belligerent lion, but he was not prepared for what he saw. In that instant his tiny searchlight, sharp and white, had shown him what a thousand years would not enable him to forget—a man, huge and blond, yellow-haired and yellow-bearded, naked except for soft-tanned *moccasins* and what seemed a goat-skin about his middle. Arms and legs were bare, as were his shoulders and most of his chest. The skin was smooth and hairless, but browned by sun and wind, while under it heavy muscles were knotted like fat snakes.

Still, this alone, unexpected as it well was, was not what had made the man scream out. What had caused his terror was the unspeakable ferocity of the face, the wild-animal glare of the blue eyes scarcely dazzled by the light, the pine-needles matted and clinging in the beard and hair, and the whole formidable body crouched and in the act of springing at him. Practically in the instant he saw all this, and while his scream still rang, the thing leaped, he flung his night-stick full at it, and threw himself to the ground. He felt its feet and shins strike against his ribs, and he bounded up and away while the thing itself hurled onward in a heavy crashing fall into the underbrush.

As the noise of the fall ceased, the man stopped and on hands and knees waited. He could hear the thing moving about, searching for him, and he was afraid to advertise his location by attempting further flight. He knew that inevitably he would crackle the underbrush and be pursued. Once he drew out his revolver, then changed his mind.

He had recovered his composure and hoped to get away without noise. Several times he heard the thing beating up the thickets for him, and there were moments when it, too, remained still and listened. This gave an idea to the man. One of his hands was resting on a chunk of dead wood. Carefully, first feeling about him in the darkness to know that the full swing of his arm was clear, he raised the chunk of wood and threw it. It was not a large piece, and it went far, landing noisily in a bush. He heard the thing bound into the bush, and at the same time himself crawled steadily away. And on hands and knees, slowly and cautiously, he crawled on, till his knees were wet on the soggy mould. When he listened he heard naught but the moaning wind and the drip-drip of the fog from the branches. Never abating his caution, he stood erect and went on to the stone wall, over which he climbed and dropped down to the road outside.

Feeling his way in a clump of bushes, he drew out a bicycle and prepared to mount. He was in the act of driving the gear around with his foot for the purpose of getting the opposite pedal in position, when he heard the thud of a heavy body that landed lightly and evidently on its feet. He did not wait for more, but ran, with hands on the handles of his bicycle, until he was able to vault astride the saddle, catch the pedals, and start a spurt. Behind he could hear the quick *thud-thud* of feet on the dust of the road, but he drew away from it and lost it.

Unfortunately, he had started away from the direction of town and was heading higher up into the hills. He knew that on this particular road there were no cross roads. The only way back was past that terror, and he could not steel himself to face it. At the end of half an hour, finding himself on an ever increasing grade, he dismounted. For still greater safety, leaving the wheel by the roadside, he climbed through a fence into what he decided was a hillside pasture, spread a newspaper on the ground, and sat down.

"Gosh!" he said aloud, mopping the sweat and fog from his face.

And "Gosh!" he said once again, while rolling a cigarette and as he pondered the problem of getting back.

But he made no attempt to go back. He was resolved not to face that road in the dark, and with head bowed on knees, he dozed, waiting for daylight.

How long afterward he did not know, he was awakened by the yapping bark of a young coyote. As he looked about and located it on the brow of the hill behind him, he noted the change that had come over the face of the night. The fog was gone; the stars and moon were out; even the wind had died down. It had transformed into a balmy California summer night. He tried to doze again, but the yap of the coyote disturbed him. Half asleep, he heard a wild and eerie chant. Looking about him, he noticed that the coyote had ceased its noise and was running away along the crest of the hill, and behind it, in full pursuit, no longer chanting, ran the naked creature he had encountered in the garden. It was a young coyote, and it was being overtaken when the chase passed from view. The man trembled as with a chill as he started to his feet, clambered over the fence, and mounted his wheel. But it was his chance and he knew it. The terror was no longer between him and Mill Valley.

He sped at a breakneck rate down the hill, but in the turn at the bottom, in the deep shadows, he encountered a chuck-hole and pitched headlong over the handle bar.

"It's sure not my night," he muttered, as he examined the broken fork of the machine.

Shouldering the useless wheel, he trudged on. In time he came to the stone wall, and, half disbelieving his experience, he sought in the road for tracks, and found them—moccasin tracks, large ones, deep-bitten into the dust at the toes. It was while bending over them, examining, that again he heard the eerie chant. He had seen the thing pursue the coyote, and he knew he had no chance on a straight run. He did not attempt it, contenting himself with hiding in the shadows on the off side of the road.

And again he saw the thing that was like a naked man, running swiftly and lightly and singing as it ran. Opposite him it paused, and his heart stood still. But instead of coming toward his hiding-place, it leaped into the air, caught the branch of a roadside tree, and swung swiftly upward, from limb to limb, like an ape. It swung across the wall, and a dozen feet above the top, into the branches of another tree, and dropped out of sight to the ground. The man waited a few wondering minutes, then started on.

2

Dave Slotter leaned belligerently against the desk that barred the way to the private office of James Ward, senior partner of the firm of Ward, Knowles & Co. Dave was angry. Everyone in the outer office had looked him over suspiciously, and the man who faced him was excessively suspicious.

"You just tell Mr. Ward it's important," he urged.

"I tell you he is dictating and cannot be disturbed," was the answer.

"Come tomorrow."

"Tomorrow will be too late. You just trot along and tell Mr. Ward it's a matter of life and death."

The secretary hesitated and Dave seized the advantage.

"You just tell him I was across the bay in Mill Valley last night, and that I want to put him wise to something."

"What name?" was the query.

"Never mind the name. He don't know me."

When Dave was shown into the private office, he was still in the belligerent frame of mind, but when he saw a large fair man whirl in a revolving chair from dictating to a stenographer to face him, Dave's demeanour abruptly changed. He did not know why it changed, and he was secretly angry with himself.

"You are Mr. Ward?" Dave asked with a fatuousness that still further irritated him. He had never intended it at all.

"Yes," came the answer. "And who are you?"

"Harry Bancroft," Dave lied. "You don't know me, and my name don't matter."

"You sent in word that you were in Mill Valley last night?"

"You live there, don't you?" Dave countered, looking suspiciously at the stenographer.

"Yes. What do you mean to see me about? I am very busy."

"I'd like to see you alone, sir."

Mr. Ward gave him a quick, penetrating look, hesitated, then made up his mind.

"That will do for a few minutes, Miss Potter."

The girl arose, gathered her notes together, and passed out. Dave looked at Mr. James Ward wonderingly, until that gentleman broke his train of inchoate thought.

"Well?"

"I was over in Mill Valley last night," Dave began confusedly.

"I've heard that before. What do you want?"

And Dave proceeded in the face of a growing conviction that was unbelievable.

"I was at your house, or in the grounds, I mean."

"What were you doing there?"

"I came to break in," Dave answered in all frankness. "I heard you lived all alone with a Chinaman for cook, and it looked good to me. Only I didn't break in. Something happened that prevented. That's why I'm here. I come to warn you. I found a wild man loose in your grounds—a regular devil. He could pull a guy like me to pieces. He gave me the run of my life. He don't wear any clothes to speak of, he climbs trees like a monkey, and he runs like a deer. I saw him chasing a coyote, and the last I saw of it, by God, he was gaining on it."

Dave paused and looked for the effect that would follow his words. But no effect came. James Ward was quietly curious, and that was all.

"Very remarkable, very remarkable," he murmured. "A wild man, you say. Why have you come to tell me?"

"To warn you of your danger. I'm something of a hard proposition myself, but I don't believe in killing people . . . that is, unnecessarily. I realized that you was in danger. I thought I'd warn you. Honest, that's the game. Of course, if you wanted to give me anything for my trouble, I'd take it. That was in my mind, too. But I don't care whether you give me anything or not. I've warned you anyway, and done my duty."

Mr. Ward meditated and drummed on the surface of his desk. Dave noticed that his hands were large, powerful, withal well-cared for de-spite their dark sunburn. Also, he noted what had already caught his eye before—a tiny strip of flesh-coloured courtplaster on the forehead over one eye. And still the thought that forced itself into his mind was unbelievable.

Mr. Ward took a wallet from his inside coat pocket, drew out a greenback, and passed it to Dave, who noted as he pocketed it that it was for twenty dollars.

"Thank you," said Mr. Ward, indicating that the interview was at an end. "I shall have the matter investigated. A wild man running loose *is* dangerous."

But so quiet a man was Mr. Ward, that Dave's courage returned. Besides, a new theory had suggested itself. The wild man was evi-dently Mr. Ward's brother, a lunatic privately confined. Dave had heard of such things. Perhaps Mr. Ward wanted it kept quiet. That was why he had given him the twenty dollars.

"Say," Dave began, "now I come to think of it that wild man looked a lot like you—"

That was as far as Dave got, for at that moment he witnessed a transformation and found himself gazing into the same unspeakably ferocious blue eyes of the night before, at the same clutching talon-like hands, and at the same formidable bulk in the act of springing upon him. But this time Dave had no night-stick to throw, and he was caught by the biceps of both arms in a grip so terrific that it made him groan with pain. He saw the large white teeth exposed, for all the world as a dog's about to bite. Mr. Ward's beard brushed his face as the teeth went in for the grip of his throat. But the bite was not given. Instead, Dave felt the other's body stiffen as with an iron restraint, and then he was flung aside, without effort but with such force that only the wall stopped his momentum and dropped him gasping to the floor.

"What do you mean by coming here and trying to blackmail me?" Mr. Ward was snarling at him. "Here, give me back that money."

Dave passed the bill back without a word.

"I thought you came here with good intentions. I know you now. Let me see and hear no more of you, or I'll put you in prison where you belong. Do you understand?"

"Yes, sir," Dave gasped.

"Then go."

And Dave went, without further word, both his biceps aching intolerably from the bruise of that tremendous grip. As his hand rested on the door knob, he was stopped.

"You were lucky," Mr. Ward was saying, and Dave noted that his face and eyes were cruel and gloating and proud. "You were lucky. Had I wanted, I could have torn your muscles out of your arms and thrown them in the waste basket there."

"Yes, sir," said Dave; and absolute conviction vibrated in his voice.

He opened the door and passed out. The secretary looked at him interrogatively.

"Gosh!" was all Dave vouchsafed, and with this utterance passed out of the offices and the story.

3

James G. Ward was forty years of age, a successful business man, and very unhappy. For forty years he had vainly tried to solve a problem that was really himself and that with increasing years became more and more a woeful affliction. In himself he was two men, and, chronologically speaking, these men were several thousand years or so apart. He had studied the question of dual personality probably more profoundly than any half dozen of the leading specialists in that intricate and mysterious psychological field. In himself he was a different case from any that had been recorded. Even the most fanciful flights of the fiction-writers had not quite hit upon him. He was not a Dr. Jekyll and Mr. Hyde, nor was he like the unfortunate young man in Kipling's *Greatest Story in the World*. His two personalities were so mixed that they were practically aware of themselves and of each other all the time.

His one self was that of a man whose rearing and education were modern and who had lived through the latter part of the nineteenth century and well into the first decade of the twentieth. His other self he had located as a savage and a barbarian living under the primitive conditions of several thousand years before. But which self was he, and which was the other, he could never tell. For he was both selves, and both selves all the time. Very rarely indeed did it happen that one self did not know what the other was doing. Another thing was that he had no visions nor memories of the past in which that early self had lived. That early self lived in the present; but while it lived in the present, it was under the compulsion to live the way of life that must have been in that distant past.

In his childhood he had been a problem to his father and mother, and to the family doctors, though never had they come within a thousand miles of hitting upon the clue to his erratic conduct. Thus, they could not understand his excessive somnolence in the forenoon, nor his excessive activity at night. When they found him wandering along the hallways at night, or climbing over giddy roofs, or running in the hills, they decided he was a somnambulist. In reality he was wide-eyed awake and merely under the night-roaming compulsion of his early life. Questioned by an obtuse medico, he once told the truth and suffered the ignominy of having the revelation contemptuously labelled and dismissed as "dreams."

The point was, that as twilight and evening came on he became wakeful. The four walls of a room were an irk and a restraint. He heard a thousand voices whispering to him through the darkness. The night called to him, for he was, for that period of the twenty-four hours, essentially a night-prowler. But nobody understood, and never again did he attempt to explain. They classified him as a sleep-walker and took precautions accordingly—precautions that very often were futile. As his childhood advanced, he grew more cunning, so that the major portion of all his nights were spent in the open at realizing his other self. As a result, he slept in the forenoons. Morning studies and schools were impossible, and it was discovered that only in the afternoons, under private teachers, could he be taught anything. Thus was his modern self educated and developed.

But a problem, as a child, he ever remained. He was known as a little demon of insensate cruelty and viciousness. The family medicos privately adjudged him a mental monstrosity and a degenerate. Such few boy companions as he had, hailed him as a wonder, though they were all afraid of him. He could outclimb, outswim, outrun, outdevil any of them; while none dared fight with him. He was too terribly strong, too madly furious.

When nine years of age he ran away to the hills, where he flourished, night-prowling, for seven weeks before he was discovered and brought home. The marvel was how he had managed to subsist and keep in condition during that time. They did not know, and he never told them, of the rabbits he had killed, of the quail, young and old, he had captured and devoured, of the farmers' chicken-roosts he had raided, nor of the cave-lair he had made and carpeted with dry leaves and grasses and in which he had slept in warmth and comfort, through the forenoons of many days.

At college he was notorious for his sleepiness and stupidity during the morning lectures and for his brilliance in the afternoon. By collateral reading and by borrowing the notebook of his fellow students he managed to scrape through the detestable morning courses, while his afternoon courses were triumphs. In football he proved a giant and a terror, and, in almost every form of track athletics, save for strange Berserker rages that were sometimes displayed, he could be depended upon to win. But his fellows were afraid to box with him, and he signalized his last wrestling bout by sinking his teeth into the shoulder of his opponent.

After college, his father, in despair, sent him among the cowpunchers of a Wyoming ranch. Three months later the doughty cowmen confessed he was too much for them and telegraphed his father to come and take the wild man away. Also, when the father arrived to take him away, the cowmen allowed that they would vastly prefer chumming with howling cannibals, gibbering lunatics, cavorting gorillas, grizzly bears, and man-eating tigers than with this particular young college product with hair parted in the middle.

There was one exception to the lack of memory of the life of his early self, and that was language. By some quirk of atavism, a certain portion of that early self's language had come down to him as a racial memory. In moments of happiness, exaltation, or battle, he was prone to burst out in wild barbaric songs or chants. It was by this means that he located in time and space that strayed half of him who should have been dead and dust for thousands of years. He sang, once, and deliberately, several of the ancient chants in the presence of Professor

Wertz, who gave courses in old Saxon and who was a philologist of repute and passion. At the first one, the professor pricked up his ears and demanded to know what mongrel tongue or hog-German it was. When the second chant was rendered, the professor was highly excited. James Ward then concluded the performance by giving a song that always irresistibly rushed to his lips when he was engaged in fierce struggling or fighting.

Then it was that Professor Wertz proclaimed it no hog-German, but early German, or early Teuton, of a date that must far precede anything that had ever been discovered and handed down by the scholars. So early was it that it was beyond him; yet it was filled with haunting reminiscences of word-forms he knew and which his trained intuition told him were true and real. He demanded the source of the songs, and asked to borrow the previous book that contained them. Also, he demanded to know why young Ward had always posed as being profoundly ignorant of the German language. And Ward could neither explain his ignorance nor lend the book. Whereupon, after pleadings and entreaties that extended through weeks, Professor Wertz took a dislike to the young man, believed him a liar, and classified him as a man of monstrous selfishness for not giving him a glimpse of this wonderful screed that was older than the oldest any philologist had ever known or dreamed.

But little good did it do this much-mixed young man to know that half of him was late American and the other half early Teuton. Nevertheless, the late American in him was no weakling, and he (if he were a he and had a shred of existence outside of these two) compelled an adjustment or compromise between his one self that was a night-prowling savage that kept his other self sleepy of mornings, and that other self that was cultured and refined and that wanted to be normal and love and prosecute business like other people. The afternoons and early evenings he gave to the one, the nights to the other; the forenoons and parts of the nights were devoted to sleep for the twain. But in the mornings he slept in bed like a civilized man. In the night time he slept like a wild animal, as he had slept the night Dave Slotter stepped on him in the woods.

Persuading his father to advance the capital, he went into business, and keen and successful business he made of it, devoting his afternoons whole-souled to it, while his partner devoted the mornings. The early evenings he spent socially, but, as the hour grew to nine or ten, an irresistible restlessness overcame him and he disappeared from the haunts of men until the next afternoon. Friends and acquaintances thought that he spent much of his time in sport. And they were right, though they never would have dreamed of the nature of the sport, even if they had seen him running coyotes in night-chases over the hills of Mill Valley. Neither were the schooner captains believed when they reported seeing, on cold winter mornings, a man swimming in the tide-rips of Raccoon Straits or in the swift currents between Goat Island and Angel Island miles from shore.

In the bungalow at Mill Valley he lived alone, save for Lee Sing, the Chinese cook and factotum, who knew much about the strangeness of his master, who was paid well for saying nothing, and who never did say anything. After the satisfaction of his nights, a morning's sleep, and a breakfast of Lee Sing's, James Ward crossed the bay to San Francisco on a midday ferryboat and went to the club and on to his office, as normal and conventional a man of business as could be found in the city. But as the evening lengthened, the night called to him. There came a quickening of all his perceptions and a restlessness. His hearing was suddenly acute; the myriad night-noises told him a luring and familiar story; and, if alone, he would begin to pace up and down the narrow room like any caged animal from the wild.

Once, he ventured to fall in love. He never permitted himself that diversion again. He was afraid. And for many a day the young lady, scared at least out of a portion of her young ladyhood, bore on her arms and shoulders and wrists divers black-and-blue bruises—tokens of caresses which he had bestowed in all fond gentleness but too late at night. There was the mistake. Had he ventured love-making in the afternoon, all would have been well, for it would have been as the quiet gentleman that he would have made love—but at night it was the uncouth, wife-stealing savage of the dark German forests. Out of his wisdom, he decided that afternoon lovemaking could be prosecuted successfully; but out of the same wisdom he was convinced that marriage would prove a ghastly failure. He found it appalling to imagine being married and encountering his wife after dark.

So he had eschewed all lovemaking, regulated his dua life, cleaned up a million in business, fought shy of match-making mamas and bright- and eager-eyed young ladies of various ages, met Lilian Gersdale and made it a rigid observance never to see her later than eight o'clock in the evening, ran of nights after his coyotes, and slept in forest lairs—and through it all had kept his secret save for Lee Sing—and now, Dave Slotter. It was the latter's discovery of both his selves that frightened him. In spite of the counter fright he had given the burglar, the latter might talk. And even if he did not, sooner or later he would be found out by someone else.

Thus it was that James Ward made a fresh and heroic effort to control the Teutonic barbarian that was half of him. So well did he make it a point to see Lilian in the afternoons and early evenings, that the time came when she accepted him for better or worse, and when he prayed privily and fervently that it was not for worse. During this period no prize-fighter ever trained more harshly and faithfully for a contest than he trained to subdue the wild savage in him. Among other things, he strove to exhaust himself during the day, so that sleep would render him deaf to the call of the night. He took a vacation from the office and went on long hunting trips, following the deer through the most inaccessible and rugged country he could find—and always in the daytime. Night found him indoors and tired. At home he installed a score of exercise machines, and where other men might go through a particular movement ten times, he went hundreds. Also, as a compromise, he built a sleeping porch on the second story. Here he at least breathed the blessed night air. Double screens prevented him from escaping into the woods, and each night Lee Sing locked him in and each morning let him out.

The time came, in the month of August, when he engaged additional servants to assist Lee Sing and dared a house party in his Mill Valley bungalow. Lilian, her mother and brother, and half a dozen mutual friends, were the guests. For two days and nights all went well. And on the third night, playing bridge till eleven o'clock, he had reason to be proud of himself. His restlessness he successfully hid, but as luck would have it, Lilian Gersdale was his opponent on his right. She was a frail delicate flower of a woman, and in his night-mood her very frailty incensed him. Not that he loved her less, but that he felt almost irresistibly impelled to reach out and paw and maul her. Especially was this true when she was engaged in playing a winning hand against him.

He had one of the deer-hounds brought in, and, when it seemed he must fly to pieces with the tension, a caressing hand laid on the animal brought him relief. These contacts with the hairy coat gave him instant easement and enabled him to play out the evening. Nor did any one guess the terrible struggle their host was making, the while he laughed so carelessly and played so keenly and deliberately.

When they separated for the night, he saw to it that he parted from Lilian in the presence of the others. Once on his sleeping porch, and safely locked in, he doubled and tripled and even quadrupled his exercises until, exhausted, he lay down on the couch to woo sleep and to ponder two problems that especially troubled him. One was this matter of exercise. It was a paradox. The more he exercised in this excessive fashion, the stronger he became. While it was true that he thus quite tired out his night-running Teutonic self, it seemed that he was merely setting back the fatal day when his strength would be too much for him and overpower him, and then it would be a strength more terrible than he had yet known. The other problem was that of his marriage and of the stratagems he must employ in order to avoid his wife after dark. And thus fruitlessly pondering he fell asleep.

Now, where the huge grizzly bear came from that night was long a mystery, while the people of the Springs Brothers' Circus, showing at Sausalito, searched long and vainly for "Big Ben, the Biggest Grizzly in Captivity." But Big Ben escaped, and, out of the mazes of half a thousand bungalows and country estates, selected the grounds of James J. Ward for visitation. The first Mr. Ward knew was when he found himself on his feet, quivering and tense, a surge of battle in his breast and on his lips the old war-chant. From without came a wild baying and bellowing of the hounds. And sharp as a knife-thrust through the pandemonium came the agony of a stricken dog—his dog, he knew.

Not stopping for slippers, pyjama-clad, he burst through the door Lee Sing had so carefully locked, and sped down the stairs and out into the night. As his naked feet struck the gravelled driveway, he stopped abruptly, reached under the steps to a hiding-place he knew well, and pulled forth a huge knotty club—his old companion on many a mad night adventure on the hills. The frantic hullabaloo of the dogs was coming nearer, and, swinging the club, he sprang straight into the thickets to meet it.

The aroused household assembled on the wide veranda. Somebody turned on the electric lights, but they could see nothing but one another's frightened faces. Beyond the brightly illuminated driveway the trees formed a wall of impenetrable blackness. Yet somewhere in that blackness a terrible struggle was going on. There was an infernal outcry of animals, a great snarling and growling, the sound of blows being struck, and a smashing and crashing of underbrush by heavy bodies.

The tide of battle swept out from among the trees and upon the driveway just beneath the onlookers. Then they saw. Mrs. Gersdale cried out and clung fainting to her son. Lilian, clutching the railing so spasmodically that a bruising hurt was left in her finger-ends for days, gazed horror-stricken at a yellow-haired, wild-eyed giant whom she recognized as the man who was to be her husband. He was swinging a great club, and fighting furiously and calmly with a shaggy monster that was bigger than any bear she had ever seen. One rip of the beast's claws had dragged away Ward's pyjama-coat and streaked his flesh with blood.

While most of Lilian Gersdale's fright was for the man beloved, there was a large portion of it due to the man himself. Never had she dreamed so formidable and magnificent a savage lurked under the starched shirt and conventional garb of her betrothed. And never had she had any conception of how a man battled. Such a battle was certainly not modern; nor was she there beholding a modern man, though she did not know it. For this was not Mr. James J. Ward, the San Francisco business man, but one unnamed and unknown, a crude, rude savage creature who, by some freak of chance, lived again after thrice a thousand years.

The hounds, ever maintaining their mad uproar, circled about the fight, or dashed in and out, distracting the bear. When the animal turned to meet such flanking assaults, the man leaped in and the club came down. Angered afresh by every such blow, the bear would rush, and the man, leaping and skipping, avoiding the dogs, went backwards or circled to one side or the other. Whereupon the dogs, taking advantage of the opening, would again spring in and draw the animal's wrath to them.

The end came suddenly. Whirling, the grizzly caught a hound with a wide sweeping cuff that sent the brute, its ribs caved in and its back broken, hurtling twenty feet. Then the human brute went mad. A foaming rage flecked the lips that parted with a wild inarticulate cry, as it sprang in, swung the club mightily in both hands, and brought it down full on the head of the uprearing grizzly. Not even the skull of a grizzly could withstand the crushing force of such a blow, and the animal went down to meet the worrying of the hounds. And through their scurrying leaped the man, squarely upon the body, where, in the white electric light, resting on his club, he chanted a triumph in an unknown tongue—a song so ancient that Professor Wertz would have given ten years of his life for it.

His guests rushed to possess him and acclaim him, but James Ward, suddenly looking out of the eyes of the early Teuton, saw the fair frail Twentieth Century girl he loved, and felt something snap in his brain. He staggered weakly toward her, dropped the club, and nearly fell. Something had gone wrong with him. Inside his brain was an intolerable agony. It seemed as if the soul of him were flying asunder. Following the excited gaze of the others, he glanced back and saw the carcass of the bear. The sight filled him with fear. He uttered a cry and would have fled, had they not restrained him and led him into the bungalow.

★★★★★★

James J. Ward is still at the head of the firm of Ward, Knowles & Co. But he no longer lives in the country; nor does he run of nights after the coyotes under the moon. The early Teuton in him died the night of the Mill Valley fight with the bear. James J. Ward is now wholly James J. Ward, and he shares no part of his being with any vagabond anachronism from the younger world. And so wholly is James J. Ward modern, that he knows in all its bitter fullness the curse of civilized fear. He is now afraid of the dark, and night in the forest is to him a thing of abysmal terror. His city house is of the spick and span order, and he evinces a great interest in burglar-proof devices. His home is a tangle of electric wires, and after bedtime a guest can scarcely breathe without setting off an alarm. Also, he has invented a combination key-less door-lock that travellers may carry in their vest pockets and apply immediately and successfully under all circumstances. But his wife does not deem him a coward. She knows better. And, like any hero, he is content to rest on his laurels. His bravery is never questioned by those of his friends who are aware of the Mill Valley episode.

LEONAUR

ALSO FROM LEONAUR
AVAILABLE IN SOFTCOVER OR HARDCOVER WITH DUST JACKET

THE COLLECTED SUPERNATURAL AND WEIRD FICTION OF J. SHERIDAN LE FANU: VOLUME 1 *by J. Sheridan le Fanu*—Contains Two Novels 'The Haunted Baronet' and 'The Evil Guest', One Novella 'Carmilla',One Novelette and Ten Short Stories of the Ghostly and Gothic.

THE COLLECTED SUPERNATURAL AND WEIRD FICTION OF J. SHERIDAN LE FANU: VOLUME 2 *by J. Sheridan le Fanu*—Contains One Novel 'Uncle Silas', One Novelette 'Green Tea' and Five Short Stories of the Ghostly and Gothic.

THE COLLECTED SUPERNATURAL AND WEIRD FICTION OF J. SHERIDAN LE FANU: VOLUME 3 *by J. Sheridan le Fanu*—Contains One Novel 'The House by the Churchyard', and One Short Story 'Dickon the Devil' of the Ghostly and Gothic.

THE COLLECTED SUPERNATURAL AND WEIRD FICTION OF J. SHERIDAN LE FANU: VOLUME 4 *by J. Sheridan le Fanu*—Contains One Novel 'The Wyvern Mystery', One Novelette 'Mr. Justice Harbottle,' and Nine Short Stories of the Ghostly and Gothic.

THE COLLECTED SUPERNATURAL AND WEIRD FICTION OF J. SHERIDAN LE FANU: VOLUME 5 *by J. Sheridan le Fanu*—Contains One Novel 'The Rose and the Key', One Novelette 'Spalatro, From the Notes of Fra Giacomo', and Two Short Stories of the Ghostly and Gothic

THE COLLECTED SUPERNATURAL AND WEIRD FICTION OF J. SHERIDAN LE FANU: VOLUME 6 *by J. Sheridan le Fanu*—Contains One Novel 'Checkmate', and Six Short Stories of the Ghostly and Gothic

THE COLLECTED SUPERNATURAL AND WEIRD FICTION OF J. SHERIDAN LE FANU: VOLUME 7 *by J. Sheridan le Fanu*—Contains Two Novels 'All in the Dark' and 'The Room in the Dragon Volant', Two Novelettes 'The Mysterious Lodger' and 'The Watcher' and Four Short Stories of the Ghostly and Gothic

THE COLLECTED SUPERNATURAL AND WEIRD FICTION OF J. SHERIDAN LE FANU: VOLUME 8 *by J. Sheridan le Fanu*—Contains One Novel 'A Lost Name', One Novelette 'The Last Heir of Castle Connor', and Six Short Stoies of the Ghostly and Gothic

LEONAUR

ALSO FROM LEONAUR
AVAILABLE IN SOFTCOVER OR HARDCOVER WITH DUST JACKET

THE COMPLETE FOUR JUST MEN: VOLUME 2 *by Edgar Wallace*—*The Law of the Four Just Men & The Three Just Men*—disillusioned with a world where the wicked and the abusers of power perpetually go unpunished, the Just Men set about to rectify matters according to their own standards, and retribution is dispensed on swift and deadly wings.

THE COMPLETE RAFFLES: 1 *by E. W. Hornung*—*The Amateur Cracksman & The Black Mask*—By turns urbane gentleman about town and accomplished cricketer, life is just too ordinary for Raffles and that sets him on a series of adventures that have long been treasured as a real antidote to the 'white knights' who are the usual heroes of the crime fiction of this period.

THE COMPLETE RAFFLES: 2 *by E. W. Hornung*—*A Thief in the Night & Mr Justice Raffles*—By turns urbane gentleman about town and accomplished cricketer, life is just too ordinary for Raffles and that sets him on a series of adventures that have long been treasured as a real antidote to the 'white knights' who are the usual heroes of the crime fiction of this period.

THE COLLECTED SUPERNATURAL AND WEIRD FICTION OF WILKIE COLLINS: VOLUME 1 *by Wilkie Collins*—Contains one novel 'The Haunted Hotel', one novella 'Mad Monkton', three novelettes 'Mr Percy and the Prophet', 'The Biter Bit' and 'The Dead Alive' and eight short stories to chill the blood.

THE COLLECTED SUPERNATURAL AND WEIRD FICTION OF WILKIE COLLINS: VOLUME 2 *by Wilkie Collins*—Contains one novel 'The Two Destinies', three novellas 'The Frozen deep', 'Sister Rose' and 'The Yellow Mask' and two short stories to chill the blood.

THE COLLECTED SUPERNATURAL AND WEIRD FICTION OF WILKIE COLLINS: VOLUME 3 *by Wilkie Collins*—Contains one novel 'Dead Secret,' two novelettes 'Mrs Zant and the Ghost' and 'The Nun's Story of Gabriel's Marriage' and five short stories to chill the blood.

FUNNY BONES *selected by Dorothy Scarborough*—An Anthology of Humorous Ghost Stories.

MONTEZUMA'S CASTLE AND OTHER WEIRD TALES *by Charles B. Cory*—Cory has written a superb collection of eighteen ghostly and weird stories to chill and thrill the avid enthusiast of supernatural fiction.

SUPERNATURAL BUCHAN *by John Buchan*—Stories of Ancient Spirits, Uncanny Places & Strange Creatures.

LEONAUR

ALSO FROM LEONAUR
AVAILABLE IN SOFTCOVER OR HARDCOVER WITH DUST JACKET

MR MUKERJI'S GHOSTS *by S. Mukerji*—Supernatural tales from the British Raj period by India's Ghost story collector.

KIPLINGS GHOSTS *by Rudyard Kipling*—Twelve stories of Ghosts, Hauntings, Curses, Werewolves & Magic.

THE COLLECTED SUPERNATURAL AND WEIRD FICTION OF WASHINGTON IRVING: VOLUME 1 *by Washington Irving*—Including one novel 'A History of New York', and nine short stories of the Strange and Unusual.

THE COLLECTED SUPERNATURAL AND WEIRD FICTION OF WASHINGTON IRVING: VOLUME 2 *by Washington Irving*—Including three novelettes 'The Legend of the Sleepy Hollow', 'Dolph Heyliger', 'The Adventure of the Black Fisherman' and thirty-two short stories of the Strange and Unusual.

THE COLLECTED SUPERNATURAL AND WEIRD FICTION OF JOHN KENDRICK BANGS: VOLUME 1 *by John Kendrick Bangs*—Including one novel 'Toppleton's Client or A Spirit in Exile', and ten short stories of the Strange and Unusual.

THE COLLECTED SUPERNATURAL AND WEIRD FICTION OF JOHN KENDRICK BANGS: VOLUME 2 *by John Kendrick Bangs*—Including four novellas 'A House-Boat on the Styx', 'The Pursuit of the House-Boat', 'The Enchanted Typewriter' and 'Mr. Munchausen' of the Strange and Unusual.

THE COLLECTED SUPERNATURAL AND WEIRD FICTION OF JOHN KENDRICK BANGS: VOLUME 3 *by John Kendrick Bangs*—Including twor novellas 'Olympian Nights', 'Roger Camerden: A Strange Story', and ten short stories of the Strange and Unusual.

THE COLLECTED SUPERNATURAL AND WEIRD FICTION OF MARY SHELLEY: VOLUME 1 *by Mary Shelley*—Including one novel 'Frankenstein or the Modern Prometheus', and fourteen short stories of the Strange and Unusual.

THE COLLECTED SUPERNATURAL AND WEIRD FICTION OF MARY SHELLEY: VOLUME 2 *by Mary Shelley*—Including one novel 'The Last Man', and three short stories of the Strange and Unusual.

THE COLLECTED SUPERNATURAL AND WEIRD FICTION OF AMELIA B. EDWARDS *by Amelia B. Edwards*—Contains two novelettes 'Monsieur Maurice', and 'The Discovery of the Treasure Isles', one ballad 'A Legend of Boisguilbert' and seventeen short stories to cill the blood.

www.ingramcontent.com/pod-product-compliance
Lightning Source LLC
Chambersburg PA
CBHW030348030726
47497CB00002B/230